D0984163

❀

India
Seen
Afar

❀

Also by Kathleen Raine

STONE AND FLOWER

LIVING IN TIME

THE PYTHONESS

THE YEAR ONE

COLLECTED POEMS

THE HOLLOW HILL

DEFENDING ANCIENT SPRINGS

BLAKE AND TRADITION

(*Andrew Mellon Lectures, Washington, 1962*)

SELECTED WRITINGS OF THOMAS TAYLOR THE PLATONIST

(*with George Mills Harper*)

WILLIAM BLAKE

THE LOST COUNTRY

ON A DESERTED SHORE

FAREWELL HAPPY FIELDS

THE LAND UNKNOWN

THE OVAL PORTRAIT

THE LION'S MOUTH

THE INNER JOURNEY OF THE POET

India
Seen
Afar

KATHLEEN
RAINE

GEORGE BRAZILLER

NEW YORK

First published in the United States in 1991 by George Braziller, Inc.
Published in Great Britain in 1990 by Green Books.

For information, write to the publisher:

George Braziller, Inc.
60 Madison Avenue
New York, NY 10010

Library of Congress Cataloging-in-Publication Data

Raine, Kathleen, 1908–
    India seen afar / Kathleen Raine.
        p.   cm.
    ISBN 0-8076-1268-5 ; $22.95
    1. Raine, Kathleen, 1908– —Journeys—India. 2. Poets, English—20th
century—Biography. 3. India—Description and travel—1981– 4. Raine,
Kathleen, 1908– —Religion. 5. Spiritual life—20th century. I. Title.
PR6035.A37Z465   1991
821'.914—dc20
[B]   91-22567
                                                               CIP

Manufactured in the United States of America

First U.S. Edition

❀

To all those friends
whose wisdom and kindness
has brought me to the
'India of the Imagination'
and above all
in loving memory of
Tambi

❀

অবসান হোলো রাতি।
নিবাইয়া ফেলো কালিমা-মলিন
ঘরের কোনের বাতি।
বিশ্বের আলো পূর্ব আকাশে
জ্বলিল পুন্যদিনে
একসাথে যারা চলিবে এবারে
সকলেরে দিক চিনে।

The night has ended.
Put out the light of the lamp of thine own
    narrow corner smudged with smoke.
The great morning which is for all appears
    in the East.
Let its light reveal us to each other who
    walk on the same path of pilgrimage.

Rabindranath Tagore
Baghdad
May 24th, 1932

ONE

WHEN did I set out on my 'passage to India'? Since I arrived there I must have set out, but when? Or did I arrive? Perhaps I have not arrived—am as far from India as before I set out. But I know at least that it is India from which I am still far away; and that is something to have discovered. The India of the Imagination, the Orient—for I am not speaking of any geographical country or political nation, nor indeed of India's treasuries of art, sculptures and temples and dance and marvellous cloths and jewels and paper birds and garlands of stephanotis and marigolds offered to gods without number—no, that India is marvellous indeed, and who am I to write of it, who set foot on Indian soil only after I was seventy?—but the India of the Imagination is another country; everywhere and nowhere it exists. It is universal, for is it not, finally, the place of every arrival, the term of every spiritual quest? And that being so, the frontier between this and other worlds. But that frontier too is everywhere, is in ourselves.

I speak, then, only of my own India, and even that inner country I have discovered very late, though I might perhaps— had I been prepared—have reached it years ago. But again, it is a country only those can discover who can recognize it. I

[3]

would not presume to claim that I have reached even my own India; but my face is turned to that Orient ever before the faces of Swedenborg's angels, and the 'oriental philosophy' of which Henry Corbin has told us that the 'Orient' is not geographical but metaphysical. The Golden Dawn.

India, Raja Rao (the novelist and philosopher) told me as we conversed in the India International Centre, where the green parrots come and go from the adjacent Lodhi gardens, is not a place or a nationality but a state of being: it is within the reach of all who can attain it: were these words of that Brahmin of Brahmins a sort of invitation? I did not need him to say (what nevertheless he seemed to imply) that India is the goal, the term, of the human journey of the soul. We reach, if we travel far enough, India; to find, indeed, that India is universal. In the West we have lost our Orient; we are dis-oriented. India no doubt is becoming ever more westernized, but not yet has consumerism completely prevailed over that renunciatory austerity of the Indian religious ideal, nor the universal sense that 'everything that lives is holy': although now at every major road-intersection there are hoardings advertising the television set, and where television enters all the technology and gadgets draw the disoriented of India westward. Los Angeles and Detroit also are a state of consciousness; a state already written on the many secular faces of Bombay. Not race, but a mode of being; a culture, our state of consciousness, be it of the East or of the West, determines what we are. 'The Kingdom not of this World' may also be found in America, in England, in every country of this earth; yet its secret name is (as Shelley knew) 'Asia', the beloved soul of the Promethean West. India has created its imaginary cities, its legendary kings and queens, its *rishis*, its warriors and gods and goddesses, its entire invisible land, its sacred rivers, and sacred fords, its necklaces of skulls. And the Noble Eightfold Path of the Lord Buddha—that way also leads from India. They say

[4]

Jesus himself visited India; He is still there (I don't mean the Jesus of the missionaries) among those other gaudy oleographs at the back of any of those small shops where you may go to buy a notebook or a cassette; Rama and Sita and Lakshmana and Hanuman; Ganesha and Mahatma Gandhi or Ramana Maharshi, the Lord Krishna and the Lord Jesus, beautiful too. I suppose there are crucifixes in Christian churches in India—I was never inside one—but the Jesus who has taken his place among the other gods and holy men at the back of the shop is beautiful and uncrucified; India has claimed Him.

Well, I have arrived late indeed. What wasted years, I'm tempted to reflect, why did I waste seventy years on this and that before the mist cleared enough for me to see where my way lay? Yet on that way I have visited so many countries of the Imagination, loved so many regions of the 'Kingdom not of this World'; I would not have wished it otherwise. Tagore wrote, 'When I go hence, let this be my parting word, that what I have seen is unsurpassable'. What, I wonder, is the Bengali word so evocatively translated as 'unsurpassable'? In what way unsurpassable? The poet does not say: in beauty? knowledge? happiness? terror? the attainment of some goal? None or all of these? Those who make the passage to India can expect no simple answers, no answers at all; rather perhaps to become more aware of the mystery. Those who want answers had better go elsewhere; or stay elsewhere. In India Blake's 'dread forms of certainty' melt away. Certainties are lost, rather than found.

I still find it very strange—not to say awe-inspiring—that it should be to India that my life has led me in the end. I was not making for India—rather I have discovered that it is to India that my journey of life has brought me: or towards—I would claim no more. But when did 'India' first begin to sign to me? When did my heart first leap at the magic of that name? Kipling of course, Mowgli and Bagheera and Shere

Khan and Kaa the cobra, that archetypal childhood where we all converse with the beautiful and untameable animals of the wild places (how sad we are when Mowgli returns to the village and is tamed by a girl, who combs his hair!) No, Kipling brought us the very breath of that India of beauty and death, cobra and crocodile and the sacred river, that India where all cobras are sacred cobras, all elephants royal, all lizards talk and tell that their joys are special to themselves and not the joys of the serpent-people. And always there are holy men, to whom they talk; who know some secret of wonder and bliss. Kim meant less to me—when I read it I had already moved into the 'real' world, away from Mowgli's jungle. That magical forest I found again long after in India's epic poetry—the most sublime and beautiful in the world—with Rama and Sita and the monkey-kings and forest dwelling holy men. But my mother—from whom my imagination learned everything—loved the story of Puran Das, a simple Government official, who left his city desk to become a 'forest-dweller'; and he too came to know the animals, and they told him of a flood that was coming, so that Puran Das was able to save the people of the neighbouring village. But to me that was not the point. Puran Das remained an image of those forest dwellers who renounce the world to converse with the creatures and to become wise. Is there any child who does not wonder how human beings could ever wish to do otherwise than live in the forest with the creatures and the trees and flowers and sun and rain and winds and storms and clouds? In India, I understood there were such people. For saints I never cared; truth to say I disliked saints with deep distaste—they seemed to have no love of nature or the living creatures and to live joyless lives. India's holy men lived at peace with nature and the creatures; I loved nature, and could not see why the saints were for ever in conflict with that beautiful world. Even St Francis did not listen to the birds but only preached to them Christian sermons, and I have heard too many of these. Indian holy-men, it seemed, did not preach but listened.

Then there were the myths; I first knew the myths of Greece and loved them indeed, I loved myths as such and the gods and demigods and nymphs and satyrs and centaurs. At least these were real gods, not those Christian saints who were but human and of this world. I thirsted for mythology, of whatever kind. Why did I not then come to know that rich Indian other-world with its marvels and beauty and terrors? It was simply not available to me—it is only now that having absorbed something of the *Ramayana*, the *Mahabharata* (albeit in an American prose translation) awaits me at the end of the day. The full text, I mean; I have read several abridgements but it is not the main outline of the plot but the endless stories of the Golden Age that nourish the soul. Imagination has created through numberless generations those gods and *naga* people, the brahmin forest dwellers and their beautiful, ambiguous wives and daughters of the other-world and kings and heroes to create a civilization that western cultural imperialism of the television set, the multinationals, and not least the westernized universities, threatens to destroy. Yet it has been, that great kingdom of the Imagination, and therefore will have been, for ever. Perhaps they will conquer the world after all, those people of the Imagination, Rama and Hanuman and Sugriva, and the Pandavas and the holy men. Is it not already coming to pass? Where, in the West, do seekers look but to the everlasting East—the pilgrim routes of hippies, and rich American widows, and super-subtle intellectuals like myself? The soul has an instinct, like animals, for where water is to be found.

And from how little the imagination can build (or receive) a picture of an unknown country— the silk saris, the refined features of Indian women, the turbaned bearded men glimpsed now and then in London, told something of the country from which they came, to which they belonged—I mean of course imaginatively belonged. Another beauty than ours, speaking of a different culture. Or the Indian conjurers of childhood, the rope trick and the mango tree I was eager to believe really did grow under their spells. Some magic show at the seaside; but a clue. The possibility of magic's *not* being just a shabby trick (as the grown-ups would have us believe) was somehow releasing: children naturally believe in magic. No, nothing will explain how we infer, from such slender clues, an 'India of the Imagination' not altogether false; as from broken fragments archaeologists infer a whole civilization. We become aware of these things in ways unaccountable, for the sum is so much greater than the parts. 'From shard of broken sepulchre' a whole state of being speaks, the reality itself, whose whole is miraculously present in every part. In reality I know almost nothing of India, and yet I know 'India'. No wonder if some attempt to explain this mysterious 'knowing' by re-incarnation. But to me it seems rather that the omnipresent spirit of the universe is everywhere always and in everyone. The India of the Imagination is within that omnipresence; as are the Greece, Egypt, Italy, France, Spain, Ireland of the Imagination; England also.

❀

Or was my own pilgrimage already forecast in my mother's most secret life? My mother's eldest sister, my Aunty Meg, spent most of her adult life in Ceylon. There, although she habitually spoke (as did all her kind in those days) of 'the natives', she had made friends with Buddhist monks. Of this other members of the family deeply disapproved; but did my mother secretly envy her sister who had travelled to the East, who had spoken with Buddhist monks, who had lived on fearless and friendly terms with the snake who lived in her bath pipe; who brought back, on her visits to England, embroidered cloths and boxes of ebony and porcupine-quills, and agates, and opals, and carved elephants? My mother, who lived habitually in the realms of gold, to whom the story of Puran Das said more than the Bible (she seldom referred to the Bible, so far as I remember, though my father did constantly) had that precious gift of communicating imaginatively, which had nothing to do with what she said or intended to communicate. Had my mother, that secret theosophist, already made her passage to India? Or dreamed of it? I do not know—she was native of a country which has no name.

I had been thinking of how, in a short poem I had then begun, to communicate the essence of a human life; my mother's life. I had written, 'Her name a message, whose meaning/Is herself, for whom there are no words, only a name/That signifies . . .'*—and here I began to consider what it is the word I could not find was to say. My cousin Jean had sent me, at Christmas a few years ago, a little silver brooch, bearing the name 'Jessie'—my mother's name—which she had found at the back of a drawer in a chest inherited from her and my grandmother. There it must have lain for a lifetime. A child's broken brooch: who had given it to her? When? When she was a light-hearted girl, reading poetry in her secret hide-away place among the heather moors? How express all the marvels of my mother's life, the secret and very essence of who she was? What regions, what realms of thought, what pictures in her mind of people, of flowers, of the little running burn with mimulus flowers growing on its brink that she had loved as a child, the good hands of cards—all that she was, that she had seen and known? What word can communicate what her name

*Revised in published version, see *The Presence, Poems 1984-87* (Ipswich, 1987), page 67.

[9]

'Jessie' on a little silver brooch with a broken pin, signifies? All that inner universe that is a life, a being? My mother's so rich in beauty, the beauty of little things, of flowers, of marvels of light falling through young beech-leaves, shells from a sea-shore, living medusae seen from a fisherman's boat? I wish there were some word to name that universe for which her name stands. The little brooch is bright now with being always in my pocket. My mother communicated to me many things she had loved, poetry, nature—all my own vision as a poet I owe to her. Yet her world remains secret from me, none knows another's being, another's inner world. These worlds, like rainbow spheres, are each one soul and no other the same in all time. It was she. All the times and spaces and places and houses and trees and gardens and songs and rain and clouds and moon and birds, within her consciousness. The soul's universe where times and places become timeless being? Something of the kind.

It was my mother who first opened for me the boundless inner worlds of the Imagination, for these were her native country. When my mother was happy she would tell me about 'the hostel' in Jesmond Dean where as a girl she had lived when she was training as a teacher at the Armstrong College, in Newcastle, as was my father. But the romance of The Hostel had nothing to do with my father, it was of quite another kind. There she had met a Singhalese lady named Miss da Cunha; Miss da Cunha was beautiful and possessed knowledge and wisdom beyond my mother's experience or imagining—she talked to my mother about Buddhism, and was a theosophist. At heart my mother was and for ever after remained a theosophist, though she knew little of it and was never thereafter free to pursue it, for my father who led her dutifully twice every Sunday—and myself also as soon as I was old enough to leave the Sunday School—to the Cranbrook Park Wesleyan Methodist Church, had other values. My mother, who by the same means had eluded the Presbyterian Kirk, simply absented herself inwardly from that world which was not of her imagination. The poetry of Scotland has perforce made for itself a place within the harsh doctrines of John Knox's Reformation, and what I received in my infancy from that religion through my mother was that of those bewitched Ministers, George Macdonald and Alexander Kirk of Aberfoyle who was 'taken' by the fairies. That 'green, green road' to Fair Elfland has never, in Scotland, been far to seek, and none knows whether at the end of time the fairies will be allowed to enter Heaven, though if the people of Scotland are consulted, they will not be kept out. And who would exchange Fair Elfland for Milton's heaven, or Dante's, come to that? My mother's happy gift of absenting herself from the uninteresting is an art acquired perforce in the land of long sermons. Only now that I am old do I realize what gratitude I owe to my mother that I have inherited some part of her gift of attending only what speaks to the Imagination. Would that I had made better use of that blessed gift of inattention.

Her life was not happy, though sometimes she forgot everything that bound her, and was free and merry. The living moor, Miss da Cunha, theosophy, and among her books Tagore's *Gitanjali*, Kahlil Gibran's *The Prophet*, and, much later (how she came by it I do not know) Israel Regardie's *Garden of Pomegranates*, fed her soul. She desired no other freedom but to inhabit the paradise of her imagination.

❀

As I think back I realize that perhaps it was not I who chose India but rather that India chose me. True, Tambimuttu was a Ceylonese Tamil whose language was in fact English and who knew little or no Tamil at all—as T. S. Eliot discovered when during the Second World War he tried to help Tambi by finding him a job. Yet although I did love Tambi I took his devotion far too lightly. 'Kathleen, you are a *great poet*' he used to say. Very nice to be told so by Tambi that prince in beggar's rags it took me too long to recognize for the real prince he was. No one else ever told me I was 'a great poet' nor did I expect it nor believe it; but in retrospect I can see that in Tambi it was India that chose me—that Tambi discerned in my work some quality India looks for and recognizes whereas England since the war—the England in which I have lived—does not. All is cerebral and political and mundane whereas Tambi heard in my verses some music of the soul; the music of the goddess Sarasvati who was the form in which he himself worshipped the Goddess: the Goddess as muse. For all his not very successful attempts to write the kind of poetry being written here in England in the 'thirties and the 'forties, his attempts to be 'westernized', his one impressive poem is his *Geeta Sarasvati*. Not particularly well written, as regards language, but a poem that speaks with the voice of India—India that knows how to praise and to celebrate that Goddess of joy and beauty, in all her arts. An *éloge*, as St John Perse would have understood—he too could praise and celebrate. While Tambi was as he thought conquering the West in its own terms, what he really brought with him was that great indivisible culture of the Subcontinent. I knew and did not know who he was. Tambi stories were of gatherings of poets in pubs, of fights, in the name of poetry no doubt, but 'the literary world' saw Tambi as a good joke and a figure of no account beside those prestigious names of Stephen Spender and Cyril Connolly and Cecil Day-Lewis whose values were of their time and place. Kafka well understood how in life we seldom recognize the faces of our eternal friends, deceived by their clothes, or their social status. How many recognized in the propertyless young man from Nazareth the Lord Jesus?

Tambi was my first publisher; I would above all else have wished to be accepted by T. S. Eliot for his list of Faber poets; his was the *imprimatur*. It was every young poet's ambition to be published by Faber at that time, but more so to be accepted by Eliot. Perhaps I must recognize that I *was* ambitious to be acclaimed as a poet by 'the literary world' and I did see Tambi as a disappointing second best when he produced for me that beautiful first volume, *Stone and Flower* with illustrations by Barbara Hepworth. A woman illustrated by a woman; and her crystalline coldness did at that time accord with something frozen yet intricately structured in my own work—or heart. Tambi was first and last the truest friend of my poetry and would have saved me from myself, swept me into India's Dionysiac dance had I been able or willing to entrust myself to Bohemia, but that was too far against the values of my upbringing that inhibited me even as I rebelled against them. I see now that it was with the eyes of the Orient that he saw me and read my poems, wrung from me who knows how, despite my intellectual, social, religious and every other kind of dishonesty; those poems did speak from my soul, albeit a soul in prison and chains, in exile. How blind I was; but of course Tambi himself was on a wild adventure to conquer the Western world. Only much later, since I have come to know India itself a little, have I realized that Tambi's warmth and simplicity of heart, of friendship given in total, unqualified loyalty, are no less enduring aspects of the eternal India than the holy men and the Vedanta, and no less precious.

But in those years India as a destination was far from my thoughts as I struggled to survive, to thread my way through the labyrinth swept by passion yet at the same time also on a spiritual quest. Christianity was at hand; I became, during a period of emotional turmoil, a Catholic, a convert to a Church for which I had no real liking or affinity at all. There was Jung, whose works I absorbed with avidity; and there was Blake, for whom 'all religions are one' yet who was a true Christian—unlike Thomas Taylor the Platonist, or Shelley, who knew their ways to other springs of clear water. But then as always it was Gay Taylor—she too all too undervalued by me—who possessed those small paperback translations of Indian texts that since her long-ago death are on my own shelves. When did I first read the *Bhagavad Gita*? I can no longer remember even in what translation; perhaps it was Wilkins's translation, in connection with my labours to discover the sources of Blake—the first English translation, by a colleague of Sir William Jones. But I well remember the physical sensation—of the lifting of the heart, of the hair rising on one's scalp—as my exiled soul recognized the voice of my native country. Countless times since have I read Sri Purohit Swami's translation—dedicated to Yeats— and is it not perhaps after all more through Yeats than by any other means that India has gradually, imperceptibly, claimed me? Never has the reading of the Gospels, for all their beauty, made my heart lift and my hair rise up. Gay, and I with her, explored all the avenues—Tao, Eckhart, the *Cloud of Unknowing*, Julian of Norwich and a host of little papercovered translations of the German mystics; A. E. Waite's Tarot. Gay's soul was more Christian than mine; she was capable of mystical love, whereas I wanted to *know*, through the mind, what only the heart can teach.

I had by now seen Indian dance, of course; that wonderful dancer Ram Gopal especially. There were plenty of 'ways' to India for any who wished to follow them. I even once met Dr Shastri, of *Shanti Sadan*, where, I no longer remember; what now amazes me in retrospect is how many opportunities I missed, how many ways I did *not* take. I could have been a Jungian, a Christian, student of Vedanta, of magic; in all these I have but dabbled. Blake indeed became my Master and him I have served to the best of my understanding and with much industry. Blake has been my sole enduring commitment, his golden string I have faithfully followed.

❀

Arabinda Basu I first met through Carmen Blacker, in my Cambridge years in the 1950s. He was at that time Spalding Reader in Indian Philosophy at Durham University, and he sometimes invited me to stay with him there, as his guest; as since he has often been mine over many years. I owe him much; but finally he has, to my great regret, but inevitably as I can see very well, given me up as a bad job. He used to play recordings of wonderful Indian music to me—of which he has great knowledge—and made me read long works by Sri Aurobindo, his guru. He now lives permanently at the Sri Aurobindo Ashram at Pondicherry.

But Sri Aurobindo was not for me and I fear that has in the long run lost me the valued friendship of Arabinda Basu. As I write, the Christian parable of the seed sown on stony ground, and among thorns, comes to me like a reproach; for I cannot be uncritical. I cannot turn a blind eye to flaws and shortcomings, else I would have been a Christian from first to last. Such as I 'about must, and about must go' and cannot follow the exclusive teachings of any single Master, though seeing in all and taking from all grains of truth. I suppose Blake I have followed as my Master without criticizing any of his shortcomings—I cannot see any shortcomings in William Blake which I suppose goes to disprove what I have said of being incapable of total commitment to any of the many from whom I have learned so much. But three things I could not accept in Sri Auro-bindo, or perhaps two (for do not 'evolution' and the 'superman' go together?) or perhaps just one thing, for the third of these things I could not accept is his poetry; a poetry of superlatives; 'superpoetry' his devotees would say. I found the philosophy interesting, though with reservations

[15]

about 'bodily immortality' (who would want such a thing?) and the Nietzschean—or seemingly Nietzschean—'superman' and 'evolution', ideas he doubtless re-created in terms of Indian spirituality but which a western reader not sympathetic to their Western versions must find difficult to accept. Of course there is much besides in Sri Aurobindo, who was by all accounts a remarkable yogi. But Arabinda Basu read me poems by Sri Aurobindo and would from time to time hand the book to me and ask me to read them aloud; and I could not bring myself to lend my speech to those blends of Victorian clichés and superlatives, and would politely hand the book back.

Arabinda put me in correspondence with a colleague at Pondicherry, Dr K.D. Sethna, who had written on Blake's 'The Tyger', and sent me his manuscript, for which unfortunately I was not able to find an English publisher. But a lively correspondence arose; and of course, inevitably, the subject arose of Sri Aurobindo's poetry. Arabinda had lent me his book *on* poetry, *The Future Poetry*, a very perceptive book in its judgements both of English and French Romantic poetry, and with whose thesis—that poetry comes from levels of greater or less spiritual awareness, and only the highest poetry (Shelley's for example) from a glimpsed spiritual vision—I deeply agree. Towards such a vision, according to Aurobindo, poetry must increasingly aspire and evolve, but I see no sign of such an evolution during this last phase of a secular materialist civilization, whose future Eliot saw rather as a new 'dark age'.

I have valued my correspondence with Dr Sethna, who has published a volume of it (in India). He cares deeply for the writings of our one poet-prophet, Blake; as an Indian follower of a spiritual path is likely to do. For the materialist West in whose accepted ideology the higher worlds and perceptions of those worlds are as if non-existent, such a view of poetry as is shared by Dr Sethna and others among Indian

[16]

critics who are not hypnotized (as are many in the universities) by western values must be self-evidently true. I too share that view, so clearly formulated by Sri Aurobindo. It must to these Indian friends be particularly disappointing that I cannot see Sri Aurobindo's *Savitri* as such a poem as they would have me think it, the supreme realization of the poetry of the 'overmind'. Tagore is another matter, a very great poet, but though deeply imaginative not strictly speaking a religious or a prophetic poet, or a mystic. But how could India, aware of the multiple levels of experience, fail to see supreme poetry as the natural, the inevitable language of a vision of the sacred? And that being so am not I the 'best bet' on an English poet prepared to read sympathetically the poems of Sri Aurobindo? The more so as *Temenos*, the review of 'the arts of the Imagination'—founded by myself and three friends in 1980—was started to make precisely this affirmation of the sacred source? Doubtless Sri Aurobindo had seen the deep and universal import of that issue, and thought he could perhaps provide such poetry by writing it himself. *Temenos* also would like to discover such a poet; I myself would wish to write such poetry. Edwin Muir, Vernon Watkins, David Gascoyne, T. S. Eliot also, have done so in flashes; Yeats more continuously in his later poems. I am willing to believe that it may lie with India to produce such a poet; but India has hitherto (modern India that is) so far as I am aware, (Tagore apart) not done so. I can very well understand why devotees of Sri Aurobindo would wish to see in *Savitri* a realization of their Master's view of poetry of the 'overmind.' I wish I thought Sri Aurobindo such a poet; I wish—I hope—India may produce such poetry. Yet I doubt whether such an Indian poet would write in English. It seems to me that English as a world-language is not the English of the poets, which must ever be related to 'the language really used by men', for whom every word has its resonances through the whole of a literature, indeed of a civilization, its aura, penumbra, its overtones.

[17]

Perhaps it is precisely in his so accurate use of English words, yet without these resonances, overtones, auras, that Sri Aurobindo fails; nor is his correct use of the English language related to any speech really used by men.

Yet these resonances and penumbras and auras are not merely something inherent in the language, they come from those higher worlds of imagination and miraculously transform language itself. And is it not in our very nature to stir in our sleep, like Caliban, when that far-off music sounds in our dreams? If *Savitri* were the super-poem its admirers claim it to be, would I not—I or any poet or lover of poetry—stir to its far-off music? As I do, even in poor translation, to Indian epic poetry, and Kalidasa's wonderful *Meghaduta*, or Tagore? I did not mean to introduce my 'passage to India' on this negative note, yet a note of bewilderment is inevitable. The Himalayas far off on the horizon look like a crumpled ridge in a relief map or a toy landscape; the nearer we approach the more difficult, the more repelling and unapproachable they appear.

We receive, finally, only what we are ourselves capable of receiving. How should I be able to read the enigma of India that draws me by the majestic splendour of its thought, and bewilders me by its paradoxes?

Dr Sethna sent me his own book on Mallarmé precisely about a poet who so well understood penumbras and resonances. His book contains excellent things, but leads up, of course, to Sri Aurobindo's poetry, seen as proceeding from where Mallarmé's ends. Yet is there not something trying to be said, 'groping', in Teilhard's word, for expression? I wish there might be, I hope there may be such poetry in a world that seems rather to be experiencing a darkening of thought than an evolution of higher consciousness. But although western civilization is perhaps spent, it seems possible that India feels the urge to create what we no longer can, in whatever language.

I hope my correspondence with Dr Sethna has not been all negative; I have invited him to send *Temenos* something on Sri Aurobindo's view of 'the future poetry' whose interest is after all applicable not to the 'future' only but to poetry as such at all times. It is a view much needed to be understood in the West, is, I would agree, the simple truth, taking into account who and what we are, as human beings, most of whom are living in this materialist age not in the traditional four 'worlds' but in a state of what Plotinus calls, and Blake after him, spiritual 'sleep'. The preoccupation, in our present situation with the material order alone, David Gascoyne calls 'the celebration of the commonplace'; unapparelled in celestial light. There must be a rejection of such trivialities as at present seem to preoccupy our versewriters. But I do not believe that 'evolution' will lead to anything that is not here and now visible to such as William Blake, who claimed to experience the fullness of imaginative vision:

> *Now I a fourfold vision see,*
> *And a fourfold vision is given to me;*
> *'Tis fourfold in my supreme delight*
> *And threefold in soft Beulah's night*
> *And twofold Always. May God us keep*
> *From Single vision & Newton's sleep!*

I could, then, have entered India through Arabinda Basu's proffering of Sri Aurobindo; either I was not ready, or maybe had other tasks in life. Meanwhile I devoted myself to my Blake work. 'All religions are one' Blake said; who was himself a Christian. Was I not therefore once more 'stuck'—I find no other word—with Christianity? Had I hoped, when first I asked advice of Marco Pallis, himself a

Buddhist, who had lived in India, to hear him say, 'How well I understand you, no-one of your intelligence (that is of course a word I like to apply to myself but what fools the intelligent can be) could stand for one moment the Christian Church as it is in these days, why do you not become a Buddhist?' ('Buddhism is the religion for grown-ups' my son James once remarked—he too paralysed by his own super-subtlety). But Marco said nothing of the kind. Since all traditions, he said, have originated in a divine revelation, all are valid, one must discover which it is appropriate to follow, and follow that tradition meticulously, not taking a little from here and a little from there, and leaving out the difficult or disagreeable aspects. Alas, what excuse had I for not following the religion of my culture and inheritance? I went away sorrowing but reflecting that Blake at least had been 'a worshipper of Jesus' and had seen in the Gothic cathedrals of England the expression of the one spiritual religion of all humankind. Had I thought a little more deeply I would have been able to console myself by remembering that Blake's Master, Swedenborg—and Blake himself—had held that a 'Last Judgment' was passed in 'the heavens' (the inner worlds) on the Apostolic Church in the year 1757; and that thereafter, although the form might remain, the spirit had departed from the organization to be replaced by the Church of the New Jerusalem of which my father so loved to quote the words of St John: 'And I saw no temple therein, for the Lord God Almighty and the Lamb are the temple of it'. I wonder if Marco had spoken his own truth, instead of by the Guénonist book, he might have spoken other words. But the responsibility after all was my own, and I would have been no happier in any other religious organization. Who at this time, in any case, can conform to any single religious pattern? All of us, whether we like it or not, are in a situation in which we have learned from many traditions, and are formed by the whole inheritance of the world not just some one part of it. Religions are a matter of culture; are, besides, as a Quaker friend said long ago 'for those who do not know God'. I was not ready for India, and had much work to do for my master William Blake. All things considered I served him well. And through him I was able at least to see Christianity as one among other religions and to read my Christian texts in the light of the *Bhagavad Gita* and the Upanishads, of the Lord Buddha, the Holy Koran of whatever words heaven has spoken to earth in any tradition.

Marco—Arabinda Basu also—recommended me to read Eckhart; I did so but although doubtless he was the Christian theologian most nearly to measure up to Indian standards, he never made my heart leap or my hair rise as does the *Baghavad Gita*. Besides, the Church did *not* follow Eckhart and the way of the Inner Light but Thomism and theological conformity and obedience to the authority of the Church. Nothing like that in India. The Neoplatonists and the Platonic tradition were rejected for Aristotle and Aquinas. Not the God Within but the Papacy and the Inquisition. As Gay Taylor used to say, there is too much blood on the hands of the Catholic Church. I well remember Arabinda saying to me, 'Don't let them get you again!' In retrospect I don't know why I tried so hard to conform myself. Inwardly, and, thank God, in my writings, I was free, (my second scholarly book was on Thomas Taylor the Platonist). I was no Christian inwardly, but with Blake, with Shelley, and Yeats, and such Indian scriptures as I knew. Was I perhaps a simple coward, unwilling to lose my friends Helen Sutherland, and that best of men, Hubert Howard, who were such wise supports in my chaotic life? Hubert it was who led me through the Churches of Rome, Assisi, Subiaco, who showed me all the grace and beauty of Italy. These were the sacred places that spoke to him all the beauty and mystery of the Gospels. How well did Hubert understand me, I wonder? He valued my poetry, I know; he valued deeply the English poets, Keats as well as Shelley and Yeats, and held Rilke perhaps to be the greatest of his time. Perhaps after all I did not lie to that dear and good friend; or in so far as I did he would perhaps have forgiven me.

❀

I never was, nor could have been, a 'Catholic poet' like that great writer David Jones—whose personal destiny did coincide with the Church culturally. He made good use of all that. But, as a young Egyptian scholar who has written his doctorate thesis on Kathleen Raine as a mystical poet, reassured me, he discerned that I was not a Christian or a Catholic mystic; a Sufi, he did me the honour to say. Insofar as at the heart of all mysticism there is total freedom and immediacy that may be true. But in my disastrous outer life I could not trust myself to follow the inner light and tried continually and unsuccessfully not so much to live by the rules but to tell myself continually that I ought to do so.

My instinct has always warned me to avoid organizations of whatever kind; my father's Protestantism has remained strong in me through it all, warning me that every soul's way is unique, there are no short cuts, and that nothing must come between the soul and its own divine source, on which each depends like a leaf on the Tree of Life. Might I not have benefitted from attachment to any one of these organizations had I known how best to use it? I can only say that my only true teacher has been my too often neglected and unheeded daimon who has always said No to formal affiliations.

Even so, there was a moment in the early 'seventies when I did, through a friend who was a member of that organization, very nearly join Dr Shastri's Shanti Sadan group in Holland Park; a scholarly dignified group not advertising itself. I went right up to the final ceremony of joining and at

the last minute withdrew: why? Because, I told myself, Blake
was after all my Master and because as a Westerner I must
not desert Christendom. One cannot 'become' this or that,
we are what we are. 'Improvement makes strait roads', Blake
has written, 'but the crooked roads without improvement
are the roads of Genius'. My 'Genius'—my Daimon—has
led me by crooked roads indeed. It is when I have attempted
to get onto the strait roads that I have lost my way not once
but many times. But again, I am indebted to Shanti Sadan
and in particular for their excellent publications, especially
Dr Shastri's own English translations of Hindu literature
and scriptures. I have, reader, as you must long ago have
realized, 'dabbled' in almost everything; in a Magical
Society akin to Yeats's Order of the Golden Dawn; in the
activities of the College of Psychic Studies; the insatiable
and superficial curiosity of the Geminian mind? I have
learned much from all; I have renounced none—I write for
Light (Journal of the College of Psychic Studies), for the
(Catholic) *Tablet*, for *Harvest* (the Jungian journal); I am on
friendly terms with a Buddhist community in Croydon, a
Sufi community in Scotland; all these are seeking and
teaching some aspect of the one truth all seek. I find nothing
inconsistent in these multiple affiliations. One group only
do I feel nowadays somewhat coldly towards, and that is the
Guénonist 'Traditional' school. From this group also I have
learned much, in the excellent expositions of traditional
sacred teachings to be found in the works of many of its
exponents, but what they seem to me finally to lack is a
living sense of the secret workings of the Holy Spirit. They
offer an intellectual security to seekers for certainties;
whereas I find with advancing age that one can be certain
only of the Mystery itself to which alone we can entrust the
mystery of ourselves. And this I do.

I regret none of my eclecticism—'dabbling' if you like to
call a way that has brought me to no final commitment to

any of the groups in which I have 'dabbled' and from which I have learned. I do not even regret that 'India'—which is but another name for that 'knowledge absolute' to which we all strive, was only—is only—a far destination. India has never been for me—as were Blake and Thomas Taylor the Platonist—an area of scholarly study; still less a 'conversion'. But 'India' is the name of that country to whose frontiers, as it proves, my long journey has led me. Perhaps not even a long journey, this single moment of life, this single life among multitudes of lives, my own or those of others, for what does it matter since ultimately all are within the One. The 'India', that is, which Raja Rao called a state of mind. In everyone, could we but attain to it. For it is the paradox of 'India' that it throws us, ultimately, back on ourselves; let us expect no help from dressing up or changing the names of the gods. Yet Indian civilization and culture does embrace and offer a fullness of sheer knowledge (both written and unwritten) not available in the West; Meister Eckhart and a few Protestant mystics are but stray swallows who do not make a summer. Mystics and gnostics were never encouraged by the Catholic Church, and an already impoverished Protestantism is not to be compared with six (is it? or much more) thousand years of continuous spiritual civilization embracing pre-literate aboriginal oral tradition and the Himalayan summits of philosophic thought and mystical practice; not to mention the multitudinous expressions of these in a culture in which none of the arts has ever lost its roots in the spiritual knowledge India has hitherto preserved. Hitherto. The impact of Western secularism could of course destroy in India the wisdom of ages. As it has done here. But no matter when and where we may say of Western spiritual tradition that it went wrong, the fact remains that the Christian mainstream of the modern West has lost its vision and its soul, and where can we turn but to India for a renewal of that vision? Perhaps before India loses her soul as well. Dom Bede Griffith who has lived half a lifetime in Southern India has in his remarkable books written on such things and of a 'Christian Vedanta' which he believes could restore a spiritual vision to the West. But one might say that the Church took the way it did take and became what it has become, and the history of two thousand years cannot now be reversed. 'Christian Vedanta' may indeed offer a way of release to those who are 'stuck with' the Church so to speak; but many more I believe will go straight to the source itself. No Hindu would, after all, ask any to deny the Lord Jesus. India has seen many divine incarnations and has taught that whenever the world's darkness is greatest, then the ever-living will assume human form to restore and heal the sad soul of the world.

Sri Aurobindo's teaching, as well as that of Dom Bede, envisages a 'marriage' of East and West; his followers would doubtless say that in adopting the Superman and Evolution and the 'Oversoul' and that whole complex of nineteenth century European terminology, Sri Aurobindo was seeking such a universalism. Certainly the spirit of the 'India of the Imagination' is at work in the world in many forms; not to mention the Rishis and Maharishis of various sorts who on a more popular level have drawn followers to 'transcendental meditation' and other forms of practical yoga. It may well be that already we have entered the time Yeats foresaw of a reversal of the premises of the materialist civilization of the modern West.

I thank the invisible Master of my life for my Indian friends; for the India of the Imagination I have seen afar, to whose threshold I have been led. And if I have now in a manner of speaking made a commitment it is rather in the course of successive liberations from false positions than in the adoption of some creed or Master. And if India has come in search of me it is through no decision of mine, but in the most natural way in the world. Not a guru but, after all,

Tambimuttu's friend Prince Kumar. Through simple affection, friendship, poetry, after all my intellectual detours it has come about unsought. And the only poetry Kumar wishes to press upon me is—my own; a recall to duty. 'The Indian Caste system', he says, 'rests upon the simple principle that all should follow their leading gift'. And the only 'initiation' he offers is a whole-hearted affection (like Tambi's own) which makes me, so to speak, one of the family.

❀

So it comes back to poetry. If I have vacillated continually and suffered endlessly from the sense of guilt incurred by the conflicts between my undone or ill-done human duties and my poetic compulsions Tambi had no such doubts: to him I was the poet, and to him poetry was paramount. In all Tambi did for me—and I have been slow to recognize how much that was—it was of the poet he was thinking. Did he not deliberately bring Gavin and myself together, in the goodness of his heart, thinking no doubt to do good to us both? And so it should have been had I been more poet and less mortal woman. But that is an old story I have told elsewhere.* He also brought me Prince Kumar, knowing or hoping perhaps that there would be the same kind of mutual recognition—oh, not love, love for Tambi was but a means to poetry—but in Kumar Tambi brought me (what indeed he had already brought me in himself) India. It was many years ago (in 1968 Kumar tells me) that Tambi brought with him one day a young Indian prince (of the House of Rana—one never knew whom Tambi would bring) by whom I was certainly much charmed but whom I never expected to see again. I gathered that when not in India he

* See the third volume of my autobiography, *The Lion's Mouth* (London, 1977).

[26]

lived in New York City; and have since learned that he looked after Tambi in his wild American adventures. Clearly Kumar loved Tambi—and poetry—and had poet-friends in India also. But some time later—a year later perhaps, I don't remember—Kumar visited me again, alone this time, and spoke of his spiritual life a little, and I was (need I have been?) surprised to find a friend of Tambi's so committed. He continued to come to see me on a number of occasions, when he was in England, always unexpectedly; even once telephoned me on my birthday, from Los Angeles or New York. Little by little he had told me 'who he was'; how, having gone to teach Indian philosophy at Columbia University he had (suddenly or gradually) realized the futility of this, that spiritual teaching was the only thing that mattered. His widowed mother had long practised austerities and lived in great simplicity the Indian religious life. After her death he showed me the photographs of that imperious lady who in traditional Indian style had made her old age a preparation for whatever awaits us at death. I listened of course with much interest, touched that Kumar spoke to me of these things. The sister of one of his followers, who had been a friend of Tambi's, sent me the last of those treasured manuscript books that have been sent me by a long succession of friends to write poems in.

Meanwhile Tambi had died; suddenly and unexpectedly Tambi was not there any more. I seldom saw him in those last years, myself occupied in all those scholarly and other detours which took me from poetry—and I had no liking for Bohemia as a way of life—but I took part in the memorial service for Tambi at 'The Bhavan' in West London. Meanwhile I myself had been to India for the first time, and knew, that day, that the great river of India had reclaimed Tambi from us. There was an enlarged photograph of Tambi's beautiful face, so full of fire and love, garlanded with marigolds, incense burning before him, flowers brought by friends—David Gascoyne had asked me to take, as from him, a bunch of red roses—and of those present half or more must have come from India or Ceylon. In that gradual, imperceptible way of India, the tanpura and then the tabla began to lift us away from this world, and the singing began, and I sat and looked at Tambi and he at me and I promised him, 'yes, Tambi, I will be your poet again in whom you believed even when I have betrayed myself'. For in the face of death what does it matter whether or not I paid my bills and polished the furniture'? Tambi had known that poetry alone mattered. Various old friends, and two of Tambi's brothers, read several poems and tributes, I know not what, as I did myself, but to me that meant but little, it was not the Tambi of Fitzrovia but the Tambi of the Subcontinent whom I that day saw leaving us, the Tambi who had written his *Geeta Sarasvati*, his hymn to the Goddess as inspirer of the arts, whose river 'flows pure from the mountains to the sea'. Her river carried him away from Fitzrovia, reclaiming him for 'the India of the Imagination'.

Jane Williams, Tambi's literary executor, used to come and see me from time to time, to seek advice, and to bring me those contributions she had received for a memorial volume. Many of them began 'I met Tambi in the Hog-in-the-Pound' or the Fitzroy Tavern or some other like place in New York; but of the many people who were fond of Tambi, who had sponged on him, whom he had befriended, how many had seen him as he was? Probably the spongers had known him better, in his princely giving, than the poets, who in general are self-centred and unimaginative by nature. How often it is only after death that we truly see who the companions of our life really were; Gay Taylor; my father and mother; Tambi. Some who die and we have known go their way elsewhere; but Tambi's presence has continued to accompany me. As did Kafka's 'K' (in *The Castle*) I have again and again failed to follow the signs, been deceived by appearances. Yet I should have known that Tambi, himself no guru, was nevertheless true to essential living values; true to poetry, true to people. 'Did you', Kumar asked not long ago, 'ever hear Tambi complaining of all those scroungers and hangers-on and drug-addicts and the rest, who surrounded him?' No, he treated all alike, in their full human dignity, whoever they were. Tambi loved us. And loved my poetry. I had missed the signs yet again. It was through Tambi, not through those high-places Blake also distrusted, 'The Church, the Court and the University' that I was always put back on my true way; Tambi, whom I shall always remember dancing in innocent glee as he sang what I think of as 'Tambi's song':

If you really love me, darling, buy me a motor-car! (repeat)
If you love me take me to the epidiascope! (repeat)
If you want to marry me darling, come in the proper way,
Don't come through the window, darling, what will people say?
(and so on)

As I also remember Malcolm Lowry's song, sung to his 'taro-patch':

This year, next year, sometime, never,
Love goes on for ever and ever,
What makes the world go ro-ound is Love!

Is it not love, after all, that is the touchstone, that guiser in so many forms, unrecognized again and again?

Kumar, a prince himself (in both senses of the word) had known who Tambi was—also in both senses of the word, for it must have been a wonderful relief for him also (with his household of adoring American *satsangis*) to relax with Tambi as one of his own class and kind—as men from the same public school or Cambridge College can relax in their

[29]

own background. I believe it must have been that Tambi had spoken of me with Kumar, who as it were assumed Tambi's role of bringing me back to my task as a poet.

On my second visit to India his was the first familiar face I saw in the India International Centre, where I was staying. His face was not in fact quite familiar, for he had shaved his beard: he had come to India to scatter his mother's ashes in the sacred rivers, as she had wished. He knew many of those Indian friends I already knew or have since met—had known Kamaladevi's husband; others also. Now he was meeting me as a State Guest in his own country and perhaps for him it was something of a relief to be on his own ground and away from the *satsangis*. He came to meditate in my beautiful room at the Centre, and attended the Yeats conference to which I had been invited. It must be very exhausting to be *Babaji* all the time!

Only a month or two ago Kumar came to London on his way from Paris 'You may be very good at doing many things', he said; scholarship, editing *Temenos*; but my true *dharma*, the law I should follow, is that of the poet and I must, even in my last years go back to that. I explained that I have never been sure that I had the right to be a poet, and looking with remorse on the pain I had caused others in being so I was still more in doubt. 'You thought it your *karma* but found it to be your *dharma*' he replied. 'Thy duty binds thee,' said the Lord Krishna to Arjuna, 'From thine own nature it has arisen. That which in thy delusion thou desirest not to do, that very thing thou shalt do!' Tambi, he told me, (whether in life or in a vision I do not know) had said to him, 'Tell Kathleen to write poetry!' To feel that I am under orders to write, rather than that to do so is in some way deeply wrong, certainly lifts a weight from my spirit. And I must write hymns—*éloges*! what else at my age can a poet write but praise? Perhaps after all Tambi was the only person—save my mother—who has ever loved me for what I (alas) am, asking of me nothing save that I should be the poet they saw in me.

These things happen, I realize, of their own accord; I was not looking for a guru, or for any support or shoulder to lean on, still less an Indian Prince of the Solar dynasty. ('My family ruled India for six thousand years', he said) Rama was his ancestor; the Lord Buddha a sort of second cousin. Speaking of Rama, he was the first mortal, Kumar said, to be the theme of a poem—formerly Indian poets wrote only of the gods. 'But (he added) god or man, what's the difference?' That was one of those profound, liberating Indian remarks that lifts and releases the soul. All is miracle and mystery. Blake would have understood. 'I am the seed of all being, O Arjuna! No creature moving or unmoving can live without Me! O Arjuna, the aspects of my divine life are endless. I have mentioned but a few by way of illustration!' All life is that illustration.

Nor does the Lord Jesus present any problem to this princely heir of the Lord Rama: on the contrary. He has a deep devotion for the Lord Jesus. He told me of a visit he had made to Jerusalem. There, on the Via Dolorosa, he had experienced a vision. It seemed that the houses on the roadside changed their aspect; were smaller, poorer, little whitewashed houses; and the road was deserted. Then he saw approaching a procession; it was Jesus carrying the Cross. Small, He was, and dark, Kumar said, and deeply humble. Kumar was overcome and made his way into a little monastic Church; the monks, seeing the state he was in, locked the outer door and left him there until he had recovered his normal state. Fact or imagination, what's the difference? one might say; what is seen in the *mundus imaginalis* is reality of another kind. In arriving in the India of the Imagination those who wish to do so will find the Lord Jesus already there. Not indeed the fictitious demi-god of the church or the 'historical' figure of the seekers for 'factual' evidence that He lived, but 'an aspect of My divine life'.

❀

As for the, I will not say 'real' India, since what is more real than the quintessence of a nation's genius which the Imagination distils from the works and days of this world, but the so-to-say untransmuted India—which none the less is still in great part what has been created by the India of the Imagination, people and their skills and dreams and thoughts are not after all the mere products of material and mundane causes—that India also awaited me at the end of the long journey of my life. I put it in that way because I have always been scrupulous about visiting other countries. Simply to say 'Wouldn't it be lovely to go to...' whichever country it may be, seems to me meaningless, we must await the sign. The hippies at least went as pilgrims. For that matter I have never had enough money to travel 'for pleasure' and if I have travelled widely it has always been by invitation—to some conference, to read a paper or take a seminar, or indeed to visit friends. I could never myself have afforded to visit Washington D.C. and New York City, Dallas Texas, Crestone Colorado, San Francisco, Los Angeles, Toronto, to say nothing of dear Paris, Athens, Madrid and Cordova, and Rome and Dublin and Sligo, and at last Delhi. But there is a profounder reason, our lives must conform to a destined pattern. One does not visit the countries of others, any more than one would visit the houses of others, just to look at the furniture. And should not the guest take something to the host, go to give as well as to receive? I have always felt that to visit another country is a responsibility to be undertaken seriously—what do we take with us, what task do we perform, for others and for ourselves? I have gone where I have been invited, and always with the fear—the knowledge—that what I have had

[32]

to contribute has been far from enough. Wherever I have travelled, throughout my life, I have always received infinitely more than I have given.

❀

It is now more than ten years ago that I was asked by the University of Delhi to act as external examiner of a Doctorate thesis on 'Yeats and the Sacred Dance', by Santosh Pall. I had already seen a paper by her, of high standard. The thesis in due course arrived, and it seemed to me not only scholarly, but to represent a way of reading Yeats's poetry, with imaginative insight grounded in a knowledge of that spiritual tradition to which he himself turned; all too rare in the academic world. In other words, the author had read Yeats in the light of her Indian culture and values and not (as all too many Indian thesis-writers) by abandoning those values to adopt some theory current in Yale or Cambridge in order to read western (or eastern for that matter) writers in the light not of permanent values, but merely in terms of the latest 'ism of modern Academe. Such converts to the prevailing Western values have nothing of any significance to contribute to Western scholarship but rather more or less smudged carbon copies of our own. Fortunately, the American external examiner shared my good opinion of Santosh's thesis and the author was awarded her degree. And in due course she wrote to tell me that she was on her way to England (intending also to visit Ireland) and asking if she might come and see me. I was very pleased of course to welcome this gifted young scholar, and looked forward to entertaining her for a pleasant cup of tea, perhaps thereafter to answer a question, to write a testimonial or the like, as I have done for others in similar circumstances.

But with Santosh it was to be far otherwise. I did indeed send her on to the Yeats Summer-School in Sligo, but she soon returned; that was not what she had crossed the world for. Much as she had loved Ireland and the people of Sligo, she had nothing to learn, she felt, from the (predominantly American) academics there assembled. She wished to learn from me and from no one else. If Kumar elected himself to be my guide in matters spiritual through no act of mine, so likewise did Santosh elect me as hers in matters of scholarship. Not a matter of attending a course of lectures, or arranging a course of study—no, I realized that this relationship too was, in Indian terms, something far more real, more like the discipleship Plato or Ammonias Saccas or Plotinus would have expected, or the Ismaeli teachers in the *madrasahs* of mediaeval Isfahan; perhaps this relationship did continue to exist in the Universities of European Christendom through the Middle Ages, the sense of total commitment of pupil to Master, and therefore of Master to pupil. A sacred relationship; do not the Upanishads begin and end with the words 'May He (the Supreme Being) protect us both, teacher and taught. May he be pleased with us. May our study bring us illumination. May there be no enmity among us!' And indeed in every University there are such teachers and such pupils. So here I was, out of the blue, as it were, asked to be guru in matters of scholarship to a beautiful Indian dancer with total (not merely academic) dedication to Yeats studies because she understands Yeats to be a bridge to communicate knowledge not from West to East but also from East to West. There are all too many Indian students at India's westernized universities who are prepared to write theses on Sylvia Plath or Dr Johnson or some other irrelevance in order to receive a grant from the British Council or the American equivalent and a scholarship to a western university, paying as price their Indian inheritance. Not so Santosh whom nothing would induce to abandon her own cultural values in order to adopt those of the Occident.

Santosh was the guest, on her arrival, of some friend or

relation, but was not able to sustain the culture-shock of crossing London this involved—the faces of the Oxford Street crowds, so different from those of India—and moved to Crosby Hall, a few hundred yards from my house.

Santosh then, armed with her new Doctorate, returned to her University of Delhi and shortly thereafter founded the Yeats Society of India with herself as President, and in that capacity invited me to go and give the inaugural lecture. It was therefore as a Yeats scholar that I was invited to cross that invisible, sacred threshold of India—I could wish no fitter reason. The British Council refused to sponsor my visit; doubtless—and rightly—deeming that I do not represent British culture as this is defined by the media and the *Times Literary Supplement*. 'Let those who want her invite her' Santosh was told. I therefore went to India as the guest of the Indian Government. A charming young diplomat from India House visited me and asked me what I wished to see and do in India? I replied by asking what I could do for India? His magnanimous reply was, 'We wish you to see and to enjoy India'. What places did I wish to visit? Thus confronted with my ignorance of Indian history and geography I said a few names—Agra, Varanasi, Fatehpur-Sikri, the Ajanta caves; Konarak, for Santosh had described to me the great temple of the sun-god Surya. And so it befell that I found myself with India spread at my feet, the recipient of that wonderful hospitality India extends to her guests. It is not permitted to send or take money out of the country, but, once there, guests are given everything that fabulous India can offer. Strange things come about.

I hoped I had something—anything—to offer India in return; only perhaps my willingness to learn, my desire to understand. I am glad that I did not visit India as the guest or delegate of an official British organization since if I represent anything it is the desire to change, not to represent, the current secular humanist values of the English literary world; *Temenos* (the review of 'the arts of the Imagination' which I founded with a group of like-minded friends) represents another kingdom—the 'kingdom not of this world' which is in its nature, not perhaps 'international', but rather universal. One cannot, of course, avoid bringing with one one's culture—dress, manner, speech, voice—even if it is not our wish to do so. Even though my battle has been against the values of prevailing materialist ideologies of our Western majority culture; my very presence no doubt proclaims and disseminates the culture of my society. Our faces, our presences, are what our lives have made them and we take these with us perforce. It is a deeply searching judgement that is passed on those who set foot on foreign soil. In France I am entirely at ease, (indeed euphoric). Of Italy I feel myself deeply unworthy—unworthy of so much beauty and knowledge and grace. In America I slip very easily and happily into that openness, often united with very beautiful formality of manners, that I have ever found in the United States; where indeed one can find so many different Americas. But how, I wondered, must I appear in Indian eyes? True, I gave papers on Yeats and Blake and their indebtedness to India; I read some of my poems at the India International Centre; but who could measure up to such a confrontation? Yet I for my part had the sense of arrival at a destination.

❊

So my 'passage to India' became an actuality. My granddaughter Sonia, at the end of her university course, had time to be free; she saved up her fare, and I asked the Indian authorities if I could bring her with me—she of course to pay her own hotel expenses as she travelled with me. I don't think that even once was she asked to pay for her share of a double room we occupied; India is a country where families hold together, where granddaughters are welcome as a

[36]

matter of course. On a number of occasions notes were passed to her attempting to make assignations—she is a very lovely girl and it is assumed in India—alas for our reputation—that white women are not virtuous. As it happens my granddaughter is in this respect commendably 'old-fashioned' and was besides in love and lived in her dreams of the young man she has since married. Thetis Blacker the painter also arranged her stay with the Deputy High Commissioner in Delhi, her friend Richard Samuel, and she too accompanied us on most of our travels. So we set off on an Air India plane where we received VIP treatment and glasses of champagne which delighted my little granddaughter. (She had travelled with me before, we had flown together over the Atlantic, to Colorado over the Rockies, to San Francisco and Tassajara in California, where we had stayed as the guests of Baker Roshi, then Abbot of Zen Center in its happy days.) Far from Sonia's being with me presenting any problem to anyone, I began to realize very soon that no-one is ever alone in India; the family are so to speak thrown in. Sonia was to stay on in Pune to work on an agricultural project then being run by an American friend of her other grandmother, Jane Drew (the architect, who with her husband Maxwell Fry and Le Corbusier had designed Chandigarh) where we left her at the end of our travels, to discover her own India.

It was dark when we arrived at Delhi airport; Santosh and her Sikh husband, Mohan, were there to meet us. Thetis drove off with Richard Samuel, Sonia and I in Mohan's car. Darkness and trees. Indian trees! At one point we were stopped by a group of men draped in grey blankets (I had not realized how cold the nights are in Delhi and had not brought enough woollies). Sonia trembled and kept close to me. Brigands! No, just the police. Santosh in her concern to look after me herself had arranged that we were to stay, not at the India International Centre—I have stayed there since—

but at a much humbler and simpler graduates' hostel where the University puts up visiting lecturers and the like. This hostel is but a short walking distance from her own house in Civil Lines, across a pleasant park where there are monkeys and peacocks and many birds and beasts, cared for, it was obvious from the food left on little platforms which seemed to have no other purpose. India loves her animals. I am glad that we stayed at this rather simple pleasant hostel, for thereby we were immediately not VIPs but simple visitors, seeing life as it is lived rather than from the remoter luxury of the delectable International Centre. A watchman in a raggedy turban and a blanket gave us our keys—we had each been assigned a room, but my tremulous granddaughter felt safer close to me, so in the middle of the night her bed was carried into my room next door. They were indeed kind at the hostel. We woke to see a pleasant garden at the back, our verandah opening on to it; and a garden at the front too, beyond the corridor from which our rooms opened, and a series of gentle servants brought us tea, newspapers, called to bring and return our washing, and so on. Gardeners were at work some with their children playing near them—it is a delight, in India, to see many people doing simple tasks that in the West would be done by one machine or not at all; do we not destroy the very texture of human life, with its exchanges of smiles and kindnesses and daily comings and goings with our enslavement to technology? When does 'labour-saving' become the destroyer of the simplicity of life itself? A plain simple dining-hall gave us pleasant breakfasts of hot milk, tea, boiled eggs or the like. Monkeys came into the charming garden at the back, much to Sonia's delight; although one had to leave nothing about that they could carry off with them over the wall into the park where they lived. There was a bathroom of sorts where the water, from wherever it came, streamed over the floor. A Heath Robinson style geyser heated the water; bits of electric wiring aroused misgivings. I had not yet learned the Indian way of washing with a bucket and a dipper to pour it over your back—simple and economical. The geyser alarmed me but it did not in fact blow up or electrocute us—I was slow to realize that the Heath Robinson water heater was a luxury by Indian standards.

By day the sinister atmosphere of the night was banished. There were men watering plants, or cutting the grass—instead of technology there were always friendly people about, doing things. There was no clear demarcation between life and work. This sense of human beings occupied in the many humble tasks, far from arousing in me that kind of left-wing or American democratic indignation at being 'waited on' I found, on the contrary, heart-warming and human. I realized that the poor of India are not so much unemployed as under-employed; but under-employment saves self-respect that the dole queue destroys. By Indian standards I and such as I represent wealth untold whereas in England—although I do not know penury and what it is to be hungry, I am certainly not among the rich—I could not, for example, afford a car. But certainly I am not rich enough to feel ashamed in England, as I did in India, to see with my own eyes how many beautiful men and women and children are quietly and unviolently poor. There are beggars, and what can a few coins from a tourist do to alleviate their need? But then again, that happiness of people without too much to do, enjoying the sharing of simple tasks, in the mild winter sunshine (like an exceptionally good English summer) and how much happier five men cutting the grass with one ox than an efficient mechanical mower, one bored man, and the other four in the dole queue? Humanity is what in India first and last most deeply impressed me—at all levels; the simplicity of human life, the affection for the many children and their affection for one another, mildness, kindness one felt among the 'crowds' of India. Not 'crowds' like those in Oxford Street or the King's Road, multitudes of isolated individuals coming and going; not aimless, because Indian people seem not to be forever going from where they are to somewhere else, but to *be* wherever they are. During my stay a young man set up as a bicycle repairer at the corner of Santosh's road; quite simple—a piece of canvas to keep the sun off suspended between a tree-branch and a wall, his tools, the ground to sit on, and the rest, one hopes, followed.

The human beauty and richness of life itself is every-where heartwarming; India has not lost her soul as the price of technology—as yet. It is not the *rishis* and the 'Masters' alone who are the custodians of that spiritual civilization of beauty and crafts and skilled handiwork, it is the people. It is not, certainly, the westernized 'intellectuals' who are the custodians of 'the India of the Imagination'. Yet that India is everywhere, like a fragrance—the beauty of the cotton saris of the women who carry earth to the men repairing the road; the family outings that seem to be a part of every journey in a *tonga*—always any vehicle seems to be laden with the whole family, old and young; days' work and life have not yet, as in the West, become separate worlds, they flow together.

I digress—but life is endless digression. I gave my Yeats paper, and another paper on Blake and India, and then I was asked to give another, on Blake's Arlington Court tempera and Porphyry's *de antro nympharum*: Kapila Vatsyayan took the chair for me on that occasion and I felt immediately drawn to that fine scholar and administrator—she was at that time in Indira Gandhi's Ministry for Education and Culture. I met also the great Kamaladevi Chattopadhyay; friend of Mahatma Gandhi, leader of the women's move-ment, and of world-wide renown for her work to establish India's craftsmen (and above all craftswomen) and to market the products of those threatened skills—threatened by the machine. Their work doubly threatened, for when those hand-made things of beauty are themselves produced for export, they become less joyous and the work less fine. Kamaladevi had also established a beautiful small crafts museum in Delhi, where rare treasures—puppets and masks and all crafts to do with the popular theatre (another of her concerns) are to be seen, and the work of living craftswomen is on sale. A losing battle? Who knows, and all battles are lost by those who do not fight on. I should know that, for is not *Temenos* such a battle for values?

Kamaladevi arranged for a company of puppeteers to play for us a scene from the *Ramayana*: again, the joy of human skill, but how long will such simplicities prevail against the ubiquitous cinema, and the advent of the television set, streaming in the currents of an alien and unlovely secular culture? One did not ask such questions if one was Kamaladevi. Imperturbable (she was, after all, for eight years of her life in prison under the British Raj), she simply, quietly, did what had to be done. Kamaladevi was remarkably kind to me and supportive of that not easily definable order of things to which I am dedicated. Perhaps she saw me also as one who works against the current: not indeed that I have been persecuted and imprisoned; in the West things are done differently—those who do not conform are not nowadays attacked unless they are much more conspicuous than I—the technique is to disregard our existence. Not a bad review but no review at all prevents unwanted books from being read; and both in my Blake studies and in *Temenos* this has been my treatment in my own country (in France the sales of my books even in translation has been many times greater than here in England—I was once even, briefly, a 'best seller'!). Perhaps the reason is that at an official dinner given for me I did commit a diplomatic *faux pas* for which I ought to be sorry—certainly it has done my public credit no good—and yet I don't know that I am sorry. I am, in my fashion, deeply loyal to 'the England of the Imagination'—the England of Shakespeare and the poets, of Purcell and Blake and Samuel Palmer and the Shoreham Ancients and the Gothic Cathedrals and all the kindnesses and simplicities of my childhood. I am an entirely non-political person. But when at that dinner I heard a strong north British voice saying to our host (à propos Mahatma Gandhi whom Kamaladevi had known so well) 'but you can't compare these *common criminals* with Gandhi!' (the IRA hunger-strikers of the Maze Prison, that is, eleven of whom were allowed to die) I heard myself saying that those willing to give their lives for a cause can hardly be called 'common criminals'. 'England has treated Ireland even worse than she treated us!' I heard Kamaladevi say at the other end of the table, in ringing tones. Be that as it may, Kamaladevi thereafter treated me very much as a friend. Not so, to be sure, the British Council; but then I was in India as the guest of the Indian Government not as the representative of my own. Those who like myself owe our first loyalty to the 'Kingdom not of this world' which has no national frontiers generally find ourselves in trouble on specific political issues. I should I suppose have kept silent, but the Ireland of the Imagination is also dear to me. Those who are less concerned with the 'Politics of Time' than with the 'Politics of Eternity' must be prepared to take the consequences. The situation of our world has gone far beyond the power of politics as such to remedy. *Temenos* is concerned only with the Politics of Eternity. But Ireland's minstrel boys who continue to swell the Ranks of Death—those tragic fanatical products of centuries of British occupation of Ireland—belong also in their way to the Kingdom of the Imagination: 'When Thought is clos'd in Caves, Then love shall shew its root in Deepest Hell.'

It was the women whom I met in India on this first visit

who most impressed me. I am no feminist—quite the contrary, for the feminist image of woman seems to me without the attributes most valuable, powerful, beautiful and loveable in womankind; they are what Robert Graves called 'honorary men'. Kapila, Kamaladevi, and Mrs Gandhi's friend and adviser in heritage and cultural resources, Pupul Jayakar—friend also of my dear American friend Nancy Wilson Ross—seemed to carry India's cultural heritage and much besides in their hands while carrying their beauty and femininity with ease. All three had lived rich lives of the Imagination: Kamaladevi had been the first Indian woman (of her class that is) to appear on the stage as an actress, and had been deeply engaged in the theatre before the struggle for Independence called out in her more heroic qualities. Pupul Jayakar has made known to the West India's heritage through the Indian exhibitions which she (as Mrs Gandhi's and later Rajiv Gandhi's Minister of Culture) has sent to the West. All three have been contributors to *Temenos*; and I wonder if there is another nation in the world three of whose ruling élite—or even one—we would ever have considered as contributors? Mrs Gandhi herself it seems knew and approved *Temenos*, which Professor Lokesh Chandra had shown her. It seems that it is the women of India who would most wish, in entering the future of a young nation, to take with them the cultural heritage of India's ancient civilization.

A young Parsee student, Shernaz Sethna visited me at breakfast one day in our hostel to speak of her wish to study Blake in the way my work has indicated, rather than in terms of the secular values offered by the universities. This she has since done, writing her thesis on Blake's knowledge of Zoroastrianism with great success; she too—as well as her sister—a lawyer—outstandingly beautiful as well. When I say beauty I do not mean simply a beauty of physique and feature, but something else which belongs to a woman's sense of her own being which can make even plain features radiate that magical gift, a beauty reflecting India's Goddess of many names. The sari is a garment designed to enhance that beauty, but the inner gift must be there. Most of India's women, rich or poor, learned or simple, possess this gift; inheritence of a culture which deems sexuality sacred. It is the women who most preserve traditional dress; though in the country more men are to be seen wearing *dhotis*. In Delhi most wear mass produced western-style suits, though men of the higher classes wear those elegant long coats that better become the Indian physique. But the women of all classes are like multicoloured flowers in their saris, the cotton saris of the poor no less beautiful than the silken saris of the rich. Sometimes one sees, with a shock reminiscent of Gulliver when he realized that the Yahoos of the land of the Houyhnhnms were human also, hideous pink blistered torsos and thighs and recognizes these as Westerners, (useless to pretend that all come from America), blue-jeans or shorts the uniform of their culture. India is never forgetful of beauty while the West seems oblivious of ugliness. No wonder that Santosh, on her first visit to London found the shock of London's streets almost more than she could bear. Alas, will India follow Western fashion? One fears so; and it is hard to imagine Western women following that of India, that creation of six thousand years of refinement. Here there is no trace in dress of sacred tradition; even priests have given up 'dog-collars' and the beautiful robes of nuns have been curtailed to silly skirts and short veils. Here I'm thinking of Ireland, where religious dress is still worn and to be seen; in London it is rare indeed. Peoples' clothes, in India, indicate their identity—the lock of the Brahmin, the strange headdress of the Parsee *Dastur*, the Sikh turban, the white Gandhi-cap; the *tilak* mark, the veil of the Islamic women, the Punjabi women's pyjamas and kurtas, but above all the sari, as ancient as the *Mahabharata*—

[44]

Draupadi's sari that miraculously grew longer and longer as her mockers pulled it in their vain attempt to reveal her nakedness. In the West identity is affirmed by wearing a tee-shirt stamped with the name of some pop group or football team or film-star; such being the identities to which our culture aspires.

The sari is, besides, (so in the Indian climate one realizes) the most practical of garments, protecting against sun, dust, and mosquitoes too, while letting the cool air flow over the body. You can cover or uncover the head in the heat of the day; draw a sari over mouth and nose in a dust-storm; it displays beauty, or conceals the deliquescent figures of the middle-aged; it is at once seductive and dignified; its colours are infinitely various, and for travel is easily folded and packed. But there is nothing in it for the dress designers who profit by ever-changing fashions and the 'rag trade' that deals in these. There is nothing for this huge commercial empire in the sari, whose beauty is timeless and simple. Indian women's education, besides, lends them grace. It is still the rule rather than the exception for girls to be taught to sing, to dance, to play an instrument; education in the arts and graces of life is still part of family tradition. Women here pay little attention to these things, seeming to prefer some skill which will enable them to earn more money, even though at the expense of the richness and also the responsibilities of life itself as it has been lived in families from time immemorial. Besides, who needs to sing or dance when there is 'the telly'? In place of the beauty and seductiveness of song and dance there is crude 'sex' advertised not by concealment but by exposure of the body or as perpetrated in American (and not only American) films. The French still retain a certain elegance of deportment, and Italy more sheer virtuosity of its own particular mode of outrageous and satiric decadence; at least in the Italian there seems to be more pleasure than in the crude and slovenly English brand.

In India there are no 'protest fashions'—nor indeed in Spain or Greece, other than those worn by English or American tourists. But if India loses its traditional dress, its traditional image of womanly beauty, the loss will be irreparable. And yet in India one finds women directing the affairs of the State—the slim lonely figure of Indira Gandhi driving in the Republic Day parade on her gun-carriage, preceded and followed by regiments in their gay plumage; Kamaladevi that uncrowned queen; Kapila and the many other women in various positions and professions whom I met have all one thing in common—all are beautiful.

My granddaughter Sonia was much delighted with the marriage advertisements in the Sunday papers: Solicitor (or doctor or merchant or whatever it might be) wishes to meet a girl who must be—and always in the following order—'beautiful, fair (by Indian standards that is, an Aryan, not a black tribal or Dravidian woman) tall, and often (but this comes last) with a university degree. Always beauty comes first; and surely rightly so, if, as Plato understood, the Beautiful is the aspect of the Good. Or as Shakespeare said, 'Is she kind as she is fair/For beauty lives with kindness'. One notices, with the culture-shock of a return to London, the sheer uncouth ugliness of our populace, the ugliness of the women's dress and deportment. Rarely does one see a beautiful face, young or old. Sexy and uneducated youth withers into disgruntled age. Does one ever get used to the absence of beauty? How long can our culture survive without it? Yet it is the technological culture of the West that invades, for it is effortless: 'effortless barbarism'.

Of course India is a deeply wounded nation. Not only do the universities absorb and disseminate western values, but so also, of course, does commercial imperialism. That it is not race as such but a culture, a civilization that bestows its beauty on India's women, one can see from the secular faces that have already appeared in Bombay. I recall my first visit to New York City, where one sees faces of every ethnic origin but all, alas, stamped with the cultural imprint of the American 'way of life'.

❀

It is said that we forget nothing—that every trace remains for ever in memory. Yet the memory differs from the sensible event as an image reflected in water differs from the bricks and mortar of an Islamic Mosque by whose means the builders of mosques and tombs and other buildings of beauty made use of these weightless replicas as gateways to transpose the material object into another order of things. So one remembers places without the insect-bites, the dust, the shoe that tortures one's foot, the heat, the fatigue. We enter, in memory, 'through the looking-glass' where we find only what we are capable of reflecting in that magic mirror. And what, from memory, do we ask? To live again happy moments, as with snapshots brought home from a holiday and projected on a screen to delight the host and bore the neighbours? Or something else? What did we really experience, as we bumped along the road to Agra in our official Government Ambassador car, Sonia and myself, Thetis, Santosh, our driver and (much to Sonia's delight and amusement) a military guard? Nothing was as I had foreseen or imagined—temples, I discovered, were seldom large buildings, but what we would call shrines (one finds plenty of these in Greece) brightly painted and with a tinselled picture of whatever god they are dedicated to—Hanuman or Shiva's lingam, a little pennon fluttering from the pinnacle. Unadorned Islamic tombs pointing their dead towards Mecca.

On the road two currents flowed, the old India and the new; there were still horse-drawn *tongas* (whole families, three generations, travelling in these) ox carts, elegant camels drawing great loads of fodder or sugar-cane; cows and their calves; buffalo with their laid-back horns; holy

[47]

men in little groups, snake charmers and performing monkeys; the animals always adorned, their horns painted, rickshaws and tongas adorned with tinsel and lotus flowers and the Goddess. The bicycle is a family conveyance, the husband pedalling, wife and infant behind, sometimes another toddler on the handlebars. The bicycle is almost merged in the archaic stream; while the world of the machine—not yet many cars, but endless Tata lorries with their over-loads with the rear sign requesting 'Horn please' inviting a constant trumpeting, not of elephants but of those too generously invited horns—affirmed and inserted and imposed another culture. Yet India can leave nothing unadorned, untouched by that beauty-creating genius that paints the tough hides of elephants, the horns of cattle and buffalo—the Tata lorries decorated with tinsel and lotuses and peacocks and goddesses, the windscreen hung with charms, and along the road strung-out villages with their stalls selling food and tea and coffee to passers-by. No doubt the road is a main source of income for these villages; and I was told the story of Chandigarh having planned for a new road which would not pass the villages but leave them to undisturbed quiet. But when the road was made the villages moved to be near that current of life and maybe source of income. India is very obviously a country of poverty; and if I write of another aspect it is not because I am unaware of what everyone knows, but simply because poets have eyes for other things, which are also there. Houses—if those bare thatched shelters can be so called—that might seem of extreme squalor in a photograph printed in our northern climes are less so in a land where people are seldom indoors; where the old men of a village often sit on a raised platform under some venerable pipal or banyan tree, or the women at work on embroidery or toy making, the babies tumbling beside them, gossiping in the leafy shade. Houses are as much for storage as for living in.

[48]

The Indian landscape between Delhi and Agra is not particularly beautiful; in India it is the people, old and young, and the many children, who are beautiful, I found, down to the poorest women in their bright saris who carry on their heads baskets of earth to the men working on the roads; dignified and beautiful, and the little clusters of children, the six-year-olds in charge of the two-year-olds and the four-year-olds minding the babies just on their feet. All are beautiful, the old men, the youths who drive the rickshaws, as often as not with a young brother or two there for the ride. Old women also seemed to fill up any spare space in those more ample *tongas*, so that all on the road seemed, whatever burdens they might be transporting, to be never far from a pleasure-outing. Or maybe I saw with Western eyes a scene that seemed bathed in happiness as with sunlight. Although there were grimmer roadside scenes—stone breakers at work with as it seemed tools no better than other stones in their bare hands. Such sights cannot but trouble Western eyes, nor is it surprising that India wants machines to carry out such menial tasks as in the West no labourer would be asked to perform. Yet, without sentimentalizing a country with so much material poverty, a sense of the richness and beauty of life itself is ever-present. Not, perhaps, in the shanty-towns around Bombay whose stench meets all who approach the city; but these I did not visit, nor Mother Teresa's hospice in Calcutta. I can only say that in India there are, poverty notwithstanding, many happy and beautiful faces to be seen; and that (spiritually speaking) the 'culture-shock' is the return to the streets of London which ever bring to mind Eliot's line, 'I had not thought death had undone so many'.

One cannot fail to notice in India how many happy and beautiful faces there are—the two go together. In the ample gardens of Nehru's *Samadhi* by the Yamuna river, five gentle brown-eyed men and a bullock cutting the grass; when the container was full it was emptied for the bullock to eat, while the young men sat and enjoyed the moment. Or the lovely gardens of Qutub Minar on a Sunday, no transistor radios, no need when all the family is there, three generations, the grandmothers, uncles and aunts, young people, small boys practising cricket with bigger sisters bowling to them; fathers holding the hands of baby daughters walking carefully along the tops of little walls; outspread blankets and baskets of food—everywhere in India there is food, gaily displayed in baskets of sliced coconuts, samosas, sweet-meats—and no one vandalizing trees or those abundant beautiful flowers. It was in Pune, in the garden of that little palace where Gandhi was imprisoned, and where his wife's *samadhi* is now among those beautiful blossoming trees, that a notice read 'Do not pick the flowers and we will delight you eternally'. The word eternally used correctly, I noticed; as in Blake who saw 'eternal centres' in hawthorn and meadow-sweet. People are still able to enjoy simple happiness, the 'eternal' beauty of flowers, the company of children and old people, in the sun. There is no rowdiness or slovenliness, a quiet decorum rather, no shouting or smashing or that resentful vandalism one finds in London and doubtless other 'inner city areas' vandalized in a kind of social resentment and uncivilized truculence that seems peculiar to present-day England.

One has but to cross the channel to see how well the French treat their parks and public places. The Luxembourg Gardens where the old gentlemen read their newspapers, the grandmothers knit, the toddlers toddle, and lovers hold hands, the young athletes run, the joggers jog, the ballet-students exercise, the gardeners garden, and everyone seems to be quietly doing what they want to do and no-one is idling and slouching and vandalizing and looking for trouble. And in India also people treat their cities—even the poorer cities—well and cheerfully, their markets of fruits and spices and dyes and brassware and flowers and textiles and plastic buckets. These are displacing the old beautiful water-pots women can sometimes still be seen carrying on their heads, and displacing the craftsmen who from time immemorial have been a part of India's village economy; and so no doubt other products of the machine. One knows that technology will triumph and in so doing will destroy many ingenious lovely things. Yet the vegetable stalls and florists still put out stale greens or tired roses for the cows and their calves who wander gently through the streets. I missed, when I returned to the King's Road, the creatures, the camels and oxen and the little pigs and dogs also who help to clear up the litter. All very insanitary no doubt but the natural life-cycles have their own virtues; belatedly we are learning that to poison the land and the seas and the air with our clever chemical inventions may prove not merely insanitary but lethal.

Such were my wandering thoughts as we bumped along the road to Agra, my first Indian road. I will not describe the Taj Mahal, that marvellous beauty received by pairs of eyes without number, carried over the world, innumerably multiplied. It is not the photographs (too many of these) but what has once been created multiplies itself endlessly in a million living minds to which that beauty speaks—those alabaster poppies and lilies, those translucent gems that adorn the tomb of the beloved—Shah Jehan's beloved, and the beloved of all those multitudes past and to come. 'Love's all worshipped tomb/Where all love's pilgrims come'. The Beloved herself. The bees nest in the niches on the side overlooking the great Yamuna beyond, with its sandy shores, and the beauty of that shrine of perfect proportion remains inviolate as it speaks to those who can read it the language of eternal beauty. As I write, I look out on a London brick wall: I look inwards and behold the crescent moon poised over a minaret, I behold the Yamuna's waters and those sandy channels, the bees' honey-combs built according to the same beautiful geometric laws that adorn the *iwans* with those geometric stalactites the genius of Islam created. All that beauty and sorrow of mortality Tagore's poem on Shah Jehan has captured, I and millions participate for ever its wholeness and perfection not divisible by no matter how many our millions, but experienced and known by each 'eternally', like the flowers.

We bought some jewels in the marble-factory just outside Agra, and inlaid boxes still made by craftsmen with those same skills as adorned the Taj; in whose realization the skills of the whole world, from Italy to Persia, were brought to Agra, to realize an eternal vision captured in the transient tragic life-time of Shah Jehan, whose slaughterous son Aurangzeb was the survivor of war to the death of the four brothers; a man who made war not love, and despised his father for spending on beauty what he should have spent on slaughter. He refused to build a second Taj Mahal for his own wife; but his son built for her (a 'poor man's Taj') a plaster version near Udaipur. But you cannot repeat perfection a second time, all works of imagination are unique. As for Aurangzeb, his tomb is a plain one, as befits a warrior, in the courtyard of a mosque and school; the sort of grave that makes one think of such truths and truisms as that the paths of glory lead but to the grave. All his armies are dust, and the Mogul rulers of India long gone, while in the Taj Mahal an intangible vision speaks to all ages still the universal language of love and beauty, for it is always our own, be we whom we may.

❊

Beauty is on all sides; where was that small ruined temple where we lingered—somewhere in Rajasthan—by a little lake, with water-birds and a few papaya trees, where the father was leading his bullock that raised the irrigation water buckets, and his small children came with posies to sell us? The water birds, the children, the rich carvings of that small deserted temple, built half-out over a little lake. Yeats wrote that when he was young he had wanted to write poems about some little temple of India's Golden Age. *Shakuntala.* Here for an hour it was, the temple, the fertile fields, the children with their posies, at peace with the heron in the lake, the ox at his task. Here animals are not hunted or disturbed. Yes, you will say, but are not the cattle starved, those sacred cows it is forbidden to kill? What about those laborious stone breakers? What about the mutilation of children by 'protectors' who send them out as beggars? What of the burning of brides whose dowries have not been paid? What of the lack of water and sanitation, and so on, and on and on. But how can a visitor from a civilization that has gained technology at the price of so much that makes life precious, fail to see the beauty and happiness of the children playing in some gutter of Brindavan where the refuse floats down, (like the egg-shell and the darning needle in Hans Anderson's children's world) and the only water tap is at the top of the street? Beauty in India is not a luxury but a necessity: how would India endure the poverty, the hunger, the lack of sanitation, the disease, the shanty-towns, the breaking of stones, without the paper birds, the bangles, the garlands of stephanotis and marigolds, the tinsel and the glitter, the gods and their bright tawdry effigies and the sacred animals, casting on this world the reflection of another? That man does not live by bread alone is a message plain enough to those of us who visit India from the affluent West. Will it be possible, we ask ourselves, for India, needing those water taps, electrical plant, stone crushers and equipment of all kinds modern technology can supply, still to keep that soul we have lost? Two things, Kapila said, are the enemies of her task in the field of education and culture: Star-wars; the wholesale destruction of the natural environment; and I would venture to add, surely the television set. I asked her if she thought India would have to make all the Western mistakes without learning from our experience? Yes, she said, all of them; but the problem surely is, there is not time!

Overall impressions are hard to define and perhaps valueless—it is the 'minute particulars' that signify—and if I were to say that my overall impression of India is one of quiet, simple, happiness, half-a-dozen westernized Indian novelists and a legion of journalists would take pleasure in proving otherwise, would tell their deplorable tales of 'conditions' and injustices and corruption and of course poverty without limit, all perfectly true. But how describe that sense that India knows what happiness is, people know how to be happy, something the West seems almost to have forgotten. Happy, that is, when not doing anything in particular, people just being where they are, tend to be happy. Where would one begin to look for happiness in the United States, where almost anyone one meets seems to be 'under analysis', to feel their weekly visit to a psychiatrist to be as necessary to life as the supermarket, as a matter of course. Happiness is something too simple for American urban-dwellers, who are, I believe, ninety six per cent of the population. New York City is a wonderful city but you don't feel happiness to be a part of its vitality, its intoxication. Just brothers being with one another, or fathers and baby daughters and grandmothers with daughters-in-law. Families are loving to one another as a normal thing. To a Westerner it's amazing! The people of Delhi, walking in the Lodi Gardens, or the quiet garden of the tomb of Humayun seem to delight 'eternally' in the flowers, or, like the 'eternal' flowers in their own lives, their families and companionship, children, young girls walking together quietly, the old, the young. Innocence! What has become of innocence among the young people of London? The pair of lovers walking in the garden of Humayun's Tomb who asked Thetis to take their camera and photograph them together? The old man washing his garment with a garden hose then spreading it to dry in the sun while he performed his ablutions?

That innocence of life seems to go with a pride and a happiness in being Indian. I don't mean Raja Rao's kind of Brahmin pride in India as the ultimate realization of our human potentiality, but something much simpler, a pride in being, perhaps, citizens of a new nation no less than heirs of an ancient civilization. Those new tombs by the Yamuna river tell of a new sense of glory no less than the eloquent witness of the glory of the Mogul emperors, builders of the most beautiful tombs in the world, surely. The *samadhi* of Mahatma Gandhi is holy ground. We leave our shoes at the entrance to that beautiful cloister-like court where the young trees are already richly grown. An old man with a spinning wheel is spinning in the shade. A school party of girls and their teachers sitting on the grass in respectful meditation, as it seems—it is the anniversary of some memorable event, I am told. There are people circumambulating that all-worshipped tomb where burns an inextinguishable flame. Flame that is not merely fire but the god also—Agni—a sacred fire. I first paid my respects to India's great leader whom my father, a pacifist, had so revered—whom all the world revered—with Santosh, on my first visit to India, and three years later with Satish Kumar and other Indians and Westerners taking part in the conference for which we had come, and again circumambulated that shrine, at which Satish recited a prayer, in Sanskrit. I had paid my last respects to our great Winston Churchill, slowly walking in that unending procession of those who had lived through the Second World War under his leadership, over Westminster Bridge, and winding our way into the Great Hall of Westminster where he lay in state. All there were full of memories as we slowly wound our way through London's dark misty evening; we had loved that great war-leader who had used the English language as one of Shakespeare' dukes might have done, to stir some sense of glory in us modern groundlings, who delighted in that rhetoric, somehow still in the blood of the English nation at that time—for the last time as it now seems to me. But Gandhiji was something else, the tradition in which he stood not the procession of history and its kings and leaders, but of holy men, renunciates and ascetics, representing on earth some divine principle. The veneration given to Gandhiji is not merely accorded to a great historical figure and national leader, nor is it even that he spoke of non-violence to the whole world, a message whose simplicity all understood: he represented a divine principle. But then, in India, how easily persons and places become endowed with a quality of the sacred!

And how will it be with Indira Gandhi, so fallible and alone, whose *samadhi*, only a little beyond those of her father and of Gandhiji himself, still remained, when I saw it—a year before I had seen Mrs Gandhi herself standing on her gun carriage to receive the salute of her people in the Republic Day parade—a raw wound in the naked earth, unhealed? The still open wound of her assassination.

What I am trying to understand—to communicate—is a certain sense of the universal participation of the soul of India's multitudes in her recent history; in the sense of glory of a heroic moment, still living in the memories of many; the 'India of the Imagination' within the politics of time. Every nation has such moments; perhaps once only. Churchill apart—and has not he too receded already into history—do we visit the graves of our Prime Ministers or remove our shoes and circumambulate them? Do we even know where they are buried? The sense of personal participation in India as a nation (something different from, though surely not unrelated to, India as a civilization) is something I distinctly felt to be very real. And besides, Nehru and Gandhiji and Indira Gandhi were still remembered and loved by the very people I was meeting in Delhi and how many more besides. It was like straying into the enactment of an epic—at least of an epilogue. It must have been like that for Shakespeare, those recent memories of kings and queens who still inhabited the national imagination. With all India's 'problems', political and otherwise, yes, I felt that India's people inhabited, in this sense, a dimension of the Imagination that creates and sustains nationhood. The television has not yet eroded that India; although doubtless it will. Fashionable violence is on its way—Santosh, who always used to walk through the charming park that separates her house from the campus of the University, unmolested, would no longer venture to do so. What has taken millennia to create can be so quickly destroyed. But I seemed to sense a happiness and a hope (for how long? Who can say?) that it would no longer, I fear, be possible to find in my own country at this time—we have the sense that our history is in the past, not in the present or the future.

Perhaps that sentiment is something incompatible with the secular; and yet it is true that in the United States the heroic and the poetic aspect of history is still a very living presence. All those battlefields of the War between the States, their history told in those long detailed inscriptions placed on the sites of this or that regiment or encounter, heroic tragic moments made enduring in bronze. Huntingdon Cairns of the Andrew Mellon Gallery used to take those of us who visited Washington to visit Harper's Ferry, and Antietam and the rest. One expedition was to a moving and beautiful memorial to the war-reporters and war-artists (of both sides) of that war, in some beautiful woods—I no longer recall the place. 'How quickly nature heals over history's wounds' or something of the kind, I foolishly said. 'Not in my heart it doesn't' was Huntingdon's reply, that son of West Virginia. Farmers still plow up bullets in their fields, as they do in France and Flanders.

For whatever reason, then, I could not but feel that happiness prevailed over discontent among the simple people of India. There was a Sunday when Mohan Pall took us on an outing to Qutub Minar, little more than an hour's drive outside Delhi. We came to a level-crossing where the gates were closed, and we, with all the rest of the travellers, had no choice but to wait until they opened. Engines were shunted, came and went in a leisurely manner, a few trains too, but the gates remained closed. We became interested, watching like children playing with a model railway. It became quite a drama, we could see the men in the signal-box and other railway employees who came and went from time to time. Sometimes hopes would rise, only to be disappointed once more. There was a bus just in front of us, and soon people got out and sat by the roadside. Youths with trays of food appeared—as they always seem to appear in India, ready to make a pleasant picnic of a traffic-jam or other occasion that brings people to a stand-still. No one seemed impatient, no-one complained or stamped up and down in Western style, it was no less possible to be happy in one place than another. The roadside was as good a place to be as any other. And so it went on for a good half-hour or more. A cyclist or two lifted their bicycles over the gates, applauded gently by the onlookers, nervously followed by the wives or sisters they had been carrying behind them. But I cannot imagine any Western country where life would have gone so serenely on, regardless of time and the fantasies of the signalman, as here. It even came into our minds that the delay was a ploy, with the connivance of the signalman, to allow those youths with their baskets of oranges and slices of coconut to sell their wares. Their presence there at least suggested that such delays were a normal part of level-crossing life.

Jaipur, Udaipur; a little deserted temple by a lake; moon-light over the great temple of Puri, the saris and the bangles. But what of the dark side of India? I, a guest of the Indian Government, was not given my Ambassador car and a guide to meet me at every airport to be shown the dark side, the worst. 'The poor are always with us', Jesus said. And has not our own welfare-state its drug-addicts, its AIDS victims, its mass unemployment, its 'inner city areas', its Ulster? No need to be taken on a guided tour of Mother Teresa's Calcutta, of Bombay's shanty-town, there are beggars and lepers in New Delhi's Connaught Circle and those mutilated children. Our guide to Ajanta and Ellora had been one of those who had attempted a rescue enterprise for such children, and was about to be kidnapped, he told us, by the 'mafia' who organized this trade in young lives, to be saved only by one of the children giving the alarm. I knew of such things and saw them from the other side of the glass windscreen of an Ambassador car. However, in holy Varanasi—older, Kumar tells me, than Babylon—the gods do indeed show their dark faces, no less ancient than the six-thousand-year old masks of beauty. In Varanasi as elsewhere.

Sight-seeing in India involves sleepless nights—sleepless lest we do not wake in time to set out for some airport to catch one of those internal flights that leaves before sunrise or soon after, doubtless to avoid the heat of the day. Thus granddaughter Sonia, Thetis, Santosh and I, with the representative of the Indian Council of Cultural Relations responsible for me, found ourselves waiting at Delhi airport at about 4 am. there to remain for several hours. Our flight was delayed because the Indian Airforce was rehearsing for the Republic Day celebrations. Thus we arrived many hours late at Varanasi; and my memory of that all too brief visit is a

somewhat painful confusion. Our guide who met us there—
he had presumably been waiting for several hours too—had
assumed or been told that I would wish to visit the
University to give a lecture; and immediately rushed us out
through roads which I recall as lined with trees in which
numbers of peacocks roosted—to the University where a
group of students and lecturers from the English Faculty
were waiting to meet us; presumably they too all those
hours. Poor things! Profuse apologies; no lecture. But we
did sit in a lecture-room round a table and talk about
poetry—I forget what—and I was sorry I had come unprepared, had been the ignorant cause of keeping these also
waiting all those hours. Santosh had by now told our guide
that I wished to see the ancient city, not the fine University
nor the Museum (this I regret). So in an uneasy mood, far
different from the shimmering light-hearted well-being in
which we had in irresponsible leisure seen the beauties of
Agra and Fatehpur-Sikri, somehow we were hurried and
bundled through Varanasi's winding streets. The first
Indian temple I ever entered was large and modern, I
believe attached to the University. Idols of Shiva in the same
mass-produced style as one might see in any prosperous
Catholic or Anglo Catholic church, neither better nor worse.
What I had expected I don't quite know, nor from the
beginning to the end of my visit to Varanasi did I ever catch
up on that original sense of disorientation, of a kaleidoscope
of unlooked-for, unforeseen impressions for which I was
unprepared not only to a degree for which I was unprepared
but in the kind of my unpreparedness. It was a series of
shocks, irritations, panic and fatigue, frustrations, discon-
certing insights into myself; and yet, if I were ever to visit
India again—in another life it could well be, for now I would
find such harassing days of sight-seeing beyond my
strength—it would be to Varanasi I would most wish to
return. Holy Varanasi. But not holy as the word is under-

stood in Christian countries—what, indeed, is the holy? Snakes and idols and monkeys and ant-hills and the lingam. Start again!

The second temple in which I set foot was far other than the clean respectable modern one; dark, rather dirty, very strange, we passed as if through a show of wax-works idols of Rama and Sita (or was it Krishna and Radha), gods daily dressed and undressed in their grubby finery, put to bed (the beds were there) roused in the morning, a devotion strangely literal, I found, in that land of metaphysical wisdom. But in India 'good taste' is a concept unknown. I had to give myself another bad mark. These are not 'works of art'—more like dressed-up dolls—crude but not ancient. Very powerful images, often, like Kali's black mask and protruding tongue, frightening; Shiva with moustaches; all as strange and unexpected as a ride in a ghost-train at a fair, and as swiftly over-leaving the same impression of dis-orientation. Another temple, with a little courtyard where the lingam of Shiva was set in a sunken basin on the ground, a stone snake wriggling in the basin where it stood. Santosh brought us, with our garlands of stephanotis and marigolds purchased from a flower seller on the pavement outside into the temple itself where Thetis fell foul of the priest who wanted a quite exorbitant sum of money from this rich English lady. I offered my garland of flowers and little packet of sugar (this shocked granddaughter Sonia that I should do so, but I would treat with respect the gods of any country). The priest withdrew for us a grubby curtain to let us see the most ancient and sacred effigy of Shiva. An uneven rock surface painted in terrifying scarlet more vivid than blood. I could not, to be truthful, discern features there; but Santosh later explained that such temples were indeed often the sites of some vision of one of the gods (as on this rock-face) thereafter consecrated. Sonia (dreaming of her missionary) was deeply shocked and shocked that I was not.

I on the contrary was shocked to find how shocked I was, again so deeply disconcerted by the unforeseen. I had thought myself well prepared to enter the India of the Imagination as I had imagined it to be. But this India was unimaginable. I was among the unimaginable. Another temple too holy to admit Europeans; Santosh, a devout worshipper of the gods of India, entered to worship. Always the fear that our guide, who seemed always to be rushing ahead round dark corners, would lose us and we would emerge no more. Somewhere in that turmoil of memories a Hanuman temple, with monkeys strolling around—real monkeys—and their holiness notwithstanding the guide with a stout stick to chase away these avatars of the god should they attack us (they did not). All was strange, all was India, nothing was 'art' or any such thing that I could hold on to mentally, all was too real, too archaic, I had no prepared responses to anything I was encountering in these ancient dark dirty streets or to the little boys begging for 'one rupee'—how could we with a few coins in our pockets resolve the problem of India's starving poor, or of our consciences? Bare-foot beautiful ragged little boys, the poor everywhere. No wonder our guide had wanted to deposit us safely at the University and the Museum. But if I wanted to see the real Varanasi, then let me have it—I don't think he much liked these English ladies who had been wished on him in the course of his duties: why should he? There was no time to establish any real relationship, Varanasi had all the reality—unreality—surreality—of a surreal fair-ground. I was shocked at my own reaction to temples and 'idols', finding these as unassimilable as if I had come straight from the Sunday-schools of my childhood—I was disconcerted, out of my depth altogether.

Sonia being with me, I did not ask to see the burning-ghats beside that holy Ganges whose waters divide the world of the living from the other world. Varanasi is indeed

Shiva's city; 'the dancer in the crematorium'. Besides, would it not be an intrusion on the world of the mourners and the reality of death? But as through more crowded (now lit with artificial light) streets towards those ghats where people gather to bathe in the holy river, not to bury their dead, we saw all that the Lord Buddha had seen: sickness, old age, death. A corpse veiled in yellow muslin with threads of gold carried on the shoulders of her mourners. On foot we went nearer that great river of life and death and there were the poor, the sick and the dying. Under a sort of sack what looked like rhythmic death-throes; all that in our own world is shut away from our eyes behind gleaming antiseptic tiled walls, was here; Death. People come to holy Varanasi to die by that sacred river that divides this world from that. Sickness, old-age and death—these at least I could understand. Should I have been shocked, horrified? They will come to us all some day. 'So here it is', I found myself thinking; with a kind of sense of kinship of flesh and blood, of familiarity with something I had always known but forgotten. Something more akin, the death and disease, the poverty and squalor (if such human life indeed is) of human suffering, than those frightening gods in their dark temples that are not at all like churches. Let those who come to search for 'the wisdom of the East' in India enter by that low door, that extreme of the human condition that none can elude, the terrifying scarlet rock face—as though painted in wet blood—under the dirty curtain, the garlands of flowers, the little packets of sugar to offer those awesome gods.

In the morning we visited the ghats again—beautiful steps going down to the wide serene river. Perhaps some of those still figures holy men in meditation, all life and death is there, the dying under old sacks, the beggars, the lepers, the pilgrims, the holy men. We can no longer bear it, no longer read it; not safely at a distance as on a television screen, but the beggar-children asking for 'one rupee, one rupee', hunger beyond the reach of political reform or Mother Teresa's nuns. (Yet I was told by Ned O'Gorman, who works in Harlem where he has a school for infants, that Mother Teresa had found Harlem infinitely sadder than Calcutta. India is not sad.) No, the holy men in silent meditation and those terrifying featureless gods who haunt rock-faces and caves and whirlpools are more true to implacable, mysterious life. Reality? Humankind cannot bear very much of it, as Eliot—the poet who withdrew from the study of Vedanta to the comforting shelter of Christianity—well knew. That serene sky, that serene river, those ancient steps down to the water where the pilgrims bathe in holy Ganges. Have I conveyed anything of what I saw, and did I understand anything at all except that I understood almost nothing? I set myself a task, it seems, in 'wishing to see and enjoy India' far beyond my capacity. Not India alone, is not life itself far beyond the capacity of the living to understand? We can but live life, we cannot hope to understand it.

Then to Sarnath; the sacred mound where the Lord Buddha had preached his first sermon; under a sacred peepal tree (not the one in Sarnath from which I carried back a leaf for a Buddhist friend in America). He was prepared to die of starvation—there are those representations of the emaciated Buddha before he received that enlightenment—and did not of course know that illumination would come; nothing is certain, there are no easy 'beliefs' for those prepared to meet reality on its own terms. He could have been a prince and ruled his father's kingdom, but what of that for one who has seen sickness, old-age and death? For the prince who has everything, what remains but to possess nothing, to wash the feet of the sick and the dying? Sarnath, serene, beautiful; those wonderful sculptures from the reign of King Asoka, embodying a vision that illuminated all the Eastern world and now seems to have come full circle, to the materialist West, where it seems that Buddhism is the fastest growing religion. Whatever it was that Prince Siddartha understood—that flower-sermon, that smile—humanity has understood for longer than the Christian crucifix, whose meaning seems in our world so self-evident. But the smile of the Lord Buddha, that grave smile—if indeed that composed serenity of the human features be a smile—that is older, has been understood, transmitted, contemplated—has brought peace, wisdom—has brought itself to us, the answer of the human soul to the phantasmagoria. All this in two uncomfortable days in Varanasi; in utmost unpreparedness I saw what Prince Siddhartha had seen, and I had seen his answering smile. Not that I have any intention of 'becoming a Buddhist'. We must, as Herman Hesse understood so well, find each our own way through the phantasmagoria. India, for me, was little better than spiritual tourism. What could my drop of life bring to that eternal river? Or how could a drop of India's eternal river wash away my own *karma?* Yet those powers that direct our lives did take me to India, did give me that glimpse. They decreed India for me, and that must mean something.

❦

Ajanta; that cliff-face whose caves must have seemed to invite those celibate renunciates who followed the example of Prince Siddhartha. Yet with what cultured refinement they depicted on these rocky walls a king renouncing his throne, laying aside his silk garments, parting from his swooning wife and her court ladies with their braided hair. What an exquisite world they were renouncing! Yet—one thinks of Yeats's phases of the moon—what more remains for princes to attain unless it be renunciation, the begging bowl and the saffron robe? What young princes nurtured in every refinement of India's royal palaces painted those

[65]

crumbling murals? That exquisitely braided hair, those silk garments and flowers? One thinks of Italy where, again, monasticism drew the young aristocrats to Subiaco and to St Francis' barefoot fraternity, they too from the most civilized of human societies, rich in all the arts of life. It is told that those caves once populous with monks were forgotten for centuries, until a British hunting-party lost the tiger they were after, who leaped through a curtain of creepers on the cliff face and was gone. The English, ever full of curiosity, went to investigate—that is, one Englishman did—and found the caves, testimony to one of the highest moments of human culture and spirituality. India has not hitherto needed to care too much about preserving 'works of art' and a 'cultural heritage', knowing that the Self moves through many forms, in continual renewal. When a village idol grows old and worm-eaten, it is put aside or cast into the river, and a new one is made. (Kamaladevi's Crafts Museum was in part collected from such disused relics) and the Western notion of 'conservation' of ancient buildings and works of art perhaps owes much of its force to our knowledge that there will be no such self-renewal. In the early Christian centuries the thing was to demolish, not to conserve, the heritage of Hellenism, the temples and the libraries. We saw the like recently in China's 'Cultural Revolution'. We are shocked, of course, at such things; but have we lost that ability to renew that made India indifferent to those abandoned cities overgrown with jungle, those cave temples with their silent record of one of the world's supreme moments? Even close to Delhi there are walled cities where now the monkeys are the sole inhabitants, loving clusters of monkey families undisturbed by tourism, for few but a handful of passing foreigners would think those ruins worth a visit. Is it not precisely when a culture has lost its power of self-renewal that it thinks of 'preserving' its ancient monuments? Christian Rome did not trouble itself over-much to prop up the temples and baths and theatres of the Forum. They knew they had—or thought they had—something better to replace the old. We, who know we haven't, shed tears for the 'many ingenious lovely things' that are gone. Perhaps we are wrong, perhaps we too should trust to the living spirit that renews itself, discarding civilizations in its flight?

Now indeed bus-loads of school-children and tourists do arrive at Ajanta daily—I being a VIP for the moment, our guide took our party early, in advance—only just in advance—of the crowds. In that rarified atmosphere I, who failed the test of the all too living gods of Varanasi, breathed again. There was much climbing up and down involved in visiting these many caves—of course we did not visit all—and not all were Buddhist, some were Jain (these also very beautiful). As an old lady with a heart that is not as good as it might be (the physical organ, that is) I allowed myself to be persuaded to be carried in a sort of sedan chair on the shoulders of bearers. I felt helpless and frustrated but it was a timely reminder that in one lifetime none can see all the wonders of the world, there are too many. I don't know how it has come to pass that I have seen so many countries and wonders and met so many people far and near. I have had to renounce Japan; I was invited after I had visited India, (by the Yeats Society of Japan) but not only did the journey daunt me, but I felt, no, I can't take on any more countries, wonders, people in my life. Only the one Self in all can know us all. Gradually of course one learns that the wonders are everywhere, these monks of Ajanta—as monks elsewhere— found and created their own wonders in these caves that the tigers later took over from them. Perhaps they had already chased out the tigers who were there before them? Surely those monks who followed the rule of compassion for all sentient beings would have been glad for Mowgli's wild creatures of the jungle to take over after them.

As for tourism, I wonder. A spiritual tourist is what, alas, I simply was.

We saw of course but a few of the many caves; some adorned with those sophisticated murals depicting that vanished civilization so poignantly; others whose more austere sculptures revealed not the courts which these young aristocrats had renounced, but the vision which they had found. (Again I remembered Subiaco). Such temples were, as I read them, depictions of an inner world. From the blazing light of the terraces, where no doubt the monks lived, and taught, wrote, carried on their daily lives, you enter a dim nave, somewhat like a small Romanesque church, adorned with sculptures of episodes in the life of the Lord Buddha and his disciples; 'works of art' here, of a kind I was well accustomed to, and I was so shocked not to find in holy Varanasi. Here, I, sophisticated European, found the finished product we in the West expect and rely on. How the monks who built our cathedrals prayed *before* these were built, we tend not to enquire, or to remember that their builders did not have these great soul-inspiring churches until their own vision and skill had created them. We too much admire the product, not the vision; it has become 'art' for us, but for those builders their art had no 'history'. It came from another world. We sit back and enjoy the marvels of others' visions, and that is what we are accustomed to expect. Or we study 'history of art' and go to Italy, less often to Greece, where those fanatical Muslims with their burning faith defaced so many Christian icons, because these were real to them in quite another way. How dreadful, we feel, to deface 'works of art'! But it is not 'art' to those who create such beauty, nor is it to those who destroy it.

So I relaxed in as it were familiar surroundings. Art. Sculpture. Almost architecture. Very beautiful. But it was something more as well. A man—sometimes a girl—with a great sheet of metal, reflected sunlight for us into those dim

[68]

caves so that in the half-light we might examine the carvings. But then, beyond these, there would be an inner sanctuary, and serene in that dimness some carving of the Lord Buddha in meditation; or perhaps a stupa— a formalized carving of the tomb of the Lord Buddha; the heart of the sanctuary. I recall one great still figure that seemed to embody the very essence of that marvellous vision; as it were an apparition, in the almost-darkness, of the hidden Self within every soul, Blake's and Swedenborg's Divine Humanity, the Self of the Upanishads, seated enthroned in the heart of the hearts of all humankind. The divine presence. That serene presence all recognize. All the world recognizes the aspect of the Lord Buddha—knows who He is. Years ago my old Cambridge friend William Empson wrote his book entitled *The Faces of the Buddha*—he had been living and teaching in China and Japan. The manuscript was lost; I am one of the few who read it and I wish I could remember more. The argument—or one theme—was, as I recall, that whereas the face of the Lord Jesus has never conformed to a single, simple, easily recognised form or formula, but is, on the contrary, infinitely complex and variable as the personality, so highly developed in the West, tends to be, any village carver can evoke from a log of wood or a stone those lineaments of the Lord Buddha. As if these already and for ever exist. All know that Face.

On a later visit to India I was invited by Professor Lokesh Chandra to visit his remarkable International Academy of Indian Culture in New Delhi—a collection built up by his father, on the theme of Indian cultural influence as this has spread to the four quarters of the world, as from an inextinguishable hearth of spiritual enlightenment. Above all of course Buddhism, which although no longer a religion much practised in India (except by a new wave of refugees from Tibet) is perhaps the greatest expression of India's spiritual genius. Those books of bark and palm-leaves written in such fine learned script, carefully wrapped in cases of embroidered silk. Some can perhaps read them still, but who can evoke the vision, the knowledge, the life of the soul to which they bear witness? How vast are the realms of human experience that have been! Civilizations vanish, our own is near its end, yet the undying spirit remains itself. In India they don't let such issues as the end of our civilization trouble them overmuch. Vanished cities have from time immemorial been a part of India's heritage, not as 'art' to be preserved, but precisely because cities—Ayodhya, Hastinapura, Lanka, Mohenjo-Daro—do vanish and can never return, and the monkeys live there, and the green parrots and the snakes, no doubt, while the majestic heartbeat of India's life never ceases as generations are renewed.

As to Buddhism, has not the vision travelled full circle? Only the other day three monks from the Croydon Buddhist centre visited me—(Croydon—'can any good thing come out of Croydon?') one of whom, a cultured and intellectually discriminating young man of total commitment, was about to return to Bombay, that most westernized of Indian cities, to rejoin a group of some twenty Buddhist missionaries working there—some of them Indian, others from the West—with the aim of re-converting, if not 'India', at least some Indians to the world religion which has been in some respects India's greatest contribution to the world as a whole. In Bombay's stinking shanty towns are gathered many who have left their villages in search of work and a livelihood, and with their villages their gods and their identity within the caste system (which terribly upsets people from Western democracies of course though Yeats understood that it was caste which so long sustained Indian civilization). Like Christianity and Islam, Buddhism offers freedom from caste (at all events as it has developed outside India) yet unlike the former has many elements in common with the more subtle spirituality of Hinduism. Certainly in

[70]

the United States Buddhism is widespread. I did stay once or twice at Zen Centre in California and was moved and impressed to see so many serious young American men and women learning to behave with 'mindfulness' and other Buddhist disciplines. But from Sarnath to Croydon and back to Bombay is a long transmission of that Face whose meaning and message all mankind can read.

❀

Ellora, where next we went on that Grand Tour of but a few of India's inexhaustible wonders, there were other Buddhist shrines, but there is also a Hindu temple, carved out of the solid rock, with sculptures of the gods and scenes from the Vedic myths and from the *Ramayana*, marvellous in their celebration of those powers and triumphs of life the Buddhist monks were so passionately impelled to renounce. It was not the Brahmins, the philosophers and holy men, (so Pupul Jayakar remarked to me later) who created the gods of India, the god-forms and their aspects, but the craftsmen, anonymous sculptors of temples and shrines where we see the gods depicted in all their serenity and power and glory and beauty. Illiterate and anonymous (as also were the sculptors of the European Middle Ages) those creators of the India of the Imagination. I think of that grubby curtain drawn aside in a Shiva temple in Varanasi, of that rock-face redder than wet blood where those who came could or could not discern the lineaments of a vision. By what marvel of the Imagination, of human genius or inspiration, are invisible thoughts, spirits invisible, inaudible, wordless presences, terrors, dreams of the mind, made visible? There at Ellora in all their freshness, demons and goddesses and gods, those powers in us depicted in all the clarity and unhesitating knowledge of the human imagination. In the face of the Buddha, as in the human faces of the Christian saints, a progressive discovery that humankind, that we ourselves, are the universe whence the gods emanate 'uncurbed' as Blake would say, 'in their eternal glory'. At Ellora I was aware at the time mainly of extreme physical exhaustion and the necessity to be courteous and attentive to our very charming and cultured young guide. (Most of our guides had gone through the University—usually reading philosophy—but just missed getting University teaching appointments. So much the better for us.) But memories of such moments resonate for ever after, and now I can recall Ellora without fatigue! I was of course once more on safe ground with 'art'; whereas my granddaughter, dreaming of her missionary, at the end of that day insisted on our stopping as we were driving past a neglected half-ruined church of the British Raj; on our going inside, surveying the pulpit and the empty pews, and remarking, with feeling, '*This* is the most beautiful thing *I* have seen today!' Perhaps she was nearer the heart of the matter as those renunciatory monks would have understood it than I at my sophisticated safe distance. Certainly in Varanasi those terrible and beautiful gods live on; as does throughout the world 'Buddha's emptiness', or plenitude. From that mystery what new forms, civilizations, worlds, solar systems, universes may come? In India one gathers a faint inkling of the inexhaustibility of that divine Self of which the Lord Krishna said to Arjuna that this universe is but one small part. So in the dust and the exhaustion, the lack of sleep and the confusion and stresses of my first visit to India I began to learn. Too late for this life—unless I can communicate to others some small part of what I seemed to discern—or perhaps next time; it was our young guide at Konarak who said that 'next time' I should be his mother. (I asked what about his own mother and was told at length and affection-ately about his family.) Sisir Kumar Ghose wrote me (long before we met) that he must have 'known me in a former life'. Literally or metaphorically. All lives, in India, are the one Life, interconnected, interwoven, unbroken, immortal. So why not in former lives, other lives, the lives of others, lives to come?

What I am trying to say—or rather am trying to understand—about my impressions of the gods in their naked unformed reality as I seemed to sense their presence in Varanasi, and the marvels of 'art' in which those forms have been realized, is not at all Conrad's 'the horror! the horror!' No, though some might see it so. Rather I seem to see the serene face of the Lord Buddha as already implicit in the sick, the dying, the poor, the lepers, the beggars, the half-starved children, the resignation of the old, the terrible life-force of the lingam the Lord Shiva was before he was adorned with those moustaches, or showed his full beauty as that *Nataraja* icon of the eternal dance, almost as familiar in its fearful asymmetry of ceaseless change as the stillness and serenity of the Lord Buddha. No, rather I see that drop by drop, blood-drop, tear-drop, drop of semen, sweat of labour and sweat of death, humanity has distilled from what Conrad called 'the horror' all the glory and the beauty of the world, poetry and sculpture, music, wisdom, holiness, Nirvana itself. Meaning, value, beauty, truth, goodness, harmony, faith hope, charity, mercy, pity, peace and love, *Om; Shanti*. All these and the treasury is not yet exhausted.

I take up the theme of my highly subjective Grand Tour with Konarak. Again the Hindu vision, this time made safe from all terror as 'art' indeed. The great temple of Surya at Konarak is no longer in use. Extinct, one might say like a volcano whose fires are out.

I write from memory alone. I dislike photographs—to me they are ghosts. And over the years I have learned that precisely the times when the days are fully occupied are the times when one has no time to keep diaries. I have been a great keeper of diaries in times of solitude. Besides that, I prefer to let memories mature. I am not recording facts in any case—these can be found in abundance elsewhere—but experiences; experiences of the imagination, the things that have remained, and have taught me or changed me. I care little whether what I write is factually accurate, and what does it matter whether this or that happened on this or that date? Time, that moving image of eternity. It is what is mirrored, not the mirror, that matters; and of that moving image I am not very retentive. My father had an almost total recall of facts and dates. 'It was thirty-two years ago today' he would say, that so-and-so died, or was defeated in an election, or became Home Secretary—and very wrongly I became very impatient with this way of remembering; so that I perhaps deliberately—or no, I fear I never possessed my Father's gift—organise memories after another pattern. But I do wish that I had remembered the names of our guides, the places we visited by name and not only by some image of a red lion by a yellow temple wall or a papaya tree growing by a pool where three little children were offering posies.

Our guides were all of them charming and interesting. Our Varanasi guide was the only one with whom we seemed to be at cross-purposes—he was determined to show us certain things, not at all the things we wanted most to see. Only as we were about to leave did we discover his real gift—he was a singer! Too late! Our guide in Rajasthan was the one who had been (I think I have it right) a social worker among those mutilated beggar children, controlled by their sinister 'protectors'. We learned many things from him. But he, like our Konarak guide (both had studied philosophy at their University) were endlessly willing to discuss ideas—the Indian gift of metaphysics is by no means—such was my experience—confined to specialists. It's in the culture. But our Konarak guide had another gift.

He knew some of the tigers in the (was it Orissa?) wildlife sanctuary. They were his friends. He could put his hand into their gentle mouths. He was sorry we did not have wildlife on our itinerary. So was I. So was Sonia. Little could he have known how dearly we would have loved to know those tigers. That is the trouble of being a traveller, or rather a visiting VIP on a Government conducted tour. Indeed the Indian Council for Cultural Relations and Santosh herself had gone to great trouble to make it possible for me to see those things I had almost at random asked to see. It would hardly have mattered if all these had been different, one has but to pull a thread anywhere to be led to some wonder. But then one is there only for a moment, no time to sit under those sacred peepal trees in temple courtyards, or to follow those dusty roads whose turnings lead to villages and temples endlessly, or to get to know tigers. One life is far too short. Our Ajanta guide told us there are still a few wild tigers roaming in that part of Maharashtra. If there are they must be hungry and starved in what remains of the Jungle of India where Shere Khan and Hanuman and Bali and Sugriva held their courts. I would have liked to visit that wild-life reserve.

We approached Konarak by way of Puri, a town of amazingly 'unspoilt' beauty with its great temple encircled by four walls, each with its lion-guarded or sphinx-guarded portal. We tourists might not enter the sacred precinct (Santosh as usual enthusiastically did so) but we others were led up some precipitous outside stairs to the roof of a nearby building, thence to look down on those elaborate elongated domes of the Hindu style, with the moon, a crescent over the minaret of the Taj Mahal, now nearing the full and flooding the mysterious precincts of Puri with its golden light. You could buy in the market reproductions of those incredibly primitive effigies of the god Jagannatha and his *shakti*, remote primordial gods, their formalized

[75]

features reminding at once of children's drawings and aboriginal art, their eyes circular and somehow inspiring terror. India certainly does not sentimentalize the powers of life. In the market place, beautiful with its trays of dyes and spices and food and printed cloth, Sonia bought a silk scarf and Santosh a dance-sari. I also remember walking in the spicéd Indian air by night round the four walls of the temple while Thetis and Santosh argued about the origin of the Sphinx. Thetis knows a great deal about bestiaries, and Santosh is a scholar who would claim all such excellent things as sphinxes for India. The Sphinxes of Egypt and Babylon she swept aside as of no significance. Sonia and I quietly considered 'how sweet the moonlight sleeps' upon this temple wall. The living night, the golden moon.

My next memory is of the sea—the Indian Ocean itself! Pasternak somewhere describes the romance of when, as a boy, he had crossed in one of those interminable Russian railway journeys, from Europe to Asia. Then the pine trees he saw from the window were in *Asia*, continent of marvels, gateway into the *mundus imaginalis*, that other country! So the Indian Ocean. Breaking on a shingle-beach outside the formerly British clubhouse where under mosquito nets and with a bathroom of the style of the pre-1914 war one sometimes still finds in country houses, spacious and deep with excellent mahogany fittings but not much hot water, we spent the night. The ghosts still haunted. We stayed in several such places. There is a sadness about recently abandoned houses or places that time has long dissolved from older ruins. In my own girlhood I might have danced there, with shingled hair and a Chinese shawl such as I had in vain longed for as a student at Girton. Later, in Pune, my eye was caught, in a shady road lined with bungalows left by the Raj, by the names 'Sunnymead', and 'West View'. In such a bungalow might my Aunty Meg have lived. My parents' house was called 'West View'. When my Aunty

Meg retired to Bournemouth her bungalow was, predictably, called 'Lanka'. In India it all stopped abruptly in 1942, preserving for ever a certain imprint. Indian manners have to this day something of the British decorum of that period I myself remember as my own girlhood. There are front gardens with trim patches of lawn surrounded by narrow flower beds, with standard roses, geraniums, lobelia, and cosmos. India loves flowers; and the flower beds of New Delhi overflow with all those annuals whose abundance in England is usually confined to the coloured pictures on the seed packets; but in the Indian sun the reality exceeds these pictures themselves. Perhaps this is an inheritance from the British. (They are very beautiful and the fulfilment of every English suburban gardener's dream.) But the Indian habit of growing individual plants in rows of closely-lined single pots seems to be their own. The 1942 style persists also in Indian indoor furnishing of the rather well-to-do. In their sitting-rooms are those meticulously polished tables with nothing on them, and electric lamps supported by half-divested nymphs (from Italy by way of nineteenth century France and the Army and Navy Stores) upholding a pink silk lamp-shade. On the walls colour reproductions of paintings of Scottish glens in the manner of Landseer. I felt strangely taken back, in such rooms, to my own suburban childhood. My mother's sisters had such rooms, whose chief use seemed to be kept immaculately polished. One would not have dared to put down on those polished tables anything so disturbing to symmetry as a book or a pile of papers. It was all very familiar.

But those sad rather grand clubhouses that seem still haunted by ghosts of their former occupants, were pleasant to stay in. Everything had slipped a little, of course; in India (outside New Delhi or the grand modern tourist-hotels, that is) things work up to a point; if the water is hot there is no bath plug; or the mosquito gauze has holes in it or things mended with bits of string that really need replacements of parts that are probably hard to obtain. Such things are not Indian priorities. I was happier with the ghosts. But what a too-good-to-be-true life the Raj must have had, away from the 'servant-problem' (there would always be plenty of servants available among 'the natives' for people like my aunt who would never have had any form of domestic help in their own country). Yet unaware of the rich civilization around them these people (again like my aunt and even a good deal higher on the social scale) brought back little more than ebony elephants, Benares brass, and a few tales of snake charmers and holy men, whom they regarded as very much the same thing, heathens all. (I speak of the commercial majority, not of the cultured elite.)

❀

The night before our visit to Konarak we spent in a smaller, delightfully simple guest house, whose custodian cooked for our evening meal delicious small fishes straight from the ocean, and our simple spotless rooms opening on a verandah and a simple garden were a welcome change from the more luxurious unreality of the (except in Bombay where there were cockroaches) excellent tourist hotels in which we inevitably stayed. Our plan was to rise some time before dawn and drive to the shore of the ocean, there to see the great disc of Surya rise from his orient on his daily progress across the land where he is worshipped by that name. It was February. But our young guide, deep as he was in metaphysics, had not taken into account that Surya's rising is not always at the same hour throughout the year. We were ready at about 4 a.m. to drive to the shore of the ocean where we were to attend his advent. In the dark we set off again to ocean's endless shore. At no time of day or night is any place in India 'deserted'. On that shore were lonely figures; a young beggar-woman who looked as if the

[78]

hand of death was upon her; other beggars; a sort of Indian equivalent of a coffee-stall; a few fishermen taking their boats down to the water—those slender skiffs that in Far-Eastern paintings look so weightless on the rivers and lakes of China's landscape-paintings. One man standing, a boy sitting, such light craft they seemed, though indeed the ocean was calm enough. I don't remember on whose mind it first dawned that sunrise would not be yet for several hours. No matter, the beauty of the night, the strangeness, sufficed. And more, our eyes—mine and Sonia's especially, she new from her biology course at Durham University—were delighted by the sight of the surf breaking in cascades of emerald. I had read of *noctilucae* a life-time ago when I too had thought of becoming a marine biologist, but never thought to see those emerald waves breaking on India's shores, green with those minute phosphorescent creatures, luminous life in fecund subtropical waters.

We waited long; the sky lightened a little. Thetis did her 'Tai-chi' exercises; Sonia and I watched the breaking waves, the magic wearing off a little. The sky was overcast and hazy, and as it grew lighter no sun was to be seen, his face barred by dim clouds, until the triumphant Surya did arrive at last. As the (for the moment) VIP of the party it of course fell to me to make a sign when we should go. Sonia murmured something about breakfast. Thetis too approached, with a breakfast-bent air. I looked round for our guide; for Santosh, that earnest Yeats scholar. Both were deep in their devotions to Surya. Breakfast was not uppermost in their minds.

But breakfast was not yet. Santosh had not come so far just for sight seeing; her dance guru taught the Orissa form of the Indian classical dance. The great sun temple of Konarak, with its famous sculpted dancers is the source of the movements and postures of the Orissi dance. Santosh had come to dance in Surya's temple itself. We must therefore be there before the crowds arrived—and in India sightseeing begins at sunrise, before the heat of the day. Already there were people arriving at the dancing hall where the temple's *deva-dasis* formerly danced (the temple is now a ruin and the *deva-dasis*, their sacred function having declined into simple prostitution, suppressed by law). So we went on to the smaller temple behind, dedicated to the Shadow, *shakti* of the sun-god; and at this small charming spot, before a little altar, (already there was an offering of flowers). Santosh donned the orange dancing sari she had bought at Puri, and danced her invocation to the Sun. Before she had finished she had already an audience watching her—with much quiet appreciation, be it said.

When if ever there was breakfast I don't remember—doubtless there was at some time. But I do remember, at Konarak, as elsewhere, that delicious coconut juice we drank, that is so reviving. The coconut-sellers neatly slice off the top of a young coconut, provide a straw, and the cool refreshing gift of nature meets all needs of body and soul. I have made a point of never having drunk the ubiquitous brew Coca Cola, a beverage generated by a machine. Such a product, and a technological civilization which disseminates it, seems to me an outrage, and although but a gesture I have adhered to this small insignificant ritual protest. Illogically perhaps, or paradoxically, I have taken, when at home in London, to drinking bottled spring-water because in London only so can one obtain what earth once gave freely to all life, pure water, untainted by chlorides or whatever other chemicals are deemed necessary to purge the nine-times-recycled sewage-water of the Thames water-board. The Government of India has, since the seventies, kept Coca Cola out of India, which alas has not prevented other equally obnoxious indigenous brews from springing up, in India as elsewhere. However, there is still coconut juice for the monkeys, I hope, or for super-sophisticates like myself, who are prepared to pay more for what nature gives than for these synthetic products of consumerism. My conscience permits me wine, Scotch and Irish whiskey, Chartreuse, Benedictine, Drambuie, Punt-e-Mes, ouzo, retsina and whatever gift of the earth and work of human hands the genius of each nation has created or some god has inspired. No doubt an all-American Coke-drinker would deem the gift of Dionysus sinful and the alcohol-free machine brew pleasing to a very different god! But who in India would want anything better or other than the delicious orange or sweet lime juice to be had in such abundance, neither bottled nor canned?

Through such irrelevancies do we approach the precincts of the gods. The great Surya with sublime indifference, sheds his light on backward sellers of coconuts and crates of bottled Campa-cola and Limca. (Presumably we had now breakfasted and our strength returned.) He was well risen into his cloudless Indian skies as at leisure we strolled, or sat, in contemplation of that amazing temple the imagination of India had raised to him. This temple can't be called 'architecture' in the Western sense, or in the sense of those superb tombs and mosques and palaces of the Moghul rulers of India. As at Ellora a temple is hewn out of solid rock, so here the sun-god's temple takes the form of a huge chariot of stone rising as a pyramidon carrying all sentient beings, the sun's retinue, all praising and delighting in that god, source of life of the sensible world and all its creatures, from animals to the gods themselves. Round the base, in that deep relief carving that in India so subtly plays with sun and shadow, are elephants, creatures of earth; next, the beautiful naga-women, human above, serpentine below; next, friezes of dancers, and musicians, each with her instrument of music, tabla or flute or vina or mirror, all adorned as for the god with earrings and ankle-bells, girdles, bracelets, dancers beneath the overarching branches of some tree; all is joy—religion in India be it of Durga and Shiva themselves, not only of the life-giving sun, is celebratory, and expresses a delight, be it terrible, like that of Kali with her black mask and protruding tongue, or Shiva whose indifferent foot tramples all that is mortal and deformed; or as here at Konarak ecstasy and bliss in all its modes. For above those dancers and musicians again, and mingled with them, are those famous 'erotic' sculptures of blissful embracing lovers. All is expressive of life and delight and fecundity. Nor are the lovers life's sublimest expression, for higher yet are the *apsaras* and the gods themselves, and high on each face of his chariot laden with all life, Surya himself is depicted, his round solar face shining on the four directions of his world, as those magnificent stone horses draw his chariot for ever from the East. His lions overwhelm earth-born elephants, animals of fire triumphant over creatures of clay. In what country has the solar kingship of the fiery lion ever been challenged? Yet here in India the hooded cobra also, the deadly one, is not without honour in that teeming fourfold chariot of life.

Here I sat in the blissful shade to enjoy, but, as everywhere in India, one has but to pause to be surrounded by sellers of beads and trinkets and postcards and the rest. I did of course buy some strings of beads alleged to be coral but probably not so, though just as pretty; and Thetis took photographs. Sonia, as always suspicious of the gods of India, stood somewhat aloof (art as such means little to her) and refused to enter a building a little apart, where, if I remember aright, there are goddesses or muses of the arts. At this point Sonia rebelled and would have no more of this sensuous heathenism. And perhaps she was nearer the religion of India in deeming their religion, their temples, their temple dances, 'evil' and 'dangerous' than spiritual tourists like Thetis and myself—I hope not but fear it may be so—who see all through the delighted eyes of aesthetic detachment. It is true that I have long venerated the Vedantic wisdom and since visiting India even more so, but shall for all that retain for ever the seal of my Christian baptism and a fear of the faces of the dark gods to whom the Indian religions (Buddhism also) offer their due of worship. But, brought up as I was to believe reality to be Beauty, Truth and Goodness, and the virtues of Faith, Hope and Charity all-sufficing, those hooded cobras, those necklaces of skulls, those demon-trampling feet of the Nataraja, those fangs, the blood-lust of Kali, all these *m'effrayent*, like Pascal's infinite spaces and send me running back for shelter and security of the all-good all-merciful all-protecting Christian pantheon. No, I had not yet made my peace with the wholeness of what is, whose joy and ecstasy is celebrated in Surya's temple at Konarak more fully, surely, than in any other *temenos* on this earth he enlightens.

❀

Memory is a thread one can draw out endlessly, but a lifetime's succession of beautiful images, a myriad lifetimes of beautiful images, these might be the delights of eternity but here there is no time to recall each beautiful roadside tree, the vivid green of the little rice fields of Orissa, or some temple surrounded by a tank where doubtless the worshippers bathed. Guardian lions, temples painted in glowing yellow and red, peacocks in trees, nests of weaver-birds; vultures, sugar-canes; and everywhere people more beautiful than in any other land. One temple I remember, painted in those bright Indian colours, where I found myself permitted—indeed forced—on making a small contribution of money, to set a little child doll of the Lord Krishna swinging. I was not tourist enough to do this light-heartedly, nor Christian enough to refuse. These childish things are little different indeed from the lovely *presepios* of Italy with the shepherds and angels and the ox and the ass and the three magi—the electric lights that go on and off to show the Star of Bethlehem and the angel-host. To me the

[83]

Krishna of the *Mahabharata* stands with the Lord Jesus, truth universal; but the little swings for the child Krishna at his play are cultural and I felt it was not for me to play with that child, yet I would have given offence to the temple people had I refused; like some Protestant refusing to genuflect before the Blessed Sacrament in a Catholic church. In India's popular temple-religion it is not the Lord Krishna of Vedanta, but the child Krishna who stole the butter and tamed the river-serpent, and Radha's lover who plays with the Gopis in the Forest of Brindavan, not the charioteer and teacher of Arjuna, who is dear to the hearts of his worshippers. Truth is universal, but religious cults belong to 'The Tutelar of the Place'.

❀

Jaipur with its jewelled palaces; I think it was in Jaipur I would gladly have spent hours and days looking at a superb collection of Rajasthan paintings; workmanship so fine that the painters use a brush made of only three hairs of a squirrel's tail; (we were assured that no harm is done to the squirrel by those who steal his hairs). But others have written of Jaipur and Udaipur and the princely cities of Rajasthan, the luxury and glamour; too akin to Harrods' advertisements, 'Enter a Different World'. Beautifully planned eighteenth century towns all in pink. Thetis, a painter, was to return to spend several days delighting in the mural paintings on houses in Shekhavati, and later to set afoot a project for their preservation and restoration. There are so many Indias. Sonia's was to be a project centred in Pune for discovering and if possible doing something practical to help with such problems as village water supply, the quality of farm stock and so on. Her degree in botany and geography suited her for this congenial work, and she remained in Pune working with her American employer and his Indian wife, and with a Sikh colleague did write a report, of which she has not yet succeeded in obtaining a copy. But Sonia after all found her way to *her* India and if her project did not succeed in changing very much she certainly tried to help. Sonia would make herself helpful and loved anywhere she might be; she has since become a trained nurse.

For the rest, images rise in my memory as if floating in space; a great banyan tree where at one time—I think fairly recently—a Muslim holy man had taught; the plaster 'Taj Mahal' Aurangzeb's son had built for his mother; Aurangzeb's own austere grave in the courtyard of a mosque that was also I think a school; a sort of Indian *Madrasah?* A performance in Delhi of Kalidasa's *Shakuntala*, with Kamaladevi—she who has done so much to preserve and revive the classical theatre—in the front row with a flower (true woman of the theatre as she was) in her gray hair; the acting highly stylized, with stylized voices also, an impressive technique that must take many years to learn. The King was perfect in this style, and so was the Deer (a small part) but Shakuntala alas was just a pretty young actress. Other times and places have superceded such schools of acting and dance as demand total and lifelong commitment, all but impossible to find in the modern world; unless the Japanese Nō theatre which still holds its own, I believe, though I have seen superb Nō companies playing in London to half-empty houses.

A beautiful temple somewhere—Sonia refused to enter it—with Rama and Sita with their great unblinking eyes 'like lotus-petals'; Hanuman. Ganesha. Marvels of beauty everywhere. Bridegrooms dressed in shabby velvet regalia braided with gold, riding rather shamefacedly in their unaccustomed finery in bridal procession to the bride's house, with their retinue. Holy men; little monkeys dressed in tunics and skirts playing their tricks so nimbly; Santosh's Brahmin music master with his beautiful voice and the exaltation of his face as he sang hymns to the gods. (Kumar, accustomed to India, remarked to me—*à propos* Tambi's *Geeta Sarasvati*—how 'shy' westerners are in expressing that ecstasy which illumines Indian faces when they worship); the abandoned luxurious grounds (seen only from the gateway) of Rajneesh's villa in Pune. There was no Rajneesh or his following of American devotees; he had been asked to leave Maharastra some time before; but there was a little conjuror sitting at the gate who did his conjuring for us very skilfully. Again in Pune, the little palace where Gandhiji had lived as a prisoner, and where his wife's and secretary's *samadhis* are in one of those lovely quiet gardens one finds everywhere in India. That refinement of soul that touches everthing in India from the poorest village (those beautiful faces) to the richest sculpture. But I cannot tell it all. I can but echo the words of my Spanish friend, Rafael Nadal, who once said to me, (in that Spanish style that makes speech aphoristic, and aphorisms resonate with proverbial wisdom) 'My life is divided into two parts: the first, before I went to India; the second, after'. How can it be otherwise?

❀

At the end of my two weeks' official tour as guest of the Indian Government, I became Santosh's guest, and she had arranged to take me to the Radha Soami Ashram at Beas in the North Punjab, where her father and mother live (as do many other retired professors, lawyers and other professional people). In Indian life it has from time immemorial been recognized that, having in turn fulfilled our role as student, then as householder, the last years of life are those when we would do well to devote ourselves, increasingly and at last perhaps exclusively, to the spiritual life. Western monasticism as a life-long vocation can be damaging for the young who in their enthusiasm devote themselves prematurely to the celibate life; and can also leave the old without meaning and purpose during years that could be rich. C.G.

Jung has done well to point out that in the natural course of a life, we spend the first half in adjusting ourselves to this world; and could do no better than to turn our thoughts, in the second half, to the inner life of the soul. So we drove north through the beautiful fertile Punjab, with its handsome turbaned 'lions', by those Indian roads shaded by trees, strung with villages, with their stream of life, the tongas and buffalo-drawn and camel-drawn carts, and the new stream of Tata lorries and Ambassador cars that have arrived since Kipling wrote *Kim*. It was on this road that at dusk a great form loomed up in front of us—an elephant, laden with the belongings of a group of yellow robed men, as they walked their pilgrim's way. For the roads in India still retain to some degree their sacred function as pilgrim's routes; men with *tilak* marks painted on their foreheads, their hair matted, taking nothing with them, travel on foot, sometimes in little groups, from one holy city to another. It is all 'still' there.

However, to return to Beas. This large and modern ashram, surrounded by many miles of fertile ground—and the movement of the course of the river Beas is, as if miraculously, giving them every year more—is a large estate, somewhat like the 'campus' of a university. A large Temple, hostel for western visitors like myself, even larger buildings for the reception of pilgrims where these may sleep; a library, as well stocked with esoteric literature as Watkins' Bookshop in its great days; a hospital, a homoeo-pathic clinic, shops where food and all small necessities can be bought; all is immaculately tended, and at all times pilgrims are fed at the traditional Sikh communal meal, the *langar*, and not only for festivals, when doubtless they come in their thousands; sitting on the ground in rows, as it must have been when that earlier Master the Lord Jesus fed the 'five thousand'. There must have been nearly that number sitting in a field for the morning worship at which the Master, Maharaj Charan Singh, appeared and sat on a dais under a canopy of yellow cloth while cantors sang hymns from the *Adi Granth* and by Kabir. He was not there to preach, or to perform any ceremony, but simply to be present to those innumerable devotees, many of whom doubtless practised the form of meditation he taught.

On my return to London I visited Mrs Jeannette Jackson, moving spirit of RILKO (the Research Into Lost Knowledge Organization which had promoted the work of one of my co-founders of *Temenos*, Keith Critchlow), and to my surprise there was a photograph of Maharaj Charan Singh on her Hammersmith mantelpiece! She had long been among his followers. (How often does one not cross the world only to find on one's return the thing one had crossed the world in order to discover?)

I attended an evening visit the Master pays to the Western visitors' hostel and saw for the first time this imposing serene spiritual Master. The Westerners had well learned the lesson from India of a devout veneration, even to the rush to a balcony to see the Master enter his car as he left. Indeed, the Pope commands such veneration; but I knew in my heart that I could never do it in quite that way—I am too Western and sophisticated to imagine that any 'Master' can assume the personal responsibility of his disciples which each of us must carry for ourselves. Yet such is an element in the Indian devotion to whatever Master it may be who accepts and initiates his followers. Unlike the Pope, however, or all the multitudes of Bishops, a Master is not so *ex officio*; a perfect Master is one who has attained a certain degree of spiritual knowledge (not intellectual knowledge) and who is of course a *yogi*.

Next day I was received by Maharaj Charan Singh. He is certainly a presence of spiritual authority, and at the same time a joyful and humane man with considerable knowledge of the world, West as well as East. He teaches, he explained, only what Jesus himself taught, what all former

[88]

Masters have taught, for there is but the one knowledge. The only difference is, that whereas Jesus was in his day the teacher of those who had the good fortune to encounter him, he is no longer in this world: only from a living Master can a disciple receive the knowledge. He himself teaches nothing different from the teaching of Masters of all times: how fortunate are those who meet in this life a Master who can thus transmit it to them. The same teaching he finds in, for example, the Pentecostal experience of the rushing mighty wind heard by the Disciples of Jesus and has indeed written books on the Christian gospels from the standpoint of his own esoteric teaching of a form of yoga that involves 'listening' to the sound current of the universe. I said that I had always supposed the 'wind' of the Spirit to be meta-phorical; not at all, he said, it is a reality of spiritual experience; Pythagoras' 'music of the spheres', Pentecost, the ever-sounding cosmic music. I knew that I had but to assent, I could have asked for that initiation. I had been aware of this as I thought over, earlier, this encounter: had my life perhaps led me to a Perfect Master in order that I might receive this greatest of blessings? But I knew it was not so; I had lost and rejected so many proffered initiations in the past, both Christian and otherwise; drawn back in part from the knowledge of my own life having been so irrevocably spoiled, and in part from the knowledge that no 'Master' can give what we cannot receive.

With my spoiled life I had no pretentions to take that path. 'Even a criminal can follow the spiritual path' he said; to which I replied that it was probably more difficult for an intellectual. 'There I agree with you', he said; but then added words that I have since found very consoling, as they are also very true. The faith of the simple, he said, can easily be undermined and shaken; but an intellectual, once con-vinced, is unshakeable. This I have good reason to know to be true. I would—do on occasion—merely laugh at the solemn attempts of 'agnostics' or clever Nobel prize-winning scientists—to give their alternative accounts of the universe. Fred Hoyle's theory that 'life' originates on 'other planets'—as if we were not already in 'outer space'. Perhaps microbes—or centipedes for that matter—do rain down on us from the star-dust of passing meteors rain down on us, but what has that to do with the origin of life or of universes? Or of star-dust? For if on 'other planets' why should that be more marvellous than on this? Perhaps we are the 'other planet' to other planets. I hope that the Master knows this at least is true of me—nothing in heaven or earth could undermine whatever it is—I can give it no name—that I know, from however remote a place, of the sacred source.

I also found myself speaking of the danger the world is in; I think I said something no doubt stupid about the end of a cycle, the Kali-Yuga or something of the kind. 'Whether we live in the Golden Age or the Iron Age', he said, 'is a purely personal matter: some live in the Golden Age, others in the Iron Age'. Doubtless, I said, but then never before has it lain within human power to destroy the planet. Maharaj Charan Singh laughed: 'Would it matter so much?' he asked. To the Indian scale what are a few solar-systems more or less? The divine is in any case indestructible. And yet, for those few of us who in the West believe even in the immortality of the soul—or maybe not even of the individual soul but of the eternal Spirit—do we for a moment live as if we possessed this immortality? I am, I must own, totally—or almost so—identified with this brief person who holds my pen, writes this page, has lived this life, read all those innumerable books, uses the English language passable well, and has loved France and known Italy a little, where from the standpoint of my own European civilization I stop short by far of what that civilization to which I belong has known and understood and done and made. Yet once again I found myself weighed in India's balance and found wanting.

Nor indeed does it seem to me to matter very much whether I am personally illuminated or saved or redeemed or whatever it may be, so long as I faithfully perform my appointed task, which I am for ever trying to evade: that of the poet I am or was meant to be, and perhaps those other duties I have laid upon myself. If I would ask even now one thing from life, it would not be to listen to the cosmic sound current but to be able, despite my own deafness to that music, to transmit it; to be the lyre of that Wind—every poet's prayer is Shelley's prayer, there can be no other. 'Make me thy lyre, even as the forest is,/What tho' my leaves are falling, like its own?' I have lived too long to care very much for personal enlightenment. Did I not lose it at birth into this world? As we all do. In any case, I knew it was not for me, that I must not ask.

Back in Delhi, giving an account of my visit to Beas to Kamaladevi I had told her of how moved and impressed I had been by those multitudes sitting in that great field in the presence of their Master; and I asked (her or myself?) how it would be when all these people have television-sets, intruding in India as everywhere in the world their material values, advance-guard of consumerist imperialism? Perhaps I was thinking of the Master's own words about the fragility of the faith of simple people. 'Then', said Kamaladevi sadly, 'it will all be over'.

It was all very beautiful; those paradisal fields running down to the Beas river, where crops are grown to feed the ashram; the sense of an oasis in this troubled world, pure and beautiful. The little house where Santosh's parents live reminded me of my own parents' last house, and for what else had my own father lived than to obey his invisible Master? They were like my own parents; Santosh's father rode his bicycle about the grounds of the ashram (and that too recalled my father, who in my own schooldays had ridden his bicycle to school and back, daily, for a few years with me beside him). He had been librarian for some time but was now in charge of the flower-garden. Such flowers he grew, opening in the Indian sun! I said to him that in England he would have carried off all the prizes at any flower-show. He modestly said he had done so in India and at last had been asked to become the judge, so that other competitors might have their chance! Some dozen brown young gardeners carrying baskets of soil on their heads, under the shade of trees where green parrots lived, were under his command. There in the Indian array of pots, superb single specimens grew of pansies and pinks and dimorphothecum and annuals of every kind known to the printers of seed packets. Sweet-Williams and dahlias, Canterbury bells and carnations, sweet peas and roses, all blooming together as we sat drinking tea on a little lawn with rose beds that might have been in some English country or suburban lawn but for the glorious sunshine and those green parrots. It all reminded me of the home I had so scorned and rebelliously rejected.

❀

On my second visit to India—to a Yeats Conference organized by Santosh—I again visited Beas with her. This time, because of the political unrest, western visitors were not being issued with visas to the Punjab; as a Government guest (for a second time) I was given my visa, but found myself the only resident in the Hostel reserved for foreigners. At night I heard howls and groans outside, and thought if these are 'terrorists', they are indeed evil men at work; it was however, only the jackals going the rounds of the dustbins. The Master, now, was constantly under the protection of four armed guards; for he was under threat for his tolerance of all religions.

Again—with Santosh this time, who has meanwhile received his initiation and lives by his rules—I was received by this serene and charming holy man. We spoke of the projected conference which I had suggested on my previous visit to India, a conference on values, to be attended by East and West. I explained that my own small contribution was the review, *Temenos*, dedicated to a re-affirmation of the true task of the arts, as the expression and language of the value-systems of any civilization. (It all seemed rather small and irrelevant in that simple presence of the Master.) He said, 'I have no doubt you do your best' but repeated that the one thing needful is to meditate on the one spiritual reality.

But I remember the Radha Soami Ashram (which in fact was the only ashram I have visited in India) as something quite extraordinary; a place of pilgrimage of all those thousands of men and women and children (India moves in families) whom I saw sitting on the grass like the five thousand Jesus fed; a place of habitation for those who there, like Santosh's parents, have in their later years assumed the religious life. And what is more, before I left the Master lent his own car to take Santosh and myself and her parents to visit the big hospital—the largest, I understand, in India—given to the local town of Beas by the ashram. A fine modern hospital indeed, lacking nothing— five operating theatres, maternity ward, casualty and out- patients clinics, beautiful hostels for the nurses and houses for the medical staff; hostels also for relations of the patients to stay, and excellent shops and delicious food for sale there. Small wards—six people or less—each opening on a little court with well-tended flowers, and trees. Those handsome Sikh 'lions' in their turbans, the medical staff. Extensive grounds; everything. It was only half completed but already functioning.

Doubtless much of the contribution to this splendid hospital at Beas must have come from outside India, for the Master has a great following also in England and in North and South America and elsewhere. Truly the Indianization of the West is taking place without help from such as I. And yet I too have perhaps my small part to play; as Maharaj Charan Singh said (and in saying it reminded me of the vanity of such things as occupy my hard-working days) I no doubt do my best. But a sense of proportion is all-important. India is grateful to Mother Teresa, of course, but none in India would therefore regard her as a spiritual Teacher. That is a quite specific and very different, matter. I refused my opportunity to receive his form of initiation from a 'perfect Master', and happy are those who come to his *langar*. But if I have a duty, as my Prince Kumar with Rama's broad shoulder always reminds me, it is to my own innate gift (or caste) which is that of the poet. And yet I day-dream, as I approach my eightieth birthday, of ending my days in some ashram or *kendra*, among others devoted to the spiritual life; partly because I panic at times when I wonder what arrangements I can make for my last feeble years. But then, in holy Varanasi I surely saw for myself that as to death, one can die anywhere. One cannot make plans in advance for receiving death.

❈

I consider every day of my life as given for some purpose other than my own, and as my years grow shorter feel that I must waste no more time, given so generously as it has been to me. I wondered for what task I was called to India. It was in my mind before I went, of course, that there is to be found the spiritual wisdom that the materialist West lacks and needs. It goes without saying that India needs many of the technological skills of the West—that is not in question. Where we are rich, India is poor; but where we are poor—spiritually poor—how rich is India! I found myself discussing this very matter with Mrs Gandhi's Secretary for Foreign Affairs (formerly India's Ambassador in Paris and now High Commissioner here in London) Mr Rasgotra. Since he is also a poet, we conversed at a level of truth: what, then, he asked, did I think was wrong in England? Trivialization of values, I suggested; and put to him a thought that had been forming in my mind; could there not be, in India, a permanent centre where East and West could meet, confer, and discuss how values (those values of which India is even now the custodian) could be brought to bear on our skills and powers to make and do in the material world whatever enters our heads? India, I said, must surely take the lead in guiding the whole world out of and through the dangers and darkness of the spiritual ignorance which seems to accompany material knowledge at this time? Should there not be a continual examination of the wise use of our dangerous knowledge, conducted according to those first principles? China has for the time being renounced its age-old wisdom; Holy Russia is also silent. Many of us, I said, who realize that the problems of our world are beyond the scope of political solution, know these things, and where but to India can we look?

There are of course minorities, here and there. Many people in the West are ready to learn, to consider and to discuss values, and surely India can in that respect lead us? Mr Rasgotra thought the idea a good one; others besides myself—from the United States for example—had put forward similar ideas. He put the idea to Mrs Gandhi and she too thought the idea a good one; so that one of the last documents she signed before her assassination was a recommendation that such a conference—at least a conference, although what I had had in mind was a permanent centre, more like Casa Eranos, the Jungian centre in Ascona —should exist. That I myself might be expected to play any further part in this did not cross my mind. I had still not absorbed the belated lesson I began to learn only from my American friends during my stay with the Lindisfarne

Association, that what we would like to see come about we must work to bring about ourselves. Useless to say, 'Would it not be a good idea if . . .' If, then we ourselves must play our part. I did, after all, bring about *Temenos*. A poet cannot simply sit under a rose bush writing poetry, my conscience or my sense of guilt has told me; if indeed value-systems are created and disseminated by the poets (Shelley's 'unacknowledged legislators of the world') we cannot disregard that world's silent cry. Some such thought had been growing in me as year by year I had indignantly and with sorrow seen the decline in my own country, not least in the Universities themselves, no longer grounded in any integral (universal) knowledge; a decline brought about, as is surely obvious, by the lack of a spiritual life in our consumerist, permissive, money-ridden, secular, materialist society. Or would I have done more to heal the 'sickness of Albion' by withdrawing from the world and writing poems?

Mr Rasgotra had suggested to Santosh (a propos our visit to Beas) that I should visit another ashram, very different, he said, that of Satya Sai Baba. At the time the name conveyed nothing to me—is not one ashram like another, truth and the spiritual path being one? I did not press the matter, nor did Santosh allude to it again. This I now deeply regret, for, if anywhere, I now know that it is at the Sathya Sai University at Prasanthi Nilayam that the new model for universities of the future, in India and throughout the world, is in process of realization. I have since learned more of this through Mr Rasgotra, who himself addressed the twenty thousand students and a hundred thousand supporters at the eighth Convocation, and actually alluded to our seminal discussions. Too late perhaps for me to make that journey now: but no matter, the seed is already growing.

❀

Some months after my return to England I received an

invitation from Professor André Mercier, on behalf of the International Academy of Philosophy (centred in Switzerland). Professor Mercier had been invited to arrange, through that Society, a Conference in India, with visits to places of interest and meetings with various personages. This was scarcely what I had had in mind; and at first I declined his invitation, the more so as I was invited to go and read some of my poetry, along with a number of other poets (unnamed). My idea had of course nothing to do with poetry readings for which in general I have no liking. However, I received a second letter saying that the Indian Government had specially requested that I be invited (I doubt whether Professor Mercier had heard my name otherwise) and rather than behave discourteously to the Indian hosts of the Conference, I agreed to go, and to write a short piece to be read on the occasion. I had expected, not a single European organization to be made responsible, but rather that the Indian side would invite a number of representative individuals from many parts of the world. The exercise seemed rather a pointless one, since 'philosophy' is but one among many fields in which values operate. However, what intrigues and counter-intrigues were involved I shall never know, but as I awaited my ticket for my Air India passage to Delhi I received first a letter to say that the Conference was 'indefinitely postponed', then a furious letter from Professor Mercier (not furious that is with me but with the Indian Council for Cultural Relations) followed by another letter asking whether *Temenos* would be prepared to publish all the papers written for the Conference in a special issue! We could not of course consider this, it would have been of minimal interest to our readers. I was sorry not to be going to India but doubtful whether in any case I would have wished to go under such circumstances, and as a character in someone else's dream, so to speak.

Meanwhile Santosh summoned me to give a paper at a conference on Yeats that *she* had arranged at the India International Centre; taking, perhaps, a leaf from my book, and seeing (very rightly) Yeats as a bridge for the kind of exchange of ideas beyond the normal academic process. I was glad to go, with a Blake-Yeats paper, and Santosh had arranged a very lively academic conference that was grounded not in Western literary fashion but in the values of the *sophia perennis* that were of course Yeats's own, who had himself looked to India. Santosh was now busily promoting what she now saw as 'my' conference, and it now seemed that she was to be its principal organizer on behalf of the Indian Council for Cultural Relations. I was a bit aghast, and realizing how little I knew of India, was dismayed to find myself thus playing a principal role in a conference I had never had any wish to organize myself.

But it seemed in itself a good idea; Santosh and I went to tea with Mr Rasgotra; Kamaladeviji (to whom Santosh was very close) was totally supportive. And in due course the conference went ahead. For a few days before the Yeats seminar I stayed with Santosh, and we discussed names, themes and the like—based somewhat on the plan of our first *Temenos* Conference, held at Dartington Hall in 1986. So I became involved in something in which I was too well aware of my own inadequacy, and unpreparedness for the part I seemed to be now forced by circumstance to play. I had a sense of walking blindfold amid intrigues of which I knew nothing. The teacher at whose feet Santosh had wished to learn now became a pawn in some game of chess whose pieces and squares were for the most part outside my ken. Thank heaven I have never been involved in politics, for which I am totally unfitted. Such a mixture of motives, good and bad, power and idealism, who can walk the slippery surface of that chessboard? Had I not already, with *Temenos*, taken upon myself a task requiring all my small store of strength and wisdom? *Temenos* is within my compass, India is not!

❀

On my second visit to Delhi I was happily surprised to find how many from the kaleidoscope of unknown faces of my first visit seemed now to be quite simply friends. Indian loyalty I knew already, from friends I already had, to be total or not at all; so unlike the subtle sliding-scale of relationships we Westerners live by—degrees of civility, acquaintance, friendships confined to some single aspect of our multiform lives, and a very, very few total, deep and enduring friendships. Perhaps I exaggerate; but there is a difference, perhaps that with us feeling plays a relatively small part in those links we form within our kind of society, where circumstantial or mental affinities predominate. Tambi had no such sliding-scale; and now in a different way Santosh, who had chosen that I should be her guru in her academic studies, was a challenge I found I could meet only up to a point. Thus yet again I failed to come up to, not merely Indian expectations, but my own expectations of myself. My 'passage to India' was a confrontation with myself in which, again and again, I found myself wanting.

On this second visit to India, then, I stayed throughout Santosh's conference at the delectable India International Centre where it was held. Kamaladeviji there presided. There she had her room where she daily received visitors, and her kindness to me, on my Indian visits may, perhaps, rest on the hope that I can do more than lies in my power (for India? for that invisible land of which 'India' is but a symbol?) in my own country, where I represent only a minority opposition to current values in the world of letters. Or perhaps she reads me aright as one whose sole concern is 'the politics of eternity' on which the whole world, and India itself, finally depends. Without that inner dimension of 'the

India of the Imagination' would not India cease to be India, that state of being Raja Rao spoke of? Certainly in my own country there are at this time all too few among the poets whose loyalty is to this country of the Imagination where alone the fire burns of those values by which every culture is enlightened. In my youth there were poets enough—Eliot and Yeats and Edwin Muir and Vernon Watkins and Dylan Thomas; Rilke, Valéry, St John Perse, Robert Frost, and many lesser poets who were true to their calling. Now in England how few; for the invisible worlds are now seldom reflected in the work of those who go by the name of poets; poetry is a 'pop-scene' or a therapy or a hobby; something everybody writes but few read. We have still one great poet—David Gascoyne; some gifted younger ones, struggling to keep the imaginative vision. In the absence of better poets I carry a responsibility that in happier periods would fall to those abler than I to 'keep the divine vision in time of trouble'. Perhaps it would be better to say with Yeats, 'Let all things pass away!' Long before my time he wrote,

> We were the last romantics, chose for theme
> Traditional sanctity and loveliness.

Yet so to despair (if despair it be; Maharaj Charan Singh would not see it so, with that Indian long-term view of the inbreathings and outbreathings of universes) is not permitted to the living. I could not give up so long as raising the standard could still gather those concerned to affirm eternal things; some among whom may take that standard from me when I have to relinquish it. Stella Corbin has decided to relinquish Henry Corbin's Université St Jean de Jérusalem; I have almost made the same decision for *Temenos*. One must have faith that there will be others to come. They alone know who they are, those prophets and torch-bearers of the future. I can but carry out my own task. I am no Kamaladevi; but perhaps she too saw that I am 'doing my best.'

This second Indian visit was not another round of sight-seeing. I could not stay on for I had tasks in England. Rather it was a confirmation of friendships and a preparation for the conference which now it was settled should be hosted by the Indian Council for Cultural Relations, and by the India International Centre, which in effect meant by Kama-ladevi, who had taken Santosh under her wing. As these things come about almost the first face I saw in the sunny courtyard of the Centre where I was staying was that of my Prince Kumar; who had come to India to scatter his mother's ashes in the holy rivers; he attended the conference—he already knew Kamaladevi—and used my room for his evening meditation. On this occasion also I first met the singer and musician Sheila Dhar, who had already contrib-uted to *Temenos*; and Ramachandra Gandhi. In any gather-ing Ramu stands out by that special Indian quality of impassioned thought; his philosophy inseparable from that age-old spiritual fire which burns in him. He gave me his book on Advaita, *I am Thou*; which I read on my return, with absorption. Kapila Vatsyayan, Keshav Malik (Kapila's brother, the poet and art critic), and others I now seemed to be meeting as old friends; Biren De the painter I had not met before, who seems to me to succeed in having created work deeply rooted in Indian Tantric art, yet in modern terms. Indian poetry I have found more difficult to track down, because I can read only what is written in English, and therefore of necessity mainly the work of poets who have chosen to place themselves under Western influences. I still don't know, or even know about, those poets whose work I would most want to know. Or perhaps circumstances are against those who reject the international language of English; as also against those who use it. Ramu Gandhi believes that it is providential that English has become India's chief language of communication, because so Indian thought can be taught to the West in countries where

English is spoken. Perhaps he is right; as Christianity in its day spread along the roads of the Roman Empire. Is not the question rather of whether the West can learn from India before India succumbs to westernization? Krishnamurti seems to have been similarly concerned with the future of that India which is a synonym for a certain kind of wisdom. Indeed it was to that question—which concerns us all; concerns the saving of the soul of the whole world—to which our conference, held in the India International Centre in February 1987, entitled 'Tradition as Continual Renewal', addressed itself.

By one of those strange fatalities I find myself today—December 26th 1987—with only a red ink biro to write with. The beautiful Schaeffer pen I bought in October, someone had thrown into the fire on Christmas Day, doubtless with the litter of wrapping paper, where next morning I found its remains. The transient *Nikko* I walked away with from Mercure de France on the day in October when I signed copies of Pierre Leyris's translation of my autobiographical book, *La Gueule du Lion* is exhausted. So here I must write in rubrics; and ask myself the significance of this. Perhaps I have to be reminded that, wish it otherwise as I may, I am writing no longer as a private person, for my own pleasure or for whatever reason poets write in our attempt to capture some glimpse of beauty or truth. However inevitable it may be, after a certain moment, we who publish our thoughts are no longer alone with them; there is a time-lag, lifelong it may be, and happy are those for whom this is so—before we cease to be alone with our invisible selves when we write. When did I cease to be the Kathie—or had I any name at all—who ranged the free wild places of a bleak Northumbrian moor; who fled to Martindale there to wipe away my life, who buried my stained face in the forgiving moss? I still thought that life could be wiped away—thought so again when I bathed in the waterfall pool at Sandaig, enveloped as I was in a dream of poetic love—and love seems always to absolve. No, all that is over, I know that nothing is ever cancelled or absolved or wiped away in the pure dew of the solitary places of the hills.

I have published my writings, I have completed my work, not all of it worthless; and now I find that I stand, if not alone, yet as a kind of representative or symbol of certain values and attitudes I represent. I cannot withdraw now from the part I have taken upon myself—gradually, imperceptibly, by choosing this rather than that, never in a dramatic way, but over the years, little by little. How reluctantly we discover that we are not invisible, as all children surely feel themselves to be! Or those invisible spectators of our dreams! Yet there must have been a day when I crossed a rubicon, and must now expect, heaven help me, to be read and heeded and treated as a prisoner at the bar of life. Even those secret things my poems. These too will be read and heeded and play their part and live a life of their own, and how I wish they might bring 'good tidings of comfort and joy', tidings of beauty, truth and goodness, of mercy, pity, peace and love. I fear it is often not so. As Ramu Gandhi told me, I carry with me too much sorrow. Sorrow is no virtue, though Christendom almost makes it so, with its Stations of the Cross and the rest. No, joy is the mark of truth. Yet my poems still I hope keep faith with lost Paradise insofar as I bear the sorrow of exile without forgetting or wishing ever to forget. I would remind. But then, I do not enough give myself to thinking and living as a poet, I have laid on myself or am involved in all sorts of tasks, editing *Temenos* and giving papers at conferences and things of that sort the world asks of me. Not for me to wear a white dress, like Emily Dickinson, playing the recluse in her father's house; enviable? I recently read a paper on the austerely

[103]

precious role she assumed, and know only that I live in harsher, coarser, times. Emily Brontë I know better. I *was* Emily once long ago, but being old I have gradually become someone else. Would she perhaps have done so? For me it has been 'put your head in the lion's gullet and don't be surprised if the lion bites it off.' I have courage—plenty of that—or perhaps rather sheer scorn and indifference for what I perceive or deem to be valueless. But I lack wisdom, I lack prudence, and also I get extremely tired, angina hinders and slows me. I need the strength of my youth to perform tasks which have come to me only in my old age. I was not ready to assume them in my youth, nor could I have done so. Perhaps in another life—if we go on to other lives, continue our slow task of learning—I shall be ready a little earlier. But after all what matter, things come to us in their due time, and we must face them there and then and not sooner or later.

It must seem absurd—and yet so it was—to say I discovered I had a part to play—a public part that is, from which I could not draw back—only when in the sunny courtyard of the India International Centre I heard myself being thanked as the organizer of the conference that in February 1987 became a reality. Its hour come round at last. Yet there was Kamaladevi, who had been in prison, in the forefront of India's struggle for independence, a leader and a figurehead. There was Pupul Jayakar, adviser to her friend Indira Gandhi, and to Rajiv Gandhi. All of them artists no less than I for the theatre had been Kamaladeviji's first love, as crafts were her last; Kapila Vatsyayan, who has written many books on Indian dance and sculpture; Pupul Jayakar, organizer of wonderful Indian exhibitions both in the West as well as in India. All these holding high office in their country's affairs. So naturally they would see nothing strange in expecting of me, a poet and scholar (of sorts), what they themselves have achieved. I felt almost an impostor, yet I had not sought the situation in which I found myself and must carry as best I could, not indeed for the honour of my own country (which has nothing to do with the matter) but for the honour of that other kingdom. Isaak Dineson's story of *The Flood at Nordernay* tells such impostors as I how we must play our part; the bishop's valet who must assume the great and sacrificial role of the man he was only pretending to be; or Pirandello, he too understood. Perhaps we are all such impostors who enact our own lives. Who are we?

Well, when the moment comes such questions are vain—we must act—enact—the part assigned, whether Lear or Hamlet or Cordelia or Ophelia or only an attendant Lord, without breaking down.

I had not of course organized the Conference nor was I ever asked to do so; as poor Professor Mercier (whom I have never met) must have been asked by someone or other to do so for the conference that never was. True, with the help of my *Temenos* colleagues and of John Lane of Dartington Hall, I had put together our *Temenos* Conference, that was held there in November 1986. Santosh was present on that occasion and no doubt gathered ideas and met *Temenos* people suitable for India the following year. Yet even Santosh was not the official organizer; nobody was finally responsible. Yet I should have been able to take the whole thing in hand and bring it to life. If it lacked the coherence of our two *Temenos* Conferences, yet much I think did after all come of it; people met, came to know one another, went away inspired to follow up those fiery ideas that leaped like flames among us. What more can a conference achieve? Kamaladevi had very firmly decided the year before that we did not want a public conference with lots of speeches and official people; we wanted a working conference, at that long table in the conference-room of the India International Centre, we wanted discussion among a closed circle of participants, and not lecturers posing before any kind of public. It was more like what must have taken place in the days of King Akbar in his beautiful and very small room in Fatehpur-Sikhri, when the best minds of the world gathered there. Best minds are at any time but fallible and human; yet I believe I can say that those who gathered in that conference room included some of India's best minds and not a few from outside India; not the kind of television-screen personalities who hold forth on this and that but committed and dedicated scholars, artists, philosophers; citizens of that other kingdom. Whoever organized or did not organize that conference the Holy Spirit played some part. Helped or hindered by some spirits of comedy and mischief be it said. Those Jesuits who held aloof at Fatehpur-Sikhri from Akbar's symposium were more aloof and uncooperative than anyone who participated in ours. All contributed something.

Looking round the table I saw indeed many faces of friends – many *Temenos* contributors in both teams, so to speak, not only of those of us who had come from the West. Santosh had faithfully invited all the people I had suggested to her on her many telephone calls from Delhi; and she had certainly studied well the contributions to *Temenos*. From England there were not only Keith Critchlow and Philip Sherrard and myself and Martin Lings, but from France Gilbert Durand and J-L. Vieillard-Baron, both friends of Henry Corbin, and members of his illustrious Université St Jean de Jérusalem; from USA Huston Smith; young John Carey from Harvard and the painter and mystic Morris Graves; from Australia James Cowan. Tarkovsky had been invited but died before the conference took place; Czeslaw Milosz refused; Osten Sjöstrand from Sweden accepted then withdrew. Wendell Berry and Joscelyn Godwin were absent; but Dartington Hall and *Resurgence* were represented by John Lane and Satish Kumar. John Montague came from Ireland. Among Indian *Temenos* contributors were Kamaladevi herself; Kapila Vatsyayan; Pupul Jayakar; Santosh; Professor Sisir Kumar Ghose (whom I now met for the first time) Ramachandra Ghandi and Raja Rao and the painter Biren De who have since contributed to *Temenos* also. My old friend Arabinda Basù was there and gave an excellent paper on Sri Aurobindo. There was a certain amount of splendour—a banquet given by Sri Venkataraman the Vice-President (now President) of India who kindled the symbolic torch.

Yet I was not altogether happy, finding myself involved in a network of, I hesitate to say, intrigue—at all events a network of relationships in another country in which I felt traps and pitfalls on all sides. Where did I stand in all this? I shall never know and after all what does it matter! Someone at some stage had decided that there must be more delegates from the Commonwealth—a perfectly good idea in itself—and lots of poets!

From the Eastern Bloc there was that dashing and brilliant Jugoslav philosopher Borna Bebek; whose father had been a Partisan with Tito; Borna looks every inch a Partisan himself, yet is a philosopher, and—somehow he manages it—a Catholic, besides being economic adviser to his Government. (Years ago I had reviewed a book of his in *The Tablet*, and meeting him later at a Dartington Hall conference he greeted me with the words 'I did not think a *woman* could have reviewed my book!' Perhaps if there were more Jugoslav partisans in England—or the United States—there might be fewer 'liberated' women, and that would be an excellent thing.) So there were as it were two conferences that did not quite fit together, and yet everyone contributed in a mixture no stranger than the world itself. So, balanced uneasily between the official and the real, the conference took place. And what has taken place is thereafter a part of the texture of the world, whose threads are woven into

[107]

distant times and places for ever. At least India saw and came to know Western minds who had a standpoint other than official policy of 'selling' British (or American) cultural values to Indians all too eager for Fellowships at Cambridge or Yale or Harvard or to have their own books (carbon-copies of Western authors and scholars) published in the West, thus spreading the infection of Western values which could but destroy the true India. And perhaps will, though God forbid. I would like to think we contributed even one drop helping to stem, or perhaps even to turn, Yeats's 'filthy modern tide'.

In that long narrow conference-room at the India International Centre, with its idyllic garden (a piece cut out of the beautiful Lodhi Gardens, just beyond) we spoke from the heart. We met as scholars and those concerned with wisdom have met over the millennia of civilization, in Nalanda and Fatehpur-Sikhri, in Athens and Florence and Paris, in Oxford and Cambridge once, in America now. There our beleaguered handful from the West, dissidents from the materialism there predominant, encountered some of India's great minds; or shall I say we met the great mind of India? What if anything did we achieve? Certainly we did more than many who come (and who can blame us?) simply to 'see and enjoy India' at the expense of the wonderfully hospitable Indian Government. Friendships were I believe made that will continue to bear fruit in incalculable ways; we from the West may have come to realize in how many important matters we are but mice at the foot of the elephant, but that in itself was something. Perhaps we warned our Indian counterparts of some of the dangers that confront us all as inevitable consequences of 'westerni-zation' with all its easy and effortless but soul-destroying technology. Is there such a thing as Schumacher's 'appro-priate technology'—or in Keith Critchlow's words, 'wise technology', or is wisdom compatible with technology—the

[108]

answer should be yes but seems more often in practice to be no. In any case the predicament of the world is the same, essentially, for our one planet earth now, and we must pool our wisdom as we in any case pool our folly. Tempers were lost, home truths were spoken. There was comedy, there were tears, crises; Indian food prostrated Keith for a day; there were parties, formal and informal—but, yes, it was something more than can be described by such words as 'failure' or 'success': of these who can judge, and how? It happened. We were changed by having encountered one another to discover the best or the worst—in other words the truth—of which we, each in our own way, are what Plato called 'the guardians'. Not a rank, an appointment, an office, a decoration, or a matter of power, or class. None chooses to be a Guardian: rather the truth we serve chooses us.

That conference room I knew well by my third visit. I had read poems there on my first; and before that poems of mine had been read there by Tambimuttu, in a none too sober state I dare say. On my second I had given a Blake-Yeats paper, and had seen already what Indian conferences are like. Indian formal manners derive in part from the formality of the British Raj—manners that in this country belong to the past, to that 'greater, a more gracious time' that is gone; in India's still gracious formality we confront that decline. I had already seen, at Santosh's conference, those sensitive, intelligent Indians, the formalities completed, kindle in turn like little flames, instantly ardently alight; no posturing, as in the modern West for the personality to be projected (whether or not the television cameras are there) but fired with the thing itself—the idea, the knowledge. An inextinguishable passion for imaginative—spiritual—thought. I don't know what discussions may go on, or have gone on,

[109]

in other conference rooms, but would guess that in Akbar's small conference room at Fatehpur Sikhri, at Nalanda, at the court of King Asoka, or at any Indian village gathering of pundits, the same little flames would kindle. Like those flames that used to be painted on the brows of saints or angels. Pentecostal is perhaps the word. Perhaps Pentecost was like India, that spontaneous combustion of flames 'that cannot singe a sleeve'. But between the formality of the opening and the reading of the first paper one was aware of being taken in, observed, read, understood not only by outward but by inward signs, understood all too well, alas, by courteous Indian eyes. Observed kindly no doubt—which does not make it any easier; given, as it were, the benefit not so much of the doubt, as of that long Indian view of the progress of the soul through many lifetimes. Far have I come and far must go. What would they make of us, what had we to offer, we Western suppliants?

So it began, with Philip Sherrard reading a carefully prepared paper setting forth the spiritual dangers of Western secular materialism. Philip enjoys diatribes and did not fail to point the finger at what he likes to describe as 'atrocious and diabolical science'. Science. Silence. These westerners who have it all don't want us to have their technology, so essential to our national development; to the immense problems of the Indian economy, the battle with starvation, flood and drought, with disease, poverty and the birth-rate. Pandit Nehru had written into the Indian constitution an insistence on the part science must play in India's future. The school of Guénon (of which Philip is a follower) is inclined to see all developments of thought since the Renaissance as atrocious and diabolical, though Guénon's words are less colourful than Philip's which derive in this respect rather from Greek Orthodox theological writers. Still, there were excellent things in the paper; an admission of the great harm India has suffered at the hands of the British and since through the imposition of western values through education and otherwise. India was prepared to reserve judgement. Kapila Vatsyayan came next; with a sliding pile of books and documents before her Kapila spoke—as she often does—extempore, without notes. With beautiful eloquence, with the eloquence of her beauty. Of things as they are. Of those behind who cry forward and those before who cry back. Reality. Things as they are. Theoreticians don't like to be reminded of it overmuch, it's too untidy. Kamaladeviji sitting in her monumental listening silence. Discussion. Raja Rao, India's distinguished novelist and metaphysician (or was that on the second day?) uncoiling himself like a dry and aged python to ask Philip 'Just what do you mean by the word "God"?' Here in India we don't say God this and God that—God is a concept used sparingly, and rather a long way down from the summit of mystery. I was electrified—others too?—by the realization that reality, not theology, had spoken. Things were beginning. We had learned our first lesson.

Lunch in the shade of the garden, tables spread with delicious food, formal informality, courtesy. Arabinda Basu, my old friend, was there, but holding himself somewhat apart. He came to speak of Sri Aurobindo. He knew I would never quite accept Aurobindo, because of the poetry. Arabinda no longer quite my friend? Sisir Kumar Ghose, however—though also a follower of Sri Aurobindo—friendly. 'We have surely known one another in a former life' he had written in one of his charming letters; and in another, in reply to some book of mine I had sent him 'I can only say one thing: I wish I had written it myself'. We have published several of his papers in *Temenos*. Arabinda has for years made excuses for not writing for *Temenos*. Not only in the West is sectarianism divisive.

Of course I realized that I was out of my depth; I should have been a great presence, inspiring the conference with my wisdom, single-mindedness, and great knowledge. I was none of these things. I realized, besides, the extent to which I did not know what had been said or done in my name. Things now, however, must take their course. There were, besides, clear spirits emanating invisible light. There was the American painter Morris Graves, who already knew India well, and was a friend of Pupul Jayakar—for all these great women were present, Kamaladeviji silently (until her time came to speak, and then she spoke with authority indeed) constantly supportive; Pupul Jayakar, Kapila, now Director of the Indira Gandhi National Centre for the Arts. Kapila *flows*; and as she said on a later occasion of her purposes for the Centre, 'I am planting trees, not annuals'. There is something altogether remarkable in seeing a young nation still with a heroic vision of its destiny, especially when that new nation is also an ancient civilization. On the Indian side also there was Biren De, schooled in Western life-drawing, now using his knowledge of art in the present world, to paint his radiant Tantric paintings (some we have reproduced in *Temenos*) showing, as does Morris Graves in America, that there can be fruitful and creative meeting of East and West in the field of the arts; something that is not simply Western influence on Indian writers, or naïve Western imitation of Eastern iconography by starry-eyed children of the New Age. Each day there was in the evening beauty, that indispensible part of Indian life. No one can live without beauty and not become savage and violent, or apathetic and zombie-like; a barbarian. The arts, Maxwell Fry has written, are 'not a luxury but a necessity'. The Dagar Brothers expounded, and sang, Indian classical Dhrupad temple chant; there were dazzling musicians from the desert of Rajasthan that swept us all into their joyous world of song; there was a classical dancer with her guru—not her guru only in the sense of her dancing master, she assured me, also her guru in the spiritual sense, for in India the two

things—art and spiritual knowledge—are in fact inseparable. 'It took six thousand years to create that face' Ramu
Gandhi said of the dancer's mask she assumed with such
grave devotion. In the spicéd Indian air by night in the garden
a tall and splendid village woman reciting in Hindi a scene
from the *Mahabharata* (Draupadi watching the assembled
heroes competing for her hand). Behind her on a rough
platform, musicians: tabla, flute, tanpura, and a cantor who
marked the caesurae of the long *slokas* of the recitation with
exclamations of 'He?' and 'acha!' which as it seemed represented the response of the listeners, first a question 'then
what happened?' as it were, and at the end of the line 'yes
we see' or 'now we know'. Formalized, yet archaic relationship between the storyteller and the listeners. I wondered
what Homer's listeners might have exclaimed. Most poetry
was, after all, pre-literate, we who read books too seldom
remember this and the living circumstances in which the
poems we burn midnight electricity over, arose. I was sitting
beside Mr Lalit Mansingh, President of the I.C.C.R.; he took
the occasion to indicate to me that he saw our conference as
somewhat beside the point; India must modernize, must
have strong military defences, etc. And yet perhaps India
was never so strong in the world as in the times of Mahatma
Gandhi. Yet Necessity, or Fate, or Destiny, pursues its
irrevocable course, and perhaps there is no retreating from
the disaster towards which we are all rushing lemming-like.
But we ourselves, after all, are the tide which turns, or does
not turn.

It is only in memory that certain self-evident things have
struck me that in India were plain to be seen—or heard—
and constitute so great a difference between India and the
West. One of these is the coherence of 'the India of the
Imagination' (where not impaired by westernization) from

the highest to the simplest, of that 'unity of culture' without which as Yeats said there can be no 'unity of being'. Yeats longed for such a world, and in Ireland found its traces, and himself worked in his poetry and through the Irish theatre to repair its foundations somewhat. He both admired, and perhaps envied Tagore because his work rested on such a unity. Where but in India can that unity now be found in the world? Unless Disneyland be a culture of the nadir whose unity is submerging all? Music above all—and did not both Pythagoras and Confucius declare music to be the foundation on which a society must stand or fall? India's music remains entire, though infinitely various, and speaks in the same language from the simple temple singer with his beautiful exalted face who came to give Santosh singing-lessons and who accompanied her dance, to the beautiful refinement of the singing of Shiela Dhar, sitting on her carpet beside her vina, to the Dagar Brothers, those consummate singers of Dhrupad temple music, the nineteenth generation of their family to have preserved that tradition. After their performance in that ever-remembered concert hall at the India International Centre, Arabinda Basu (who long ago in England used to play me such fine records of Indian classical music) said, as we left, 'You will never hear finer performance of India's sacred music than this'. What indeed can surpass perfection of the sound-current of creation itself?

But always from silence comes, softly sounded on the tanpura, the note played in unison on five strings by gentle accomplished fingers, creating, as it were, a living sound-medium from which the ragas are born, as the singer or instrumentalist, at first softly, imperceptibly, brings the music into being, weaves its pattern, slowly and softly at first, then the tabla or Pakhwaj brings in its subtle, ever-approaching rhythm, long complex bars that I could never succeed in following, always losing count before that subtle pattern is back to the beginning again of that earth-beat that accompanies the cosmic music of singer or player of flute or sarod. And so the music comes from afar, with slow approach, arrives like a retinue of the gods, without our knowing how or at what moment they came, yet we know they are there, we are taken up into the cosmic music, for the sound current of the universe flows through us also, through our unawakened occidental senses and crude flesh like unfired clay, yet of what else are we made, being within the one creation, unless of that music, that octave that is colour, sound, light, the flow of tides and rivers? On that ever-advancing sound current the gods arrive in their splendour. The Dagar Brothers, so refined by that music, seem almost luminous, and carry with them, even in a room full of people, a listening stillness. Seeing them, always, as it seems, together—or when in the same room listening, as it were, to one another—it was as if the music flows through them always, when silent no less, or only a little less, than when they sang; like two wonderful instruments—violins— their human frames sounding-boards of the unheard music. Like the sound *OM* their music is a bridge between men and God, transforming and purifying the dull senses, so that even we for a moment seem to discern those unheard sounds of which Pythagoras taught that heard sounds are but a crude approximation, and who

> *Fingered upon a fiddle-stick or strings*
> *What a star sang and idle muses heard.*

No, even Yeats's words are too Western, too secular for that absolute:

Million times prayer brings devotion
Million times devotion is equivalent to continual recitation
  of the name of God.

[115]

Million times recitation of the name of God is equivalent to music.
This music is the greatest of all.

This Dhrupad singing brings within earshot of even our dull hearing the absolute cosmic music, and that music depends not on the virtuosity of the musicians, nor on the imagination of a composer—great as that virtuosity may be, supreme indeed in Ustad Fayazuddin and Ustad Zahiruddin Dagar, but rather on the sound of the Universe itself.

And that same sound-current flows through all India, one hears it under an awning in a village festival, in temples, in homes, everywhere. It is the sound of India, the India of sound. On that sound-current Tambi was floated away in 'The Bhavan' in Londsdale Road, w.11. On that sound—*OM*—India is upheld. Here, the raucous mechanical sound of 'musack' disseminates disintegration from every supermarket, café, building-site and factory, disco, pocket radio-set; here as throughout the secular West. Are we not doomed by our music? In India one can understand the truth Pythagoras had understood, that a civilization is sustained or destroyed by its music. One sees that truth reflected in the very refinement of the bodies and bone-structure of a race whose poorest villagers—whose beggars—seem to participate in, to be formed by the sound *OM*. For how long? Can disintegration defeat the sound of creation? Does not our popular music proclaim our irreversible dissolution? Will that bridge, that rainbow-bridge, that sound current, carry us to heaven after all? But we think too much in terms of the future, for, after all, there is only the present, and every present infinite. Every moment of beauty is eternal.

During those happy days at the India International Centre I did not dream that we, in our turn—*Temenos*—would be able to play host to the Dagar brothers. I write this postscript following our second *Temenos* Conference, at Darting-ton Hall, with the sound-current still flowing through me on which that music, sung on our last evening by Fayazuddin and Zahiruddin Dagar, lifted us. The great hall was packed, some unable to get seats. Yes, we in the West did hear, did listen, did enter that current of sound. The brothers had recently been in Russia. There too. Everywhere humanity vibrates in harmony with the music that created and sustains us. Everywhere. 'We came because we love you' they said to me on that last evening after the concert. The love that unites all who respond to that sound. All.

Kapila also came—her paper, surpassing the rest of us with such ease, sustained as she was on her civilization. Whereas we of the West are striving to rediscover the holy ground that has been lost, she communicated a knowledge and a wisdom refined by millennia of human fidelity to the source—and she is a dancer also, the dance too is that music. India was received, in her person, with a standing ovation.

Yet we can discern, catch glimpses, of a Europe of the Imagination once unified by the singing—the Plainchant—of the Church and a popular tradition of folk-music not far removed from that *temenos*. In my childhood—even now? —the Scotland of the songs and the pipe-music took its deep-felt unity from certain cadences, certain modes—in the Gaelic-speaking Highlands and Islands above all, though these I knew only much later. That traditional music was participated by all. I have heard the pipe-music in the hills of Wester-Ross; the pipes of a MacIsaac at Laig Farm on the Isle of Eigg could be heard on most of the scattered crofts of the Isle; heard 'big Hector' MacKinnon on the Isle of Canna from Sanday across the bay. That music evokes—creates—is, Scotland. Yet already the television set has moved into every kitchen on the remotest Isles, where formerly the songs were sung and the stories told. Was it a divergence of the sacred and the secular that in the Renaissance broke the old 'unity of culture'? Or a divergence between learned and popular in a society no longer held together by Christendom's vision? Now we have indeed a repertoire of great musical compositions, still widely—ever more widely—performed, but there is another sound coming from the radios transmitting a popular culture quite unrelated to that classical music, a music crude and mechanical. There is no longer unity of culture in western music. And is not the secular unity everywhere imposed by the television-set as great a threat to the soul of the world—the universe of the Imagination—as any weapons of physical destruction? Whatever unity the television screen may impose on the entire world is itself a disunity, for it builds no unseen bridge between earth and heaven on which the gods may arrive. The temporal world it briefly unites is transient as the moment itself, without past or future, and bringing its news from no eternal realm. Europe's greatest art celebrates the tragedy, brevity and poignancy of mortality; India's the undying, the arrival of the eternal Presence that 'comes, comes, ever comes'. *Asi, asi, asi.*

❧

Fine papers by Raja Rao and Arabinda Basu. Kapila was chairman for a morning session at which Dr A. K. Saran went on for an hour and a half with no sign of coming to an end of his paper. Kapila stopped him at last, because poor Professor Nagaraja Rao, a Brahmin from South India, had practically no time left for his paper. Dr Saran was huffed and did not reappear at the Conference. Since it was Marco Pallis who had insisted that at all costs Dr Saran must be invited to speak, I was responsible for having insisted on this; it was my fault, though not directly but because Marco here represents the Traditional school of thought, is Guénon's translator, and highly respected by Philip, Dr Lings and Dr S. H. Nasr (who had been invited but could not, mainly for policial reasons, come). Marco had later confirmed to me that Dr Saran is inclined to go on and on. I should have trusted India to judge its own representatives. My fault. Worse and worse. I should, besides, have realized that the Guénonian view of 'sacred tradition' was all very well for the West, but of little significance in India, which is the thing itself. It was decided to limit the time of any paper to forty-five minutes. Pupul Jayakar was next day's chairman, for Keith—very appropriate since Keith is the architect of a new building at the Krishnamurti Centre at Brockwood Park. (Pupul Jayakar was a lifelong friend and has written a biography of Krishnamurti.) Keith too is inclined to overrun time limits. However, the Chairman this time spoke for nearly twenty minutes, and it was Keith's turn to be curtailed. However, he gave a splendid lecture (with slides) on Chartres Cathedral in an evening, to a delighted audience; many from outside the Conference.

Ramachandra Gandhi, whom I had met the previous year, kept a little aloof for some time. Keith felt—I also—that much depended on Ramu Gandhi. Fortunately, after Philip's initial false start in his total unconditional dismissal of 'science', an Indian physicist gave a paper on science so elementary and inadequate that Ramu lost his temper and left the room; the score was now more equal. Fine papers by Sisir Kumar Ghose; Kamaladevi; Pupul Jayakar; some of the Traditionalists did not like to hear the views of Krishnamurti, who renounced the role of the guru and denounced all reliance on religious institutions or organizations whatsoever. Pupul quoted the words, 'I maintain that Truth is a pathless land, and you cannot approach it by any path whatsoever, by any religion, by any sect . . .Truth, being limitless, unconditioned, unapproachable by any path whatsoever, cannot be organized; nor should any organization be formed to lead or coerce people along any particular path.' There were some among the Western followers of the Guénon traditionalist school who deeply disliked these frightening words. Essentially such people are insecure and in search of certainties that, as I grow older, I realize life does not offer. Krishnamurti, like C. G. Jung, admonished us to 'think your thoughts to the end', to seek truth within. Like the Lord Buddha—who likewise offers no answers other than reality itself—Krishnamurti tells of a vision for which there are no words, but unlike the Lord Buddha offers no rule of life, no Noble Eightfold Path in those austere regions.

Martin Lings showed beautiful slides of Islamic Korans; Biren De of his Tantric paintings, which so admirably unite a knowledge and command of modern Western methods of painting and a vision profoundly Indian. All were beginning to enjoy and participate. Then came another set-back, from an unexpected source—Huston Smith, that dedicated and courageous American follower of the Traditional school, who already loved and knew India, elected to show a film on the sacred places and arts of India: temples, dances, bathing-ghats, sculptures; not a bus or a power-station or an Ambas-sador car or a Tata lorry or even a bicycle to be seen anywhere. This film would have told much in America, but, in India, it again awakened suspicions: so they want to keep their picturesque India for spiritual tourism! Alas, not well received. Better, had he wished to show the contrast between sacred India and the secular West to have shown landscapes of Brooklyn or Detroit or the Pacific coast of Los Angeles, or Disneyland. And is it not a true reflection on western followers of Guénon's traditional school that they would have wished to stop the world as it was at the end of the Middle Ages and before the Renaissance, (not to mention the Industrial Revolution) rather than addressing themselves to the problem which is the same in every present, of em-bodying a vision? And did not followers of that school of thought look a little odd in India: rather a kind of intellectual (in some cases literal) dressing-up?

❀

Another side of India was less likely to attract the spiritual tourists: by a quiet, impressive Indian countryman from the forests of the Himalayas—Sunderlal Bahaguna—we were told something of the devastation there wrought by 'progress', greed in alliance with technology against the gods, and the women who heroically hugged those sacred trees to resist the destruction. His was indeed a heroic presence to shame mere discussion. Satish Kumar, returning to India where he had walked with Vinoba Bhave in his campaign to persuade landowners to give land to the landless, was able to speak with equal urgency of the destruction and poisoning of the environment in my own country. Greed is by no means new in the world but possesses now means of devastation formerly restrained by the lack of the power—and indeed the will—to ravage the earth at the expense of future generations. From the Himalayas to the tip of India (so Keshav Malik also told me) tree-felling has been laying waste the land and changing the climate, causing flood and drought. In his own youth—not long ago by my standards—to cut down a tree was deemed a sacrilege, unless for good reason. As against that, however, it is true that extensive tree-planting along the canals and elsewhere is taking place; perhaps it is not too late?

Keith went down with food poisoning; and perhaps the strain of the situation, of which he was very much aware. John Montague arrived reeling from a domestic crisis and required whisky and comfort; the whisky was administered by Matilda, Duchess of Argyll, who is a follower of Keith. I who normally at the end of a day drink one Scotch, scrupulously avoided alcohol as a guest of the Indian Government, except one evening when the Contessa de Robilant (a friend of *Temenos*, and former student of Henry Corbin) was hostess to a party at the Swiss Embassy; and

[121]

again (need I say) at a party at the Irish Embassy, where later
the Ambassador, Paul Dempsey, and his wife Janet invited
John Montague to read his poems, and me to introduce him;
home ground for John, and for myself to some extent, since
for so many years Liam Miller of the Dolmen Press had been
my publisher as well as John's own, a dear friend of us both,
and of Santosh also (whose book on Yeats and the sacred
Dance he had planned to publish). Liam at that time was
already very ill with the cancer that took so prematurely that
great artist of book design—a last figure of the Irish renaissance and a man whose gifts Yeats himself would surely have
appreciated. The Dempseys, John, myself and Santosh had
Liam much in our thoughts.

I behaved 'badly' too; the officials of the I.C.C.R. had, in
the commendable attempt to broaden the base of the
conference, thought fit to invite a sprinkling of Commonwealth poets. There was a Korean lady whose butterfly-like
clothes were a delight to look upon; the Australian Aboriginal poetess, Kath Walker, just back from a conference in
Moscow, who was demanding the right of all aboriginal
housewives to have the benefits of modern technology—
washing machines, for example. She was, very rightly, a
political activist speaking for her people; and most of the
Commonwealth poets also seemed on the whole to see
poetry as the language of political activism; they must have
wondered what the rest of us were talking about. There was
a Maori poet, very shy. There was a poet from Indonesia
who explained to me how you can attract and summon bees.
I would have loved to be taught by him how to summon
bees. Kathie of Bavington would have been at home there. I
wonder if he was intuitive enough to discern my own
far-away peasant love of that world so close to the earth?
Thus there was a sprinkling of poetry interspersed with very
different matter. So in the time allotted me to read poetry I
simply did not do so, considering it as being an irrelevance,

and made instead a statement of the function of poetry and the other arts, as the natural vehicle for the dissemination of value systems within a society; on *Temenos* lines. But John Montague and I did read poems one evening, informally. And however much things slipped, misfired, infuriated, a clear current did at last flow.

Gradually things sorted themselves out; we became less two 'teams' and more committed to a common search for the problem and its solution, in the course of that rich blend of differences, imaginative beauty, comedy, irritations.

The burning words I remember were spoken by Ramu Gandhi. (Is Ramu like his grandfather? I asked Kamaladevi who had known Mahatma Gandhi so well. Yes, in many ways, she said). 'We live in dark times', he said; 'the shadow is indeed heavy on our world'. He then told a parable about a man who set out to bury his shadow in a deep grave; but as the grave was filled up, the shadow also rose, and was there as before. There is but one way to overcome the shadow, Ramu continued: it is to look always at the Sun. Then the shadow will fall behind you. That, he went on, is perhaps what Jesus meant when he said 'Get thee behind me, Satan'. We must look always to the Sun, to the source; the present world (and that is especially so in the West) is obsessed with the shadow but forgets the light which alone casts it, and banishes it. 'God', Ramu reminded us, 'cannot be destroyed'. Keith and Ramu understood one another, at the end, as two men of entire purity of motive. And after the conference, Kamaladevi pronounced the words, 'We must follow this up'.

Later Ramu wrote to me and told me I must meditate more; attend to my breathing; and be less sad! To him (after the conference) I had said, 'Ramu why do you not start a Review, of international scope, on philosophy and meta-physics?' He replied that he had long intended to do something of the kind, but meanwhile had a book to complete. I hope that one day he will start such a Review; but I always felt, in his company—as indeed with other Indians I have known—that although he was there at that moment, he might, like Puran Das, disappear into the hills to become a *rishi* with his hair matted and one of those rosaries of a hundred and eight beads made of the seeds of a forest tree. Meanwhile, he is in California. Borna Bebek left saying 'We must have such a conference in my country'. (Jugoslavia). It is only, he said, a matter of wording; say 'human values' instead of 'sacred values' and all is well. But rivers flow on, their waters irrigate many lands, who knows, we are but a drop in that flow.

Raja Rao invited me to lunch. 'They tell me you are England's greatest poet', he said. No, I replied, we have only one great poet, David Gascoyne (I was not going to refer him to the British Council or their list of accredited poets representative of British culture, etc). Here at least, at the India International Centre we were not concerned with cultural imperialisms, British, American, or otherwise, but with true, not contingent, values. And in the end Truth I believe did prevail. Raja Rao said that next time I must visit India as a poet; must see southern India. India, he said, is experiencing a great cultural renaissance; in India during the last century there have been philosophic minds as great as any in her Golden Age; Ramana Maharshi; Vivekananda; Radhakrishnan; Sri Aurobindo; Mahatma Gandhi; Krishnamurti; and others living now. I believed him for had we not experienced this for ourselves? And also, he added, the world must be saved by woman—tell them that! he concluded. He did not mean 'women's lib' but the thing itself that women's lib denies. That too I had seen for myself in India.

These are but a few of the moments I remember; shall

always remember. Others will carry different memories; but all of us were, I believe, changed by the experience of India, that state of being. Doubtless I could recall more; but of what use is 'total recall'? What mattered was those Pentecostal flames, those sudden flames of thought which in India is not conceptual but spiritual, imaginative, ardent, beautiful. And what mice we of the West felt ourselves in the Himalayan presence of those living heirs of India's unbroken lineage of beauty and wisdom! Unbroken, that civilization, as Ramachandra Gandhi also pointed out, from the aboriginal to the most highly developed culture, unbroken and continuous within a single texture. But for how much longer who can say?

❀

My official visit over, I lingered on for a few more days at the International Centre as Kamaldeviji's guest; as did the Contessa de Robilant, who had attended the whole Conference as a guest, and who understood very well what the need was of which we had attempted to make our Indian hosts more aware—the need to summon and bring together an association of Plato's 'Guardians' responsible for 'the politics of eternity' in this transitional period. All periods are no doubt in some sense transitional, but I am a follower of W. B. Yeats not only in having made my 'passage to India' but also as a student of *A Vision*, as seeing the present transition as involving a change—a reversal—of the premises of our civilization; a transition from a materialist civilization to a reaffirmation of the values of the human soul and the realization that spirit, not 'matter' (whatever matter may be) is the ground of reality; the old myth of the reversal of the Iron Age and the Golden Age, each in turn, the reversal of those 'gyres'—Plato writes of them in *The Laws*—foreseen by Yeats as already stirring at the time he wrote *A Vision*. At such a time—at the present time in which we are—the changes are of a kind and on a scale for which political solutions are inadequate; politicians cannot remedy the sick soul of the world, and those of us who owe our allegiance to the 'Kingdom not of this world' must do what we can. The old religious forms can probably do little and the truth of this time is that 'pathless land' of which Krishnamurti spoke.

Maly de Robilant and I, when all was over, thought it was perhaps worth making one more effort of a practical nature. Maly has access to—or rather perhaps knowledge of—certain sources of funds (in Switzerland, where she herself lives). Kamaladevi had been extremely chary about any proposition that involved funding from abroad; it seems that India is wary of the sources of any such funding which is often traceable to the United States and the CIA and therefore imposes conditions. However, Maly thought that this is probably not so in the present case; and it so happened that Dr Karan Singh (hereditary heir and one-time Governor) of Kashmir—who as a fellow poet has always behaved in a very friendly manner towards me, sending me his books and so on—was the Indian representative of this mysterious (to me mysterious, as all to do with money and funding is mysterious) source. We therefore visited Dr. Karan Singh; he and his beautiful wife received us with much interest and sympathy for the whole idea. Dr. Karan Singh, who had been a cabinet minister under Indira Gandhi, seems also to be turning his thoughts rather towards the 'politics of eternity' than any longer to the 'politics of time'. He has, he told us, a palace in Kashmir, a beautiful spot: why not make that palace such a centre? Such a meeting-place of the Guardians? The money could be available, a Director would be needed: why not Arabinda Basu? I knew that Dr. Karan Singh had studied philosophy under Arabinda. I knew he would refuse even as I said·to Karan Singh what a good idea to invite him.

Arabinda refused of course; and he is after all already busily occupied in going off to conferences all over the world, on behalf of the Sri Aurobindo Ashram, of whose school he is now in charge. Arabinda has devoted himself to being the delegate of a not inconsiderable modern teacher; from whom for no good reason—unless his poetry be a good reason—I hold a little aloof. Maly de Robilant and I talked long of these things. She too wishes to serve. For many years she has attended the Eranos conferences at Ascona; she was a student of Henry Corbin and is a friend of Stella Corbin. Soon after my return to Europe I was in Paris and talked at length with Stella; I have several times attended the *Université St Jean de Jérusalem* conferences, whose papers, published annually under the imprint of *L'Ile Verte* are, somewhat in the manner of Eranos, and in the spirit of *Temenos*, symposia of the best thought France can offer in the field of 'the Learning of the Imagination'. We have, in translation, published some of these papers in *Temenos*. The U.S.J.J. was represented in Delhi by Gilbert Durand (a follower also of Gaston Bachelard, and a regular lecturer at Eranos) and by J-L. Vieillard-Baron. Gilbert himself has founded schools in France, Portugal and elsewhere, for the study of the 'imaginal'. All these links and currents and cross-currents, a network of kindred minds to which *Temenos* is our sole English contribution, unless one includes the Guénonist *Studies in Comparative Religion* which has probably outlived its usefulness, and *Resurgence* whose themes are rather the practical issues of ecology and its accompanying value-systems, as these can be presented to a wider public. Stella Corbin and I had discussed the situation and decided to ask Maly de Robilant if she would consider—if she would give her mind to something that would pick up the threads of the U.S.J.J. (now ended) *Temenos* (soon to end) of India, of Eranos, and of whatever other living centres there may be; in the United States, in Australia, who knows where? Almost we had persuaded ourselves, Stella Corbin and I; but then, about to part outside my little hotel in the Place de l'Odéon, I said what had been unsaid through all these discussions, 'But we have no great inspiring figure. No Henry Corbin'. What am I but a poor stand-in for someone—a Yeats, a William Blake—who is not there?

No river springs from a single source; but it is enough that *Temenos* has been one of the tributaries of the great river, and of a later project—again it was Satish who gave it words—which may realize in England something I had thought of as rather taking place in India. At a meeting of the Fellows of the Schumacher Society, in the winter of 1987 (Keith and I were present, Christian and Diana Schumacher, and the President of the Dartington Hall Trust, John Ponton, John Michell besides others of the like-minded) Satish suddenly proposed that a small University, grounded in the traditional, sacred knowledge of the true nature of mankind and our universe, of the earth and our human task as its guardians. The unanimity in which this proposal was greeted was as if Satish had but given words to a need we all knew was essential and vital; as if the words had been given him from some unseen inspirer. Once again I was shaken by the realization that everything is possible to those who serve a living idea. Fritz Schumacher, after all, achieved so much by putting into operation a very simple one—'intermediate technology'—and the words 'small is beautiful' have in themselves done much to transform the world. What gives such ideas their power is surely that—as in the case of Schumacher himself—they are grounded in a service and dedication to a vision of the sacred, an understanding that humanity and our earth are rooted in holy ground. Greed and consumerism may seem to prevail—the Great Battle is for ever being fought—but they have not the transforming power of a clear and selfless vision originating on another plane altogether. There was Gandhiji; there was

Vinoba Bhave; there was Fritz Schumacher; there must have been countless men and women who have discovered—surely many of them with no less astonishment than has been my own experience—that the invisible powers of the Spirit never fail when these are summoned into operation, for it is they who direct and sustain the world. By some unknown law or principle, money and means appear, as if by miracle, in the service of such seminal ideas. At our first Temenos Conference, Satish—he had after all as a youth been for eight years a Jain monk—expounded to us the principle of *Yajna*—sacrifice—as this forms part of the Vedantic view of the world. It is not by greed but by *Yajna* that the world operates. Why am I always so surprised when these things prove to work in practice? So ingrained in my western formation is the notion of material causality, despite Blake's words that have so often comforted me: 'Every material effect has a spiritual cause, and not a natural; a natural cause only seems.'

A culture can only live if it is rooted in a true understanding of the answer to the ancient question, 'What is Man?' India has long had that answer; as did Christendom once, before education from the universities to the schools, to the homes where the television screen is the new domestic oracle, had lost its orientation to this source. Much now disseminated, no less in our Universities than in our schools is rather mis-education than education, and in place of a 'university' grounded in a recognition of the 'universal' single ground of all knowledge, we have the diversity of endless specializations lacking any significant unifying context. From our collective experience of mutual support, and our common purpose, defined and discussed in India, such a venture—a 'university' in the ancient and true sense of being grounded in a total knowledge, as understood in India, by Plato and by Blake, might well come about. Or perhaps in more than one centre, serving rather different needs, at different levels; *Temenos* maintaining a post-graduate rather than an undergraduate standard. My own part in this is of course marginal; yet I believe that the 'invisible college' *Temenos* has at this time re-convened, has been a means—one amongst others, but there are not so many 'others'—and may have its part to play. Of course the project may fail; or if put into operation may deviate from those first principles, fall into the wrong hands, fail to find students (this however I doubt) or run into those conflicts that beset, as it seems, any venture that seeks to put into effect some seminal vision. Yet, at this time when the materialist premises of the modern world are everywhere being called in question, as Blake's 'new age', Yeats's time of the reversal of the gyres of the Great Year is upon us, there must be such new centres of true learning in order to contain and to direct the change. There must, besides, be such centres as I had originally envisaged where the 'guardians of the City' themselves may meet. A new *Akademia*, whether in India, England, America, or in any of the four quarters of this planet. It is in another 'place', on another plane, that the 'invisible college' now as at all times meets. I may not live to see any practical outcome, yet I hope I may; for these things are not a dream of a far future, but the world's great need here and now.

❦

Before I left India I was invited by Santosh and her husband, Mohan, to prolong my visit as their guest and participant in two more experiences of 'the India of the Imagination': Brindavan, and Haridwar. Brindavan—magical name of that sacred forest-country by the Yamuna river where the Lord Krishna spent his childhood, grew up among pastoral people, hidden from the enemies who would have killed him as Herod sought to kill the Child Jesus. There he stole the butter, played with the *gopis* (those beautiful milkmaids of Indian art) and playing his magic flute in the forest enchanted their hearts and lured them from their domestic duties into the eternal other-world of the soul. The Krishna of Brindavan is the Krishna of Indian popular religion. It is said that he could divide himself into as many Krishnas as there were (or are) *gopis* in Brindavan. And above all it is Radha, the Indian Psyche, who loves him and is his beloved. Again and again in a thousand paintings, in dance, in sculpture, in poetry, that immemorial story is embodied. At the festival of *holi*, the *gopis* dance their circle-dance in the streets and temples of Brindavan. Santosh suggested we go to see the immemorial dance. The drive was long, we arrived late; the temple dances were over, or would not be until the evening. But that joyous festival when coloured water is thrown by everybody (especially by little dancing-eyed boys with water pistols) over everybody was in full swing. Crowds of people, of children, of pilgrims. Our car was conspicuous and separative, and I felt deeply how far off, how separate I necessarily was; a spectator, a tourist. Happier when, leaving the car, I found myself being helped up the streaming wet steps of a temple (our shoes and stockings left in a sort of cupboard off the street blow, itself streaming with water and mud of various kinds and plenty of dogs and little pigs strolling at their task of scavenging) among children, among old women much like myself, helped up by our charming teenage boy guide, everyone joyous among the jets of dyed water, and all the idols in their best finery, Radha and Krishna, worshipped because the soul and her love for the Lord Krishna is a sacred mystery of joy. Everyone is Radha, the old women, the young girls, the wives, now as ever, lured away to the Brindavan of the imagination by that flute.

In Brindavan the idea of private property seems minimal— the streets, the whole town, the temples, belong to everybody, including small boys and pilgrims; excluding, I sadly felt (for I too had run barefoot on the streaming mud of Bavington's one street if street it could be called) white visitors in Ambassador cars. But fat white woman though I might be in that temple, 'whom nobody loves' could not have been said, my old feet squelching with the rest in the filth of the street, in the streaming temple, no-one treated me as a stranger and a tourist. *Cras amet qui nunquam amavit, quique amavit, cras amet.* I was beginning to get into the spirit of paganism. The children don't behave like children in a church; they jump over everything joyously—a festival in the true sense of universal excitement and participation of young and old. A Bacchanalia but no-one drunk of course, this is a sacred city, the town full of processions of pilgrims to all the temples. The invisible poet in me was with them, though my English flesh and blood saw it from that 'afar' our visible selves impose.

Down those filthy streaming streets gutters flowed in which the adorable bands of beautiful children paddled; no sanitation. Water was fetched in pails from taps at the corners of the streets. Mounds of sweetmeats on sale everywhere; and in the soul's country of the Imagination doubtless also covered with germs, whatever these are. But with it joy and beauty and the works of the human imagination and human hands. You don't go to India to admire the landscape but to understand how beautiful are the young and the old, the women and the men, the youths, the bearded pilgrims. In Brindavan I saw universal rejoicing that owed nothing to alcohol, commercialism and the profit-motive, or anything but the innate joy of life there is in people, delight in the ever-living presence of the Lord Krishna and his beloved and the *gopis*, those dancers on deathless feet whom we never managed to see. But in all hearts the music of that flute. Everyone's shirt was splashed with purple and green and orange and I wished I had not been but a spiritual tourist, a spectator of that day's rejoicing

[132]

in which the world we see with our eyes is permeated with the reality of the *mundus imaginalis*.

But if the dancers eluded us, we came, by chance, upon a great yellow awning under which a stage had been set up. Grandmothers (old men too, but those joyous old women and little boys seemed to be everywhere) sitting on the ground and grandchildren weaving amongst them, behaving pretty well, for this was a sacred enactment of an episode of the *Ramayana*, where the unfaithful wife of a Rishi of the forest obtains her pardon only when Rama comes to release her. Indeed the sort of bad, rowdy or purposeless behaviour of English and (even more) American children, who, given that uncharted 'freedom' American demagogues and journalists are forever proclaiming, seem never to know what to do with it, wave their arms and legs about, draw attention to themselves, and totally lack concentration; not so Indian children; who are, of course, more loved, by more people. Not only parents but grandparents and uncles and aunts and cousins, brothers and sisters. Also there is not a hard and fast line dividing pious behaviour (not much of that left in the West in any case) and secular behaviour, for in Brindavan the small boys jumping over the rails of some temple are perfectly aware of, and imaginatively delighted by, the sacredness of the place, those staring idols in their finery, but then, pagan religion is joyous. So in watching a performance of the *Ramayana* the occasion is at once like going to the theatre and going to church. 'What is a church, and what is a theatre?' Blake asks, 'Are they two, and not one?' Here in Brindavan they are most certainly one. The stage was adorned with curtains of scarlet encrusted with plenty of gold. As Rama and Lakshmana were royal princes, India's villagers young and old expect them to wear their regalia all the time, even in the Forest, just as they do in the holy picture I bought also in Brindavan, spangled and glittering over a Rama of divine beauty, accompanied by the

[133]

peerless Sita, Lakshmana and the devoted Hanuman—those high princely conical crowns, earrings, bracelets, jewels. This was a performance by local talent: a narrator with one of those musically unattractive portable harmoniums that India has wrested from the culture of the Protestant missionaries of the last century, and somehow absorbed. The beautiful adulterous wife was played by an embarrassed teenage boy, uneasy about what to do with the heavy plait of hair which was part of his costume, who when it came to the line (all the grandmothers knew the lines by heart of course) about her being 'the most beautiful woman in the three worlds' (her lover was a god) all the delighted audience laughed while this embarrassed actor did not know where to look. The play was already in progress and we were standing at the side, but the old ladies kept beckoning me forward—wanted me to miss nothing—and I found myself gradually pushed and beckoned to where I had a perfect view of everything; not because I was a government guest from England but because I was old like them, or just from courtesy to any guest to Brindavan, whose Golden Age seems never to have ended. They all knew the lines and joined in from time to time at exciting moments. And I too, when at last Rama himself entered, accompanied by the faithful Lakshmana, their cardboard princely headdresses tottering a little, I too felt my heart swell with emotion— 'He's really come, Rama himself!' Because Rama had come, not only would 'the most beautiful woman in the three worlds' be pardoned, but so would we all, everything at last made right by the long-foretold advent of the god-like Rama. Kumar's ancestor, I recollected, and Kumar's words too 'Man or god, what's the difference?' But in this performance every inch a god in those symbolic adornments. All too brief his presence on the stage! It seems that Peter Brook whose magnificent *Mahabharata* Satish Kumar and his wife, and John and Truda Lane and I later saw in Glasgow, has learned from India that theatre can be, even in 1988, a sacred art.

And where was that temple looking over the great fertile basin of the Yamuna, where there are two child's footprints carved into a little marble slab, where the child Krishna had stood when he overcame the water-snake that was ravaging the land? The Infant Hercules, St George and Apollo himself also overcame serpent-dragons, and of course slew them, as any Western god or hero would. But not the Child Krishna. Santosh gave me a little brass figurine of the little Lord Krishna, his foot on the head of the serpent as he holds its tail high in the air. Victory. But it was at that moment that the serpent begged for his life: 'After all, you made me!' Unanswerable. The Child Krishna spared him and let him off with a warning to stay where he belonged, in the river-bed.

There were other temples; courtyards filled with votive tablets. I saw many great peepal trees (and perhaps other species also) that grow in temple precincts leaning through the walls, which seemed to blend with their venerable trunks. This, Santosh gave me to understand, is because when a tree grows in such a way that its branches endanger the wall, it is not in India the tree that must give place, but the wall. Here the tree would be lopped; in India the temple wall is taken down to make room for the tree-trunk. Hence much beauty. Trees are sacred; walls are but walls. Beautiful golden age when all nature is sacred, trees, water snakes, monkeys, anthills—all is sacred. I was beginning, I found, to get on better with idols too. Another car ride to another small town nearby took us to the birthplace of Radha, beloved of the Lord Krishna. There were many pilgrims, some approaching the temple on their knees, others pros- trate on the ground moving serpent-wise, in the posture of total, absolute worship of the gods, those gaudy dolls who yet are the expressions of the soul's deepest dreams. I find it

extremely painful, nowadays, to kneel, yet I followed Santosh into the temple—yet another temple—made my offering, realized how near and real that world of the
imagination is to India, how far from myself! Everywhere
that inter-world of the imagination is near, is embodied; all
the Indians I met, or was able to see, learned or simple, are
open to poetry, drama, music; beauty; they expect it, it is
their daily food. At our conference the Punjabi poetess
Amrita Pritam read poems; I understood no word but
watched the faces, listened to the gasps and sighs of deep
appreciation and reverence. They expected it of me also;
they expect from one another song, music, dance, poetry; as
from that beautiful singer Shiela Dhar, whom I came to
know on my second visit to India (again through *Temenos*)
and as Santosh herself danced daily her worship of Surya.
Or the musician who accompanies her dance, a Brahmin
descended from generations of temple singers. His raptu-
rous beautiful face. A poet in polite society (polite-ish;
society is no longer particularly polite) would no more recite
a poem at a dinner table than a parson would talk about
religion. I remember when Tambimuttu did just that at the
luncheon-party given in my honour by W. H. Smith when I
was awarded their book prize for a collection of poems one
year. Everyone was embarrassed, of course, including
myself, and tried to quiet Tambi. No doubt he was drunk,
but now I understand better, yes, dear Tambi I understand
better now what it is to live in a country where a poet would
come as a poet to any occasion, and not wear the vapid mask
of anonymity. It is we, not Tambi, who are disoriented, who
have lost our vital continuous communication with those
beautiful and terrible worlds over which the Indian gods
preside. Did not Tambi write his *Geeta Sarasvati* his hymn
to the Muse? A purely Indian poem, although written in
Tambi's artless English.

And let no one ask me if I did not see the poverty, the

insanitary conditions; no doubt the social injustices are there too, and degradation, and corruption. There was a girl-dacoit (Phulan Devi) whose story was running in the Indian papers on my first visit—her colourful story of rise to leadership through a series of rapes, bereavements, betrayals, murders, splendours and miseries was itself a kind of popular legend in the making. Yes, of course there are these things, everywhere and always. But the beauty and the meaning and the joy of life is there too. That impressed me the more because it is what my world most lacks. Of course Brindavan should not have to fetch its water in buckets from a tap in the street; of course every house should have a water-closet and a kitchen tap. And would that spell the end of those bevies of children playing in the squelch of the streets, among the little dogs and the little pigs, and the women adoring the Lord Krishna as if he were their lover also? Will people still gather to see Rama and Lakshmana step on the boards of a country stage when the television and the video make their inroads? Alas, must the world choose between the riches of this world and of the other? Are there not moments of equilibrium? In India souls are rich and bodies starved, leprous, suffering. Here it's the opposite, so forgive me, Indian friends, if I seem indifferent to your country's poverty, sickness, injustice and all the rest of the world's woes. But the Lord Buddha's answer to ever-present sickness, old-age and death is India's answer to those woes, given to the world long ago and still speaking to multitudes in the West as in the Far East. Is technology so rich a gift as the wisdom of the Lord Buddha's grave and serene compassionate smile?

Back in Delhi we met Borna Bebek and he could hardly wait to catch the first train next morning to Brindavan. I hope he found the dancers, the *gopis*, the magical world we had seen made of tinsel and dreams. Of what else is the world ever built? My 'holy picture' of Rama and Sita and

[137]

Lakshmana and Hanuman bought in Brindavan for five rupees, I see when I look up from my writing. Do I, a poet, need, then, to go as far as India to find what is everywhere? England has not, after all, quite forgotten King Arthur and Guinevere and the Holy Grail and the Fisher King and Merlin and the Round Table.

❀

And last of all, Rishikesh and Haridwar. A tourist poet, what right have I to write of India's holy places? 'Where are the holy places of America?' One of Herbert Read's sons asked his parents that question when taken there many years ago. Ireland has its holy places still; and England's younger generation visit the Tor of Glastonbury and the somewhat factitious holy well where the late Wellesley Tudor Pole found a chalice of blue Roman glass—or maybe it was not Roman, what matter? And there is the Glastonbury Thorn, Avebury and Stonehenge. The Christian holy places— Walsingham and Canterbury and St James of Compostella that left its traces even in England where the pilgrims gathered at 'the Spaniards' in Hampstead to join the pil- grims' way—these went long ago. Now we have glossy travel brochures thrust through our letter-boxes. Buy buy buy. A holiday in some sunny crocodile-isle with nude bronzed women and men in rude health displayed on the covers. We must discover or create our own holy places. Poet and saint confer the quality of their vision, as Words- worth upon the Lake District, as Blake on 'lovely Lambeth'; Yeats on his Norman tower. On what have I ever conferred holiness? Perhaps at most on moss and trickling water on some bare hillside long ago. But the well at Bavington has long been piped into houses now occupied by commuters from Newcastle, their native inhabitants long gone. The houses of Wordsworth and Ruskin and Thomas Hardy and Yeats's Tower are turned into museums not shrines; a blue

[138]

plaque on the wall of Eliot's flat in Kensington Palace Gardens—these are better than nothing, but no, the best we can do is to commemorate, not to sanctify. It may be said that all is interiorized in our culture; but what of the wholeness of inner and outer, the dream that builds temple and cathedral in likeness of itself? What is within will express itself in such embodiments. How, for us, now, can that expression come about? We can at least endeavour to keep the seeds of future vision alive. But what beauty do our industrial cities express? Our Disney-land fantasies? Yet I did visit India's holy cities, and I hope rather as pilgrim than as tourist. In the clear swift waters of Ganges I bathed my old tired feet. And are not all rivers the same river? All human feet pilgrim feet?

Last of all to the holy city of Haridwar. Again those Indian roads, so full of life, themselves rivers where life flows, that by now I had come to know so well; the strung-out villages, the washes of blue flowers, the Mango groves, the Papaya trees, the little temples with their fluttering pennons, the Muslim tombs oriented to Mecca; once a pullulating flock of vultures that had descended on some dead dog or other creature on the road (for that pullulating swarm covered whatever the carrion was). Strange, the vultures wait on dead trees, motionless; or do the trees the vultures perch on die? Death is their world, their lust. For once I saw them at work. Nothing would have driven them from their feast of carrion. Awesome nature! I Am that I Am. So with the pythons in the baskets of snake charmers, so with the little scavenger dogs and pigs with their piglets; with the wondrous peacocks, the weaver-birds, the hoopoes and the green parrots. The gentle monkey families. On and on endlessly along the bumpy roads of India, past road ends leading to villages and temples I shall never see, so all is interwoven, there is no break anywhere. Everywhere we are everywhere, so why travel at all? Yet what endless marvels!

[139]

Haridwar, holy city where the Ganges descends to the great plain. We stayed this time not at one of India's grand tourist hotels but at a government hostel, simple, plain, clean, downstream from the city with steps leading to the river. Perfect but for the mosquitoes (they got in without difficulty through the holes in the netting over the windows). But first we drove on and up towards the first foothills of the great Himalayas, to Rishikesh, so named because there from time immemorial the rishis—the forest-dwelling ascetics—have lived in ashrams or come down from their solitary retreats. I a stranger, like an observing camera, yet insofar as I too am a pilgrim soul on this earth, a participant in some measure (what of those Indian friends who 'knew me in a former of life' or intend to be my children in my next?). I have seldom seen Mohan so relaxed and happy; for this was country he knew from his school-days, and the burden of responsibility he carried as a merchant, he had left behind him. That Sikh tradition which appoints the man the guardian and protector of the woman was extended to me, as a guest, receiving through Santosh my share of that reflected courtesy of the Sikh way of life. 'Mohan treats me like a queen!' Santosh had once told me—in England. Now I saw that this was really so (are not Sikh women addressed as 'princess'?), and what a rare luxury that is, the ever-present strength and protection of the man to lean on. Always Mohan would be waiting with the car to meet Santosh wherever she was; to plan her journeys, see her off, meet her on her return, forestall her needs and wishes, and when she is in England, telephone her daily. This is not 'romantic love'—quite the contrary—it has the unquestioning dignity of a code of conduct. It is not 'love' or anything of that kind which dictates the conduct of man and woman towards one another in such traditional marriages, but *dharma*, right conduct; the 'law' of life itself. And in the woods of Brindavan there is always the divine

[140]

flute-player who brings Radha the ecstasies of another kind of love: who has ever heard of the husbands of the *gopis*? Had Radha a husband? Not marital infidelity, in the French style, which no doubt has relieved the tensions of many a marriage, but of something else, which the West has very largely forgotten. Perhaps that, ultimately, every soul loves only the Lord Krishna, or the same Lord by some other name.

So, in Rishikesh we stood and watched the flow of the waters of Ganges down from the wooded hills (for they are but wooded hills, such as one finds in England, the great mountains are far beyond) a swift pure flow that turns in a bend, flows past the welcoming ashrams on her banks, then flows on, spreading through a network of channels that unite again above Haridwar. Abundant, everlasting flow. On the far side, the brightly coloured ashrams; on the near, steps down to the water where the beggars and lepers sit in the sun. Not many, but always they are there. 'Down by the river, where the ragged are'. The river seems to draw the derelict, the dying. To watch the flow of the water?—what is it in that flow that so heals and comforts? That is an aspect of *l'eau et les rêves* that Gaston Bachelard did not write of. Is it that the flow of water carries away our thoughts, our sorrows, as it does leaves on its surface? That we, like the river, forever 'rest in changing'? Little ferry boats come and go, across not down the river. How often have I boarded such boats, the ferry to Eigg; to Iona; boarded Bruce Watts's *The Western Isles* from Canna; from Sandaig; to Rousay and other isles of the Orkneys where the selkies raise their heads to look at us from their cool seas. Here the same precarious scramble aboard an unsteady boat, among men and women and children, offering helping hands to an old woman not now nimble as once.

So once again on the waters of a holy river I floated on that joyous laden ferry; the children excited by the great shoals of carp in the water gathering to be fed; kindness, laughter; peasant people the same the world over, people of the place, knowing one another and that place their world. We tourists see it all as from the other side of a glass partition. Those friendly hands for a moment offered. No matter, I could say to myself—and to whoever reads my words—'I was there, I was borne on the holy waters of the Ganges'. But was I? For that holy Ganges is not of the outer, but of the inner world, the 'interworld' of the *mundus imaginalis*. Pilgrims know those holy cities, those holy fords and rivers and mountains; but do tourists? Americans write about little tavernas in Greece where they drank cool retsina and ouzo, or ate and drank something else in Japan, consuming a culture they did nothing to create, whose creators had other values, whose genius (you can add Florence and Rome and Ispahan and Granada and Toledo, or Katmandu, or where you will) was rooted in some experience of the sacred. Whereas the consumerism of tourism brings no such vision, merely enjoys aesthetically what was the quintessence of the devotion of a civilization, for whose values tourists care nothing, which if they discern them at all, they enjoy as mere aesthetics; not tears and prayers and a vision. Consumer culture. Expatriate culture: what is the expatriate but one living a secular life in squandering the spiritual riches gathered by sacred civilizations? Not all of course, for some Americans also are pilgrims. Not so Thoreau or Emerson or Frost; or Faulkner or my friend Wendell Berry indeed, who set themselves to create 'the America of the Imagination.' We must know what is ours, we must consecrate our own holy places. And the texture of earth is seamless in all its times and places.

❀

Towards evening at Haridwar. To the ghats we hurried through that beautiful ancient city, down to the river as dusk fell. Santosh and I bought each our little basket made of the leaves of a plane-tree, laden with rose petals and stephanotis, with a small candle-end and a sprinkling of paraffin whose smell among the scent of flowers made a strange discord; that disturbing discord of flowers and incense, and death or corruption one often finds in India. We had left our shoes in the car and hurried barefoot across a bridge to the farther bank, opposite the temples; low steps to the water, and Santosh and I sat on those steps, our feet cooled by the flow of the river—Mohan our protector; but Sikhs do not offer flower-sacrifices to river-goddesses. Across those swift waters all the temples were open, the priests chanting, the torches alight, lowered and raised, lowered and raised in worship of Mother Ganges. Thousands of pilgrims on the ghats—not a special day, but on any day there are such pilgrims who have travelled to Haridwar. And afloat on those swift waters hundreds of these fragile flower offerings, each with its candle-flame, floating down the river so swiftly into the darkness. Beauty speaks a langauge all understand—those offerings of flowers, who does not understand, these precarious offerings with their little lights afloat on the sacred river?

Yeats, who understood the language of symbols, has somewhere used an emblem of a candle in waves; Liam Miller had taken it to illustrate one of his Dolmen books; and it was used in my *Yeats the Initiate*. When I visited Liam in Our Lady's Hospice, in Dublin, where he died—not long after my return from India—he asked me to send him a photocopy of the Candle in Waves; 'and I will make you a drawing from it'. I sent the photocopy but that drawing was never made. But to me that was Liam's last message to me. A message that needs no words, mine or another's—those baskets of leaves bearing their offering of flowers and a candle-flame alight, on the one river of life. Where do they come ashore? Where do those lights drown? I think of a

[143]

song I knew as a child—from Robert Louis Stevenson's *Child's Garden of Verses*, and the 'green leaves a-floating'. My beautiful daughter-in-law, Jenny, so lately dead, had described to me the beauty of those little lamps in India's evening worship; our lives those little gardens of dream floating down the river. Holy Ganges accepts our offerings on her abundant flow, and carries them away for ever into the darkness. But how cool, how clean, how healing those waters to pilgrim feet.

Santosh loves temples—she is a true Hindu in her love of the arts and forms and embodiments imagination gives to the meanings and values and invisible, intangible apprehensions in dance, sculpture, ceremony, dress, all the multiform arts of life. And after the worship of the river with torches and chanting and offerings we walked back over the bridge, retrieved our shoes, and Santosh, guarded by Mohan, descended to visit the temples by the riverside. I felt unequal to climbing up and down those many steps, and said I would wait for them at a certain spot at the top of the steps, surrounded indeed by as many temples as booths in a fair-ground. For a long time I looked at Hanuman in a little shrine, his monkey's jaw and his blue human eyes; he could watch me and I him as I thought how close the understanding between human beings and the animals, and how touchingly Hanuman's aspiration to be human is expressed in the role he plays of the faithful but sometimes forgetful devotee and servant of Rama; the Hanuman in our common humanity that is sometimes the irresponsible monkey, and then again remembers Rama and our aspiration towards something we perceive but do not understand. At a nearby corner was a small Shiva-lingam. A little twelve-year-old-girl briefly came and prayed and dropped a flower-offering and slipped away. In a country where sexuality is sacred adolescent girls accept their womanhood with beauty. In a nearby temple much smaller children were climbing on the knees of the priest; perhaps they were his children. Temples in India are like that, children play there as the gods in their finery of the imagination stare with their great unblinking eyes. If the roads of India reminded me of a gypsy camp on the move, here among the temples as night fell and their lights were kindled I was reminded of the fairground lit up with that magic of the imagination that has no price.

When Santosh and Mohan returned, we wandered in the market where I bought sandalwood beads and rosaries of forest seeds. One hundred and eight beads is Shiva's number. I have kept one, distributed the rest as gifts on my return; to Buddhist or other believing friends.

If sometimes I have seen Indian temples as one huge gypsy encampment full of tawdry magic—those doll-like idols with their great eyes and the tinsel and the glitter of which the *mundus imaginalis* is continually made and re-made, at other times—as with those flower offerings to the River—the magic touches a level of understanding so deep that it merges with the highest poetry. And beyond that are the yogis and those bearded rishis in their dhotis and heavy rosaries whose faces reflect their vision of sacred things. The temples are not 'works of art' and neither are the idols. No more than is Disneyland. But what a different vision! I fear the gods of Disneyland, more diabolical by far than India's idols, and more hideous and dangerous, popular idols of a religion whose dreams are star-wars, the 'conquest' of outer, not inner space, not the beautiful flute player in the forest, the king who rules justly and his consort Sita, beautiful and chaste. Disneyland is vulgar and vulgarity is the expression of evil, for it diminishes and makes ignoble and undignified what in us aspires to nobility and dignity and beauty. The opposite of beauty is not the ugly, but the vulgar and the trivial. At all levels of Indian culture, the vision of the beautiful is expressed at the level appropriate to those who perceive it. Even the tawdry is not vulgar. So I waited for

Santosh and Mohan, a little afraid in an unknown land, but fascinated by the glitter and dazzle of India's dream, that lit up the night.

Later still, sitting in the dark with Santosh and Mohan on the steps by the river below our hostel and its little well-tended garden, night was without dreams. Darkness; just a few lights reflected from across the river. Yet the deep river flowed through that darkness as it had flowed through that beautiful pageant of dreams. All of us, I think, were deeply satisfied. India says everything to those who can read its language.

Have I been to India or have I not? I have seen it from afar. For India *is* the *mundus imaginalis*, the 'savage and beautiful country' of our dreams where all has meaning. In India also lies the way through and beyond all dreams to the heights and the silences. It is all there, and yet not more there than here or any 'where'. And have I been, or not been, 'there'? As I write in London am I in India? When I was in India did I leave London? Did I ever go? Did I ever return? The heights and the silences, be they outer or inner, lie beyond the place where I am.

❀

TWO

❀

'Tis not so sweet now as it was before'

❀

I NEVER thought to return to India—not, at least, in this life. Two years ago I had said to Kamaladevi, as we sat in the sun of the garden of the India International Centre one happy day, that I would probably never be in India again. Why should this have mattered so much to me? I am over eighty now—I was nearly eighty then—and had lived a long life before I reached India, and yet as I write, back in London once more, it is with the kind of pain at heart separated lovers feel that I reflect that, this time, it may be true that I will never again return to India. There must always be a last time, and there is also a probability, when one is eighty, that some long exhausting journey to a far off land may be the last. But Kamaladevi would not have it: 'You must not say you will never return,' she said, 'it is inauspicious, and perhaps you *will* come back.' Sad to say, it was Kamaladevi herself who had gone from her old room in the International Centre when I returned in February 1989. Her absence was everywhere present, and not only from her room, but from India, I feel, as I add this postscript to a record I had thought was concluded. 'A greater, a more gracious time, is gone,' she the last of Gandhiji's friends who with him made India's history, and as the bronze-age ended when the feet of the Lord Krishna no longer touched the earth, so perhaps it is with modern India's heroic age. It is said that 'beginnings are better than endings'—but they are also less easily recognized: who knows what child may not already be present to bring renewal? All children bring renewal! But renewal was not to be my experience, rather in India, as elsewhere, the imagination of the world seems to be confronting themes of endings. But, as Maharaj Charan Singh had said to me on a previous visit, golden age or Kali-Yuga is a personal matter.

So I am in India once again. I came to participate in a half-centenary celebration of the death of Yeats, arranged by the Yeats Society of India (that is, by Santosh) to which Anne Yeats, the poet's daughter, and his daughter-in-law Grania, the harper and singer of Irish songs, were also invited, and my Lebanese friend Professor Suheil Bushrui, who this year gave the annual Yeats Memorial Lecture. Now they have left, and once again I am Santosh's guest—perforce, imprisoned as for the moment I am, following an infection which has left me convalescent and rather helplessly deaf. I write on the airy roof outside the guest-room in Santosh's house in Civil Lines. In the cloudless blue above me the kites are 'turning and turning' in the thermals. I look across to the rich gold-grey cracked crumbling wall of an old house mysteriously broken by a few meshed openings on whose sills sit the doves. Between my roof and the wall is a jacaranda tree where two tree-squirrels chase each other, and bright finches, crested bulbuls and 'seven sisters', green parrots and crows come and go. I have been answering letters and sipping a homeopathic solution which I hope will finally dispel the virus infection or whatever it is I brought with me from England. I feel that this virus is only another symbolic form of a poisoned land, for this has been the winter of salmonella infected eggs, listeria infected cheese, hormone infected meat, water polluted by chemical nitrates and pesticides, radioactive waste and all the other poisons with which we are destroying the fields of the earth; and heaven knows what other pollutants are killing our seal colonies and our dolphin—lead polluted air, acid rain and radioactive seas and hill pastures still infected from the fall-out of Chernobyl. A third of the seas and of the creatures that are in the seas, a third of our rivers, destroyed by those so profitable poisons. A star called Wormwood.

I speak apocalyptically, but apocalypse has itself become literal, a daily banality of the newspapers. We prefer to believe the official cover-ups and denials that there is 'enough evidence' to link Windscale's nuclear discharge with an unusual incidence of leukaemia, or the death of the seal-colonies with anything we have been doing to the sea their habitat, because it is less disquieting than to know the truth of the pollution and destruction of England's green and pleasant land, and indeed of Mother Earth herself. Had I not, in beautiful Italy, seen the atomic cloud from Chernobyl drift over Ninfa's paradise? That news has grown stale, but our mountain pastures are still tainted. Only this winter James Lovelock spoke with sober truthfulness at the annual meeting of the Schumacher Society, of the destruction of the ozone layer that protects the earth, the burning of the Amazonian forests, destroyed not even for their timber, just destruction of an area the size of France, to replace the age-old forests with cattle to convert into hamburgers and the like. Of all the threats, James Lovelock told us, the destruction of the forests—the 'lungs' and rain-gatherers of the earth—is the most dangerous and immediate. In India too, the devastation in the Himalayas. It's irreparable, we know at heart, and it goes on apace. The profit motive, and something called 'progress' goes on of its own momentum. A tide that may turn, or a river that flows only one way? All traditions—the *Mahabharata*, the *Koran*, the oral tradition of

[151]

the Hopi people, have their prophetic foreknowledge of the end of this world. Now we have no need of prophets, it is upon us, we know it in our bones. A Master can laugh and say, 'would it matter so much?' if earth is destroyed. But, like my mother who, confronting her own departure, said, 'but this is a nice little world!' I too think of the gray atlantic seal and the blackbirds and the snowdrops. And here in Santosh's jacaranda tree the little tree-squirrels, and the green parrots; and the vultures, those cleansers of corruption who cannot cleanse the aftermath of Bhopal. It's gone too far!

The whole foulness of England in the winter of 1988–9 is itself perhaps only the 'correspondence', as Swedenborg would have said, of an inner foulness. And I, for all I may think of myself as devoting my life to attempting, (through *Temenos*, and in other ways) to dispel the miasma that is poisoning soul and body, I am it seems the bearer of that miasma, that foulness, by my very presence. Santosh has been telling me what a good thing it is I am in India, and treating me with small homeopathic pills. This imprisonment is not what I had planned or anticipated, but since I am here, what better place to continue at leisure this record, for what it is worth?

When I was invited to return to India I asked Satish Kumar (he is to publish this narrative in his series of Green Books) to hold the earlier sections, already in proof, in case I should add some more pages. Pages and pages and endless pages we write from the one Book of Life, whose every page is a mystery, of which we who are at once its authors and its readers can catch here and there a phrase or a word, or a letter—or even less than a letter. Not more and more pages but only a deeper understanding of the one ever-open page can avail. Of this I can read so little, write less. And yet, unless by this unending discourse of human beings with one another, how have civilisations arisen? We tell one another our thoughts and dreams, in poetry, painting, music, conversation and laughter, all the adornments and ceremonies, and daily loves and kindnesses, and only so do we come to have Hamlet and Lear, Rama and Hanuman, Draupadi and Helen of Troy, Dante's topography of the heavens and the hells, and the Thousand and One Nights, Kalidasa and Kabir, and that other immortal weaver, Nick Bottom. And all the saris and jewels and turbans and the shield of Achilles and the temples and cloud capped towers, for what is the world but an edifice built in the image of our dreams, those emerald cities?

How far have my own dreams led me from my cottage among the hills and the winds and the secret places, but the Golden String in its windings takes us away from loved places, and yet the choices are ours, all those innumerable minute unnoticed choices of a lifetime that have brought us to where we are. Mine, it seems, have brought me to India; and India had not, after all, rejected, or even just forgotten me.

It had made me very happy when, last Christmas, a messenger from India House had come to my door bearing gifts from Mr Rasgotra, now India's High Commissioner in London—beautiful Darjeeling tea—and presently came Mr Rasgotra himself. We exchanged our thoughts about the conference of 1987, and of mutual friends. I was glad of the opportunity to explain some of my own bewilderments, but had no need to do so, for Mr Rasgotra had already a very clear picture of the situation, even clearer (very naturally) than I. It was a relief to find that I was still in good standing with India; even to the point of his saying *en passant*—something I love in relationships with my Indian friends—that meetings in this life come about through links in another. 'Is it that in some brighter sphere/ We part from those we meet with here?' Shelley's words, here in England deemed a poetic fancy, become in India a truth of the soul's history— as indeed it was for Shelley's masters, the Neoplatonists.

Truth literal or imaginative, this is a footing on which I feel at ease; these things have meaning. Warren Kenton, my Kabbalist friend, assures me that he 'remembers' knowing me in 16th century France, where I was a nun, he a Jew (of course—how but through many wanderings could he have learned his wisdom?) and Keith Critchlow thinks we may have known one another in some Pythagorean school, and Arabinda Basu too long ago, said he thought he had known me in eighteenth century France. A manner of speaking it may (or may not) be, but it is true to certain vistas of one's own and another's being, shared vistas. Vistas within Spirit that knows all?

But when a High Commissioner invites himself to tea it must be for some more pressing reason than links in the *mundus imaginalis*. In this case I was unprepared indeed. On January 30th, India's Martyr's Day, a bust of Indira Gandhi was to be unveiled in India House. Mr Rasgotra's imaginative idea was that only women should participate in the ceremony. Mrs Thatcher was to unveil the bust, the present Mistress of Somerville (Indira Gandhi's old College) was to speak and would I be the third speaker? But, I protested, I had never even met Mrs Gandhi. Jane Drew, I said, had known her well. We telephoned Jane but there was no reply—as I had feared she was in America. In the end I gave in and agreed to speak of how paths may cross even of those who do *not* meet. I hope that in the brief speech I wrote with much labour I said what the High Commissioner had hoped a poetess would say—that Mrs Gandhi, in her concern for the politics of time, was also aware of the necessary role of Shelley's 'unacknowledged legislators', the poets, and the politics of eternity. I hope I wrote with honesty—draft after draft I tore up; but my worst anxiety was that I supposed it would be proper for me to wear a hat. I never wear a hat, poetesses do not wear hats. But for the sake of India I went to Harrod's accessories department and bought in their sale a beret somewhat more formal than the two (one black, the other navy blue) that I keep for wearing in the rain. But in whatever way I tried it on I knew that beret was a lie, a sin against poetry.

The day came and a car (much too early) from the High Commission, and a member of the Staff to escort me. I was put to wait in the High Commissioner's room, and presently brought downstairs to await Mrs Thatcher's arrival. To my immense relief our Prime Minister was wearing a cheerful pink suit, and no hat! Unobserved (so I hope) I discarded my beret under a chair, and took my place beside her. Our Prime Minister was very affable; I said I believed we had a friend in common in Laurens van der Post, to which she replied how well he wrote, and I with what wisdom and we were off! The High Commissioner on the great role of women as Prime Ministers; Mrs Thatcher recalled Mrs Gandhi's expression of sympathy at the time of the Brighton bombing; not long before she was herself assassinated. She then took up the theme of international terrorism—no merely abstract or political theme for world rulers. The Mistress of Somerville spoke (as would any Mistress of any College) of Indira Gandhi's (not particularly distinguished) record as a student. I said my piece about the Politics of Time and the Unacknowledged Legislators, Mrs Thatcher leaned towards me to say she wished she had my command of words. The world of *maya* has its amusing moments. My reward was three leather bound volumes of the works of Nehru. I was able to say that I had already read—and enjoyed—*The Discovery of India*. The other two I am not likely to read—at my age time has become too precious, one has to make choices. Had it been the works of Mahatma Gandhi it might have been otherwise.

Maya indeed, all that charade; yet here in Delhi Mohan Pall, himself a Sikh, told me of how Mrs Gandhi had been warned against retaining Sikhs in her bodyguard, angered as they were by the attack on their Golden Temple, where the militant separatists were storing arms. It was Indira Gandhi who had herself pleaded for the two men who killed her to be kept on—she knew them, how could she not believe them loyal? They were young, they were subverted, Mohan told me, when home on leave; no doubt, again, by people they themselves knew, friends and family. How hard it is for Caesar to believe that Brutus, whom he knows and loves, will join the conspirators! How hard for a woman not to become fond of those about her, whose faces she knows, sees every day. Yet it is always friends, seldom strangers, who conspire and betray. I found this account moving, it had the ring of human truth. I would have done just the same, acted just as she did. Most women would. Shakespeare could have written the script, from the fatal order to attack the Golden Temple, an act which the Prime Minister of India must have known was to sign the death warrant of the woman, that simple human creature who had admired the Sethna family's delphiniums in the next door garden (that detail from Shernaz Sethna). To attack an arsenal is a measurable risk, to attack a symbol is fatal. Is it not all *maya*, the political world? But for a daughter of India, her script had been written by India's epic writers long ago, and not in terms merely political, but in the language of the Imagination.

Dining two days later at the Indian High Commission, Mr Rasgotra pronounced on the proofs I had asked him to read. Yes, he passed all my conceivably tactless references to persons, but thought I had been too hard on idols! He thought some of my adjectives should be toned down: 'We Indians love our idols', he explained. I took his reproof. Who am I to recoil from Kali's black mask whose own religion of 'love' has a record so blood-stained? Next morning I left for Paris, where I was to read poems at the Maison de la Poésie. I must not say of beloved France either, perhaps my last visit. But with age comes an intensity of living in every present moment, the Now which contains all.

❁

A visit to India with my fare paid was a temptation I could not resist even though an inner voice warned me. The Yeats Society of India sounds well, but my invitation had come at the last minute. For Yeats's sake I would in any case have agreed to go to any place, and where but in India would he himself have wished his half-centenary to be celebrated? Santosh had requested me to give a paper on Yeats and the After-Life. I presumed this fitted her programme and her intention to present a performance of *The Dreaming of the Bones*. I put other things aside to write the paper, and typed it as well. It was a good paper, I thought. A telephone call from Suheil Bushrui said he was counting on seeing me in India: there were matters he wanted to discuss with Anne Yeats, Santosh and myself. There were also things I wanted to discuss with him, concerning the proposed Temenos Academy of Integral Studies. So I silenced my misgivings.

Meanwhile the High Commission mobilized my departure with truly Indian munificence, and in the early morning of February 25th, a car, with Mr Manral (at that time cultural attaché) as escort, was waiting at the door; at Heathrow I was received with every courtesy, a wheelchair awaited me, and Mr Manral, who seemed to think that the laurel halo of the poet belonged by right to anyone who bore the name, quoted long passages of Shelley and Keats and Meredith and Tennyson to me, which I was at a loss to match. I promised him, on my return, a copy of *Defending Ancient Springs* with my own 'Defence of Shelley's Poetry'. I find that Indians still know the classical English poets—those, at least, not engaged in literature, who, like our own post-war generation, probably no longer do.

I was already becoming aware that I had caught an

[157]

infection, but Indian sun, I thought, would soon melt away that miasma that has hung over England this winter. So, carrying my small parcel of all England's current poisons of body and mind I relaxed into my seat, believing I was leaving all these things behind me.

It was night in Delhi and there again was Santosh to meet me, and her son Ajay (Timkoo) the young photographer who had slept on my floor the previous winter on his visit to London whose obscurest suburbs he had scoured in quest of photographic equipment. Once more I breathed the spicéd Indian air by night. But I was deaf from the flight, infected with my virus; glad to reach the India International Centre and a bed at last.

Anne and Grania Yeats had already arrived; Suheil Bushrui by a later plane the same night, no longer from Lebanon but from Amsterdam. He had telephoned to ask me to read his paper if he did not arrive. Fortunately he did come, but without his luggage, which followed a day later, bringing a white Arab robe which quickly transformed him from a Western Professor to an Arabian *Seyyid*.

The words that spoke themselves to me as I stood waiting for Timkoo to bring the car to the kerb at the airport, where Santosh and I awaited him were (again Shakespeare) 'Tis not so sweet now as it was before'. The music, that is. Why these words? Is it that I am an old woman, that I have no longer the energy, or that the sense of 'Oh brave new world, that has such people in it' I brought with me to India eight years ago, has faded? Is the change merely in myself? I hope so; yet something in the air has also changed. As we drove into New Delhi I saw few cars or lorries adorned with tinsel and lotuses and the goddess, as if the belief that the machine can be humanized, can be translated into that India of the Imagination, in which elephant and buffalo, tonga and oxcart, still moved in a world created of tinsel and dreams, had faded. The impression was to be confirmed—Delhi's traffic flows now in the light of common day, as in other cities—or almost so. The little herds of cattle are losing the battle against the herds of machines, as these inevitably displace them. They try in vain to cross the dual carriageway of Delhi's new circular road to a few patches of grass on the side of the Yamuna, patient, bewildered, thin. The gentle Nandi bulls can no longer lead and protect them, the traffic never slows. They will, I hope, be taken somewhere to augment India's 'white revolution'—to increase the milk-supply. The Tata lorries, the scooters, those buses jam-packed with beautiful slender youths hanging on precariously outside as well, move in a different world. No dream can transmute the machine: will the machine destroy the dream? Or is not the machine itself a 'deadly dream' that has possessed us? Time flows but one way and in a few years the cows and their calves will be gone—who in that world will care for the sacredness of life? In the age of the machine nothing is sacred, and the animals are leaving us. There are posters with forthright (much needed but not much heeded) warnings against dangerous driving: 'Speed thrills but kills'; 'Drive recklessly, kill a man, spend two years in prison', and so on. Warnings against heroin too. Yet in some sense there still seems, even in Delhi's chaotic traffic and disregard for rules and regulations an abundance of happiness on those beautiful faces.

The India International Centre was, as ever, a pleasant place to arrive; but the absence of Kamaladevi, her welcoming room, her glass bangles, her grey hair adorned with a flower, the cups of tea she offered us, were no more. At her Crafts Museum, assembled with such love, there is now a case commemorating her: photographs, public honours, private treasures. There too her absence is present. She knew as well as we that she could not turn the tide, could only in a measure preserve those skills that arose out of joy in life's simplicities, the theatre masks, the royal puppets, kings and queens of the India of the Imagination, who enacted the Golden Age still to be found in villages and emerging for festivals in country towns where television has not yet supplanted the six thousand years of the dream they inhabit. With her death the India that might have been if Gandhiji's vision and not Nehru's programme of 'progress' had been followed is gone for ever. Kamaladevi had prepared, inspired, and taught younger women who will succeed her; like Sima Sharma who now edits the excellent quarterly journal of the India International Centre; Premola Ghose, the programme organizer; Santosh is herself one of those talented protégés, not to mention all the craftswomen (craftsmen too) all over India, whom she befriended. But their work, Kamaladevi already knew, was declining in quality, made, as it inevitably is, for export and profit rather than as a spontaneous flowering of joy growing from the necessary tasks of life itself. When the machine can weave effortlessly and endlessly, the handloom and the spinning wheel are already deposed and Gandhiji's dream has no support from necessity, that mother of invention and agent of change.

❀

The Yeats Society programme was, it proved, a very sketchy affair. The little exhibition, brought by Anne Yeats, of Cuala Press publications (combined with a memorial exhibition of masks from Kamaladevi's theatre museum), was charming. Grania spoke of Irish songs and on the last evening gave a concert of harp and songs, from which, unfortunately, I had to retreat, such were my fits of coughing as my malady refused to go away. I just managed to take the chair for Suheil Bushrui's eloquent paper on the Arabian elements in Yeats's poetry. This was the Yeats Memorial Lecture, but because the Yeats Society has a very tenuous existence, had no printed programme, and had sent out notices only at the last minute, we had to move from the half-empty auditorium to the conference room; the paper deserved a wider hearing, as did our great poet of the perennial wisdom on this half-centenary of his death. Next day Suheil also read and commented on 'The Gift of Harun al-Rashid' with fiery passion, to an even smaller audience. After a variety of charming samplings of Tagore, the Upanishads in Sanskrit and the Yeats-Purohit Swami translation, a talk on Yeats's Irish background, illustrated with slides, by Paul Dempsey, the Irish Ambassador, it was already afternoon and clearly there was no time for my paper, for which no specific hour had been assigned. What should have been a professionally produced and rehearsed performance of *The Dreaming of the Bones* proved to be an unrehearsed reading of the play without costume, lighting or other props—again the situation was saved by Suheil, whose ardent speaking of the chorus brought fire; a musicologist colleague of Santosh's, Ranganaiki Iyengar, had adapted for Indian instruments the not very distinguished music written for the play's original production by the musician Rummell. However, the three children of Santosh's dance-guru mimed (barely rehearsed) the dance parts of the play, and these gifted young people, born (and trained) dancers, brought an element of skill and magic which suggested that *The Dreaming of the Bones* could, indeed, be produced in India with just those elements of music and dance Yeats was at a loss to find in the West. Perhaps this will be done at Yeats's centenary! I read my paper in the afternoon to a handful of friends, Anne Yeats (who had to leave) Suheil, Santosh, Piloo Nannavutty, Ramu Gandhi and one or two others. My work, I felt, had been wasted, and so for that matter had the cost of my air fare, paid for by the Indian Council of Cultural Relations. Keshav Malik was my chairman; to whom at the end I said, 'Keshav, why don't you and I give a poetry reading?' I felt I owed something to my Indian hosts. Keshav had just published a book of poems, a copy of which he had given me, and my own collection *The Presence* had appeared since my last visit to India. In due course we did this, again in that now familiar conference room where so many invisible flames have burned so brightly.

However, as a meeting of friends under Indian skies this should have been a pleasant occasion. Suheil, that man of inspiring and energizing ardour, wished to put to us all—(Anne Yeats, Santosh and myself) his project of an International Yeats Society. It was more than time, he said, that Yeats should take his place as the world-poet that he is; he had many hard things to say about the small academic clique who present him according to provincial standards as a minor Irish politician, perhaps, a stylist, a leader of a literary movement, as anything to evade any consideration of the central concern of his life, his spiritual quest, his part in proclaiming and defining the premises of a New Age, in turning the tide of 'the three provincial centuries' of Cartesian materialism, as the greatest disciple of his prophetic Master William Blake. Such considerations are the last thing the academic world would wish to see; the living Imagination is ever a threat and a mind of the depths and heights of Yeats's cannot be fitted to that bed of Procrustes. 'Father was too big for them', Anne had once said to me *à propos* his Irish successors. It was India towards which Yeats himself had turned and towards which his intellectual quest had led him though he never visited India. He had planned to do so, to join his teacher, Sri Purohit Swami, but had been unable to make the journey. Anne was to have accompanied him. I remarked to Anne, (such being the theme of my paper) that it seemed to me that Yeats's thought about Indian doctrines of reincarnation was inspired not so much by his desire for spiritual liberation, as by the hope of living in this world 'again, and yet again'. Yes, she said; 'Father was insatiable'.

It was, above all, to disclose and discuss this plan that Suheil had come to Delhi. I shall, however, play no part, since my energies must now be used only for essential things. Others—Suheil, Santosh—can look after Yeats's reputation; indeed that reputation can look after itself, regardless of the academic 'Yeats industry'. But for myself, for what purpose had I been brought—or brought myself— on this inauspicious visit to India? I had returned even though I knew—and at heart I had known—how little I would 'enjoy' a visit under these obscurely wrong circumstances. The choice was mine, perhaps simply to complete my record of *India Seen Afar*. Or rather, where India is concerned, its spell summons me at a depth beyond choice.

❀

To return, then, to my obscure unease. There had of course been T. S. Eliot's centenary celebrations. It was certainly not only the fault of the Yeats Society that the elder poet lacked acclaim, for Eliot rates both as a British and as an American poet, and all the cultural propaganda apparatus of those two countries was available in support of an Eliot centenary, whereas Ireland, a poor country, lacks means, for all the official and also personal backing of Paul Dempsey, the Irish Ambassador. But that is not the deeper reason: Eliot lies within the compass of Western culture and the received values of this time. He is eminently teachable in any 'Eng. Lit.' syllabus, for his allusions are to the corpus of European literature. When Eliot uses the word 'tradition' it is in a historical sense, as the history of (mainly European) ideas. The last major poet of Christendom, his work stands within that context, his allusions and resonances within that culture. With Yeats it is otherwise: 'tradition' is for him human kind's sacred and perennial relation with the timeless. In his exploration of the frontiers of his universe he read many

[163]

books outside the canon of European culture—or of any culture, books on magic and alchemy, on psychical research, the works of Dee and Paracelsus, the Kabbalah and Swedenborg, works not to be found on any University syllabus; but then, neither, in our secular academic world, are the work of Plato and Plotinus, Porphyry and Proclus, the Hermetica, and the Upanishads. Yeats's scope is greater than Eliot's, but he leads into lands unknown, whereas Eliot's ground is familiar. Yeats's reading, and besides books, all his explorations of regions of the mind to which no books give access, relate to what Coleridge calls 'facts of mind', a 'learning of the Imagination' excluded by the very nature of modern Western materialist civilization. Yet that excluded knowledge comprises the sacred texts and greatest art of all the great civilizations humankind has created, not excluding Christendom itself in its finest expressions. Whereas Eliot sought to situate his time within European history, Yeats's task was to situate history itself within the greater context of the soul's history. It was indeed his quest for this 'knowledge absolute' of the spiritual universe—or rather of a metaphysical understanding in which no dichotomy between matter and spirit, body and soul, is perceived— that had led Yeats to India's threshold. It was the same quest that had led me, in the footsteps of Yeats and of our common Master, William Blake, to search for that India which, as Raja Rao had said, and has written, is also a universal realm. Yet in the Universities of India, although the British rulers have departed, Western values prevail, and Western cultural imperialism is undermining the very knowledge, the very Indian culture Yeats's quest led him towards, and which inspired his greatest poetry. The lesser culture prevails over the greater. The way down, in things intellectual as in other spheres, is the easy way. It is sad to witness the waning of a supreme civilization succumbing to those values which Yeats, in his great labour to reverse the premises of Western materialism, had rejected. As the finest imaginative minds of the West are ready to learn from the 'oriental philosophy', India is throwing away its age-old heritage of wisdom. As science itself is discovering the inadequacy of the materialist premises—as the great physicist David Bohn set himself to learn from his friend and teacher Krishnamurti—Sanskrit is dropped from the syllabus of Indian schools.

Of course that is not the whole story: America and Europe are well aware of the Indian universe; from the Maharishis who address the ignorant and the young, Krishnamurti and Sri Aurobindo who address the sophisticated and learned, India speaks to the heart and to the mind, at many levels; the story could be told from the opposite standpoint, as an ever-growing process of infiltration of the West by Oriental thought. Yet in India itself the wound of westernization is deep. The magnet of Western technology is a force that seems to operate of its own momentum, whereas we who seek to 'keep the divine vision in time of trouble' must labour against time and tide. Perhaps it has always been so. It seems that it is impossible to select certain elements and reject others; Western materialist civilization is the dominant current of this time, and with refrigerators and nuclear power comes the whole decadent trashy packet of Western journalism, television and whatever literary and pictorial fashions arise in the West. These are indiscriminately and uncritically received even in Indian places of culture and learning.

Mr H. K. Kaul, the librarian at the India International Centre has founded a Poetry Society for Indian poets writing in English, and he gave me a volume of poems—*Voices in the Making*—selected from the big entry of a poetry competition sponsored by the British Council. I read them all; and few differed either in quality or in content from those which come through the *Temenos* letter-box of my own front door in England—carbon copy culture, with but few exceptions, little or nothing that speaks with the voice or from the imagination of India. Or from the Imagination at all. How can the world, that has known such profound things, seen such visions, built a civilization embodying such beauty and wisdom, forget, lose, become unconscious, as it seems, of those regions that are our own creation? Yet few who today claim the title of poet seem even to be aware of these deeps and skies of the human universe. Keshav Malik had been one of the judges; I told him he was wasting his time, that what is needed in India is an Indian *Temenos*; and indeed Keshav has it in mind to start in India a serious review of the arts, to set some sort of standard of excellence. But where the vision and the fire fail, what use a literary Review?

All this—as in my own country—saddened and troubled me; too much, perhaps. One can, of course, still go to villages where splendid girls who don't speak a word of English recite the story of Draupadi and the Pandavas. Yes. Still. We say 'still' and that says all. Or perhaps it did not trouble me enough, for it is by trivialization rather than (as in the Communist countries) by outright suppression that the West imposes its secular values. I heard of one young woman writing a thesis on Sylvia Plath; another on Ruth Jhabwala. Six thousand years to create the face of beauty, the *dharma* of right living! What tyrant could destroy that culture with such ease and irreversibility as that most destructive of modern machines, the television set? In the West it all happened long ago, one no longer notices what is no longer there; what is saddening in India is to see the process at work.

Yet at all times the enduring values must be affirmed and embodied, and in the end their truth prevails; the music, the poems and the paintings, these outlast all changes of fashion or even history itself. The world of the imagination is timeless. The paintings of the Altamira caves are as contemporaneous as when their pigment was traced on the walls, and Paradise as new and inviolate in the paintings of Cecil Collins as in the beginning. These are the enduring visions.

I am disquieted by my own disquiet at this democratization of poetry, by all the poetry workshops, poetry competitions, poetry festivals and the rest, which ought perhaps to delight me, as they do those who participate in them—not, certainly for any merit in the productions, but because poetry and the other arts are 'the three Powers in Man of conversing with Paradise'. Like prayer, they are a raising of heart and soul to the Divine Vision. Perhaps the mutation of the age in which I am living is one I can neither understand nor accept. Whatever has in the past raised civilization has been the exceptional, work purchased more often than not at the price of great loneliness and sacrifice by some master-spirit in service of a vision uncomprehended by the generality of mankind, and yet in the end speaking to all more profoundly than any 'self-expression' can reach. This flooded river of self-expression (whether in England or in India) is something quite other. Does it enable those who participate in it better to understand real poetry, or does it confuse and lower the standard? At present it seems to have supplanted real poetry, and perhaps indeed civilization has done its work and is over. Instead there is a universal uniformity of universal 'originality'; people write their own poems but do not read even one another's, or perhaps any poetry of significance at all, like the American who refused to read Shakespeare lest it interfere with his own creativity! I cannot see how the universal democracy of the present time, whose agent is the television set that communicates instantaneously everywhere, but has neither past nor future, and describes only superficial appearances, can sustain or produce poetry in the old sense.

No matter what regret such as I may feel, westernization sweeps the world on its course, and Indian poets will write in English, and with the language will adopt the thoughts and attitudes of the modern West. We are one world, instantaneously in communication with the whole. Whether multinational English will produce a flowering of 'world-poetry' or prove a no-man's-land remains in doubt. Indian poets like Nissim Ezekiel (a Jewish poet), and Keki Daruwalla, have with entire success entered this current of Western civilization; they could be British or American but for the accident of local scenery. Is not the choice to write in English already a choice to enter that current? It is the modern world, and even if 'conduct and work grow coarse, and coarse the soul' the imperative of the present is not to be denied—it is as if there is one collective world-soul operating universally, and we are all its instruments, but for those few who are above the age. And where at this time, are these?

I am uncomfortably aware that knowing no Indian language I may be missing some fine Indian poets, but again, I wonder if these too are drawn into the current of the age? And if not, perhaps they ought to be? What would 'Indian' attitudes be, at this time? And yet I feel—hope—believe—that India has a unique contribution to make; for the current flows, on another level, very strongly from East to West, and, again, why not in poetry? What kind of poetry am I expecting to find? One never knows, of course, what the new voice will say until it has spoken, or where it will speak from. It could be out of Africa, or a newly-awakened Russia.

Perhaps it is because 'things thought too long can be no longer thought' that the sublimity of the classical Indian conception of man is not to be found in India's 'voices in the making'. It is the alienated, trivialized, diminished image of man current in the West that the poets writing in English are assimilating with the language. But then, as always, as in England, my conscience says to me, 'This is a new age, these people find themselves alienated, sucked perforce into the

Western vortex, the old culture can't sustain them'. H. K. Kaul has responded to a strong wish and need of the writers themselves in founding this Indian Poetry Society. But with few exceptions, alienation is the note of these 'voices in the making'. Yeats says that there can be no unity of being without unity of culture. Yet the living source is ever-present and whoever draws upon it will receive inspiration from the 'fountain of light' now as at any other time. Cecil Collins's angels have no less power and beauty than have Beato Angelico's, David Gascoyne's grandeur of language is no less than is Hölderlin's. Of course there are gleams of beauty, resonances of tragedy, in some of these Indian poems; and is it not more necessary to humankind to create than to consume the work of others? Yet I wonder. A great work is one with which many can identify themselves, through which they (we) can discover hitherto unknown regions within ourselves: we do not 'admire' great works of the Imagination, we live by them. One wishes that India's 'voices in the making' had better models than the minimal-ist trivia imported from the West. One wishes that these writers were less ready to exchange their own heritage for Western fashion. Self-expression is so easy—it is easier to write than to read with deep attention and receptiveness. I vacillate, and guilt assails me, now because I am too hard on the uninspired, and then again because such as I must never lose sight of the true measure, the high vision that leads poets and all visionaries of the Imagination away from the mass, the collective, into that solitude in which they receive from afar messages from the universal Imagination, making audible to us in their work the universal music. For the many are imitative of collective models, of one another, of what is expected and received; the true poet is the vehicle of 'things unknown', listens to no voices but those that speak the deepest secrets of the heart. And that task demands nothing less than a total dedication undreamed of by an age

[169]

in which neither the writers nor the readers of verse are aware of any higher source of poetic inspiration, of Plato's 'garden of the Muses', known to true poets. This being so, it follows that the decline of poetry at this time is to be found wherever Western materialism casts its shadow.

'Poetry is the house of the soul'. Strange words for I. A. Richards to have written, but their truth will outlast the ephemeral fashion of 'scientific criticism'. We inhabit Homer's world, and Shakesepeare's, and Proust's and Valmiki's and Kalidasa's and Yeats's and Tagore's. It has always been the rare, exceptional spirits, the inspired ones, a Rumi or a Dante or a Blake or a Goethe or a Shelley who has poured out the fertilizing stream. It is perhaps an aspect of the prevalent materialism to democratize the arts, since on the level of the shared world of common experience, we are, in a sense, interchangeable; it is only in the worlds of higher vision, of deeper venturing into the invisible and inaudible realms that lie beyond common experience that the everyday self is transcended and transmuted. In other times and places the great ones have been honoured precisely for their sacrifice of themselves in total dedication to a universal vision. 'Against the superiority of another there is no defence but love' Goethe wrote. But honouring the greatest men most is not a fashion of the modern West, rather the reverse. But we all in the end recognise what is immortal and universal, it speaks to what is deepest in all.

Such poets are rare at any time; in my own country I see only two or three at the most, few in France; I do not know if there are such poets in modern India. Yet in India if anywhere it should be understood that true art comes from levels above the descriptions of the experiences of the shared everyday. It is a tradition of India's musicians, her dancers, her poets as well, to invoke the gods, and poems and hymns of praise to the gods are an integral part of the Indian poetic tradition. No matter for the names, it is the raising of the poet's mind to the regions the gods inhabit that is essential. As Shelley addressed the Skylark; the name is nothing. Or as Blake invoked the Muses from within,

> *. . . Come into my hand,*
> *By your mild power descending down the Nerves of my right*
> *   arm*
> *From out the Portals of my brain where by your ministry*
> *The Eternal Great Humanity Divine planted his Paradise,*
> *And in it caus'd the Spectres of the Dead to take sweet forms*
> *In likeness of himself . . .*

Sri Aurobindo in his valuable book, *The Future Poetry* describes and distinguishes several levels whence inspiration flows; and paradoxically the higher the level—of soul, of spirit, of some collective overmind—the more universal the poetry, the more do we feel that it speaks to, and for, our own deepest understanding, in the Self that is common to all. We feel that we ourselves know these things, might have written these words from our own hearts; for in the deeps of the mind whence arises true poetry is indeed the one spirit that lives in all ages. That voice is immortal, and unmistakeable, and its works never fade. Works of the Imagination are unageing, they speak from beyond times and places, making the world of the Imagination contemporaneous, Homer, Shakespeare, Kalidasa, the song of a French troubadour, immediate and present in every present. It is in the service of that undying spirit that every true poet works.

The responsibility of the poet is not to the public but to the Inspirers, and it has ever been the solitary individual— the individual in solitude—who has carried that torch, never a popular collectivism. It is through the most profound misunderstanding that those great vehicles of the abiding reality are accused of personal pride or self-aggrandisement, for it is precisely by transcending in the grandeur of inspiration whatever belongs to the personal and the individual that the poet is empowered to speak to, and for, whatever is immortal in all. Often it is at a great price that the divine gift is bestowed.

❧

I had many long conversations with Keshav Malik, Kapila's brother the poet and art-critic. I well remember meeting, on my first visit to India, that handsome, introspective, sophisticated representative of Delhi's world of the arts, who yet has an altogether unlooked-for gentleness and purity of heart. He had known Tambi, and befriended him on his visits to India. Keshav likes my poetry, which may well predispose me in his favour; but I believe that the deeper reason is that we both belong to the 'school of Tambi' a certain shared imaginative country. In the West I would have expected a poet so aware of the modern predicament, so exposed to it, to be cynical, or despairing, or both, but Keshav is neither. Keshav is not such a poet as Coomaraswamy would have approved, working within the symbolic framework and terms of some shared tradition. Rather he submits to the imperative of his time, his images are modern and disturbing confrontations with the immediate. Doubtless Indians who enter the current of the English language and the secular Western poetic fashions are not looking to Indian writers in English for what I find in Keshav's work—Indianness. His is a poetry of images, the vertiginous and the perilous, the disquieting, 'earth's destiny in the balance'. His uncompromisingly awkward phrases, his images of the immediate, trashy, dangerous, fragmented world are true to their insistent immediacy. He confronts the banal, incoherent foreground of life with humility; images of the trivial and the beautyless that so obsess modern poets trapped within the secular materialist

ideology are imaginatively resolved into Indian spacious-
ness. The trivia and fragmentation of the immediate opens
onto a cosmology that rests, no doubt, ultimately, on what
Raymundo Panikkar calls 'the Vedic experience'. An experience rather than a religion or a philosophy. The Indian experience may be spacious, may include beauty, even joy; but it
is not consoling.

❦

Pupul Jayakar gave one of her delightful parties for Anne
and Grania Yeats, Suheil Bushrui, the Palls, and I really
should not have gone, but was, of course, tempted against
my better judgment. Among her guests were Dr. Karan
Singh and his beautiful wife. It went through my mind to
tell him about our plans for the Temenos Academy but I felt
that the theme had taken another direction from that Maly
de Robilant and I had put to him two years ago. When the
plan becomes a reality will be time enough. Suheil Bushrui
with his Arabian gift of story-telling kept us all hanging on
his words with his ability to bring all to life, whether great
or small. Yet he had lost all he had, his house in Beirut, his
library three times destroyed before at last he left his
beloved Lebanon. In this total loss, he said, he had found a
new kind of total freedom. It was my privilege to catch a
glimpse of that tragedy and I will never forget another
conference, one that never took place, which Professor
Bushrui had planned to hold in Beirut to celebrate the
centenary of that man of peace, Kahlil Gibran. I was invited
because of Blake; and accepted because Gibran's *The
Prophet* was a book my mother had loved. I was decidedly
scared at the prospect of going to Lebanon, where the
Druses were shelling the airport and so on. But a telephone
call from Suheil was a royal command and I gave him my
word that I would go. Also my friend Dorothy Carrington
(daughter of that headlong General Carrington famed in the

Matabele War) was staying with me at the time, and she took it for granted that I would go, it would be by her standards unthinkable to flinch in the face of danger. So go I did. For the sake of Blake, of my mother, from personal pride, because Suheil in his war-torn country felt that an affirmation of the values of peace might be of some avail. From the confused mixture of motives from which human beings generally act, I went; having somehow failed, at the last minute, to take in the message sent to the Airline that the conference had that day been cancelled, I had thought Suheil's telephone-call the previous night was my final order to go. I was therefore bewildered when there was no one at the airport to meet me, and decidedly indignant. However, by good chance someone who knew about the conference rescued me and drove me across Beirut to the sad scene of what should have been an affirmation of peace, and had become a casualty of war. There were the exhibits, photographs, manuscripts, drawings, arranged in à room in which no conference would now be held. A young musician had also come—other participants had already cancelled or received the last minute message I had failed to register.

I was to have stayed in what I suppose was the guest-house of the American University; but Suheil took me home to his house (his second house, the first had already been destroyed) where, besides his wife, his daughter and a young baby were staying. I remember that, of all things, the American series *Dallas* was showing on the television. It seemed an abode of peace, and I spent that night in what I remember as a large ceremonial bedstead, with the pine scent of the Mediterranean in the soft night air, reminding me of Greece. Yet I had driven past the recently destroyed Palestinian camp, recalling the blitzed sites of wartime London; a group of young Italians of the peace-keeping force in operatic poses driving round on their armoured truck; a youth in his late teens, budding moustache, tin helmet and rifle slung on his shoulder, who stopped us to check our car as we passed some invisible barricade. Who he represented I never knew. I remember thinking of the poor dressed-up 'punk' generation on the King's Road, with their deadpan faces, and reflecting that youths prefer the real thing—these young Lebanese glowed with the age-old sense of glory of the war hero. The personal glory of those who gamble with death? The collective intoxication of the war-pack? Down a leafy side road a small discreet encampment of Israelis. There it all was, the Druses almost visible in their mountain stronghold—the mountains of Lebanon like the backcloth of a theatre—opera rather perhaps. Yet as Suheil drove me to the airport next day, we talked of literature, of *Temenos*, of Blake and Gibran; and for many anxious hours he waited with me in the VIP lounge at the airport—crowded, and already the ground pitted with frequent recent shelling—until at last there was a plane. Meanwhile a meal was provided for travellers awaiting departure—anxiously watching for some plane to fly in from Cyprus or elsewhere. Phrases I have never heard before or since reflected the embattled situation in a land, like Ireland, of 'great hatred, little room'. 'They are sons of Satan' seemed typical of a mood of total hostility that kept up the courage, I suppose, of beleaguered minorities in a doomed land. Two days later the airport was closed for three months.

I was glad to have made that journey, to have seen, to have been for a moment on the field of the Great Battle in that Biblical land. A useless gesture. Yet Suheil perhaps understood that, however ineptly, I had paid my homage to Gibran's values, and Blake's and to my Mother. And so it has been that from time to time Suheil Bushrui, like a djinn from the Arabian desert, appears in my life. Unheralded he comes and as suddenly vanishes. He, at least, believes in the need to affirm the values and the vision of Blake and Yeats in a sick world whose trivia cannot nourish or heal that soul.

Yet how infinitely more David Gascoyne has availed than I who battle on as I do in many activities other than poetry itself, simply by his integrity as a poet, the depth of his suffering and his dedication to the service of his genius. David's broken life has been a channel of immortal verse that will change the world more surely than all my largely futile industry. Or Cecil Collins's fields of paradise, where the vulnerable ones of this world walk in their joy.

❀

But before deafness cut me off completely, in the garden of the India International Centre, lit by fairy lights, at last I was able to converse with Ramu Gandhi, under a great moon, and asked him what he had been thinking; but if I looked for comfort from Ramu he had none to give. He has been thinking, he told me, of how we should be prepared to confront at least the possibility of the total dissolution of the world. 'But Ramu,' I pleaded, 'we have all been keeping our courage by remembering your words two years ago about putting the shadow behind us by lifting our eyes to the Light!' Yes, he said, yet we should neither fear nor reject dissolution, but rather learn to rejoice in the whole of manifest being and in non-being. All levels are present at all times, in waking, dream, and dreamless sleep—these things are familiar to us always, what have we therefore to fear? That may be so, I said, but to us in the West these things are but concepts, to you in India there are no mere concepts, for you, knowledge is existential. We divide things into categories; and I thought of Wilson Harris, the Guyanan novelist, who also seeks to restore to unity waking and dreaming, the dead and the living. All the same, admitting Ramu to be right—Wilson Harris also—that there are no real divisions in the comprehensive *advaita*, the imminent possibility of the dissolution of all things is one which I would rather evade. True, I myself cannot evade that dissolution for many more years at most, but I would like to think of my friends sitting in the spicéd Indian air by night discussing these things in their own here-and-now when I am gone. And all the people and places and forests and creatures of the world. And against non-existence, the void, the dark, there is the face of the Presence that, in Tagore's word, 'comes, comes, ever comes'. On a later day, walking with Ramu in the Lodhi gardens, he again spoke of these things. To envisage the dissolution of the world, he said, is not to despair. He will not, as a theologian, call what he is undergoing, coming to terms with the possibility that this world may be totally destroyed, despair. We must learn not to fear death, that non-duality that makes us all one. We separate into categories what is undivided. Such is Ramu's attempt to come to terms with what we would wish to evade and avoid. Nor is he, he confessed, in any way near that non-dual vision, that fear-transcending realization, *advaita* eludes him in his own soul as a lived realization. His book is stuck, he says. I must have been reporting this conversation, for someone—I don't recall whom—told me that Kamaladevi had thought that Ramu had adopted a 'stance'; not indeed merely for the sake of a theological concept but rather in order to explore an area of experience. Doubtless he would agree with Prince Kumar that these realizations can come about only through inner transformation; it is at the deepest level only that *advaita* is to be found. But have I understood him? I am a poet not a philosopher. Walking among the bright flowers, and trees, and tombs of the Lodhi gardens I explained to Ramu my own continual amazement at the marvel and mystery that anything IS; an ant in the dust, a woodpecker that alighted at our feet. Tagore had understood this, and I tried to explain how delighted I had been by a paper by Tagore on Individuality that I had recently read; things come into being only when a mind comes to bear on that unknown unknowable into whose deeps Ramu is seeking to penetrate. I pin my faith on ant and woodpecker. No matter if I were to cease to be, the IT IS of every moment has been, and therefore can never not be a part of what forever belongs to indivisible being. The deep truth, Shelley says (he should have, or perhaps indeed he had, made his passage to India) is imageless; but poets know only images, the imagination, the imaginable.

❀

The Conference over, with what relief I embarked in Dr. Jungalwalla's car beside Piloo and was driven to their cool, spacious flat in Safdarjung Enclave, where Piloo sent me straight to bed in a room where it was hard to sleep, because every textile on which my eye fell was beautiful. The Doctor prescribed inhaling steam from a saucepan of boiling water, my head wrapped in a kind of tent made with a towel. It helped streaming eyes, nose and cough but did nothing for the increasing deafness. Lovely, simple, quiet, thoughtful household. Piloo sat reading the Zoroastrian scriptures, a scarf over her head, the sacred fire burning beside her. It was good to have these days of respite with Piloo; for while on the one hand she is deeply immersed in the Zoroastrian faith and the problems of the Parsee community, on the other it was pleasant to share memories of Girton friends and contemporaries and the Blake world and visits to Geoffrey Keynes; and, of course, Blake himself. Piloo as a Blake scholar contributes what I wish all Indian students of Western culture would bring with them, that is, their Indian culture. In the case of Blake, as with Yeats, secular Western thought is alien to the whole substance of his vision, whereas the oriental—Henry Corbin's 'oriental philosophy' —that is to say spiritually 'oriented'—is in accordance with all Blake laboured, within the rather clumsy terminology at his disposal, to communicate. Much secular modern literature, indeed, there would be no point in discussing in such depth—although it might be valuable to expose its vacuity in terms of perennial human values—but an 'oriental' assessment of the finest genius of the West, of Shakespeare, Milton, the Romantics, Goethe and Dante and much besides, awaits such evaluation.

Piloo and the Doctor took me to lunch next day at the Delhi Gymkhana Club, one of those ghost-haunted relics of the British Raj, a once grand, once luxurious, once no doubt exclusive preserve of the Imperial rulers; the dance floor was dusty now, the high spacious rooms surely unpainted since those who had built them for a social life once so pleasurable, so secure, so taken for granted, had departed. That once so solid, so privileged here-and-now the more ghost-like to me, the more poignant even, because those ghosts are of my own generation. I might have danced at some May-week Ball with one or another of those young men who had gone into the Indian Civil Service and who had played tennis or squash on those courts, or who had relaxed in the swimming pool 'Presented by Lady Willingdon'. Club members are still met at the door by doormen wearing those bird-like turbans I have seen otherwise only in Army displays on Republic Day, or in the British Embassy compound. Dr. Jungalwalla, of course, remembered the thing itself. He, and Piloo, seemed still somewhat living in that past—is not memory part of one's present? They were aware of changes, I only of the presence of the ghosts, of the remains of the Worcester services, once in use, hung on the walls maybe to cover stain or crack. Only the banks of flowers were as brilliant as they could ever have been; India excels in flowers. At the Gymkhana Club one is courteously received by the past. There are of course plenty of accounts of 'the Club' (an institution rather than a place) in its glory; and reading in Ingaret Gifford's Memoirs of how an English girl of eighteen—of my own generation—had set foot in 'the

Club' at Poona suggested what the Delhi Gymkhana Club must have been:

> This enormous glittering palace made our little Club in Ahmadnagar look like a railway siding. The Poona Club had a huge ballroom with a high ceiling ablaze with lights and a raised stage at one end where the band played by day and night. The bandsmen were presumably garnered from the British regiments stationed there, and they looked most impressive in their fine regimental uniforms. There were crowds of men strolling around with glasses in their hands, or gathered together in groups, laughing men in polo-kit, men in tennis-shorts, men in plus-fours, and quite a few in kilts. I could easily tell at which end of the Club was the bar, and the men's changing-room because of the noise emerging from both! The Poona Club was the first highlight of my life in India, and I was quite breathless at the spectacle.

A spectacle indeed in the pageant of Empire; but how far from India, then or now or ever.

Two days later—it was a Sunday—we again lunched there at little tables on the spacious but no longer immaculate lawns. I admired saris, and babies and, as always, the deportment of Indian families (always families) in public places. To those ghosts, it is we who are moving in an irrelevant future of a here and now whose zenith was theirs.

Later I was to visit with Keshav Malik, the painter, Khosa, who has some official post as an artist employed by the Indian Government. He lives in a house in a pleasant housing estate, built I suppose in the late twenties, for British officers. India is strewn with such ghosts of a recent past. Ghosts because totally of the past, there is no continuity, as of a family house or continuous neighbourhood, with the present. Yet who knows how many elderly men and women of my own generation still living, probably here in England, were themselves a part of that dead present, danced on that dusty dance floor, lived in those pleasant 1920-style houses. I'm bound to say the 'hearty' recreations of the British seem remote from these decorous family groups of Indians who stroll in these grounds with no apparent desire to take healthy exercise—tennis or squash or badminton—in India's blaze of noon! Later I was taken by Ameena Ahuja (the calligraphic artist—her work also we have published in *Temenos*) to a smaller, rather similar, golf club, where some small Moghul tombs, scattered here and there, no doubt made interest and variety for those British who went round the 'holes'. The Moghuls left thrones and tombs and mosques and reflecting water, gardens, and places of dignified contemplation; cultured people when not engaged in the kingly occupation of slaughtering one another.

❧

On the second day of my visit to Piloo we were bidden to lunch with General Sethna and his family. Shiraz's studies of Zoroastrian sources of William Blake have taken second place since her marriage and the birth of Jehangir and the slender student protester is now a full-blown rose of Persian beauty. Shireen, now a practising lawyer, and other lovely daughters whom I had not met, appeared. On the Sethnas' lawn were many of the Parsee community; the Sethnas pressed me to come to the Parsee festival at the India International Centre the following weekend, which I did, on one of the three days. Seeing so many Parsees together one realized (rather as with the Jewish community here) how very different they are from the Aryan Indian race. Since there can be no converts, and only the children of Parsee men are Parsee, it is a dwindling, though highly successful, community. Piloo showed me her family photographs, her treasured saris, works of art indeed, one work of priceless beauty after another, some very old, embroidered in the Chinese style the Parsee merchants brought back from their trade with China; silverware of Zoroastrian designs, which recalled to me the menorahs in the houses of my Jewish friends.

At the Festival held at the India International Centre the following weekend there was an exhibition of sumptuous textiles and silverware, and photographs of nineteenth-century interiors and furnishings, many of them lent by Piloo. Upstairs in the conference room books, rare and old, and others new, including Piloo's children's books, written to teach the Zoroastrian religion to the young; and to my surprise a copy of the Chaldean Oracles with an introduction by myself! How in my ignorance had I dared to write such a foreword, and what had I written? ('That's *our* Kathleen Raine', Premola Ghose had said; that, at least, was heart-warming! Piloo herself had said, I don't remember on what occasion, 'you are one of *us*'). The morning's programme, in the now so familiar auditorium, festooned with flower garlands and filled with Parsees, many from, I suppose, Bombay and its environs, began with chanting; then an introductory address by Dr. Karan Singh, that politician of time who has turned his mind to the service of the politics of eternity.

Dr. Karan Singh's theme was the enrichment India had gained from those religious minorities to which she has given sanctuary—Jews (some colonies had settled in India before Jesus Christ) Parsees, more recently Buddhists from Tibet, and more recently still members of the persecuted Ba'hai community. By all these, he said, India has been enriched; and I could not but reflect on the appalling treatment of the Jews throughout European history and the current latent hostility towards negroes, and Muslims as reflected in the discreditable Rushdie affair, in which little support or sympathy has been accorded to the law-abiding Islamic community in this country. However, Partition was scarcely an example of religious tolerance, and there are plenty of community problems in India. But Dr. Karan Singh was at least stating a principle. Piloo read a fine introductory paper, followed by others; then there were tableaux in which two grave little children underwent the initiation ceremony and binding of the woollen cord, the Parsee equivalent of the sacred thread of the Brahmin. There followed a marriage-ceremony, the bride in white, as with Christians, not the red of the Hindu bride. (I learned that 'bride' and 'groom' had been married for long enough to have raised a family.) Bride and groom have equal rights of choice; but when a Parsee woman marries out of the community she ceases to be a Zoroastrian (unlike the Jewish law in which inheritance is through the mother) and her children are not accepted by the community. There was a good deal of spirited discussion on this subject—why should not women in this respect have equal rights? No agreement about this. There was a tactful veil drawn over the disposal of the dead in the Towers of Silence, that strange, ancient, primitive custom still practised in that most ancient of the world's higher religions, save for that of the Vedas themselves. Why could not the dead be burned, Dr. Karan Singh asked, fire being sacred in the Zoroastrian religion? My hearing-aid did little to enable me to follow the decidedly complicated argument which followed—I have the impression that it is precisely because of the purity of fire that it must not come into contact with corruption. What, Dr. Karan Singh asked, if the supply of vultures should fail? I understand that in Bombay (for example) this is a real problem. But here in Delhi those grey spectres whose kingdom is death are ever visible, waiting, in dead trees, for the summons of corruption borne in the wind.

Then delicious Parsee food—fish wrapped in banana

leaves, savoured with some wonderful mixture of herbs and spices, all a little less highly spiced than northern Indian food. There was also an exhibition of paintings by Mrs Frenny Billimoria; on whose lawn Keshav Malik and I read poems on my last evening in India, with again, many of that remarkable Parsee community gathered to hear us, and, again, marvellous food! But Piloo laments that the very prosperity and success of the Parsees has led to a neglect of their spiritual heritage: they are too rich, too successful, it seems!

❀

Still in a sorry state after my brief stay with Piloo, I was claimed by Santosh. I had long been expecting her to arrive in England with the manuscript of her book on Yeats and the dance. Now I had offered to take it back with me to hand over to the publisher, supposing that it was complete, but on my arrival as her house guest I found her father Professor Kocchar (on the roof, between the petunias and the carnations) pasting up footnotes for her, and her son, Timkoo, the young photographer, transforming her illustrations and captions to meet his professional standards. I wrote a brief foreword, but refused otherwise to be drawn in, having already read the book first as examiner of Santosh's doctoral thesis, and since. In spite of this pressure of work, Santosh looked after me devotedly and I have reason to be grateful for her care. On her roof top terrace I could read and write in peace and recover from my infection. But when finally it became clear that the deafness, which had continued to get worse, was not going to go away with the abatement of my other ills I asked to be taken to see a doctor, and Santosh arranged for me to see Dr. Prem Victor, ear, nose, and throat specialist at St. Stephen's, a private hospital in Old Delhi not far from her house in Civil Lines. Although the reason was unfortunate, I am glad to have had a direct experience of

India's medical care. As in all else in this country friends are the link—a friend who shares Santosh's interest in gardening, and whose husband travels India giving lectures on his 'subject', the *Ramayana*, is a voluntary worker at St. Stephen's, and arranged (all this in a rapid flow of Hindi of which I understood nothing) that I should be seen as part of a special programme—how or why I do not know but the charge I finally paid to the hospital was only seventy-five rupees (about £3)! All more informal than in an English hospital; whatever India lacks in other resources, kindness is never lacking. Dr. Victor's cubicle was small in size, little in the way of equipment—chair, and washbasin, and a couch on which a patient could be examined. On the wall a poster of a little child and the caption 'Every step into my future depends on your love'. I was to learn more of Dr. Victor's work for deaf children.

He told me, after a brief examination, that I should have come sooner, that at my age it is unlikely that I would recover my hearing, damaged by my virus infection. He prescribed some pills and vitamin injections, which I did not take, since I do not use allopathic medicines. I said I would settle for a hearing-aid. Santosh is knowledgeable in homeopathy, Professor Kochhar even more so, and most of all her brother, an officer in the Air Force, who is stationed in Delhi at this time. I exchanged Dr. Victor's pills for homeopathic salts and for small mysterious pills prescribed by a homeopathic doctor in Old Delhi who sits like an alchemist at the back of the shop of his son (an oculist) surrounded by a multitude of phials and little glass bottles and jars. His prescriptions are unhesitating and they seemed to work—so much so that on a later visit Dr. Victor asked what prescriptions I had taken—these might prove useful, he said, for other patients. This would scarcely have happened in an English hospital, where homeopathic medicine would not have been prescribed by an allopathic doctor. I do not know whether the gradual but almost complete recovery of my hearing over the next weeks I owe to the course of nature, or to the Kali. Phos., Nat. Mur. and Nat. Phos. dissolved in water which Santosh devotedly administered; or to an incantation Piloo made over me—a very strange and beautiful chant—of which she said that if deafness were my *karmic* destiny it would be of no avail, but if not, I could expect to recover. My own belief is that there must still be work for me to carry out while I am here in the world and that I have been restored sufficient hearing with which to do it. Deafness on Santosh's roof meanwhile was no hardship, with the birds and the tree-squirrels in the jacaranda tree.

Meanwhile I was handed over to Dr. Victor's assistant in an adjacent sound-proof room. The skill and knowledge of the staff is in contrast to the minimal means at their disposal—though where is the hospital without its patient, waiting, sick and maimed and poor, and its overworked, dedicated staff? People and children wander in and out informally. Dr. Victor almost immediately called me Kathleen. I soon learned that the poster of the toddler whose future 'depends on your love' meant love in a very literal and immediate sense. Dr. Victor runs a Society of Rehabilitation and Research for the Handicapped on the outskirts of Delhi for deaf children; there I was to go to have moulds taken of my ears—this, it seems, was within the 'special programme' which was to save expense. Faithful Timkoo drove us for miles into these outskirts, and, losing the way, we drove round many side roads ending at last in a cul-de-sac occupied by a camel resting in the dust, its master beside it.

I was struck by something perhaps characteristic of India, the superiority of the people to their surroundings. Here three-storey houses, poor by English standards seemed to be packed with families in small flats; minimal road maintenance, all far below English standards of 'housing' but with a sense of seemly living rare in English council estates or high-rise flats where accommodation is ample and well-built but vandalized by occupants without the standards or values of the Indian commitment to a traditional code of family relationships and conduct, or is it love that is more plentiful? Yes, I know that drugs and crime of every kind are rife in India also—there are now posters in Delhi warning against drugs—but I can only give my overall impression of people, though poor, living with a certain seriousness and dignity. True, I never saw the really poor quarters, at the other side of Jamuna or the shanty-town that has sprung up, as everywhere around cities where industry attracts the poor from the villages to a worse poverty of the industrial towns. There is both suffering and demoralization in both rural and in urban poverty—I don't doubt that Kamala Markandeya's novels describe these things all too well; yet she pays tribute also to the innate goodness of people trying their best and loving one another to the very limits of the endurable.

At last we found the Centre, again a building good by Indian standards, all to a human scale. Up a flight of stairs, two rooms, a booklined outer office and a secretary; a little room beyond with a sink and some boxes and a small work-bench, all very simple and informal. Suddenly Dr. Victor appeared with some dozen students from an American college, and asked me if I would mind their watching the making of the moulds for my ears, by Mrs Verma, the assistant responsible. Of course not—dutifully I laid my head as on a block while Dr. Victor lectured the students and Mrs Verma skilfully poured whatever it was into my ears and removed the mould. Sounds of children through another door intrigued us and we were asked if we would like to see the school. Three little classrooms, gay with children's paintings and with alphabets and charts on the walls. A nursery class of smiling infants, a middle class of five-year-olds and a smaller class of those now ready to go on to a normal school. Lovely, happy children, each with their teacher; 'each step into my future depends on your love'. The teachers were all mothers, whom Dr. Victor has involved and enlisted in the work for these little deaf children who will never hear. He has also written a book about the teaching of deaf children and how to care for them in a family; I have passed it on to granddaughter Sonia, now a trained nurse herself. Simple, practical wisdom and love is abundant, if technology is scarce.

We and the students then all packed into the outer office, where we were given bottles of lukewarm Limca or Campa-cola while Dr. Victor lectured on his work; I heard scarcely anything, of course, but understood that he spoke of the need to involve the family, of the importance of hearing words in the building up of memory and so on. Everywhere in the world there are such men, devoted to helping and healing, committed, inspiring others; the father of that little school. Greeting cards of the children's paintings were sold in aid of the work, and of course I bought some. One was by a little boy 'aged four' whose name was Verma—the son no doubt of Mrs Verma who had taken the moulds of my ears. Santosh meanwhile was explaining who I was, that I had been the examiner of her thesis, inviting Dr Victor to tea, and to my poetry reading (he and his wife came, and also to a farewell party Santosh gave for me). I was beginning to feel that the loss of my hearing had brought me at least an insight into another India than that seen on my first visit, as a State guest. Here I was 'Kathleen' and I too was experiencing a little of that love.

As against this rosy picture of skill and devotion, at what is, after all, a private hospital, I am told of a much less happy state of affairs at the State hospitals. And what of the brain drain of all those excellent qualified and skilled doctors trained in India who leave the country in a continual stream for the better pay and conditions of the West? Depleting the profession in a country that needs more and better doctors, not fewer? Granddaughter Sonia sees it otherwise—sees how much Indian doctors bring to this country, happy when she is able to work with them in her hospital at Maidstone. And who indeed can blame skilful educated young men and women for not wanting to go and live in some one or other of India's innumerable remote villages where the water buffalo plodge in scummy malarial ponds, and the villagers resort to some local idol of the Goddess to cure their ills?

Two days later we collected the moulds for my hearing-aid and the apparatus itself, and the technician in the sound-proof room adjusted them to my level of hearing. I gave Dr Victor an all too small contribution to his school and we went on our way, while the toddlers and families strayed in and out: 'appointments' are relative. But there are always the sick, the aged, the poor. India does wonders, but it is never enough. Nothing could ever be enough.

This commitment of India to its vast tasks I found also in contributions to a collection of papers by Sima Sharma, who now edits the India International Centre Quarterly. Sima is one of those dedicated and committed women taught and inspired by Kamaladevi. I had several conversations with her in her office at the International Centre. Her commitment is first of all social, but she loves poetry too, and asked me for a poem for the journal. Taking me downstairs to the ground floor she led me, one evening, by a back way so that we could see together the great crimson disk of the sun as it set over the Lodhi gardens. Indian women never despise or discard their own beauty, and beauty delights them eternally, be they sociologists, economists, no matter what. I treasure my memory of standing with Sima Sharma for the space of the setting of a sun, from the moment its disk touched the horizon to its being gone. I read all the eighteen papers in her collection, *India, the Formative Years*—papers on education, agriculture, foreign policy, citizenship development, technology, schools, health, population, women. All—or almost all—the papers had one thing in common, dissatisfaction with how things had gone in some particular field, tremendous efforts notwithstanding. After the heroic moment of Independence, now that the great ones have gone, those who now remain seem to feel themselves as it were orphans. Perhaps another generation will not feel that sense of loss. Yet with all the self-criticism is not the commitment of the writers of these papers itself the best sign of hope? Many aspects of society may be corrupt—a point made by many of these authors—yet this book stirred in me a memory of what my husband, Charles Madge, and his friends had seen in Marxism all those years ago. Theirs was a vision of a better, less selfish world for the unregarded poor, and an internationalism still reflected in India's constitution as a 'non-aligned' nation, a living vein of (failed?) socialist idealism in the thought of these pages, something India shares rather with the socialist world than with the ghost of the British Raj that still dictates so many aspects of life—good as well as bad—here. None held out great hope for improvement in their respective fields; few question the aims themselves that India set herself—'progress' and industrialization and modernization in the Western pattern. Yet some do ask—should India have paid more heed to Gandhiji's vision, rather than Nehru's programme of material progress? Too late now; and would it in any case have made any difference? Could Western economic and cultural imperialism have been stemmed by Gandhiji's programme? We shall never know.

I had not previously heard the name of Nirmal Verma, the Hindi novelist and essayist. I have since met him—he is a

[190]

friend of Ramu Gandhi. At one time a Communist, he now proclaims values more native to India. His is the last word of Sima's collection, in a paper entitled 'The twilight of an era', he writes of what he calls 'the dream principle' of Indian civilization. That principle is what I have tried to indicate as 'the India of the Imagination', and on reading Nirmal Verma I found the most profound expression of what is befalling the soul of India at this time, and my hair rose as it does only to true communications from the *mundus imaginalis*. Nirmal is writing of the Kumbh Mela of Allahabad; and I too have seen those multitudes so great that India numbers them in 'lakhs'—a lakh is a hundred thousand. Three lakhs to hear Maharaj Charan Singh preach, at Qutub, a few miles outside Delhi; I was to see five lakhs at his ashram at Beas. Nirmal Verma writes:

> 'If you want to see God, go with the flow', a bearded old Sanyasi told me, making a vague mocking gesture towards the seething mass of people, and, at the moment, I could not be sure whether by the 'flow' he meant the endless stream of pilgrims, or the river itself, to which they have been flowing for centuries. And perhaps in this vagueness lay the ambiguity and anguish of my sense of belonging to a weary river, to a rag-tag mass of people—so mournfully dim and wretched in their isolation, so profoundly rich and illuminating in their relationship. An old culture seems to have a very fragile texture. If you take one strand out of it, pull out a thread of myth from reality, the legend from life, then the entire web of meanings begins to disintegrate. Whether we save it from disintegration is for me perhaps the most pressing and profound challenge that we have to face in the next few years.

Or, as I myself felt on my first, as I have on my subsequent visits, 'If India is lost, all is lost'. Yet the truth of India stands for that texture of dreams which is, not for India alone but for all of us, human reality itself.

Those multitudes—gentle, beautiful people, but poor, poor beyond remedy. The Sunday market between the Red Fort and the new Circular Road. The beauty of Indian faces, young and old, those slender bodies, are they not formed over millenia by that dream? 'I had not thought death had undone so many', Eliot wrote of London's commuters, but in India I do not see 'the innumerable multitudes of eternity' (Blake's phrase) as undone by death, but as raised up to the experience of life and beauty by the great sun that morning by morning I have watched in its brilliant rising over this teeming land where, even now, 'everything that lives is holy'.

As to 'progress', on which there is no going back, the West could tell India the spiritual cost of that material prosperity the lakhs of India's poor must needs envy, for we have lost that something Nirmal calls 'the dream factor'. Is it perhaps our souls? 'What shall it profit a man if he shall gain the whole world and lose his own soul?' Even Ramu is speaking of the end of the cycle; we all feel that apocalypse is upon us, and yet we have to labour at our respective tasks, there is no choice. And reality has many levels. Too late for Gandhiji's India. Perhaps it was never a possibility in terms of the realities—or unrealities—of 'the politics of time'. The point of no return must seem so recent that a change of mind could even now undo what has been done. But it is not so, the recent past is as irrevocable as the Battle of Waterloo or the burning of Troy. Even as I type this record, written but a few weeks ago, the irrevocable massacre of the students in Tiananmen Square. Whatever has happened is irrevocable.

❀

With the help of my hearing-aid I was now able to hear

most of what my friends were saying and to participate in that endless converse that has woven us humans together since the beginning of time. Ramu came to spend an evening with the Palls. He has been deeply exercised by the Salman Rushdie affair. Neither he nor I has read the book—I because I am old enough to know that it would be a waste of my time without going to the trouble of reading it; 'Why should I read a banned book?' was Ramu's rather unexpected answer to a direct question. Ramu had written a letter to Rushdie suggesting that the profits of the book (or a part of them) should go to establishing a conference where the issues raised by the book should be discussed by leaders of the world religions. He never received a reply. Ramu's grandfather spoke to the conscience of the world, but the conscience of the modern intellectual world is not sensitive. If Rushdie had been a man to respond to such an appeal he would not in the first place have mocked the sublime poetry of the Holy Koran; but the sense of the sacred, whose language is poetry, and that of modern journalism, belong to different worlds. There is a spirit of diminishment and denigration abroad in the world, and Rushdie's ignominious name is floated on a tide swelled by multitudes. Here in India the journalists produce carbon copies of the West, proclaiming the 'freedom' of the 'writer'. To be a 'writer' at this time nothing is required but a typewriter: why should the 'writer' say his say at the expense of any number of non-writers? The only voice of protest raised in India that I have seen is that of the Jewish poet, Nissim Ezekiel: 'Behind our anger is the mockery of Islam by Rushdie'. As a Jew he well knows that racial hatred can fire a holocaust. The whole shabby affair serves only to expose the supremacy of the profit motive. Ramu would do well to forget it!

Timkoo has on several evenings shown me beautiful slides of his expeditions to Rajasthan and Orissa, to the Kulu valley. Since my first visit eight years ago Ajay has grown from a schoolboy and to a student at the University where he was unhappily reading economics. Now he has made the decision to follow his leading gift and heart's desire and become a professional photographer. He has risen to immediate success, with features in India's official 'glossy' magazines—on the Pushkar camel-fair, the festival of the Goddess at Jaipur—a very elegant idol who lives in the palace of the Raja, and once a year is carried in procession round the town with much state, elephants, musicians and royal attendance; another festival, celebrated on the seashore near Konarak; a crafts village in Orissa; tigers; Hidimba, the demoness lover of Bhima, the Pandava hero, in her forest shrine; and the festival of the little golden idol of Raghunath, made by the sacred hands of Rama himself. Raghunath reigns supreme over all the other village gods of the valley, who once a year come to pay homage to him;—strange structures of the many masks of the gods, like trays of fruit in a window display, who circumambulate the shrine of the smallest and most powerful of the gods of the valley. The rites end with the sacrifice of five animals, ox, goat, hen, fish and crab. Timkoo had captured the priest-butcher, robed, with sword raised in both hands, about to decapitate a tethered ox; and in the next photograph the decapitated body, still standing on its legs; the elderly Raja of Kulu presiding. (At which English University had he been, I wondered.) The glossy magazine had not included that moment, scarcely likely to attract tourists. And Hidimba—how archaic, how primitive her forest shrine! She, Goddess of the woods, the Rakshasa who fell in love with that wild man, Bhima, strongest of the Pandavas, son of the wind-god and half-brother of Hanuman himself. Their half-demon son, Ghatotchak, fought and died in the Great Battle of Kurukshetra (how movingly Peter Brook recreated that scene for us in his production of the *Mahabharata*), and to this day Hidimba, whose higher nature had been awakened by her love for the Pandava, is tutelary spirit of the forests of her Himalayan valley. There was a photograph of her shrine, which I shall never see, remote from my life in a place I shall never visit. And yet she reaches me—when I was a country child in windy Northumberland, would I not have offered my wild flowers to Hidimba, the spirit of the wilds? I would have known her then, when I laid my offerings on a certain stone on a certain crag, among the polypody fern, as I sat looking out to the sunset from my sacred, secret place. What little country girls have offered their flowers to Hidimba! And what of her forests, the Himalayan forests stripped bare, the soil erosion, the floods, the devastation? Will Hidimba survive the desecration of her sanctuaries? How the child I was would have mourned the destruction of the wild places, how that child I was does mourn!

When Ajay is as old as I am how much of that archaic India will remain? Will his photographs remain only as a record of a vanished past? The beautiful doomed India of handcraft skills, of a myriad village gods and their festivals. That India of the Imagination is already vanishing. Kamaladevi, who did so much to sustain its life, is gone, and the television aerials sprout from the roofs of India's poor. Those dreaming faces of village craftsmen and women, makes of silver filigree, carvers of stone and wood, those 'illiterate' bearers of six thousand years of civilization, women, and men also, who paint on the humble plaster walls of their houses the joyous stories of Radha and Krishna, and the ancient god Jagannatha and his sister and spouse, with their terrifying circular eyes, who in the timeless world of mythology have mingled their archaic presences with the eternal love story of the beautiful Lord Krishna with his flute, who lures the gopis away from the domestic world into the forest of Brindavan. And will not the publication of all these photographic 'features' in itself only help to bring about the vanishing of the ancient world, as the tourists arrive, and the quality of work made to sell to these intruders, inevitably deteriorates? The 'gods' will depart before the television screen, and the beautiful 'work of human hands' made in their honour will be carelessly made for the tourist trade. 'Literacy' will replace the values of an age-old civilization, 'documentaries' the timeless stories of the gods, *'in illo tempore'*. Almost I am glad that I am one tourist who will not disturb those sanctuaries.

❀

Mohan sometimes tells me stories over the glass of Scotch which he offers me as we await the evening meal—we dine late, at nine or after, as in Spain. One such story is of a friend of his grandfather. The story is remarkable enough to have survived the passage of time. This gentleman, who lived in Uttar Pradesh, found on his estate, or was brought, an abandoned leopard cub. Had its mother been killed? The story does not tell. Be that as it may, he took the cub home, fed it and loved it, and between them grew that special devotion possible between humans and animals. I think of Balzac's *Un Amour dans le Desert*; of Goethe's remarkable story 'The Hunt' Pierre Leyris sent me in his French translation last Christmas, of the lion and tiger kept by a little family who toured with their small menagerie, and of the boy who spoke and sang to the escaped lion to bring him back, while the whole retinue of huntsmen from the castle held their breath, rifles at the ready. So blind are we to that power of love—of all such stories Goethe's surely the most beautiful.

When the leopard cub of our story was fully grown, it became impossible to keep him any longer as a domestic pet, and the man who had reared him with so much love and trust decided to take his leopard to the Zoo, in Lucknow (I think it was Lucknow, but no matter), where he could be kept in safety. A year later he decided to visit his friend, and went to the Zoo, where he made his way to the leopard-cage, in which there were two fine young leopards. He called his leopard by name, and at once one of the two bounded towards him with every sign of loving recognition, and allowed him to tickle him behind his ears and pull his whiskers, purring with pleasure, accepting the tit-bits offered, and responding to the old endearments. Presently the keeper arrived, dismayed to see this loving exchange going on between the gentleman from Uttar Pradesh and the young leopard—this, the keeper said, is a dangerous animal, (and so on). The former owner of the cub made light of these alarms—this was his old friend, who knew him well, there could be no danger, just look how pleased he is to see me, how playful and friendly! But, the keeper replied, your cub died some months ago; this is not your leopard.

By what mystery is such a story to be explained? I do not doubt that it is substantially true, or that many naturalists would believe it. One thinks of Rupert Sheldrake's new term, 'morphic resonance', coined to describe apparent telepathic communciation of knowledge and skills from animals in one place to others of the same species at a distance. A fine new word for a reality only our own iron-age materialism has ceased to know. These are mysteries of life, of the soul of the world. Seen simply, one could say that the strange leopard responded to the fearless love of the human who called a leopard he believed was his own; responded to that love which restored the old harmony between man and nature, whose covenant we broke when we left Eden. A sufficient reason? Perhaps. Why then did only one of the leopards respond? 'The first leopard must have told him' was the response of Piloo's husband, Dr. Jungalwalla, himself a lover of animals. We do not know if for a time the two leopards were together; or how, supposing they were, leopards exchange pictures of the mind. Or is there indeed a plane on which the collective soul of leopards resonates? Or was it, again, perhaps a case of 'mediumship' in leopards, in which the soul of the dead leopard 'communicated' with his old friend through the second leopard? And why had the first leopard died? Had he pined in captivity? The love of the animal is total. How infinitely mysterious are these invisible bonds and living resonances—between human beings far apart, between the living and the living, the living and the dead, between, it may be, the individual and the collective mind of the species. Did that dead leopard caress his old master through the intermediary of the living leopard? It is awesome, the mystery of life we so little regard; we can but revere that unknown Presence. Had man and leopard found their way together into that lost Golden Age which is ever-present for those who can open eyes and hearts to re-enter that lost kingdom we have but to remember? Not with the mind, but, surely with the heart—is not love the way to that lost domain? Is not India's mysterious wisdom, after all, grounded in an unbroken bond of love that has united her masters and *rishis* with all the poetry and joy of life, of the single indivisible universe?

In India people notice different things—a different paradigm. So it was that Piloo's comment on the story of the leopards was to describe to me how once she had found herself (I suppose in a Zoo) looking straight and deep into the eyes of a tiger. 'I am a king in captivity' the tiger had told her. Here in the West we might say 'The tiger looked like a king in captivity'; here in India mere simile becomes metaphor, and myth, and truth.

Santosh's father, Professor Kochhar, also told an animal story that no Western theory of 'morphic resonance' or the like could explain, and which can more easily be simply disbelieved, although it rests on a belief integral to the

Indian 'dream'. It concerns the second Master of the Radha Soami ashram at Beas, where Santosh's parents now live; 'the Great Master', as he is called. One day this Master had visited a Zoo with some followers, and had gone to an enclosure where there were monkeys. The Master had taken with him some *gram* to feed these monkeys, amongst whom was a female. He had called to this monkey, and she had come to him: 'Tell me, tell me!' he had coaxed her; and the little female monkey had wept real tears. Such is the story. He had recognized in her, Professor Kochhar explained, the soul of one formerly human, now for some fault born in animal form; and had promised her liberation in a future life. That is the whole story. Not a matter of fact, but a way of being, of experiencing nature; poetry not science, nor are 'belief' or 'disbelief' appropriate responses. These things are imaginal vistas, experiences we cannot measure by the criteria of measurable quantifiable fact.

Since my return to England I have attended a lecture by Rupert Sheldrake in St. James's Church Piccadilly, which formed part of a programme arranged by Satish Kumar, for *Resurgence*. The church was crowded to hear what this young scientist had to say; which was, after all, what all civilizations prior to our own have taken to be axiomatic— that the world can best be understood if we assume it to be alive. He is a modest and intelligent young man, and made no claim to 'originality', declaring himself, on the contrary, an Aristotelian—Aristotle having written of the 'souls' of all things in nature, animals, plants, stones; of the world itself. The surprising—and pleasing—thing is the stir his writings cause, the number of people drawn by their desperate desire to hear such a statement, remarkable only because so long forgotten in our Western culture, and made by a 'scientist'—as if 'Science' were the ultimate arbiter of truth, rather than a method of measurement and calculation of the quantifiable appearances of nature.

All these are, of course, love-stories; stories of love, that cannot be quantified, but only experienced. To which Professor Kochhar (that superb gardener of flowers, which must indeed love him, so freely do they grow for him) added a third, from the plant world. A botanical experiment was set up, not, in India, but, he thought, in Indonesia. Two plants of the same species were set side by side and a number of men made to file slowly past. Of these, one was instructed to take one of the plants and throw it out of the window. The remaining plant showed reactions of shock, recorded by some fine electrical recording apparatus. After some time—weeks, or days, I do not know—the same men were asked to file past the remaining plant, which showed no reaction, except to the man who had thrown its companion plant out of the window, to whom it again responded with reactions of shock. It remembered! Of course plants are sentient beings, Professor Kochhar commented, they know whether hands touch them with love, or harshly. Another love story?

And the plants judge us, and the animals, and the sun and the other stars, and is it not the knowledge of that judgment that hangs over us now? And is there not some universal archetypal dismay of our world, shaken by the condemnation of universal nature we have incurred? All those cock-sure intellectuals who believe, as they did in Blake's day, 'that there will be No Last Judgment', and who, as Blake declared 'flatter themselves'. Ourselves. We are judged by universal nature, whom we have violated.

Say these are but the stories we tell one another (and what else is Western science?) what else is a civilization but stories told and shared? Plato's 'likely stories'. I find a deeper truth in these love-stories of nature, than in 'science fiction'. Or science fictions.

❀

The stories we tell one another are of what seems significant to us, personally or culturally. In the West a story tends to be some event or fact of the outer world; in the East, of the inner world, of soul's country. Another story I chanced to hear is, again, a story of love. Two little boys of different religions shared a desk at school, and they were friends. Because his employer, a Hindu, followed a policy of favouring members of his own community, the father of the non-Hindu boy had been made 'redundant' and through no fault of his own was now unemployed and in extreme straits. Everything the little family possessed had been sold, down to their very clothes. The son, asked by his school-fellow why he was so sad one morning, confided to him that next day the bailiffs would be coming to evict the family from their home unless they could find the sum of money needed to pay their arrears of rent. With a child's generosity, the Hindu boy went to *his* father and begged him to take the needed sum, first thing next morning without fail, to his desk-mate's family—made his father swear on the Ganges water that he would do this—which he did.

Meanwhile the needs of the little family had become known, through another of the children, a little girl, (and again love is the link) to a charitable worker who tried to find work for the father of the family. But some strange fatality seemed to work against him—every job suggested had just been filled, or was in some way unsuitable. At last he heard of a job, many miles out in the country, and went to apply for it. He was a small frail man, and the employer to whom he presented himself merely laughed—a huge machine had broken down and he wanted a man to work the pump—by hand! On his way home a man in the garb of a *sadhu*, the yellow robe old and shabby, approached him and said. 'Stop! Listen!' The poor man walked away, only to meet the same *sadhu* coming now from the opposite direction. Three times he refused, but at the fourth encounter, he was unable to get away, pinned down by a crowd in a market, and he listened. The *sadhu* told him, 'You were born in such-and-such a place', and there followed a catalogue of exact incidents which had occurred in his life right up the present moment. 'Remember! No man is tried beyond his strength—I have been sent by a higher power to tell you that you *will* get a job by such-and-such a date. Now go in peace.' 'But if this comes true how can I ever repay you? Shall I ever see you again?' 'Perhaps I may come to ask you for one rupee and a quarter'. Saying this he vanished into the crowded street.

And so it was. The charitable worker who had not hitherto succeeded in finding a job for the poor man, was telephoned with an urgent request to find a clerk, not some smart young man but someone older and likely to be reliable. The very man for the job, this time. The poor man was so moved by the mysterious providence that had changed his life that he always had the sum of 1¼ rupees sewn into his shirt so as to be ready for the *sadhu* at any time. But he never came.

There is evidence in India of the existence of a secret Order, a 'white' Brotherhood, whose watchword is 'sevveyas'. It so happened that the lady social worker who had befriended the family had known that such an Order existed, and of their sign, a request for 'One rupee and a quarter'. The Order bestows charity and does good works, and it is deemed a great spiritual privilege to be approached by one of them. Years passed, and another crisis arose in the family—a little daughter needed, for her health, to spend a period in country air, away from Bombay, but her parents hesitated to let her go. At this moment the *sadhu* again appeared; his advice was to send her to the country, that she would recover, and that all would be well. This was done. The father who had all this while kept his 1¼ rupee in readiness, now offered it to the *sadhu*, who refused it, saying he would come again some other time; but he did not appear again.

Again, was not love the mysterious agent? The two little boys sharing a desk at school; the Hindu father who paid the debt; the charitable lady who found work for the man in misfortune; and running through all the mysterious providence that holds together all life, whose agent was the holy man, the *sadhu*, one of those sensitive to the living current of that unseen universe in which, again, love is the bond?

Once again I felt, 'That is India!' not because of marvels and mysteries but because these marvels and mysteries are carried on the simple flow of love, the secret law. Yet it is not only in India that these things happen—which of us has not at some time caught some glimpse of the laws of the inner worlds that are other than those in the West believe the laws of nature to be? And do not holy men and women wherever they may be remain attuned to the flow of love, whether in leopards, or plants or in human beings, the simple laws of life the materialist West has long forgotten?

If such things form no part of our culture it is because we have no coherent cosmology to which they may be related. During the centuries of 'the reign of quantity' the premise that the only reality is the material order, definable in terms of weight and measure, has prevailed; the figure of Sherlock Holmes, so popular here in England, represents the received opinion that there is a natural explanation for everything: the Hound of the Baskervilles is only a large dog made up with phosphorous paint—catch the dog and the cause of fear will be removed! What naïvety—but that is by the way. Yet the inexplicable goes on happening, and people whisper their experiences in secret, afraid of being disbelieved and laughed at. Yet there are plenty of records of such things as telepathy, precognition and the rest, the well-known 'second sight' of Scotland—one of my aunts was afflicted with these previsions of deaths and disaster. The ever-growing body of 'evidence' gathered by the Society for Psychical Research, the College of Psychic Studies, and now even in accredited University departments, is no longer to be swept aside.

The mistake, I believe, is to suppose that such things can be subjected to 'scientific' investigation at all; that the emotionally neutral conditions of a scientific laboratory are appropriate to events in the realm of immeasurable life. All records support the view that it is at moments of living intensity that a mother knows the need of a distant child, a seer receives foreknowledge of a death. There is surely an element of love even in such everyday experiences of knowing we shall receive a letter from such-and-such a friend, a call at the moment our own hand was on the telephone to dial that person's number. Animals—even plants—receive their knowledge, it seems, through this living medium so that the more the scientific researcher purges the experiment of 'subjective' aspects, the more negative will be his results. I think of a dream in which a voice repeated the words, 'A rocky death! A rocky death!' at the time a dear friend of my youth, Humphrey Jennings, had fallen to his death from a cliff on the island of Poros; and there followed deep grave words, 'However we may seek sanctuary in life, sooner or later we must leave'. Only several days later did I receive the news of his death.

An odd recent experience relates to my Indian friend, Dr. Sethna, whom I have never met, but with whom I have corresponded over many years, mainly about our common interest in Blake. Dr. Sethna is a devotee of Sri Aurobindo and has most likely practised *yoga;* so that he is, no doubt, more sensitive to that invisible medium than I. We were, about a year ago, engaged in a lively correspondence on literary matters, and I was well used to receiving thick envelopes from Pondicherry. On this occasion I was surprised to receive a thin airletter; Dr. Sethna's message was brief—he had, on such-and-such a day (he gave the time) received a 'visit' from me. I was in distress and carried a copy of the TLS; there was also an odd detail concerning—of all things—a comb. I had not thought of Dr. Sethna or consciously directed such a message to him, but the facts were authentic. *Temenos* had received an insolent review in the TLS which had both distressed and angered me. On the same day I had seen, by pure chance, on a stall in the Chelsea Antique Market, an ivory comb that had caught my fancy to the point of my asking my daughter to find out the price for me. Much too expensive, and I quickly forgot about it, but all the same the detail was confirmatory. Why and how did my thought reach Dr. Sethna? 'Love' may be too strong a word, yet are we not all, in reality, sending and receiving continually thoughts and knowledge within the one indivisible Self? I had neither knowledge nor intention of directing a thought to Dr. Sethna—or indeed to anyone. It is an awesome realization that our love and hate, our prayers or curses, our song or music or sorrows and violence have no bounds within that unity of being, whether or not we are aware of it. How rarely do we catch a glimpse of that world of which a holy man—and maybe a little croton plant, or a leopard cub—is aware always. As young children are, before, like us, they are 'sunk in deadly sleep'. Yet if we knew all, could we bear it?

❀

The day before Easter Sunday I had asked what the truth was about the expulsion of missionaries after Independence, for there seemed to be any number of Christian schools and hospitals, both Catholic and Protestant. Ajay had attended the Jesuit School in Civil Lines; St. Stephens' Hospital was a German Protestant foundation. Ajay's comment was that missionaries had been widely replaced by Indian priests. Then who had been expelled from this subcontinent where religions coexist in the ambience of Hindu tolerance? True, Christianity is the religion of the Imperialist West—first the Portuguese missionaries in Goa, later the British in the wake of Empire. Professor Kochhar explained that it was for political, not religious reasons that the expulsions had taken place, mainly of Americans. When, after Independence, India elected to become a non-aligned nation, this, in American eyes, amounted to being pro-Soviet ('that evil nation') and anti-American. Fundamentalist American missionaries began to arrive who attempted to 'de-stabilize' the Indian political balance by bribing Indians (the poor and those of low caste) to become converts to their sects, and further bribing them to vote against the Congress Party. Thus it was on purely political grounds that expulsions and the discouragement of missionaries took place. Christianity was always of course most successful among the lower castes, to whom it offered that same sense of dignity and self-respect that early Christianity had offered the slaves of the Roman Empire. In medicine and education Christianity has done much for India, and no one is more loved than Mother Teresa of Calcutta, for her good works, though she is by no means regarded as a spiritual Teacher, which is quite another matter.

However, I felt that on Easter Sunday I ought perhaps to go to a Christian church; William Blake had, after all, been a follower of 'Jesus, the Imagination', although Blake's Jesus is scarcely that of the Church or the churches, but rather the Self of the Upanishads and the *Bhaghavad Geeta*, the 'God within'. Mohan, himself a religious Sikh by upbringing, offered to escort me. Truth to say, I was curious to see a relic of the British Raj more living that the Delhi Gymkhana Club. Near and convenient, in Old Delhi, was the Church of the Christian Brotherhood, an Anglican missionary foundation, one of whom often visits Santosh to talk about gardening. Mohan accompanied me, a splendid figure in his

Sikh turban, to the rather beautiful spacious Anglican church I had often passed in Old Delhi. On Easter morning (the service was at 9 a.m. before the heat of the day) India's lovely pots of flowers led up to the Church porch; in a corner of the grounds a cemetery with big tombstones, and stone angels commemorating, most of them, no doubt, British civil servants or army personnel who had died in India in the days of the Raj. In the airy spacious interior were abundance of Easter flowers, Easter candles, many Indians and a few English ladies in those hats one would have seen up to a few years ago in any English parish church on Easter morning. It was like re-entering a world long past. Lovely airy unglazed windows and two of late Victorian stained glass of the kind so widespread in the heyday of church building in England, where no doubt they were made. As at the Delhi Gymkhana Club it was abundantly clear that the British who had built this rather beautful Anglican church had no intention or expectation of quitting India at the time it was built. Hymns Ancient and Modern, but the modern-ized prayer book, which paradoxically made the service seem even more alien, a fossil lodged in a recent stratum of Time Past; for the King James prayer-book would have introduced a timeless note of poetry and beauty. The modern service had been designed for British congrega-tions, people who were not there. The insistent Englishness made no concessions to 'Indian English'. With my new hearing-aid the sound of bells and music was painfully distorted. I had of course known most of the hymns all my life. All was a replica, from the thanks to the ladies who had brought the flowers, the welcome for newcomers (pointedly including myself, for Mohan had telephoned to discover the time of the service and had announced my coming). Some women and girls were dressed in rather quaint modest old-fashioned English-style dresses, though most wore saris. The wings of C. of E. angels were over us. Although I could hear little of the sermon, I have heard so many like it, imparting the literal, factual, historical version of the Resurrection that this hardly mattered. I reflected that this was the religion of my father, to him that story was a historical fact beyond question. There I sat, as it were, between my Father for whom that story was the ground of his faith, the Gospel, the words of life, and my Mother, that secret theosophist.

Yet when we begin to unravel mythology from history, to draw a distinction between them, to unweave the rainbow, is not the magic lost? And is not my own inability to share my Father's faith a failure of love rather than a mark of intellectual superiority? Never did my father act in any important matter without asking himself what the words of Jesus would bid him do. How admirable, noble, and simple he was! Yet, here in India, I listened to that familiar Easter sermon (I had heard it countless times) unmoved. In what way did it differ from the queer unedifying story of the little god Raghunath? Moulded, it is said, by the hands or Rama in the City of Ayodhya? A nobler myth, to be sure; the Gospel of Jesus equals, in some ways surpasses, even the teaching of the Lord Krishna, and is matchless. I don't doubt that those Indian Christians (how good Indians are at carbon-copy culture!) are full of virtues and good works; but as my Father was present beside me on one side, on the other side was my mother, whose wings were for ever clipped by that unimaginative moral literalism, and whose blessed gift of inattention, her dreams, and her store of poetry learned by heart, stood her in good stead through many a sermon longer than this morning's. Of course Jesus was a great Master, the story of Easter has become a part of the Imagination of the world. But here I found myself—I too carried back to the nineteen-thirties, so embalmed in this church in Old Delhi—and for once I found myself in complete accord with my long-ago rebellious self who knew

[208]

that the Christian Church was not for me, but took a lifetime to dare to admit this, even to myself. How many sermons I have heard that reduce the Christian faith to a cliché, delivered in the formulations of a vanished age! And to what can the preaching of clichés lead but the living of clichés? I wondered, as we left the Church of St. James, to what extent these Indian Christians were not perhaps living a cliché at second hand? Or did they find in Christianity some trace element—the human love of the Lord Jesus perhaps, the concern for the poor—missing from their own religion?

This Anglican church is a fossil so recent, resembles a living mollusc so closely that the stone winged angel who presides over the little Anglo-Indian cemetery behind the church might not have noticed the change. Every fossil has been living once, and fossils are very beautiful. Are not truisms exhausted truths, once living realizations, the forms into which some vision has crystallized? My unease at the sight of these Indian C. of E. Christians living within the fossilized shell of a relic of the British Empire was, in part, at the incongruity. These people were no doubt the second and third generation of converts who in adopting the religion of the imperial rulers may have sought some advantage, advancement perhaps through Western education for their children or maybe they genuinely admired the British. I did not have the impression that these were the children of the kind of low caste or untouchable Indians who might well have found in the Gospel of Jesus a dignity and freedom denied them in their low place in the Indian social hierarchy. But the mimicry was too complete, the manners, the faces, the whole bearing subtly un-Indian. I remembered the ecstatic worshippers of Radha and Krishna at Brindavan, and the little lights afloat on the Ganges at Haridwar as the sun set. That is popular religion, of course, a long way from the Brahmin super-subtlety of Raja Rao, or the sophisticated philosophic teachings of Sri

Aurobindo's 'Integral Yoga', or from the illuminated vision of India's holy men, who are held to be above and beyond the practises and creeds of 'religion'. India's temples and her idols are no essential part of these higher reaches of India's spiritual life, indeed these popular practises may well be discouraged—so I understood from Arabinda Basu in the case of Sri Aurobindo (although not necessarily so by every Master). Even so, that popular religion (now I am defending India's idols!) serves, as Yeats and A.E. had wished to see in Ireland, to wed the imagination of the race to river and mountain and forest and to a history that merges into the mythological and the spiritual order that sustains it, historical persons become sacred persons, kings merging into archetypal kingship, history into epic, and epic into the enactment of archetypal events and myths that are the timeless foundation of the identity of a nation. The India of the Imagination is not an elsewhere, but to be discovered in the rivers and trees and little shrines of India, not in Zion and Sinai and Jerusalem—the Holy Land, indeed, of the Jewish people. But Blake understood what was lacking when he named as Britain's holy mountain 'Snowdon sublime'. In France and Italy to be sure the Christian story has become naturalized in the beauty of Italian painting, the Virgin and the Angel of the Annunciation transposed into a balcony with tubs of little orange-trees or the familiar surroundings of some little Italian town on a hill; or French villages where some sculptured village Madonna smiles in the dusty market square; perhaps the Church of England is wedded to those old English parish churches where the rude forefathers of the village sleep in those leafy churchyards that Thomas Hardy so loved. But not here; I was embarrassed, saddened and irritated, and wished I had stayed away.

Santosh recalled how when she was a little girl there had been a small temple at the end of the lane that ran behind the garden of her grandparents' house, where the children used to play, and how when at sunset the priest used to ring the temple bell all the little girls would stop their play and run and crowd into the tiny temple where the priest of Krishna and Radha or whatever god it was would give them *prasad*—parched meal and sugar. So I too had played with my school-friends by the little stream that ran across the 'kirk loning' by our remote holy place on the Border, no Jordan's stream purer than the water we drew from the well whence flowed that little burn. But here, in a land where Ganga flows from Shiva's locks, a few miles from Rama's ancient city of Ayodha, in the very city of the Pandavas, a few hours' drive from the battlefield of Kurukshetra, the ancient land over which Mount Kailasa has ever stood between earth and heaven, why were all these good people who were not Jews singing English hymns about Jerusalem and Zion? One might of course ask what all these starry-eyed young Americans (and English too!) who follow Buddhist or Indian or Sufi teachers are doing with their fine vocabulary of Eastern terms and a diet of dahl and chapatties instead of sliced bread and baked beans? Perhaps on both sides the glamour of the alien? But perhaps also on both sides (discounting the social factors) these Indian Christians, no less that the Western followers of some Tibetan or Zen or Sufi or Hindu Teacher (some of these most decidedly dubious) may find in the alien religion some element lacking in our own heritage? 'All religions are one' of course, 'according to each nation's different reception of the Poetic Genius', and even Christians may in the end be forced to concede this. But at the Church of St. James in Old Delhi I could not but feel an atmosphere of that all too familiar Christian impervious complacency, as when I was a child and a rebellious teenager, and when my mother's sister so shocked the rest of the family by conversing with Buddhist monks in Ceylon.

On that same Sunday morning, after church, Mohan, ever courteous, drove me across the city to see the new Ba'hai Temple—not, it seems, known by that name, but the woman who finally directed us to it knew it only as 'The Lotus Temple', and not surprisingly. Suheil Bushrui, himself a Ba'hai, had already visited it. That passionate man, although himself a descendant of the Prophet Mahomet, had, not surprisingly in war-torn Lebanon, adopted a religion that proclaims a universalism—Blake's 'all religions are one'. Such is the message of Lebanon's own religious writer, Kahlil Gibran; and the Ba'hais have since sealed their faith with the blood of martyrdom, in Iran and elsewhere. I had not expected so impressive an edifice—a gleaming white marble lotus built on an immense site at present adorned with flower-beds and walks, but intended later to flower into schools, conference-centres, hostels, a hospital, library and whatever else humankind's ever-elusive never-relinquished dream of setting up the kingdom of heaven on earth may require. The building would look well from outer space with its gleaming whiteness and its ninefold design of marble petals reflected in pools of water at once simulating the leaves of the Lotus and helping to cool the air. People, not by Indian standards a crowd, but many people, were streaming towards the Lotus Temple on well made tiled paths edged with brilliant flowers. Leaving our shoes we climbed the flight of steps, again adorned with well-tended flowers. There is, however, no lift from the lower buildings—a library and so on—a mistake surely on the part of the planners to take no account of infirmity and old age. Helped by Mohan's strong arm, I managed all those steps, however. One could not but admire such a building, albeit more suggestive of a newly-alighted spaceship than a work of human hands. It belongs, to be sure, to the age of universalism, it is built for large numbers, and an internationalism purged of whatever is local is perhaps what it states. ('Like Esperanto' was the comment of a friend to whom I read this, who remembered, as I do, that well meant attempt after the First World War to unite Europe in a common language that vaguely resembled all, but none actually—then or now—spoken; eliminating of course all cultural traditions of which each language is a vehicle.) The architect I was told is an Iranian, the marble was imported into India from Greece, where every section was already cut for assembly. The Taj Mahal, though likewise a monument to an alien faith, was none the less built in all its beauty of marble and alabaster from India, and by multitudes of Indian craftsmen, housed in an enclosure where to this day one may imagine the skill and industry they brought to this great work.

Inside the Lotus Temple silence is enjoined. It is cool and spacious, nine arches support the inner vault—not marble, but white concrete, each arch proportioned a little differently, which gives an organic beauty rather than a mechanical symmetry. Rows and rows of beautiful seating, wooden backed marble benches, stand empty awaiting the multinational multitudes of the future. (That's another thing, the C. of E. provides pews, the Ba'hais marble seating, but Indians sit on the ground.) The glass doors have a transatlantic finish. There were great brass vases of bright gladioli, and the latest amplifiers where a hypothetical speaker might stand to address an audience who might fill all that beautiful empty seating. Those who enter the temple are invited to use it for prayer or meditation. By the usual modern misapprehension of the best conditions for prayer or meditation all is light and spacious and public, no shadowy side-chapels where a sorrower might be alone, no light burning before the Blessed Sacrament, no grubby gods or goddesses with their wide unblinking eyes, no little golden miraculous idol of Raghunath formed *in illo tempore* by the hands of Rama, no garlands of marigolds and stephanotis offered to the gods and then thrown out on the dark streets of Varanasi for the sacred cows to eat! No place to shed tears. Spacious, empty, declaring multinational unity, the no-man's land of universality. It lacks Blake's eloquence of 'minute particulars' or David Jones's Tutelar of the Place. The Lotus Temple is not a place, it replaces place. Strangely enough,—or inevitably—hardly anyone was *in* the temple. People sit for a moment, then stroll through and out. Very un-Indian. Like all that belongs to the modern world it denies and negates the human scale, the scale of the body, or the auras and astral extensions of the body. The soul is not at ease. There are of course no idols, no images, no icons, nor could there be without detracting from the proportions of the architecture; the spaces created speak for themselves. Yet the building is not, like the Gothic cathedral, or the mosque, or the Hindu temple or Buddhist *stupa*, itself an icon, inviting to a spiritual journey into an 'other-world' conducting the worshipper into some inner shrine symbolizing heart or fire, holy relic or holy of holies. There is no mystery. The nine arches represent the world religions; a 'good idea', but not archetypal, not iconic; they express the architect's conception and the Ba'hai universalism, but not the 'sacred geometry' of traditional principles, grounded in cosmology and therefore intrinsically meaningful. The secular message of the 'modern art' of this time takes no account of the purpose of the building, inevitably tasteful, abstract, and international, whether built for collective worship, or as a conference centre. Two young Canadians were distributing leaflets and giving information; and that was all.

I had not at the time formulated to myself what was wrong, that emptiness of the Temple at the end of the stream of people who flowed towards it—a temple that houses no dream, no sacred symbols, no inner world; nor does that pleasant approach through lawns and pretty flower beds, suggest an inner journey, a pilgrimage. The light outside is in no way different from the light within those functional glass doors which carry no symbolic differentiation of outer and inner space. No light pouring through rose windows 'stains the white radiance of eternity', nor those false doors and false windows of gleaming multicoloured tiles that Henry Corbin (writing of the mosques of Ispahan) describes as opening, not onto nowhere, but into the *mundus imaginalis*. No shadows, no mysteries, no hiding places for dreams or fantasies, no Green Man's pagan face peering from between the leaves of Southwell, on Christian capital or architrave, or plain village faces among the stone angels. No devils to delight us, no grubby curtain withdrawn to show a redder-than-wet-blood wall where Shiva's shadow fell, beautiful empty space, but natural, not imaginative, space. But that in itself says something of, and to, our time.

Yet could not a still silence be present in such emptiness? Again, the space is not intimate, as in some plain Quaker meeting house where men and women have sat together in a holy intimacy, with a shelf of books in one corner and simple windows opening upon country trees and sky and cattle and sheep. What kind of services will be held here, who will attend them? Space-men, or Martians perhaps? Nor is there any Teacher, or Master, whose presence would, here in India, draw a multitude like those who flock to the feet of Maharaj Charan Singh of Beas, or to Sathya Sai Baba, adored as an Avatar, and doubtless in many other ashrams, not excepting the Benedictine Dom Bede Griffiths of Shantivanam. Ramu Gandhi describes, in the current issue of the *India International Centre Quarterly* how at the passing of his Master Ramana Maharshi a peacock cried all night on the roof of that saint whose presence in the world had no bounds. The animals loved him, they too knew who he was.

No peacock will ever perch on the sterile marble of the Lotus Temple or loving mongoose streak out of the bushes to be near these latest triumphs of technology that transmit indifferently the words of saint, tele-evangelist or the man testing for volume. What, in that marble hall, will be spoken, by whom and to whom? That marble lotus from outer space is not rooted in the mud of life nor does its heart hold the mysterious jewel.

Talking it over in the evening it seems that Mohan had felt as I did: the Temple was empty. Not like Santosh's little temple into which the children crowded when the priest rang the evening bell. Mohan loves the Sikh Golden Temple with an imaginative intensity unlooked-for in a practical merchant, and has explained to me the symbolism of the Four Gates opening (as do the Four Gates of the New Jerusalem of St. John the Divine) to admit the four castes and religions of all humankind. There are other archetypal structures of church and temple and mosque and *stupa*, according to whose pattern sacred architecture has conformed. It is not, it seems, enough for a religious sect to employ an architect trained in the technology of his time and place; whose imprint is stronger than whatever personal faith the builder may hold.

In St. John's New Jerusalem there is no temple; but meanwhile the heart seeks for some local habitation, some Quaker meeting house in Wales, or New England; a smiling village Madonna in France, or Hidimba the penitent Demoness who has reigned over her forests. Or at Chartres, Rilke's Angel of the Sundial who measures the hours of the real lives of real people of France, or the quiet graves of an English village churchyard. All religions are one does not necessarily mean one world religion, or so one hopes. Or does it? A pity the choice should lie between the smugness or fanatacism of Christian (or other) fundamentalism and the no-man's-land of the multinational. Or do we not all know, now, that the only church is 'within the hearts of men'?

One other thought on the two unquestionably very fine buildings visited this Easter Sunday—where did the money come from? Who imposed, or hopes to impose, an alien form of worship, and on whom? Who built Hidimba's forest shrine is a question easily answered, she is the Tutelar of the Place; or the little stone Covenanter's Kirk at Bavington, or the great cathedral of Chartres. The monks of Subiaco or Ajanta were those who also lived and worked and worshipped there. The British Raj spared no expense to build for themselves that lovely airy church in Old Delhi to house their Englishness—a blend of complacency, good will, and want of imagination, and also, no doubt, a centre of good works of a high order in medicine, education and welfare. But who pays for the Ba'hai temples that are springing up here and there in the developing Third World? Our little Buddhist Peace Temple in Battersea Park was built stone by stone by Japanese monks. It speaks the Lord Buddha's message of peace and compassion to Londoners; who like it. It is not vandalized, little jam jars of flowers are always filled, some no doubt by Asians but by no means all. But at the Ba'hai Lotus Temple those tended banks of grass, those brilliant beds of flowers, all tell of money poured into building and upkeep, not of the little offerings of multitudes of worshippers. Somewhere there is money—too much money—promoting the Ba'hai movement. Like those Chritian Science reading-rooms quietly and persistently present among the 'better' shops in so many English middle-class suburbs. The Lotus Temple was not built without very large sums of money from somewhere, and to what purpose? I suspect whatever goes beyond the human scale; but then we live in a world that has done just that.

❀

It was important that I should see Kapila, and with my hearing-aid it was now—just—possible to do so. I wanted to discuss with her our projected Temenos Academy for Integral Studies for which we hoped to have her support; since Kapila herself represents in India and on a national—indeed an international—scale, that essential knowledge of which we would hope, in England, to be a small but seminal centre. I did not want to leave Delhi without discussing these things with her; and also I wanted for *Temenos* the paper she had given at our Dartington Hall conference in 1988. The site of the great Indira Gandhi Centre for the Arts was still as I had seen it two years ago, twenty-three leafy acres in the heart of New Delhi—building will begin later in the year, and when completed this will be the most important piece of architecture built in this city since Lutyens' Government buildings. A centre for the arts of India, past, present and to come, this will be something more than a piece of architecture. It is now India's turn to disseminate the universal knowledge of which she is, now as always, the custodian; a knowledge which, perhaps, the West is ready to receive. Scholars from the four quarters of the world will look to this great centre that is arising here in New Delhi, literally from the ground. While in England it is with the utmost difficulty that the great museums—the Victoria and Albert, with the rest—are keeping their staff Kapila's appointed task is to set and maintain a standard of the highest excellence.

At present Kapila is encamped in a former British officer's mess, but no ghosts here, for although the roof leaks and large drops of rain drip on the stairs, ghosts cannot survive where new life springs from tables laden with papers, boxes of manuscripts, a room below where recently hung an exhibition of calligraphy, Kapila's spacious untidy *atelier* where already seminal work is being done where the Tree flourishes whose roots are above and branches below.

I came away with much literature on present and future projects of this great renaissance of Indian culture for though there seems to be much political discouragement and disappointment (as shown in Sima Sharma's *India International Centre Quarterly* and its many contributors) with culture it is otherwise—as Raja Rao assured me two years ago. India's ancient learning and the Bollingen Foundation's new learning are alike re-affirmations of a knowledge long shut out of a secular Academia. It is an unageing knowledge, not less the 'new learning' now, than when Gemistus Plethon brought the Platonic works to Florence; already older than Athens, and doubtless it was from India this perennial wisdom had reached Athens itself, and perhaps older Egypt. But will the world last long enough for that tree Kapila is tending to spread its branches through the world? My sense of the smallness of my own part is submerged in thankfulness to see that whether in England we succeed or fail (and through *Temenos* at least we have kept a spark alive that others may blow into a flame) to know that in India the Aswattha tree is already putting forth new shoots,.

Already there are books: works on music, the first volume of a great projected Lexicon of Sanskrit terms relating to the arts, Professor Lokesh Chandra's learned work on the icon of Avalokiteśvara, the Buddhist icon of a thousand arms. Just nine terms in the first volume of the Lexicon, each chapter the work of the exhaustive research of the finest scholars. These are terms without which it is impossible for a whole range of knowledge, of insight into India's tradition of spiritual wisdom, to be understood—all who wish to approach that wisdom will need to learn these terms. For those of us for whom the Orient is not a geographical but a spiritual region these are seminal works indeed. Yet Kapila herself must work against the tide—of academic westernization, and secularization, and the disappearance of the knowledge itself. Modern India would exclude Sanskrit from the school syllabus—there as elsewhere concentrated on technology and science—because the Sanskrit learning of the Brahmins is associated with the caste system. One might have thought it more 'democratic' to make the knowledge of the few available to the many but wisdom is itself undemocratic in its very nature, whereas to technology all is equal in the kingdom of the machine. Kapila's task is to restore to the young nation the timeless heritage of an ancient civilization.

Kapila sees that the Temenos Academy might be a centre, in England, for the dissemination of this knowledge. Programmes might sometimes be shared: conferences, exhibitions. I almost wept to think how much we might do, how far we are from realization. Yet we may, we must establish in this country that small foothold, that minimal, seminal school and centre. If we fail others must perform that task. I rejoice that such a renaissance is taking place in India. Two years ago Raja Rao told me it was so. I have an especial sympathy with Kapila's work, it is in the service of 'the learning of the Imagination' in its full splendour, fine scholarship in the service of the highest vision of which mankind is capable, that wisdom we have created from the foundation of the human world—or word—or that has created us. I returned laden with review copies for *Temenos*—the Lexicon; a volume of selections from the letters of Coomaraswamy; Professor Chandra's work; books on Indian traditional music—and how unlikely it is that any other Western review will take note of them! So much at least we can do.

One of the first friends I chanced to meet after my return to England was Satish Kumar and his response to my enthusiasm was unexpected, but perhaps predictable, had I known more of the true India; he was suspicious of all these books, for the sacred knowledge of India has ever been an oral transmission. Publication of books he sees as endangering that tradition which rests, finally, on human relationship between Master and pupil, not a purely mental transmission that books can communicate. Satish himself was a Jain monk for nine years and knew that tradition which is to me only hearsay. For all a few of us may have read Coomaraswamy's *The Bugbear of Literacy* we still, without thought or question, identify culture with education, and education with literacy, and this is profoundly wrong. Book learning is not the whole of integral knowledge and the great civilizations of the past were not dependent on the ability to read and write—craftsmen, the builders of temples, mosques and churches, the sculptors of Konarak or of Chartres were not literate, and oral tradition carried poetry and sacred knowledge for millennia before books. Indeed in this terminal phase of Western civilization literacy may well have the opposite effect—disseminating not truth but trivia, not knowledge but ignorance. If a civilisation be a transmission and participation in a certain kind and quality of experience, how can such knowledge best be transmitted but by one living being to another? Oral tradition is the ground of every civilization, every language, whose records cannot in themselves preserve it. In this sense India is to this day highly and profoundly civilized; America, for all its technology, hardly civilized at all (beyond a diminishing number who still participate, in an older European culture). With every technological invention by which knowledge and its transmission is removed from the ashrams of India's 'forest dwellers', the schools and religious communities of Christendom as it was, from the 'temenos' of the gods, so we are exchanging civilization for technology. Perhaps American counter-culture grass roots movements—here in England also—are an attempt to return to the norm of civilizations of making and doing, and human communication as against storing information, and 'literacy' that merely exposes ignorance to commercial or political propaganda. I am a highly sophisticated product of the best English education, to which I have added long years of study in the Ivory Tower of the North Library of the British Museum and elsewhere; and I was brought to pause by Satish's comment. Perhaps the education we most need in the West today is above all else the education of transmission by love—father to son, mother and grandmother to daughter, and babes, and by spiritual teachers—and teachers, for that matter, of literature, or botany, or algebra, or bookbinding or of anything else whatever—who can transmit the living fire. I was fortunate in my father who loved Shakespeare, my mother and aunts rich in their heritage of Scotland's oral tradition; the ballads they taught me came to me with the reality of life itself, something no school book ever imparted. But this is the Kali-Yuga and must we not use what means we can for the preservation of humankind's sacred knowledge and its dispersal, as at the end of a life-cycle the plant scatters its seed?

Probably we in the West are incapable of estimating this profound difference—the parting of the ways between wisdom and technology is too far in our past. Plato knew it, when he recorded the Egyptian king's pronouncement that the use of writing would lead to the deterioration of the human memory. Now we see storage of information so developed that human memory has come to seem only a short-lived and disposable substitute for technology. Yet what has been lost is wisdom; and love. It comes back always to love, that mysterious link, or medium, in which life has its being. The relationship of parents and children, of philosopher or holy man to his devotees and disciples, indeed of any true teacher with pupils whatever be the subject studied—all these are relationships of love, or information is nothing but a burden and a destructive mockery. Children learn from those they love and who love them, otherwise they leave school hating French because they had a French mistress whom they disliked, or the Church because the spirit of love has fled from it. The Indian link with the *guru* is a relationship of love, be it all those beautiful Punjabis with their Master at Beas, or Ramu in his relationship with Ramana Maharshi, albeit he had never seen him. Or Arabinda Basu, and Dr. Sethna with Sri Aurobindo. Through love they know themselves linked with the one living Self of the universe. Taped and recorded information cannot impart love, never wisdom, never that living breath of poetry, only the words. All the same, does not something from Homer, from Shakespeare, from Valmiki, from Wordsworth and Shelley, from Yeats, travel still on the living network of love, to the end of time? What are the limits of that network? Is not all present past and future ever present within the one life?

Kapila took me to lunch nearby and I told her I had been reading Sima Sharma's collection of papers entitled *India, the Formative Years*. Each writer seemed to be asking why some scheme that had seemed so good had failed, and a few asked whether perhaps the premises had been wrong in the first place. Kapila at once said—what heaven knows we know to be true yet fail to act upon—that political and social problems can never be solved at that level, but only from another level, the higher vision. Only the politics of eternity can resolve the politics of time. She agreed that India needed to retrace her steps to the divergence of modern India from the age-old civilization. Indira Gandhi, she said, was deeply aware of 'the India of the Imagination' and she sees her own task as precisely the healing of that 'wrenching apart', a return to the non-duality of a civilization of the human spirit. Democratic egalitarianism seems inevitably to lead to the lowering of standards; India is a socialist country with many Marxists, yet for Kapila there is only one standard—the highest.

Kapila has her troubles, however; she is working against

the tide of 'progress' that is carrying away the very arts and knowledge she is working to preserve and promote. The transmission of the Brahmin learning is no longer assured in modern India. She had recently been in Pune, conferring with pundits whose ages ranged from eighty to ninety four; they had trained no successors and she is concerned to send students to learn, while the knowledge is still ('still' again) preserved in an unwritten tradition of six thousand years. Yet is not the great Indira Gandhi Centre for the Arts itself in danger of becoming a museum, that grave of civilization that Coomaraswamy denounced? Only the living fire can avail against decline and fall.

❀

What with my various afflictions and Santosh's resolution to complete her manuscript, our expedition to the Radha Soami Ashram at Beas was deferred until the first days of April. For a third time I am the guest of Maharaj Charan Singh, and occupying the very room where three years ago I was the only visitor except for the little jackals making their rounds. Now Western visitors (several from England) are sunning themselves on the pleasant lawn shaded by 'weeping' ashoka trees, and a mango tree where green parrots disport themselves. Today in the *dera*, where we arrived yesterday evening, there are five hundred thousand people—five *lakhs* as the Indians say, who need words for great numbers—young and old, high-court judges and ambassadors' wives, down to the poorest, with every degree between.

Yesterday with Santosh, Professor Kochhar, and Timkoo as our escort and driver, we made the nine-hour drive from Delhi, through Haryana and so to the green Punjab, the corn-fields of the granary of India already turning gold. We left early so as to reach Beas before sundown, for although the Punjab is once more open to visitors, that by no means guarantees safety.

The outskirts of Delhi are depressing enough, although the main road to the Punjab does not pass through Delhi's shanty town district, which is on the other side of the Yamuna and I must admit that I have never seen the worst of India's poverty. We passed through a dismal area where acres of garbage is 'processed' in the sun into what in the end will be used (I was told) to fill in swampy land for, presumably, 'development'. Meanwhile the vultures are perched there as thick as maggots on so rich a feeding-ground. We passed a little group of pilgrims, carrying flags, on their way, Santosh explained, to a shrine in the Hima-layas, visiting temples on the way. Returning three days later we passed the same pilgrims somewhere in the middle of Haryana, with many days' journeying still before they reached their shrine in the hills. There was nothing, not even—least of all—occasional glimpses of the Jamuna to rejoice the eyes. India's boundless poverty. Here and there a rather fine new building is an institute of this or that, or a small factory, or a dairy centre, but the surrounding poverty, the little groups of shanties, seems in no way related to these signs of prosperity and progressive ventures. On my first euphoric visit I had noticed the camels and the tongas and the painted horns of the buffalo and the tinsel and the lotuses adorning the Tata lorries. Fewer of all these now, the trucks seldom decked out as for a gypsy fair; few camels on the fine road with its double carriageway now under construction from Delhi to Amritsar. The animals are going, the machines are coming. Poverty remains unchanged, it seems, 'progress' has done nothing for the men and women breaking stones, and there are the shanty settlements, some larger, some just a few propped-up tarpaulin shacks, such minimal shelters that, like a mathematical series that ends in zero, there is a kind of return to infinity—those who from sheer want have nothing assume something of the dignity of those *rishis* who have renounced possessions to affirm and experience the dignity of being itself. India respects the poverty of her holy men and somehow the poverty of the destitute is not without its dignity. But the shanties themselves are without dignity, ugly squalid habitations like a blight spreading on the outskirts of every town where industry employs migrant unskilled labour. Santosh tells me that a minimum wage is now statutory and that most shanty-dwellers are employed; but what wage can compensate for the squalor and rootlessness of such a life, one wonders? I have been reading two novels by Kamala Markandeya, who so compassionately depicts the life of India's poor, both rural and urban—the exodus of young men from villages where mere survival is the best that can be hoped for; or even when survival might be possible there is a restlessness as the magnet of the industrial cities pulls a generation who hope for better things than village life and the old ways can offer. Modern 'literacy' does not teach the skills or attitudes village life and the husbandry of 'mother earth' demands, but, on the contrary, awakens in the young ambitions of employment at some machine, or desk where their fine new literacy—itself the product and the instrument of a different kind of culture—will raise them 'above' their fathers and forefathers; and now the shimmering television screen holds before India's lakhs of millions images of an affluent Western society that usurps the old myths of Kubera's palaces and gardens and has no more reality than they.

India's poor are not some special category, or 'problem' in the Western sense—they are not the 'unemployed youth' or some group who must 'prove' their right to national assistance. They are, by their very multitude, simply the people of India. As such they seem to possess a personal dignity that makes them superior to their lot, their dwellings and

[226]

surroundings, women in their faded cotton saris, or Punjabi *kurtas* and pyjamas, the men whose turbans, however ragged, impart the stature of their collective rather than some minimal personal identity. They are Sikhs, or Muslims, or men from the hills, or from Madras, a cultural rather than an economic identity. The Aryan Indian race is without question the most beautiful in the world, in refinement of feature, in bodily frame. The blotched skin and the lumpish physique of the white races is not to be compared with the sheer physical beauty of the men, women and children everywhere to be seen, old women with their fine intelligent features, bearded old men who with their glowing deep-set eyes have the looks of *rishis*, and children little dancers from the beginning. They are loved, of course, usually by a number of people. From the nondescript dusty poverty of India, beauty springs, like Sita from the furrow. Indian landscapes, in those states I have visited, are not outstandingly beautiful, as such—India's beauty lies in her people. In our Western cities—above all in America—it is easy to forget that people, collectively or individually, may be beautiful. Yet to realize that Indian beauty springs from a culture and not merely from a physical frame one has but to go to Bombay where the secular modern culture that there prevails has extinguished that beauty from the many secular faces one sees in the streets.

On the road to the Punjab, as one flashes past, one sees beauty of women and children, of old men and youths. A turbaned young man leaning against a dusty truck had at that moment the physical nobility and bearing of a young king, in the refinement of his race, his unconscious posture. Personal identity takes its dignity, even in the poorest, from something else. If India's poor ever cease to embody this greater identity (Nirmal Verma's 'dream factor'?) they will be poor indeed. The Irish long kept something of this cultural dignity amid personal poverty, and the people of the Western Isles and the Western Highlands, the Macleods and the MacKinnons and the Macraes and the MacIsaacs in their storm-beaten crofts. Nor does 'our humble mother the dust' diminish the stature of India's poor, who live so near to her.

These dusty verges are somehow of the very essence of Indian life. My first (Western) reaction was, of course, 'something ought to be done', this no man's land should be tidied up, the hovels and the dumped heaps of motor tyres or scrap metals, the stacks of wood, piles of bicycles, or just heaps of earth. Then I ask myself, 'what should be done?' Sidewalks and pavements? Shop fronts in the Western style? And I seem to understand that it is just because this no man's land belongs to no one in particular (or so it seems) it belongs also to everyone. The sense of property, so well—too well—developed in my own country, where every square yard belongs to someone who is prepared to go to law to defend his right to it against any encroacher, seems to be a writ that does not run here in India. If a man wishes to sleep, he lies down on the ground, pulls up a blanket over his face (the blanket at other times an outer garment) and sleeps on the lap of Mother Earth. The proprietors of some tarpaulin covered poles where fruit or coffee is sold, or the barber who sets up under a tree with a razor and a bowl of water, do not build walls round themselves. This absence of the deplorable insistent affirmation of personal property (I live in a London square in which nearly every house is fitted with a burglar alarm) I first noticed at Brindavan; the freedom of the children who seemed to feel that everywhere was theirs. In a paradoxical way those who have nothing—or so little— have, if not every*thing,* at least every*where.* On these humpy, dusty, weedy margins, people live, children play, maybe a hovel or two is set up—impermanence is accommodating and spacious. Am I wholly wrong in feeling that the near starving multitudes of India don't feel dispossessed

[228]

from Tagore's 'humble mother, the dust'? Such as it is, the dust of India—the earth of India—is theirs, their unshod feet ('nor can feet feel, being shod') stand on their native earth; and that earth is a living earth, and sacred. Pavements are not like that, who can feel that a pavement is Mother Earth herself? Will not something be lost when those unpicturesque scruffy verges are cleared up? The children and the dogs and the pigs and the cows won't like it. In England those who occupy them would be called 'squatters' and moved on, or made to show their licences. Blake burned with indignation against London's 'chartered streets'—here it seems, Mother Earth is still, at least by the dusty roadsides of India, uncharted.

Indeed it is only here and there, even in beautiful New Delhi and its outskirts, that there is not a wide, dusty, scruffy margin between the road and that indeterminate row of shops, or shacks, that line (except in residential enclaves) every road. No doubt this conforms to some regulation about not building within a certain distance of the road but to whom this nondescript terrain belongs and who is responsible for it is not clear. The shops, or shacks, themselves seem to have ill-defined limits and street markets are even less well-defined, for when does a barrow made of an old bicycle frame laden with bananas and oranges become a market-stall? And by no means all erections of a few poles covered with thin thatch or tarpaulin denote misery—those light minimal coverings from the sun's heat may shelter piles of fresh 'organically grown' vegetables the like of which it would be hard to find in a Western supermarket, papayas and bundles of fresh spinach and coriander, or rows of shining, streaming pans of food, or tea or coffee, or light frame-beds (*charpais*) for the repose of long-distance truck drivers. What to Western eyes might seem a hovel, otherwise regarded might seem an airy market stall, perfectly fitted for its use. When we returned by the same road a few days later, as dusk fell, some of these light erections were gay with lights, white or green neon lights standing upright on poles indicating that food was available, or tea (of different strengths, '200-kilometer tea' was a strong brew for drivers with long distances to travel), and some had added strings of red and yellow fairy lights as well; a human, cheerful scene, trucks, dust, food served in the open air or under the lightest frame, with cool air circulating without the encumbrance of walls. For tourists Haryana has with imaginative taste built comfortable and attractive 'motels', many with sleeping accommodation, serving excellent food to travellers; each has the name of a bird—'Woodpecker' or 'Black Partridge' or 'Kingfisher'—all with charming leafy gardens, flowering champak trees and bright flowers. Punjab is beginning to emulate this state enterprise, which does much to make travel in India by car a pleasure and is no doubt a source of profit. Elsewhere I am told things are not so good. These are oases of a middle-class world, islands quite apart from the surrounding poverty. When the ambitious road planning development is completed 'progress' will have raised the standard of many things. For miles and miles the roads of Haryana and Punjab are lined with eucalyptus trees, introduced from Australia but now everywhere to be seen, changing the Indian landscape, but fast-growing and good for draining swampy ground, but in fact destructive to the land; no shrubs can grow under them, and, although profitable, their long-term effect is disastrous. Ecologists don't like them and are attempting to bring back the peepal, the neem, the banyan, and India's other indigenous trees; but the eucalyptus, here as in California, seems to have naturalized itself irreversibly.

I realize that anyone who has walked the roads of India—Satish Kumar for example—could tell of the bitter lot of the landless poor. Yet with property comes all the greed and avarice one finds in the wealthy countries of the world, and the wealthy classes—India's bourgeoise guard their property under lock and key with bolts and bars on every door—doubtless with good reason: the frontier between the 'haves' and the 'have nots' is always and everywhere a dangerous one.

❀

That sense that the earth they tread is their own—or God's—is sacred—I have seen these last days in the *dera* of the Radha Soami Ashram. Yesterday—a Sunday—was the feast of the second—'the Great'—Master, predecessor of Maharaj Charan Singh. As we approached this domain on the river Beas, in the evening light, on Saturday, after our long drive from Delhi, Professor Kochhar returning home after his stay with Santosh, who was celebrating the completion of her manuscript by a visit to her parents, Timkoo driving, already a green prosperity seemed to pervade the land. As we drove through the town of Beas, there was the fine hospital I had entered on a previous visit, three years ago, then unfinished, now serving the community. As we approached the multitudes were already converging on the *dera*, mostly Sikhs from the Punjab, the men in their proud turbans, the women in their multicoloured tunics, young and old, families, youths and grandmothers and infants-in-arms, the prosperous and the poor. With difficulty Timkoo steered our car through the throng to his grandparents' little house that so reminds me of my own parents' last house. The multitude. That word from the Gospel. Jesus fed 'the multitude'. Five thousand with five loaves and three small fishes. Yesterday five hundred thousand were present, to hear their Master's discourse, and of these most received food at the *langar*. I was in, yet not of, that multitude, but enjoying the great beauty of these people in their gentle streams. They spent the night on the ground, sleeping under awnings, in tents, sheds, great shelters built for them, or in the hostels where the better-off could find rooms. Many slept on bedding they had brought in bundles carried on their heads, or on bicycles, or on mats issued by the *dera*. So thick on the side-walks they lay that there was hardly an inch between these sleepers, many covered in the blankets that the Punjabis wear by day as cloaks. Or one could see with what simplicity a little family would settle into a tent, children and parents as much at home there as in any other place, under the blessing of their Master.

Again I saw how those with few possessions are at home wherever they may rest. Gentle, happy people, those united by the love of God, and their Master, and one another, beautiful indeed. Densely as their multitudes were packed, as the crowd streamed like a river there was no shoving or pushing or disorder—they flowed. 'If you want to know God, go with the flow'. But how can I, who have in these last days seen that multitude convey to those who have perhaps seen only a football crowd the beauty of human beings attuned to their Master—yes, the turbans, the saris, the brilliant garments of the women of Rajasthan, the bundles carried on the heads of men and women with such grace, all that is beautiful to the eye, but imagine, that each of that innumerable multitude—of Blake's 'innumerable multitudes of eternity'—bears the unique imprint of the divine image. When Blake wrote that 'everything that lives is holy', yes, he meant the grain of sand, the particle of dust, the flower of the meadowsweet and the May, the lark, the tyger and the lamb, but above all the one-in-many and many-in-one of the Divine Humanity. 'All is Human, Mighty, Divine', Blake declared. I shall not see the like again of that multitude; and all, all who wished, were fed at the *langar* on the harvest; fruit of the earth blessed by the Master and given freely to all. The climate of the Subcontinent, the fecundity and richness of the soil, make for a culture in which movement is easy, unfettered, unencumbered by the kind of barriers that circumscribe life in Northern and Western countries.

A room the size of a barn was heaped shoulder high with *chapatties* made of rich, fragrant wheat of the Punjab, made by teams of buxom Punjabi women squatting over griddles heated from below with fires kept ablaze with straw and brush-wood heaped hedge high on either side of the *chapattie* ladies while men stoked the fires, and yet more women carried yet more laden baskets on their heads to replenish the pile. Each of that endless stream of people was given a stainless-steel plate and a beaker for water, and a spoon. Sitting on the ground in row after row, facing one another, none went away hungry—men in turbans with shining buckets of *dahl*, or curried vegetables and lime pickles, went up and down the rows not once but several times; all ate their fill. As those who had eaten streamed away, others streamed in to be fed; men lay on the ground in the shade to rest, children tumbled in the dust that surely here too 'breathed forth its joy'. One had the impression that these people accepted as of right their being in their Master's domain, their being fed in body and soul—they had not the air of 'visitors' but rather of family. Here property does not count—does not exist—here the Golden Age lives on, the earth as God gave it to humankind as our own place. At his evening discourse to foreign visitors (and what a lumpish unprepossessing gathering we are, beside these beautiful children of the furrows of the Punjab) one eager young American thanked the Master for the privilege of being in this abode of peace and harmony. To which the Master replied that the people to be thanked were the women who had cooked the *chapatties* and the men who had prepared the great cauldrons of delicious *dahl*, the feast was their work, and those who had sown and reaped the corn. And he further reminded us that outside these gates the Punjabis live in fear of their lives, lock their doors at sundown and do not venture abroad before daylight returns. Many have sought sanctuary here—such sanctuary as the *dera* affords—for the Master himself is given a guard by the State police; the only protection here is the spirit of peace that pervades the place.

And there have never *not* been holy men in India. What when this Master is no longer here? Will they come to his successor? Who can say? Heaven forbid that this living flow of love and life should be institutionalized—meal vouchers issued for the *langar*, the women who squat for hours over hot metal plates paid by the hour. The flour is ground from wheat grown on the *dera*, the pulse, the *ghee*, the lime pickles brought as free gifts and stored for the great feasts. But the *langar* is served every day, to whoever comes.

As a guest at the guest house where foreign devotees of the Master are entertained I felt doubly isolated, for I have not received, nor do I intend to receive, his initiation; and I wanted to be with the multitude. Santosh and her mother, Timkoo and I, therefore, went to partake of the *langar* food— Mrs Kochhar likes to do this, and readily agreed to my request, as did Santosh. Not in the endless ranks of the main area, but in a smaller group where the workers here at the ashram received their food. (This was to save me the longer walk which I could not easily have managed.) I have never been able to sit cross-legged on the ground, and chairs were brought for Santosh's mother and for me; the others, rich and poor, a high ranking officer covered with medals side by side with gardeners and the women who swept the pavements, we were all served. One Sikh gentleman who served us was a High Court judge, so I was told by Santosh; another a well-known Punjabi writer. Our shoes removed, we sat in lines facing one another in the welcome shade of a wall. Again and again the *chapatties*, the *dahl*, the curried vegetables, the cool water, were brought round—excellent food of this rich land, the best *dahl* I have ever tasted. So it should be—no money was involved, nothing bought or sold, all was fruit of the earth and work of human hands.

Outside the gates of this twice five miles of fertile ground the Sikhs and the Hindus shoot one another with weapons supplied by Western nations. Meanwhile that serene, wise Sikh Master preaches the Everlasting Gospel, the same always and everywhere: Love God, and your neighbour as yourself; meditate, listen to the sound-current of the universe to which we are ourselves attuned. The beautiful voices of the cantors, singing hymns from the *Adi Granth*, and poems of Kabir, echoed that heavenly music.

Here it is so immemorially human and simple, I shall, when I return to England, scarcely be able to believe that I have partaken of the *langar* blessed by the Master; who claims, no doubt with truth, to be the bearer in this time of that same sacred knowledge that the Lord Krishna, and the Lord Buddha, and the Lord Jesus and others in their times and places have given to the world, the Prophet Mahomet, perhaps the martyred teacher of the Ba'hais—these things are secrets of the inner worlds. But between that marble Lotus Temple dropped from outer space and the human harvest grown on Punjabi soil, what a difference!

I am sitting alone in the leafy garden of the guest house. I did not go to *satsang*—I find sitting on the ground extremely painful, and, to be truthful, these hours of leisure are precious to me because I can write this record of things whose like could not be found elsewhere on this earth. The multitude: blessed are the meek for they shall inherit the earth. *Seva*, it is called, the voluntary service of those who come, from the little old women who with their switches continually sweep the dust from the streets and pavements, to the men carrying baskets of earth on their heads in a building site, or laying the bricks for yet another hostel or clinic or vast covered shelter where the Master may preach in wet weather. So must it have been when the cathedrals were built; at Chartres, as here, lords and peasants together dragged stones to the site. Women, then as now, must have been baking bread made from the wheat of *la Beauce* as here from the wheat of the Punjab. The cathedrals, like India's ashrams, were built by the unanimous devotion of the people to Our Lady or to some other Christian vision of the sacred. Again I thought of the Lotus Temple, dropped from outer space ready prefabricated; without *seva*, no *chapatties* and *dahl* and lime pickles blessed by the Master for the workers to feast as they toiled. Santosh's old nurse, from Amritsar, had been working all day in a crèche for the babies of mothers receiving initiation. Twenty-seven thousand people will, in the next twenty-one days, receive initiation from the Master.

Santosh and Ajay came for me after the *satsang* ceremony which I did not attend. Professor Kochhar drove us round the *dera*. It is like a small kingdom, self-sufficient, where all that is used and consumed is grown and made: fields of wheat and vegetables beyond the walls of the ashram, on land which has itself increased as the river Beas has moved its course, as if by miracle (they would have seen it so in the Middle Ages also). Bricks are made from the earth itself, for more and yet more buildings—guest-houses for families, and for women, great spacious airy halls to shelter the multitude for the Master's *satsang* when the weather is cold and wet; clinics, a hospital, a school, workrooms where women stitch garments, everything is there, and all the work of *seva*. There is even a clinic where every year a group of eye-specialists come for a month to give their skill. We saw the newly harvested wheat being ground into that fine flour, fragrant of Mother Earth; heaps of rice being winnowed—I have never before seen that archaic cradle of

Dionysus, the winnowing-fan, in use—and great barns where wheat and maize and rice and lentils and gram are stored, house-sparrows nesting in the perforations of the bricks in that sparrow-land of Cockaigne.

We saw 'buses departing, laden with pilgrims, others streaming out on foot, bundles on their heads, brilliantly clad women from Rajasthan, white cotton turbans from Madras, toothless old women from who knows where singing lustily, and here and there little companies of the sweeping-women, and women cooking the numberless *chapatties*.

I said, let us eat again in the *langar*; so, having taken Professor Kochhar home from the garden whose flowers so love him, Santosh, Timkoo and I returned through the service door we had entered two days ago; we were late, but a place was found for us in the shade of a wall, near the barn where the *chapatties* are stacked; again we were served with delicious *dahl* and vegetables and lime pickle, brought by a beautiful grave little boy with a ragged turban who poured our water for us like Ganymede himself, and served the lime pickle with his fingers. Here in the *dera* the water is fresh and good and I forgot about asking if it was boiled, as had become a habit elsewhere. To refuse to drink it would be like insisting that the water of the rivers of Paradise be boiled. We took our plates to wash, according to custom, under one of the taps provided, and one of the Punjabi ladies collecting the plates to finish off and return to use, asked if I would like to do *seva*. So we were set, Santosh and I, and Timkoo too, to sealing cellophane bags of *prasad* (puffed rice), the food the Master blesses and distributes. I was offered as a seat one of those wicker baskets carried on the head, supported on a little round pad (there were heaps of both these about). Hard to get down, harder still to get up again! But with the *seva* ladies there was nothing for it but the ground, so I knelt opposite my partner, who folded the top of the bag and passed it to me to seal against a hot iron bar; each bag to be given a shake before it is put into one of those numberless baskets to be heaped and carried away. I was not very good at first but improved with practice (the art is to seal the bag without either failing to touch the bar enough to seal it, or scorching the cellophane so that it shrivels up).

I was told that sixty-five per cent of the people of the Punjab are Maharaj Charan Singh's disciples. The *langar* is blessed and distributed three hundred and sixty five days of the year. Little wonder that the Master had said to me all those years ago that it is 'a personal matter' whether we live in the Golden Age or in the Kali-Yuga. At least for a moment I could almost feel 'with the flow', sitting on the ground with those cheeful peasant women—the same everywhere, hospitable, clean, simple, friendly and welcoming. They told me to come back later, and to send other guests at the Hostel, for they would be working there, they said, until ten o'clock at night. And after all I too had been a peasant child, nor did I ever wish to leave that golden age where I and my schoolfellows went barefoot on the dusty stone outcrop that was Bavington's main road that belonged to us all. So in a sort of way, sealing bags of *prasad* with the Punjabi ladies from the villages was not so very different from those long-ago preparations for a 'whist drive and social' for Bavington's stone kirk of Covenanter memory, and old Mr Howatson's long sermons as he preached the word of the one God: 'But they that wait upon the Lord shall renew their strength: they shall mount up with wings as eagles; they shall run, and not weary; they shall walk, and not faint'. I flew with the eagles then, and in old age I can at least walk with the toothless old women with glittering black eyes who come to look at me with kindly curiosity and greet me with *namaskara*. The terrorists are outside the bounds of this happy place that is grounded in life's barest simplicities, yet where these multitudes of men and women, learned or unlearned, look always towards a vision of the supreme.

❦

Yesterday, with Santosh and Ajay, I was received for half an hour by the Master. Santosh did most of the talking, for which I was glad. Maharaj Charan Singh is well aware of the things of this world, a man of practical wisdom. I gave him, having nothing better to give, a copy of *Temenos* 10 and told him that Keith Critchlow (from whom I brought a message), had been a co-founder; that I remembered his wise counsel of three years ago; thanked him for the privilege of a third visit. Unspoken was my *not* asking for initiation. If he is a true Master he must have discerned my unspoken reasons. I have lived my life, and on that life 'Jesus, the Imagination', the Judge within, has already pronounced the judgment incurred by the loveless, 'I know ye not, go from me'.* For a long minute that wise, beautiful Master looked at me. Perhaps he read all this. 'And forbye', as my mother would have said in her Scots pride—it comes to me in her tongue,

---

* A friend who wishes to be unnamed, who has read this manuscript, has passionately denied this view and writes—'Kathleen, you can never, never, *never* be rejected by the Christ. Don't you realize that you were *given* to him at your baptism? The everlasting arms have always encircled you and still do. At that level of divinity there is no jealousy, no possessiveness. Whether your spirit turns to the Christ, or Buddha, or Allah or Bhagwan, or Ahura Mazda or to none of these, matters not a whit. What matters is *freedom* and *love,* for the spirit of man cannot be fettered. "In freedom it arises, towards freedom it moves, in freedom it rests" write the seers of the Upanishads, and your own scriptures assert the same: "The wind bloweth where it listeth. Thou hearest the sound thereof" but this wind cannot be caught and imprisoned. You have suffered and gone beyond. It is enough.'

But it is not that I have exchanged one Divine Name for another, under whatever name the loveless are rejected. 'Some good I mean to do' like the Bastard in *King Lear* (not that he succeeded!) but no longer see it as important whether I am 'saved' or 'lost' so long as I can accomplish while I am still in this world my appointed task. But my friend's beautiful words are, again, spoken from the deeps of that spiritual culture I have called 'the India of the Imagination'.

although my English Protestant father would have said the same, as did my Master William Blake—that the God Within, the Inner Light, is in all, and that no Master save the Holy Spirit is needed to instruct the soul. Again and again I have found how deep-rooted here in India is the tradition that each Master gathers his flock, present for them as Jesus for his Disciples. Is there something I have not understood, perhaps never will understand, lacking the sixth sense which experiences these things as living reality? All these beautiful Punjabi people love their Master as his disciples must have loved Jesus. To me he is a wise, serene, beautiful presence, this uncrowned priest-king of the Golden Age. My friend Prince Kumar knows full well that for all the *mantram* he gave me, and which from time to time I repeat, that my only true link with higher worlds is my poetry; he is forever telling me so. Kumar does not believe in the value of mass-movements, but in small, unostentatious groups. Both no doubt have their place. For a moment I could be—or could wish to be—at one with the multitude at the everlasting sacred meal all humankind share. I have in my day 'joined' too many things—the Roman Church, the Society of the Inner Light, evaded the Communist party when my husband and his friends were seeing salvation there; Shanti Sadan was a near miss. Blake has been, I suppose, my only total commitment. But my wiser self knows that every life is an unique pilgrimage, no two alike; that we learn from many men and women on the way. My father and mother, my Aunty Peggy Black, Mr Howatson the Minister who on alternate Sundays bicycled from Stamfordham to Bavington Church there to instruct us; Germain d'Hangest, my long ago French mentor, Humphrey Jennings and Julian Trevelyan my friends at Cambridge, David Gascoyne, Tambi, Helen Sutherland, Fr. Pius the Carmelite, Gay Taylor, Winifred Nicholson (I evaded Christian Science, however), Cecil Collins, Rafael Nadal and many besides. Why then should I become a devotee of this shepherd of another flock? Yet I hope that good Master of his people knows that 'some good I mean to do', even though for him (and he would of course be right) 'doing good' would not be the point at all. Nor indeed for myself; some poetry I still hope to write would be nearer the truth.

No one, said Mrs Desai, who presides over the guest house, ever wants to leave. But my experience of the ashram at Beas, such as it has been, was complete. I have left too many loved places for this departure to cause even a mild regret: rather I am grateful to have rich memories of the Golden Age to carry away. We did not leave too early, for when the roads are otherwise empty terrorists are abroad—broad daylight is relatively safe. We travelled without incident and arrived at Civil Lines at about nine in the evening. But in the paper next morning there was an account of an ambush on the road we had lately travelled. The Chief of Police in Amritsar had been ambushed and owed his life to the bullet-proof windows of his car having proved more effective than the bullets of his assailants. Such is the green and pleasant land of the Five Rivers!

It is easy to describe external events and appearances, but how convey immeasurable qualities? To the West knowlege is information and its application; here in India knowledge is something else altogether, it is a way of being, a state of mind, it pertains to a quality of consciousness. Mental states, degrees of awareness are infinitely variable, between Blake's state of those 'sunk in deadly sleep' and the awareness of enlightened Masters, with every degree between. But what is common to all within this civilization of the spirit is a recognition of that range and scope, and the aspiration even of simple people, their orientation; and who can say that the illiterate multitudes of India do not participate in a fuller knowledge than the intellectual specialists of Western and westernized Universities whose culture-heroes are technologists who can manipulate nature to produce material results. Many of these half-million people whose beloved Master is the teacher of a spiritual path, may be illiterate, yet aspire to a sacred source, enjoy the sense of living within the context of a spiritual order in which 'we live, and move, and have our being', a context which gives meaning to life at all levels and stages of development. Their desires and aims are other than those of the Western populace, their aspirations and their sense of values and the direction of their quest. Again I remember the little stone kirk at Bavington where just such simple believers held that 'man's chief end is to glorify God and to enjoy him forever'. Just as here families converge on the ashram in tongas and buses, so those from every remote farm, on the Sabbath, drove to church in their traps, the same journey to the holy place on the holy day. In the *dera* I saw the same simple children of Mother Earth, farmers and their wives, held within what Yeats calls 'unity of culture'. Blessed are the meek for they shall inherit the earth. Whatever the future may hold, these people are here and now. Spiritual orientation is a norm making possible (Yeats again) 'unity of being' within that culture. It is not only the exceptionally endowed, but all human beings who have within us the light of understanding, which cannot be measured in terms of 'intelligence quotients'. Wisdom is to be found in fields and villages where indeed life's values and meanings are better understood than by most of our 'experts'. Here in Beas one is reminded of the 'simple rules of life' that secular Western culture with all its technology has forgotten. These beautiful faces tell a secret lost to us.

※

A brief expedition to Agra was planned and executed in my honour by Timkoo. We left soon after 6 a.m. and this time the road lay south, a route that passed through an industrial zone comprising both Delhi and Haryana; many small, new, clean factories and other enterprises built in spacious grounds planted with young trees. One sees such things but without feeling that the vast problem of poverty grows any less. A lovely road to Agra, beautiful keekar trees with brilliant yellow flowers. Why had I remembered on the road to Agra an avenue of banyan trees? Old trees there were, but the only banyan I saw is in the outer court of the Taj Mahal itself. Is there, anywhere, that avenue of banyans my memory had given to the Agra road? Doubtless my imagination deemed them worthy of the approach to the city of Akbar and Shah Jehan. We stayed at one of those excellent State tourist bungalows (Timkoo playing host) clean, simply equipped rooms with all that is necessary for a traveller, and good simple Indian food. We stopped on the way at Sikandra for an hour or two while Timkoo took photographs of the gentle monkey-families who are the tenants of that monument to Akbar's glory and his might. Monkey-families, tree-squirrels streaking from tree to tree, little deer, tame and secure under their shade. Beauty and history and sun and flowers. I bought some agate necklaces from a blind man to bring back as gifts. Later we lingered in the gardens of the Taj itself, while Timkoo photographed; and next morning visited the Fort, which I had not seen on my previous visits to Agra. Never before or since so great a castle, such a sense of glory. We lingered in that small exquisite room where Shah Jehan at the end of his life lived, imprisoned by his son Aurungzeb, victor in the war to the death between his four sons. On one wall of that room was a small glass in which he could see reflected the all-worshipped tomb of the beloved. Deserted splendour, scene of such loves and such murders, cruelties surpassing those in the Thousand and One Nights. The fanatical Islamic warrior Aurungzeb survived the romantic Prince Dara, son of the beloved Mumtaz Begum. Now all is empty and silent, the glory departed of Akbar and Jehangir and Shah Jehan and Dara; Aurungzeb too, for all his victorious battles; but so has the more enlightened but stuffier ascendency of that British Governor of India's Northern Provinces whose Victorian Gothic tomb is planted squarely in front of the throne-room of the Mogul emperors. Such are the ironies of history, but beauty remains—the incomparable Taj, and the Pearl Mosque, now unfortunately closed. The British left law, and railways, and, of course cricket and a barracks within the walls of the Red Fort of Delhi, but no Pearl Mosque, no Taj Mahal. Santosh does not like me to praise Islamic architecture, and points out Rajasthani and other influences; and yet what a vision, what a sense of glory created over a few years those miracles of beauty from the Alhambra to Ispahan, to Sikandra and the Pearl Mosque and the Taj Mahal itself. The eternal India has seen many empires come and go.

On the drive back to Delhi we began to pass, along the road, all sorts of tongas, bicycles, ox-carts, buffalo-carts, camel-carts, tractors, merry parties of the young on foot and the old crowded into every kind of wheeled transport invented from the times of Mohenjo Daro to the present, all in their glittering best, their faces lit up with delight, all thronging in one direction. At first we thought they were returning from some village fair, but we presently saw that they were making their way to the festival of a village goddess, whose temple we could presently see, a field away from the road—all that festive throng of mothers and babies, boys and girls and old women, some of them singing. As we drove on we met others converging from the opposite direction, bright saris and laughing eyes. People, I reflected, are made happy by people, all seemed happy because they were together, brothers and sisters and neighbours and relations, all speaking the same language, singing the same songs, travelling to the village shrine of the one Goddess. So they must have gathered before the Moghuls, before Alexander perhaps, that wild pupil of Aristotle, and so after the British and their organization, on just such days of early summer, and so may it always be. As so often, it was again India's simplicities that spoke to me more deeply than her splendours, as from long ago, once again, came a breath of Bavington and the Girls' Friendly Society, of sheets of foolscap written by us school children in our best cursive script, pinned up on some gatepost on a farm track where they were sure to be seen, announcing a 'whist drive and social' at Bavington school. People who had known one another all their lives, happy to be together, and whose days would be long in the land. What if the throng who now as from time immemorial, celebrate the festivals, ride in tractors and crowd into lorries, their joy is the same. In the crowded markets and bazaars the trash of the machine has displaced the beautiful work of human hands, but the people are the same, the joy is the same. And the poverty.

But that is an India I shall see only from afar, for in its nature it depends on that kinship of family and village, of knowing the same songs, sharing some village idol who from the *mundus imaginalis* presides in some local shrine. Then I think of the shanty settlements, the alienation, the slow undermining of the India of the Imagination by the Industrial Revolution and the inner desolation that follows. Or need it be so? We would like to think that material prosperity is not incompatible with the soul's country. But where there is property, greed and material interests prevail, and all the locks and bolts with which the Indian middle class guards its own. Yet in the towns too there are temples—in Agra one temple was alight when we went back to our guest house, alight with a thousand fairy lights and an overflowing crowd singing. A temple of Rama, Santosh thought, and I thought I caught a glimpse of an image of Hanuman, as we drove past the open doors. In the morning the crowd was still singing hymns, as they must have continued all night.

❈

Keshav Malik took me, one happy morning, to the studio of the painter, Kishori Kaul, and we sat among her pictures, which somewhat reminded me, in her vision of colour and light, the flow of light on water and flowers, of Winifred Nicholson, as did also the scent of paint. It was like a return to a familiar world. Her studio is in Babar Lane, near Bengali Market, in Delhi's Latin Quarter, where Ramu Gandhi also lives, where Delhi's artists and intellectuals have made for themselves that everlasting Paris of the Imagination; Triveni is close by. Keshav's wife, Usha, works all day at the Indian Council for Cultural Relations, and Keshav meanwhile lives the free life of the poet and art critic. During my remaining days Keshav played the role of my escort in Delhi's world of the arts. He thought I would like Kishori's work, and indeed I did. Kishori, again like Winifred, is the granddaughter of a painter—her great grandfather was a Kashmiri miniaturist, and her grandmother used to paint the backgrounds. Presently Ramu joined us; 'Satsang', he said—the word means 'sitting together in the presence of "being"' (sat). Such, he said, is the essence of India. To flow with the great anonymous river of the multitude, or just to watch that river flow, is moving and impressive, but to someone like myself is, after all, somewhat unreal. But to sit talking in a timeless way, with four people in complete understanding, the perfect participation of the imaginative intelligence, that is as near to perfect happiness as life can bring. Perhaps 'fellowship' might once have carried Ramu's meaning of satsang; Blake calls it 'brotherhood' (in contrast to 'love' of which Blake has a rather low opinion) and it is indeed a kind of kinship, we being all the children of the one Presence. Kishori said she would like to paint my portrait; I

[246]

accepted with alacrity, just for the sake of returning to that oasis.

Ramu was anxious to know what I had felt about the *dera* at Beas. I told him how moved I had been to see the multitude gathered to hear the word of God from their Master; but that for myself I could not accept that bond of allegiance to a living 'perfect Master' as something needful, and had at no time contemplated becoming a devotee of the Master of Beas. Keshav at once said, 'Of course not!'; being a poet himself he knows what a poet can and cannot do—what after all is poetry but listening to the universal music? Keshav had used the same phrase, 'Of course not!' when I had explained to him that I could not see Sri Aurobindo's *Savitri* as a great poem—or indeed as poetry at all. With Keshav one does not have to spell these things out. Tambi's friend Prince Kumar also knows very well that the *yoga* of a poet is poetry. Poetry, that is, that conforms with Blake's definition—'one thing alone makes a poet: Imagination, the Divine Vision'. These words are altogether in keeping with India's traditional understanding of poetry, though scarcely with that of the secular West.

But Ramu defended India's age-old traditional view, seeing in the living bond between Master and disciples a participation in *advaita*, the many-in-one and one-in-many of the Master's realization of the universal Self. As Swedenborg and Blake understood that the Divine Humanity is made up of 'the innumerable multitudes of eternity'. Ramu's Master is Ramana Maharshi whom he never met, but whom he loves. (Do I love William Blake in that way?) Ramu can no more understand why we of the West shy away from commitment to a Master than I can wholly understand why in India this seems so indispensable. I seem to see that to Ramu this bond is no more in need of explanation than why people 'fall in love'; it is just one of the profound basic experiences of life. Love again, that

[247]

universal medium or network in which our lives are invisibly united. It seems that there is something I do not understand. Perhaps it is, again, love, for our austere Western 'umpire conscience' may be a guide to conduct but to love the 'God within' is scarcely possible, there is no relationship. A Master one could love, as his disciples loved Jesus; even he since become an abstraction or a fiction.

❀

I said, that on this visit I scarcely knew whether to see India more as a tragic country or as a holy one. Ramu said he hoped as both, but of course went on to deny that India has any monopoly of that truth and reality which is one everywhere. But he did allow, with loving pride, that 'we have always preserved a certain sacred core'. May it always be so! 'Television' I said; and once more the conversation took that downward turn I have found again and again on this visit. Did I simply not notice it before, or is India experiencing a crisis of self-examination, as she is swept into the current of the modern world? Finally I said, 'Ramu, let us admit that the world may be on the brink of self-destruction, that turn where we will we see a decline in values, not to speak of the boundless want and suffering. How, then, should we face the truth that the Destroyer is no less a divine aspect than the Creator or the Preserver? We should always recognize this, Ramu said, we are unwilling to face it; destruction is also from God. Yes indeed, I reflected, the materialist West always believes that Science will provide some 'fix' to remove from us the consequences of our actions. Ramu, as a theologian and philosopher, has set himself to confront this problem, not to evade it.

Kishori led me to her painting room, that opens on a little garden of casual flowers and sparrows and a fragrant champak tree, to prepare her thoughts on the portrait. Ramu left to meet a friend at Triveni, where, presently, we all three joined him to eat a simple dish of rice, *dahl* and vegetables. Ramu eats there every day, conversing with friends in the morning, then returning to his room to work. India's daily food; followed by sweetened tea—if you ask for tea it comes ready sweetened. At last, here in Delhi, I felt not a visitor, official or unofficial, but simply sitting with my friends, as it might be in my own country or in Paris, or in Massachussetts; and almost, though never quite, in beautiful Rome, of whose 'learned Italian things' I have never felt quite worthy. Or rather, to be truthful I never felt wholly at ease at the heart of Christendom. We dispersed to our respective tasks, Ramu to think out an *advaita* that will embrace both ends and beginnings (which Greek philospher wrote 'Beginnings are better than endings'? No Indian philosopher would be so naïve as to make any distinction in an event between beginning and ending; the *lingam* of fertility already is the dancer in the crematorium). Kishori returned to her studio and Keshav and I to talk about poetry; that endless unbroken *satsang* whose participants come and go, meet now in Athens, or Ispahan, or Nalanda, Cambridge, Paris, Dublin, or Dallas Texas, but whose theme is the thread of which civilization is spun, and which runs on until the yarn runs out in Erda's music, Loge's fire or the primal waters of the Rhine maidens, or whatever sound current of the Universe the holy men of India listen to. Keshav no less than Ramu confronts the worst—not in ultimates but in his determined confrontation of unwelcome immediacies, black images on a ground of darkness, but seeking, no less than Ramu, a poet's *advaita* that includes all. Kishori's vision dissolves all into light, as does this magnificent sun of India, no mere symbol or metaphor of divinity whose epiphany moves from his brilliant rising in the cool dawn, through the annihilating blaze of noon, to the crimson magnificence of sunset.

I returned to Kishori Kaul's studio next morning. The

[249]

champak tree outside the little studio where Kishori works was dropping its first fragrant flowers on the grass patch. As I sat for Kishori, looking at the designated spot on the back of her canvas, my mind returned in memory to Bank's Head, and Winifred Nicholson's garden at ease, her rooms, her flowers, many remembered pictures I had been the first to see, resummoning them all; and to my nearby Mousehole with its garden and the garden birds, the apple trees and the roses—Celeste, Mme Hardy, Blanc Double de Coubert, Charles de Mille, Tuscany, the Schoolmaster's Rose, Those long-ago roses. They rose before my mind's eye as Kishori worked. From time to time she carried her canvas into her inner room to look at her work and allowed—requested—me to do so also, and to comment. This Winifred would not have done until the work was finished, and she herself returned to this world from that other, painter's world that would not release her until the work was done. Kishori came and went. It was balm to my spirit to be with a painter at work, she in the world of imagination reflected in her intelligent face; too long since I had looked through that door into the magic garden. She worked through the day, with a brief break for a simple dish of vegetables, and in the afternoon telephoned Keshav to come and see the result. I had brought Kishori a copy of my *Selected Poems,* and for Keshav a tape of *On a Deserted Shore.* Kishori played it on her tape-recorder. Earlier I had read her a few poems, so that she should know 'whom she was painting'. What Kishori painted on that first day reminded me of Gloriana's 'mask of youth'. I saw my presence materializing on the canvas, but not my aged features. Mohan, who presently arrived, commented on the absence of my old age; but this neither surprised nor troubled me: Kishori was 'looking for the face I had/Before the world was made'. A timeless presence.

Next morning I returned, and Kishori worked like a sibyl on the blue robe she had made of my dark cotton dress, and a touch here and there brought a presence (mine?) into her canvas. Suddenly she stopped, knelt on the floor in front of the canvas, signed her name, and it was done!

As she again prepared a simple lunch, she asked me to tell her the story of my life. I wondered what I could bring from my store of memories to enrich this painter's imagination; and found myself describing the well at Bavington and the sand grains dancing in the clear water; and how the snow for certain days built around us a sanctuary, inaccessible to the outer world—such things as these—and at last I came to Tambi, my first publisher, and how he had loved my poems and believed in me always. 'Tambi', she exclaimed, 'But I met him! 'And Kishori Kaul, it seems, had been the very last artist whose work Tambi had chosen. It was Keshav who had given her, on her visiting London, a letter of introduction to Tambi, then living and working at the October Gallery. 'But what had he done with his life!' she exclaimed. At half past ten in the morning he was already drunk, his head and shoulders bowed over a table, his lank slate gray hair, and the bottle beside him half empty: could this be that wonderful Tambi of whom Keshav had told her? He had offered her a cup of tea; and she had unrolled her canvasses. And she painted a picture of the mind, to the life, of how Tambi raised his head, he came to life; he was delighted, he too had 'seen' her work, instantly, as I had, as belonging to the only world he loved, the world of the Imagination. He had called the American girl: 'Chili! We will give her a show!' But when, a few days later, Kishori had telephoned, Tambi was already dead. He had fallen from the gallery where he used to sleep, and his neck was broken. Kishori had not 'taken to' the Americans to whom the October Gallery belonged, and had not followed up Tambi's offer to show her work there.

But neither Keshav nor I saw Tambi's as a wasted life, no, no, he was a sort of drunken *rishi* living in the inner freedom of those who do not care for money or respectability one way or the other; whether asking for money, or giving with princely unconcern to whoever happened to be in need, deserving or undeserving, it made no difference, for he loved us all. So Keshav and I chanted his praise in antiphon—not a wasted life, a wonderful, love-bestowing life. Not for the first time I silently reproached myself for keeping a bourgeois distance from Tambi in his later years—the measure of my own estrangement from poetry, not of Tambi's. When it is too late, how inevitably, how clearly we understand who are the Messengers from the Castle! How I had pinned my young foolish ambitious hopes on being published by T. S. Eliot among the Faber poets, whereas in reality with none of these poets (Auden, Spender, Day Lewis and the rest) with the sole exception of Vernon Watkins, whose work at that time I had scarcely troubled to read, had I, as a poet, anything in common. None were poets of the Imagination, but rather of its absence. But Tambi was of that world, recognized it in me, knew me better than I knew myself. I had neither the insight nor the courage to entrust myself wholly and solely to my inspiring daimon. Had I done so, who knows—would I have been a better poet if I had plunged into Bohemia, rather than into all those years of reading old books in the North Library? Who can say? Gay Taylor used to compare destiny to the veins of a leaf, whose network leads by devious routes only to the one central vein—we will, by one way or another, fulfil our destiny. So to Kishori I said, never vacillate, never lose the thread, or betray that other, the only real world, that other dimension, in which Tambi lived always. Not indeed that she is likely to do so, she has the quality of a dedicated artist, and it is I who felt reproached in the light of her paintings, that Tambi had also 'seen'. She has painted me in that light—an evanescent face; weighed down by a dark blue robe—for such my dress has become. Keshav sees Tambi as I do. We loved him. Kishori met him too late. Or perhaps not quite too late, for it was as if Tambi himself was present with us in that studio in Delhi's Latin Quarter, as we spoke of him, and of the world of poetry where he was a prince incognito.

India, I seem to discern, dissolves all into light, or into darkness. Kishori's light turns all surfaces into a blaze or shimmer of light, on river, on flower, or as I now experienced it, my own face. Surya daily brings that all-dissolving light. The Indian experience is of 'a deep and dazzling darkness' or of an all-dissolving light. So in Kishori's portrait my face flows with the river of light.

❀

Next day it was the turn of Ramu, who brought with him Nirmal Verma, whose paper entitled 'The Twilight of an Era' had electrified me. We met at the International Centre, Ramu with his handloom woven jacket and his monk-like hair, Nirmal Verma with the suffering intelligent face of a writer, a sufferer's face whose like I have seen elsewhere, but for his gentle brown Indian eyes. He had lived in Czechoslovakia for eight years, leaving India in disillusionment with the Communist Party, to which as a young man he had belonged, returning when the Russians invaded Czechoslovakia. Perhaps it was of Edwin Muir he reminded me, whose story was so parallel. Concerned, like Edwin, with the human predicament in ways deeper than a merely political thinker or writer, he speaks for the India of the Imagination; in sorrow and bitterness and love. Burning sorrow and anger at the undermining of Indian civilization by the British imposition of a system of values other than those of India. I do not know enough of India's former social structure, nor of how the British law (which India has in essence retained) undermined its workings. In all good faith the British administered British justice; if India's justice is otherwise it is surely because established in a world-order so much more subtle

[253]

and inclusive—and elusive?—than a justice based largely on property, which undermines the self-image of any Indian within a more complex structure of duties and relationships, built up over millennia. Nirmal understands that such a system cannot be tampered with—pull out one thread and the whole fabric unravels:

> Is it possible to keep alive the rituals linked with a tree, once a forest is destroyed? Can a peasant preserve the entire mythology, the innate sense of religiosity, grown out of this age-old relation to environment, once he is uprooted from his land? How long will it survive in a Bombay slum, once he is driven there under the thrust of industrialization? A river dried up, a village uprooted, a forest destroyed, they are not mere ecological and economic disasters. The wound they inflict is deeper: they destroy the physical habitat, in which a culture orders its meanings, connects its insights in a coherent vision . . .

Thus while I can still see that only from India can we of the West re-learn the values and realities of the spirit, I see ever more sadly how threatened are these age-old states of being here in India. We are one world now, and India is being swept on the tide of time, with the rest. Where will the seed of Indian civilization grow when in India the tree is felled?

Nirmal gave me the address of his London agent, who has since sent me a passage (in English translation from Hindi) from a recent novel, *The Red Tin Roof*. I felt the reproach (not from Ramu or from Nirmal, but from myself) of being a member of the nation which had inflicted the wound; of being, besides, rarified élitist that I am, not deeply 'engaged' in the sorrows and soul of 'the great human family' (Czeslaw Milosz's phrase, he too a writer engaged in the struggles and sorrows of humankind); but Ramu said, 'we are a family' and so indeed I feel we are. Having read Nirmal Verma's essays, *Word and Memory* I seem to divine how deeply he is indebted not only to Gandhiji but to Ramu himself. Both are looking into the possibility that we are at the very brink of the end not merely of a materialist civilisation, so obviously spiritually bankrupt, but of the earth itself; I seem to recognize in Nirmal Verma's writings Ramu's 'stance' and again catch an awesome glimpse of the Indian scale and scope—into what light, into what darkness will our world dissolve? Or (Ramu's image) like Abhimanyu's unborn child, will life survive the Great Battle, reaffirm itself to renew the Golden Age, the great beauty of creation?

Ramu has but to sit down in any public place and people come to him—former students, an Orthodox Bishop, an ecologist at a nearby table engaged in planting oaks in the devastated Himalayas; who was sitting at the same table with (perhaps not surprisingly) Satish Kumar's friend Edward Goldsmith, who also came over to speak with us. I explained that I was trying to persuade Nirmal Verma to contribute to *Temenos*, and he at once said that *Temenos* is the most distinguished Review, was it in Europe, in the English language, or in the West? No matter—but I was grateful and not a little surprised to discover that he thought so. Another of Ramu's friends, and his wife, also joined us, a teacher and exponent of 'communications techniques', and this gave Ramu the idea that he would like to interview me on television this week. We look for wisdom to and in one another, on our brink, in our melting pot, alembic or dream, or *satsang*. Meanwhile Ramu started putting me to the test—what led me to where I am now (and where am I now?) what in childhood, what was I seeking, what did I find lacking in the poetry and thought of my generation at Cambridge? Ramu had been at Oxford—at University College—and knows that world from inside, and what it lacks, though a generation younger than I. What I find in Ramu that Nirmal Verma perhaps does not wholly participate, is his total devotion to the sacred, combined with a total refusal to reject any human being or point of view. His *advaita* is deeply rooted, in himself and in his culture. He keeps pulling me up when I am condemnatory or dismissive. His resolute determination to exclude nothing—neither evil (Hitler) not violence, Salman Rushdie's blasphemy, the mechanistic theory of the Universe, no matter what; to acknowledge the Destroyer no less than the Creater and the Sustainer. Is it this same meaning of all-embracing totality that gives beauty to the faces of the Punjabis who find their wholeness in the initiation they receive from Maharaj Charan Singh, or those happy country people on their way to worship the Goddess at a village festival? Ramu always brings me back to the need to exclude *nothing*, not science and technology, not materialism, not evil even, all somehow must be accepted, included, understood.

Who can understand? Perhaps those holy men whose presence in this profound land, even now, bears witness. Is it that as the love of the leopard who died, for his master, had become the knowledge of another leopard—of leopards—is it enough that a holy man has experienced a vision of reality, to change the 'morphic field' of all humankind, or of a race? Ramu believes so; and added that Hitler put into our human consciousness knowledge of evil: we all now know these things, they are part of the world's self-knowledge. Obviously Ramana Maharshi did create such a 'morphic field' and the wild creatures knew this secret, closed to me. The mongoose and the peacock who cried all night on his roof· on the night the saint died. Humankind may fail to recognize love, but animals never do.

A few days later Ramu visited me in my room at the India International Centre for a long deep discussion of the television interview which we were to make together on the following Sunday. We settled the main points—the necessity that decrees that 'man cannot live by bread alone', and the exclusion of sacred knowledge from modern Western culture and education; the 'learning of the Imagination' which in a measure I have sought to restore, through my own work and through *Temenos*; my debt to my mother; my daimon; and finally 'why I love India!' Ramu was pleased when I referred to the story in the *Mahabharata* of how Hanuman explained to his half-brother Bhima (both were 'sons of the wind') that whereas in the Golden Age (the *Ramayana* tells of the Golden Age) he could leap from India to Lanka, could carry to the battlefield the mountain with the healing herbs, and perform all his mighty feats, now in the Kali-Yuga he was only a poor old monkey. For in the Golden Age humankind knew the whole of reality—ourselves and our world. At the beginning of the Silver Age a quarter was lost; at the end of the bronze age, a third quarter, so that now, in the Kali-Yuga we live in only a quarter of reality. 'That's it' I remember saying to myself when I read the passage, 'that's what it feels like to live in a world aware only of the material order', we know there is more, but it is beyond our reach. But (and this quite apart from spiritual Masters and teachers) the people of India still live within sight and hearing of higher worlds, echoes of the silver and the golden ages still reach villagers and pilgrims, the multitudes who gather to hear the teaching from some Master, and that vision still shines in those gentle brown eyes one meets everywhere. India still lives in more than a quarter of reality. 'When are you coming back?' was to be Ramu's last question. Unanswerable of course: I am an old woman. But I said, 'Space is no separation, I shall not leave you'.

The interview itself took place in the shady outdoor sculpture courtyard at Triveni, where at half past seven in the cool of the morning Ramu awaited me, with the director of the film, and the cameraman. He told us how we were to approach, from under a small tree, conversing, then sit on a stone bench, facing one another at right-angles; a simple enough arrangement, one would have thought. Ramu's questions were rich and profound, and our conversation flowed almost as well as if there had been no camera; until the moment came when the director (Balu, named from Ganesha's war-god brother) said to Ramu 'now you must repeat your questions'. It transpired that the camera had been directed only at me with Ramu nowhere to be seen. This Alice-in-Wonderland situation could only be resolved by Ramu's repeating the 'questions' he had asked me! There was much heated argument, for how can 'questions' be repeated from a flowing dialogue? Modern technology, it seems, has not (at least here in New Delhi) mastered the problem of photographing two people at once with one camera. But there was no help for it; Ramu and I racked our memories for the way the dialogue had gone. Balu insisted that it would be all right when it was edited. Meanwhile Keshav and a neighbour of Ramu's had arrived and Surya had risen high, and the moment came to move to Kishori's studio, where the programme was to continue, with the portrait. Here things went better—Balu, no longer militant, proved to be a great lover of Shakespeare and a reader of English poetry. Kishori, looking very splendid in her *kurta*, spoke of why she had wanted to paint a portrait of my 'essential self'. A friend from the Swiss embassy was with her, all eagerness to talk to·me about the Women's Movement, and was quite disappointed when I assured him that I had never found my work undervalued because I am a woman. Not for a moment, I said; women of talent are free to produce whatever work lies in our power, and those who

[258]

complain that but for sex discrimination they might have written the plays of Shakespeare, the works of Beethoven, etc., etc., make this fantasy the absurd pretext for their not having done so. Women, after all, have been in the world as long as men, we are not the invention or discovery of the second half of the twentieth century. Both Kishori and I have produced our work, nobody has prevented us from doing so. In India's crafts tradition the work of women is no less valued than that of men. All the same it is true that at other levels of society women, even now, are without due rights—bride-burnings are reported in the press; not necessarily by the bridegroom but more often by in-laws who want a bigger dowry, a television set, a refrigerator. Women of power and influence, talent and independence, are not lacking; but it's done by 'woman-power', not by 'women's lib'.

๏

Keshav took me to see the work of other painters besides Kishori. The brilliant and powerful Tantra paintings of Biren De we had published in *Temenos*, introduced by Keshav. Biren De, having passed through an early phase of life-drawing and experimenting in contemporary Western styles, has made his way back to—or forward to—works essentially Indian in spirit. Those brilliant blinding colours belong to Surya's realm. One evening Keshav took me to see work by his friend Khosa—highly skilful and accomplished, it is hard to say whether his strange vision of many heads sprouting from rocky confinement are a personal nightmare or an invasion of our sick world-soul. There is in his work in general an absence of the feminine, much as in the recent male-obsessed school of Francis Bacon. In only one appeared (as it seemed to me) a redemptive feminine sheltering presence. I suggested to him that release of these prisoners (had not Michelangelo also known them?) might

[259]

come from allowing the feminine principle to come into his work. Yet, on the wall of this painter so painfully reflecting the tensions of this time, was a large photograph of a face I could not for the moment place: Vivekananda! It seems that his wife and her mother are devotees of Vivekananda; they fast twice a month at 'the full and the dark' of Yeats's lunar cycle, and because of this his wife was unable to join us when we went out to eat. That 'more than a quarter' is never far away.

For a long time we discussed the possibilities, problems, cost and so on, of a Review of the arts which Keshav is seriously hoping to start in India; an idea I have certainly encouraged, for it seems that there is much work being done, both in writing and in painting, which would benefit from the context of a Review. Great works are not isolated phenomena, but grow from, and in, a context; 'That civilization may not sink', the scaffolding where Michelangelo reclines must be built and upheld by many, some known, some unknown. Civilization is not a solitary achievement, but the unending converse we hold with one another over the centuries and over the world. Keshav did formerly edit a Review which came to an end at the time of 'the Emergency'. But whether in France, Massachussetts, or in my own country, money is ever the problem, and Delhi is no exception. Keshav had, in fact, managed to raise enough funding for a first issue, but this had (he hopes only temporarily) disappeared. The theme of how to finance a Review, or publications of work not produced from the profit motive which so well serves the unoriginal and the second rate, has many variations.

On another evening Keshav took me to see yet another of Delhi's painters, Rameshwar Broota, and his wife Sobha, also a painter, who live and work in Triveni. Again I was following in Tambi's footsteps, who had known their work. Sobha had at that time painted birds, but now pleasant abstract circles of light. Rameshwar is a more powerful painter—great black landscapes—if landscapes they can be called—worked in a laborious technique that might be seen as a form of meditation, slowing down the composition of those dark images of the Kali-Yuga. The most memorable is a reclining rotting corpse which is also a range of hills, an image of a grave grandeur; from the decay runs one living vein, a mere thread of life that seems to promise renewal. The big canvas on which he was now working showed the slow swell of a black expanse of sea, or chaos, from which rose a black tree with coiling branches: the end of our world or the primordial darkness over whose face the spirit of life has passed before, and will pass again—from which rises the Tree of Life, if such this dark sinister tree can be called. India's painters, no less than her philosophers and her poets are resolutely confronting the worst: Broota has passed through a phase of depicting the skeletal figures of sinister ape-like beings—us?—contemplating their sinister reflections.

We visited other studios where work more or less as one would find anywhere was in progress. Khosa had also worked at Triveni—India's artists do not lack encouragement or support. But the renaissance, it seems, is not in the arts, quite yet. After my return I sent Keshav the catalogue of Cecil Collins's retrospective exhibition. With such simplicity Cecil has shown again the fields of Paradise and the faces of its Presences, to an apathetic public that has declared the ugly fantasies of Bacon, Andy Warhol and other nihilists to represent 'truth' and 'reality'. I remember Cecil describing how some art-critic had objected that his visionary land 'does not exist' to which he replied that it existed *now*, since he had painted it. Delhi's painters are indeed attempting to come to terms with an experience of our single, indivisible world, not a local one; but they have forgotten the feminine principle, the gentleness of life so fully and beautifully appearing once more in Cecil's work. The harsh maleness of Bacon and the lately widespread Western homosexual school has influenced too much the very homeland of the Goddess—it is time she returned to reclaim her realm!

The Brootas entertained us to yet another of India's delicious meals in their flat on the top floor of Triveni, where there were yet more paintings. It might have been Paris, or any city, or my own house, where Winifred stayed for a long time and Cecil worked until his death, within a few days of the revelation of the world of Paradise and its inhabitants, in all their beauty, at his Tate Gallery retrospective exhibition in June 1989. Cecil indeed was asked once (I think at the ICA), since he disliked the state of England so much, with what country was he comparing us? His instant reply was, 'Paradise!'

As for those negative images let loose on the world by Francis Bacon, whose power to obsess seems so strong, here in India no less than elsewhere, what would Ramu say, who would have us exclude nothing, who reminded me that Hitler made evil known to us, an aspect of our world? Bacon has certainly done that, his images are indeed charged with power, and are true to a nightmare shared by many. Like Christopher Marlowe with his proud affirmation that 'this is Hell, nor am I out of it!' Against this, Cecil's gentle Fools, his Oracles, his Angels, and the all-redemptive presence of the feminine. Blake was quite clear that 'all things are comprehended in their Eternal Forms in the divine body of the Imagination', and that these nightmare obsessions are 'States of the Sleep which the Soul may fall into in its deadly dreams of Good & Evil when it leaves Paradise'. Do not India's holy men teach that the Light is real, darkness the absence of light? Did not Ramu, only a few years ago, bid us, if we would master the shadow, look to the source of light?

While India's younger painters are resolutely confronting

[262]

the dark disintegrative soul-destroying dreams of the modern West, it was, paradoxically, in Lennox Massachussetts that I was able to see the recent work of one of her older painters, Susheil Muckerjee. As these things happen, by chance or an inherent pattern in things, I brought this record with me on a visit to my friends at the Lindisfarne Press, in Massachussetts, there to work on my revisions. On the very day I finished these we visited Susheil Muckerjee, who lives only a few miles away in one of those neat frame houses with a garden of flowers and a view over lovely orchards and fields to New England's wooded hills. All very beautiful, but somehow unreal. It was in his studio that I found paintings, again, with Surya's fire—sacred themes of India and no discernible trace of secular Western influences. There were symbolic Tantric paintings, an abstract representation of the Trimurti (the three aspects of the divine manifestation), another of the departure at death; and a large and splendid 'work in progress' of the dying Bhishma on his bed of arrows by the Ganges with Arjuna beside him, a powerful rendering of that heroic theme, in terms both contemporary and purely Indian. Like Joyce, who took Ireland with him into his self-chosen exile, Susheil Muckerjee in his New England paradise, seems to have become only more Indian. There were also, in his studio, some dark tormented renderings of the Crucifixion and other tortured Christian themes, reminiscent of Broota's present work, but all this, he says, he has outgrown, and Surya's golden light moves freely through his subtle abstract forms. I said, these works, especially the Trimurti and the heroic theme from the *Mahbharata*, should hang in India's National Gallery. Although living in the United States he does not exhibit there—neither there nor in India. But he would, he said, like to be able to arrange an exhibition— where but at Triveni!

Christopher Bamford made the point that perhaps Sushiel

had needed to come to America to discover his Indianness: that in India he would have felt, like Khosa and Broota, the compulsion to look at the West, at the strange unknown Other. Biren De also travelled to America and to Germany, and having done so discovered the age-old Tantric abstract painting of India. I remember Herbert Read saying that he had only discovered how English he was when he went to Europe, and how European he was when he went to America. I wonder.

❀

While I was still staying with Santosh I was visited by Zahiruddin Dagar, and the two children of Fayazuddin, who had died unexpectedly and suddenly from a heart-attack, not long after their visit to the Temenos Conference at Dartington Hall in October 1988. When I heard this sad news that never again will these two great Dhrupad singers make music together, I had written to Zahiruddin, and he had managed to trace me to Santosh's home in Civil Lines. He came one morning, bringing with him the two young people, Waziruddin and his sister Qamar, who had played Tanpura at Dartington. Wazir is now singing with his uncle; he is the twentieth generation of this family of musicians whose art has been transmitted from father to son since they were appointed as court musicians to the Moghul emperor Jehangir. It makes me happy to remember that John Lane of Dartington, and I, had insisted that the young people should come, even though this had meant that we had to pay their fares from our non-existent funds. The Indian Government had paid the fares of the brothers, and their young drummer, Mohan Shyan Sharma, but said that surely there were Tanpura players in England. No doubt there are, but John Lane and I had agreed that it was important to respect the tradition of musical transmission within the family. Now I saw how important it had been to the young people, to have

[264]

made this visit. To them it had been one of life's magical experiences—and no wonder, Dartington being so beautiful a place, and the Conference what it was—from the opening notes of Yoshikazu Iwamoto's Japanese flute, and Hideo Kanze's consummate Noh acting, with the Tessenkai troupe, to John Tavener's compositions sung by the Bel Canto singers, David Gascoyne reading his noble poetry, and much besides. Wazir is twenty, his sister younger; they told me that they had talked so much about the Dartington visit on their return, that their family was tired of hearing about it! They lingered behind when the party left to ask me to remember them to each and everyone whom they had come to know at Dartington. I remember Zahiruddin's parting words after that music in the Great Hall at Dartington (overflowing with those who had come from far and near to listen), 'we came because we love you'. Zahiruddin said how he had valued an occasion created by poets and artists rather than the kind of official organizers with whom they must often have to deal. I understood the essential spirit of India, Zahiruddin was good enough to say; if to love 'the India of the Imagination' be to understand, I would wish it to be so. But I have only dipped my small cup into that mighty river which flows on. One singer dies, another takes up the unending music, accomplished fingers are never lacking to touch the strings of the Tanpura, lifting us into that other world where the sound-current of the universe for ever flows.

Zahiruddin, who is something much more than a performing artist in the Western sense of the word (though heaven knows there are Western musicians also who are attuned to the music of the spheres), brings with him that atmosphere of higher worlds. He gave me a recording of what must have been the last programme the brothers made together. I could but give in return a tape of *On a Deserted Shore*—how faint an echo of that music of the universe their chant transmits in even the best of poetry! Would they, I asked, be performing anywhere while I was in Delhi? Immediately Zahiruddin offered to come to Santosh's house and sing for me, and so I arranged to defer my return to England. What a joy that this great singer of India's sacred music should so honour me—that these living links of the Imagination have been formed—to me these links mean more than fame. Although so many of those who have been my friends and companions in that world are now dead, yet others come into my life, and others will be woven into that unbroken pattern when I am no longer alive, so long as the earth remains.

Meanwhile Santosh had planned what was to have been a farewell party for me. She has a gift for producing, on all occasions, with perfection and speed, delicious food and is not that the simple secret of making people happy? To Santosh's party the most diverse people came, mostly her friends, and some of mine. Professor Rupin Desai came and I was able to tell him with what pleasure I had been reading *Hamlet Studies* No. 10; I hope he had been reading, with equal pleasure, *Temenos* 10, which I had given him. Dr. and Mrs Prem Victor came, Premola Ghose from the India International Centre, the Islamic scholar Akhtar Qambar, Keshav and Usha Malik; Ramu, and a number of Santosh's academic colleagues, many of whom I have met on this or previous visits to India. I found myself listening to that formal and courteous scholar, Professor Desai, recollecting how his father (a Christian) long ago had believed that the days foretold in the Book of Revelation are at hand—an unexpected variation, as we quoted the Scriptures to one another, on the apocalyptic theme which has accompanied me throughout this visit. Did I bring the shadow with me, or is the world indeed experiencing what Raja Rao calls 'an eruption from the cosmic ground', a shared inner knowledge that sets Delhi's painters and poets to wear in their souls Hamlet's black garb, and Ramu to question the Dancer in the Crematorium? But for whatever reason this was a happy and harmonious party, as sometimes happens when stars are propitious and the food is as good as Santosh's.

The following Sunday evening was the larger party for the musicians. This was a great undertaking for Santosh, still deep in preparations of the manuscript of the book I was to take with me to England. I was now back at the International Centre, where Mohan came to fetch me. On our way he picked up food in the Bengali Market, and I bought flowers for Santosh, a bouquet for Zahiruddin Dagar and boxes of sweets for the young people. Many friends came, and the garden was turned over to an assistant cook whom Santosh had, with great difficulty, found. Why, then, did I feel a shadow over that gathering? Was it the absence of Fayazuddin? The young Wazir was beautiful as he evoked the undying music which formerly had inhabited his father, and now sang with his young voice, accompanied by the subtle delicate hand movements (*mudras*) that accompany the Dhrupad singing, and that seem, in the inspired Zahiruddin, a part of the music itself: 'Shiva, Shiva, Shiva', the music praised, invoked, evoked, the greatest of India's gods, whose presence had somehow overshadowed, or undershadowed, this visit to India. The singers made Shiva present in an ecstasy that was the soul of India, was India, and I too was with that flow. Yet the shadow was there.

Keshav and Usha, and his brother the philosopher Subhash Malik, drove me back to the cool peace of my room at the India International Centre, where on the lawn in the morning I watch a pair of hoopoes, sparrows live above my window, and green parrots from the Lodhi gardens display themselves. The gentle servants bring tea, the *dhobi* washes my dresses and presses my suit; I skim the newspapers that appear under my door for nature items. What ideal conditions in which to write! But, here as elsewhere, I am only myself. Long ago I sadly recognized that the limiting factor of the boundless spirit of inspiration is oneself; and now time was shortening and my thoughts were towards departure, even the parrots and the sparrows were beginning to thin away, no longer quite real.

Meanwhile Santosh had asked her dance guru, that man of his art from Orissa, to dance for me. He recalls to me Rupert Doone, my old friend who had danced in Diaghilev's ballet until, after a bout of rheumatic fever, he had to give up the dance, and become Director of the Group Theatre, and a dedicated teacher of theatre at Morley College. All the gifts are scattered in all parts of the world but there is a family likeness, be it poets, men of the theatre, dancers, in whatever time or place. There he sits on the floor of his studio awaiting his pupils, a little harmonium on one side, a drum on the other, a string of black beads round his neck. In that spacious, plain room in Triveni (which also reminds me of Morley College), one wall a mirror where the dancer may see herself, I have on more than one occasion watched Santosh dance her Geeta Govinda Radha-Krishna dances. Today the Master himself had offered to dance for me, and to have his son Nirmal, and his gifted younger daughter Rekha dance. So, once more, with roses for Guruji and sweets for the young people, there we were, in that plain and simple space, seeing the gods of India evoked and recreated. Rekha, with her long expressive fingers and dancer's mask, performed a Shiva dance; Nirmal the incarnations of Vishnu—fish, tortoise, bear, lion-man, dwarf, the Lord Rama, the Lord Buddha; Kalki whose sword we await. Guruji and Nirmal sang and danced in turn, or played their simple instruments, or Guruji told the stories of the gods. It heals something in Santosh when she dances Radha—she goes every morning to Triveni before she starts her day's work, and says she could not live her life or do her work without these hours on the dance-floor with her guru, who teaches her more than dance, teaches the deep realities of the soul's life. How much better than the American practise of paying visits, almost as frequent, to some psychiatrist, in order to talk about themselves! Once again, it is within a family that the art is handed down from father to son, and, in this family, to two gifted daughters. Nirmal is equally gifted as a singer as he is in the dance.

❦

As the days and the hours shortened my mind turned towards such things as changing money at the American Express, in Connaught Circle (a horrible experience!) collecting a pair of shoes being made for me (at, by English standards, a remarkably low price) by one of those craftsmen who are 'still' there as technology and mass production augments and skills diminish; finding gifts to take back to England, and such things. Shirnaz came with her husband and Jehangir (five teeth now) with a reference she wants me to find for her in the Journal of the Warburg Institute and a gift for granddaughter Sonia's baby, a splendid scarlet knitted suit lined with white—such a positive garment seems already to proclaim that 'untidy muddy boy' Sonia has set her heart on (and who has since entered the world). The proud parents of Jehangir presently went their way to take their evening walk in the Lodhi gardens, and Professor Lokesh Chandra was my next visitor.

It has always given me no little pride and pleasure to know that, before he even met me, Professor Lokesh Chandra had discovered the first issue of *Temenos* and has since been a regular subscriber; he told me he used to show it to Mrs Gandhi. I have since visited his International Academy of Indian Culture, where from cabinet after cabinet he drew marvellous manuscripts in their silk cases—Tibetan, Indonesian, Chinese and Japanese treasuries of Buddhist and other works emanating, directly or indirectly, from India, from whose heart, from whose vital pulse, again and again, a current of wisdom has flowed into the world, to fertilize civilizations; from pre-Socratic Greece and Persia in the West, to Tibet in the north, to China and Japan in the East. Once again it would seem that impulse may be about to carry to the culturally bankrupt West a current from India's sacred river. From the pre-Socratics to Plato and Alexander, from Persia to Plotinus, to Blake and Shelley, to Thoreau and Emerson, to Yeats; and even now to the modern West as once to Tibet, Indonesia, China and Japan. I had been reading with that special kind of delight poets receive from works of learning far beyond our reach, that like mountain ranges on the horizon tell of regions beyond and beyond, Lokesh Chandra's learned volume on the Buddhist icon of Avalokiteśvara. Such works remind us of great regions of thought once created, inhabited once, like lost kingdoms where the scholar may discover traces of the once-living. I had written a probably not very good poem inspired by a resonance, infinitely remote, from that great icon and this I gave him; the book itself will go to Carmen Blacker, the Japanese scholar, to review for *Temenos*. Such are the works whence poets draw inspiration, as Coleridge and Shelley from books of travel, Blake from Fludd and Paracelsus— literature is not made out of literature!

Scarcely through the door, Professor Chandra launched into advising me on our proposed Temenos Academy—we must by all means bring this about, he said; his support is not surprising, perhaps, in view of the theme and purpose of his own Indian International Academy—the diffusion of sacred knowledge from India, its inextinguishable hearth. Kapila must have told him of our project and shown him our draft programme. He was sure we would find funding; offered to write to Mr Rasgotra, in our support; there are Indian expatriate millionaires in plenty (why can I not find even one millionaire, Arabian, Japanese, Indian, American,

English even? It is not in my stars to move in those currents where millionaires are to be found in such plenty!). Millionaires, Lokesh Chandra said, want something in return—flattered vanity, or perhaps what we had already thought of, the chance of buying a property in London that would go up in value. That, he thought, might prove a good bait for some Indian millionaire willing to become a patron of a centre of the perennial learning. It all seemed, as he explained how easy this would be, almost accomplished already; as if what should be, already is. But here in India many things seem possible that in England we must labour to create. The level of discourse in India's intellectual journals is at the level of *Temenos*—and I do not mean only Professor Chandra, or Kapila Vatyayan, although the presence of such scholars of the Imagination is part of it—but all those books and journals I have been reading here—K. D. Sethna, and Sisir Kumar Ghose, and Nirmal Verma, or Raja Rao, Professor Desai's *Hamlet Review*, the excellent *Aligarh Journal*, the Quarterly Review of the India International Centre —and I have but seen what has come to me by chance, and made no study of India's literary journals, of which there are doubtless many others. India understands a scholarship of the Imagination, whereas in the West—with few exceptions—only the rational materialist mind is brought into play. That 'more than a quarter' is not visible and audible in the Western intellectual world. Here in India I feel understood in a way I do not feel even in France. French culture, so rich in the sphere of feeling (Proust, Jean Mambrino says, is to France as Shakespeare is to England, the very epitome of their civilization), does not rest, as here in India, on a metaphysical ground, venerable and universal. What in the West is exceptional (in Yeats, or Shelley, or Blake, or Corbin or indeed in *Temenos*,) in India is shared ground. Nor is it only the superstructure of thought, but the 'simple rules of life'—*dharma*—that rest on that basis. Much that is impossible to explain to any but a minority in the West, here in India does not have to be explained at all! This despite the westernization in academic life, as in other spheres.

'You should make *Temenos* known to Mr Gorbachev,' he said. I replied that we had tried to find contributions from the USSR—had published Tarkovsky, and at least one Russian poet, neither dissident nor Marxist. 'I said Mr Gorbachev,' he repeated, 'he is concerned with these values'.

I was presently to join Ramu and Nirmal Verma for the rest of the evening, and when Ramu came to my room to collect me he found me not a little euphoric after my conversation with Lokesh Chandra on the subject of millionaires and how many there are, how easily we would be able to find a willing patron of our Temenos Academy. Ramu's opinion of millionaires was rather different and my brief euphoria had already faded by the time we reached the bar, which I had not known existed, at the end of my corridor in the International Centre. As sometimes happens in a dream, there was a door opening into an unguessed, unknown region. This transformation-scene, as it then seemed, so unexpected it was, behind a door I had passed every day, opened into a bar that somewhat resembled a pub. I don't go to pubs in my own country, but appreciate the value of these spaces of common ground, where intellectuals and doubtless others, like to converse, of which the French café is the supreme realization. Here, then, the scene was set for good conversation, as I saw from my friends' expectant faces. Ramu bought me a double Indian whiskey, which I had never ventured on before. This was a mistake, and within an hour I was almost blind with migraine, and could not find words, almost like a slight stroke. In justice to the Indian whiskey, I must add that a few weeks later the same thing befell me in New England—I could not remember words—on an occasion on which I had not taken any alcohol at all.

Meanwhile I produced for Nirmal Lokesh Chandra's challenging proposition, tossed in the air as in some 'glass bead' game just before he left, that the British Raj had preserved Hinduism for Islam. Nirmal disagreed passionately, of course; British value-systems based on property ownership and money-values had undermined India's very different social order, based on functions unrelated to such things and rooted in an immemorial and intricate structure in a religious society with quite other values. In the book of essays he had given me, *Word and Memory*, there is a paper on 'Indian Fiction and Colonial Reality' in which he has written (*à propos* the novelist Prem Chand)

> ... when the organic structure of relations is debased and corrupted, man's dedication to his obligations ceases to be a source of spiritual redemption; instead it becomes a cause of unbearable bondage, of untold misery and inner destitution. What was true and meaningful within the scheme of things sanctified by the spirit of 'dharma' overnight turns into something dark and ambiguous, more a matter of private creed than a normal pattern of behaviour; and what was offered by the colonial masters as a 'real and rational' norm of conduct remained something vague and sinister, totally incomprehensible.

He goes on to sum up the Indian predicament—that wound of which I became instantly aware on my first setting foot on Indian soil:

> If the Indian society had been completely disrupted by the Imperial conquest, it would have become like any other society in the 'third world', if it had remained completely integrated with its traditional past, the tragedy of compromise and distortion had never appeared. But since it was neither one, nor the other,

the Indian civilization was given to the contradiction of deepest magnitude which bifurcated it right through the middle.

What, then, would have happened had the British not come? Would not the impact of the Industrial Revolution have reached India inevitably, in any case? India, Nirmal believes, would have confronted the modern world in her own way, and on her own terms. At least the thumbs of the weavers of fine muslin would not have been cut off (as I am told they were at the time of Warren Hastings himself) in order to promote the cotton industry in Lancashire. Nirmal, more than any other Indian I met on this visit, suffers burningly the anguish of the de-Indianization of India, already instated by the British and still proceeding apace through the technological world-revolution that seems irreversible. Like Ramu he sees the virtue of Gandhiji's vision that was not to be realized; yet he believes that some options are still open. Maybe the teaching of Sanskrit will be reintroduced in the schools, and other things, here and there. But we all know, like it or not, that in this 'global village' technology is the new world order, sweeping the whole world, as it seems, with its own momentum. Yet Sri Aurobindo remained convinced that a spiritual evolution is taking place, despite all; and hope is, after all, self-realizing, which perhaps is why it is deemed one of the three theological virtues.

What is painful in India is that the fatal choices are so recent—looking back into living memory it seems almost possible to stand again where a different choice might have been made. But none knows better than I that only one step away one is already gone, from house, from home, from family, from spouse. And so also with history. Choices are made in accordance with choices and causes forgotten that made the fatal course already inevitable. Nirmal has just finished a novel and was sad. Ramu too is sad—far, far, he had confided to me, from the realization of that total *advaita* to which he aspires. Perhaps happiness—bliss—*ananda*—is altogether too simple for the likes of any of us; 'He who catches the joy as it flies / lives in eternity's sunrise'. Unless ye become as little children. Do we all try too hard?

And does not Ramu feel a bitterness, I asked him, at the usurpation of the name of India's great Mahatma Gandhi by the present ruling family? To Ramu, who at the age of eight had, with his father and brothers, set the sacred fire to his grandfather's funeral pyre, bitterness is inevitable. But not despair—not one of us has despaired. How hard we are all trying, each according to our abilities. We reached no conclusion, unless that sharing of our thoughts, that fellow-ship of what Ramu does not hesitate to call love, although love is a word I would no longer dare to use, be conclusion enough. Speaking of the Christian idea of 'forgiveness' I said I did not know what the word means; to which Ramu replied, 'I do not want to be forgiven, I want to be *loved*'. Is not that always the answer?

It is true that we must each necessarily attract to ourselves those events and people congenial to each; an engineer, a naturalist, a drug-addict or a professional diplomat would have each their own 'India'. What I experienced, and what I did not experience are what I consciously or unconsciously attracted towards myself, or failed to notice. I could not claim to have a more than accidental knowledge of India's poets and painters, and I disclaim either the ability or the intention to speak of India's literary world, happy as were my days in Delhi's Latin Quarter. All the same, the India I encountered is a reality, is no invention of mine, and for what I received I am deeply grateful.

The young journalist, A. K. Mital who has over the years

corresponded with me from enthusiasm for *Temenos* came to see me. His letters used to be exuberant and inchoate, asking me unanswerable questions about the universe, and equally unanswerable ones about practical matters. Two years ago he came to interview me with a fine new recording apparatus—he was just married, and this splendid piece of technology was a symbol of his new and reponsible state as a householder. Now as on almost my last day we sat in the shady courtyard of the International Centre he told me of a first baby expected in June, and of his guru, Swami Sivananda. The two Indias grow side by side, this young journalist loves both his technology and his guru. He spoke of his happiness in his life of meditation and gave me a little booklet entitled 'Wisdom Light' which I have duly read. The modern painter with the portrait of Vivekananda in his room; the ambitious young journalist with his spiritual Master. He asked me about poetry in England, and I told him that nowadays poetry was something people wrote, not something they read; that the standard was low but that this was probably a necessary social change. And writing poetry was for many a form of meditation, self-discovery, prayer, yoga even; a means available to all—you need only a biro and a school exercise book. You in India need it less, I said, for you have Masters and teachers, spiritual knowledge is more easily available. He knitted his young brows and asked me if we did not have saints in the West, and if not, why not? I replied that once we had saints and spiritual teachers but that in a secular materialist society dominated by technology they came no more; or if they came, were unknown in the world of the media. But we have many seekers, I told him, among the young, and many teachers come from the East, Buddhist, Sufi, Indian. What of the Church? Concerned, I said, with many good causes but little with spiritual knowledge, as such. This young man, whose profession doubtless

[276]

exposes him to every cynical and reductionist Western influence, has adopted a life of devotion to his Master and his family life is joyful and full of love. True, the cynical kind of journalists would not have sought me out, but, again, my impression is that the 'more than a quarter' is never far away. I have since heard from him of the birth of a little daughter, whom everyone spoils, while the exhausted parents cope as best they can! How beautiful—and simple—life can be! He told me that the young people like to be 'trendy' and Western, but the girls are good Indian girls at heart, and are happy to become good wives and mothers—probably he was describing his own experience. Basic, universal human simplicity, but in the West where has it gone? Such happiness would seem now to be the exception rather than the rule. The young live together without having children, have children without living together, and few young faces are filled with joy.

The hours flowed away; my bags were packed. I was waiting for a telephone call from Ramu, who was to let me know if and when we could see the interview we had made together, but this did not come—I left India without seeing the film. Meanwhile I telephoned Kishori, who came to my room to pass the last hours with me. I made a last visit, with Kishori, to buy a few more gifts at the Crafts Centre. Then Kishori bargained for me with the Rajasthani women on the pavement for work far more beautiful than any I saw in the Emporium itself. I bought for Thetis Blacker a cloth worked with little people, elephants, cattle, sheep, and a castle, full of humour and the joy of life. I wish I had bought several others, for who knows for how many more years this skill, humour and joy will inspire such work, and the happy bargaining Kishori was so skilled in. Back in my room, in the great heat, I lay on my bed, Kishori stretched out on two chairs. This companionable informality seems very natural in India, but very un-English—un-European—and for myself, who live alone, a strange resonance from long ago, sharing bedroom or bed with aunts or cousins, when lives flowed easily and unreservedly among friends and family; when, perhaps, people were simply less lonely than we are in the modern West. It was just a tremor, a resonance perhaps from an ancestral past, just something not quite audible or definable, a kind of melting of frontiers. Our frontiers, by which we define ourselves are too rigid, we pride ourselves on our uniqueness and individuality, but what does it amount to? It might have been anyone outstretched on a neighbouring chair or floor, or, as I saw the multitudes of Beas, on the ground. Not just the material earth, on some invisible ground we share, earth's bed.

Suddenly the room was full—Santosh was there, and Mohan, and Keshav, with whom I was to read poems in the garden of Mrs Frenny Billimoria, a painter whose work I had seen at the recent Parsee festival at the International Centre, and who had also some fine modern work in her house, by Khosa and others. Santosh was not coming to the poetry reading, the completion of her manuscript had now reached a final crisis, since in a few hours it would be in my hand luggage and on its way to Colin Smythe, who is to publish it. Mohan was to accompany me to the reading, then drive me back to Civil Lines, and see me off at dawn. The atmosphere of the Billimoria's house, nearby in the Lodhi estate, with its beautiful garden set with torches, and a circle of chairs, was, again, the spacious one of the world of the living arts, Mrs Billimoria both painter and patron. This was not the 'Latin Quarter' but rather the world of those patrons of the arts on whom all painters depend, not only or principally financially, but, even more, for the understanding and support of the work itself. I read I know not what, for my friends, in the spicéd Indian air by night, the green parrots circling over the trees, the mosquitos round our ankles. Keshav's infirm mother had come, and he read, I thought, better than I had heard him hitherto. As the evening faded, delicious fruit-cup and Parsee food. Lingering over farewells cannot be for ever, but this gentle finale was indeed 'linkéd music long drawn out'.

But not the end! Santosh, meanwhile, assisted by faithful Timkoo, was working to the last minute on her manuscript. A crescendo of frenzied note-checking, caption-checking and the rest, had been going on with increasing momentum. Santosh is a scholar with the temperament of a dancer, and that creates a whirl! When Mohan and I got back to the house, Santosh's finale was still on stage, but the moment came when Mohan had at last sealed up the manuscript, it was bestowed in my hand luggage, and Santosh had at last relinquished the work to which she had given her thought and heart for so many years, and through which, as these strange threads of destiny run, I had first come to India. My short Foreword Mohan insisted I should sign; I assured him that a Foreword is not a legal document! Santosh felt it was auspicious that I should transport her work and give it to Colin Smythe with my own hands, which in due course I did.

And so, somehow packed, after a sleepless night, an early start, soon I was looking down from the cabin in an Air India plane, on the awesome mountains of Afghanistan. As a child I would have delighted in their sublime beauty, but as I travelled through the air, a fragile speck in a boundless sky, that sublimity which is beyond beauty told only of dark unfathomables. Then we were flying over Russia's woods and rivers and lakes and roads and villages; then Heathrow Airport, where Thetis Blacker was waiting to meet me. What a mystery times and places are! As I sit typing this record by my window opening into my own garden where a blackbird is revelling among the unripe grapes of a vine hanging over my wall from the garden next door, these memories are so recent, so present, that I seem still living them. And what is memory, and where, and when? These and older memories, and the memories of the days of the generations of the ancestors—we call them the dead, but what is death? What has been is forever; but where, in what manner? What are places and times, so poignant and so briefly here and now? Mine with the rest. Against the awesome desolation of rocks and peaks of snow, the soul-shuddering spaces of the material universe, 'satsang'—being together with friends in the Presence. Love, the mysterious medium in which we fragile human beings are indissolubly woven together beyond mountains and distances.

Soon after my return from India I visited the United States of America, a far other country to which nevertheless I owe much and where I have many friends. On the very day when I returned to London from Kennedy Airport, a telephone call came from Keith Critchlow—he was with Ramu Gandhi, who was in transit to Honolulu there to attend a conference on his way to California; could they come round? So there at my door were Keith and Ramu in his handloom woven tunic, just as I had parted from him only a few weeks before. It seemed the most natural thing in the world that Ramu should be in my room, as if he had just crossed from Triveni or Kishori's studio in Babar Lane. Distance was suddenly made non-existent. He brought with him as a gift a videotape of our interview. A gift from my Indian friends, he said. Now it was not the sorry Salman Rushdie affair, or the establishing a Peace Centre on the site of the Great Battle of Kurukshetra, in Haryana, that occupied his mind, but the massacre of the Chinese students in Tienanmen Square: he spent some time telephoning about a photograph he wants to reproduce, of a child, with a face of grave innocence, about to be mown down by army tanks. For Christmas, perhaps, he thought, such a card would be appropriate. The Innocents still massacred; does anything change? Why a memorial in Haryana while the Great Battle goes on? Although, indeed, why not? It seemed strangely natural that Ramu should be telephoning about a photograph in the cause of peace, in my room, making nothing of the mountains of Afghanistan and the Potomac and the Ohio rivers and New England's wooded hills, that I had traversed since last we met. Space is nothing at all! Ramu took both my hands as at last he left, to spend the evening with the friend on whose floor he will sleep before catching his plane to Honolulu—and said, 'I *love* you!' Strange words—what do they mean? I seem to discern that the secret wisdom of India—the 'more than a quarter', the invisible medium, the living network that binds and unites, is something one must call love. 'God is Love'—what a silly thing to embroider on a framed text, I no doubt thought in long-ago days when these words lingered on in quiet places where life was simple. God, 'in whom we live, and move, and have our being'. Truly, I have been a slow learner—or had so much to unlearn. I find as I grow old and outgrow that best of educations I worked so hard to acquire, that it is the self-evident that fills me with a sense of boundless wonder.

❀

Stranger still was a visit from Raja Rao. This record opened with his words describing India not as a country on any map, not a place but a state of being. I had been sorry to hear, in Delhi, that Raja Rao had just passed through, on his way to Southern India; yet more sorry, on my return to London, to find a telegram saying he had hoped to see me as he passed through England—too late! Yet a third message awaited me on my return from USA—he would be passing through London on his way back to Austin, Texas, where he now lives, with his American wife. How could I let him

[281]

know that I expected him? It was too late to reach him in India. I telephoned Mr. Manral in India House to see if they might know his whereabouts. Then Mohan Pall telephoned —he had met Raja Rao, quite by chance, at the India International Centre and promised to give him my telephone number. But the date Raja Rao had given me came and went and no message came.

Then several days later came a telephone call from his wife, Susan; and she brought him to spend an afternoon with me. He was frail, he had been ill, and was expecting to undergo surgery on his arrival in Austin. Raja Rao's visit was stranger, more mysterious, then Ramu's. I felt that he had come to impart something, that this was in some sense a ceremonial, a sacred visit. He had come to England, he said, breaking his journey for but one day, only to see me. This I felt was no 'literary' visit, although I had written on *The Serpent and the Rope* for the celebratory issue of the Oklahoma journal *World Literature Today* on the occasion of his having been awarded the prestigious Neustadt International Award, and reviewed *The Chessmaster and his Moves* for *Temenos*. He introduced Susan, his wife—'She was a hippie!' he said affectionately. 'The Beautiful People'. And beauty did indeed inhabit her face. On my recent visit to the States it had been the deliberate ugliness of both the men and women, the self-image expressed in their vulgar clothes, that most depressed me—beauty, that presence of the soul in the body, one rarely saw, and the spiritually unoccupied flabby bodies, vacant faces and dyed hair I found, after the expressive beauty of India, deeply distasteful. The black people of course are beautiful, they have a different culture from that science-fiction nightmare and loveless feminism that sets the style of America in 1989; Yet any body, any face can be beautiful if inhabited by that beauty of the soul Socrates prayed for.

Raja Rao said he had not written to me these last years

[282]

because he had been passing through a darkness so deep that he had approached the verge of suicide. A 'dark night of the soul'. Yet his life, he said, had been rich, he had been in all things fortunate. How had he fallen, that seeker for the Ultimate, into darkness? Darkness again. I had not expected to encounter that shadow yet again in Raja Rao. Is that darkness a shadow over the whole world, in Raja Rao's own words, 'an eruption from the cosmic ground', in our age? He said he had found the state of India, on this visit, deeply depressing. I did not go into that question, for it was clear that he had come to speak of quite other things. He spoke about the forthcoming second volume of his great trilogy. In the second volume the hero, Shivarama, meets his guru. I asked if he intended to write about the encounter between India and the United States? That, he said, is in the third volume. Returning to his experience of darkness, the worst, he said, was now over; he was now returning from his Master's ashram, where he had received comfort. I remembered my surprise when at our conference Raja Rao had praised (as I had understood him) Sri Aurobindo's poem, *Savitri*, and asked whether Sri Aurobindo had been his guru. Most indignantly he rejected such a misunderstanding: Sri Aurobindo was, in his eyes, scarcely Indian at all in his thought. He had received, from boyhood, an English education and imbibed Western ideas and Western culture, and his ideas of evolution, and the superman, totally at variance with the deep current of traditional Indian thought. My Prince Kumar too had said that it was Sri Aurobindo's misfortune not to have had an Indian childhood—it is in childhood, he had said, that India is imbibed, and to miss that experience is an irreparable loss. I was glad to know—as I should have known already from his writings—that Raja Rao's super-subtle Brahmin mind saw the Ultimate in more traditional terms; rejected the 'new' ideas Sri Aurobindo had intro-duced into his teachings: how can there be 'new' truths?

[283]

'Originality' could never impress so subtle and learned a mind. Truth, and what is, are ever themselves. When he had met his true guru, he said, he had answered all, all his questions; there could be no doubt.

He had brought me three volumes of Sri Krishna Menon's (Sri Atmananda's) works and one by his son: *Advayananda* teaching of the most absolute, pure, and traditional kind. I asked him if he would sign this gift for me, to which he replied with a *namaskar* gesture, and said he could not possibly do so, since these were the words of his guru, sacred words. I was surprised—I should not have been so—to see in Raja Rao, most supersubtle and sophisticated of all the Indians I had met, such humility before the sacred wisdom. One does not find such things in students of so-called 'philosophy' at Oxford or Cambridge. But then, neither does one find the sacred wisdom there. Raja Rao nevertheless had studied Scholastic philosophy at the Sorbonne and at Avignon, had married a French wife, had studied deeply the Western sacred tradition. He thinks he may have been, in an earlier incarnation, a monk. But that experience, he went on to say, had not sufficed, it had not brought him to the ultimate wisdom; which now he had found in his guru Sri Krishna Menon, a householder, whose son is Susan's guru and continues his father's teaching. Now, he thought, perhaps he was ready to pursue that ultimate understanding none can possess, and yet when for an instant we glimpse it, is so simple and familiar, being our own deepest reality. In the words of his guru resonate the teachings of the Lord Krishna, and all Vedanta.

> I have no mine-ness, attachment or egoism. I am eternal, non-doer, all purity, self-dependent and self-luminous. Attributeless, shapeless and unconditioned, I am the abode of Love, stainless, the one without second, and ever peaceful.

'Love is the unfamiliar name'. His mathematician hero, like his author, is too clever to find a secret so simple, yet too dedicated a seeker to abandon his search for the Absolute, the Ulitmate. In the concept of zero he discerns the secret, the *bindu*, Blake's and Boehme's 'centres of the birth of life'. There is no bliss in concepts. Blake, who had understood the deep mystery of 'bliss' knew that 'life delights in life' and that 'every particle of dust breathes forth its joy'. One has glimpses, 'between two moments', as Blake says, of a pure, impersonal and immortal bliss, simple and universal. I said that since he has set out on such a quest, he must go on, for the sake of all who look to him, he is committed to that sacred quest. Raja Rao has not abandoned his quest, though it has led him into the 'dark night of the soul'; he is prepared to pay the ultimate price for the ultimate vision. But we sophisticates have read too much, and the divine vision is simple. We are prepared to search the world for the 'kingdom of heaven' yet we are told is to be found within, that only little children know the way to the Kingdom.

The question is not where we will find the Ultimate, the Absolute, but rather when and why we lost it. The key is not knowledge but love. Had I not rebelled against my father I might have remained with him in the kingdom of Jesus Christ, his Master; intellectual pretexts are for the loveless. In becoming a Catholic convert I did not return, was not reconciled with the home I had rejected. And so with all my searchings, in esoteric studies, in all the proffered hands held out to me; I could find fault easily enough with Sri Aurobindo's poetry, with Mary Baker Eddy's mishmash of American Transcendentalism, with Buddhist asceticism, with the intellectual arrogance of Guénon's school, with eclecticism, with sectarianism, as if these things had anything whatever to do with the heart's reasons. All these are streams at which men and women better than I have quenched their thirst. It is the loveless heart that is in exile,

[285]

and will ever be so. And did not Raja Rao leave India to study in Paris and in Avignon? Marry in a far country? Perhaps he and I are too much alike, and find ourselves in our old age in the outer darkness.

What is the comfort, then, I asked him, that he has received from the son of his guru? And again came that bewildering Indian answer that has baffled me again and again: 'Hold fast to your guru!' were the words. Love again? And I thought of Ramana Maharshi, whom Ramu loves, he says, with the intensity and reality of that kind of love we 'fall' into. Without love there is no redemption. Perhaps we can only find the 'God within' when we love? Without relationship what can we know of love, and therefore of God? In India the relationship with the guru—that love Ramu spoke of—appears to be one of those basic human experiences comparable with the love of parent and child or man and woman united in the sacred bond of marriage. Ramu had read my Autobiography, and as he saw it, Platonism—or Christian dualism perhaps—the rejection, or inability, to form a bond of love with 'the other', explained my falling in love with a homosexual man with whom that relationship with 'the other' could not be. Must we not look for the God Within also through 'the other'—the guru? Not, of course, a personal relationship—doubtless gurus have personal relationships, some are married, with families, are householders; but the bond between guru and disciple is on another level, is of another kind, within that universal medium of spirit—that is, of love. We may wander the world for ever, read all the books, we who have violated the bonds of love, but we will never find it.

My friend, Dorothy Carrington, who was again staying with me, presently joined us and we had some conversation of a less bewildering kind. Raja Rao had delivered his message, and we conversed on such things as history, the French intellect and its limitations; we spoke of Tambi, whom we had all known—for Raja Rao had known him too, had been present at his wedding to Safia, his Indian wife. I showed him my photograph of Tambi when he was young and very beautiful. Tambi again—he seems always to be there, binding the threads, bringing us together. Before Susan led him away, his frail body, his great yet unsatisfied mind, he consented to inscribe my copy of *The Serpent and the Rope*. He wrote, 'For Kathleen Raine, pilgrim of the absolute, who will find the answer to all her questions when the sincerity of her search will reach the ultimate "I-principle", the Absolute. With affection from Raja Rao.' So he delivered to me this sacred message; sacred trust, one might almost say. An invitation to cross the threshold within that admits the exile into that India towards which all travel?

Some weeks later, I wrote Raja Rao a letter, again, on bliss—*ananda*. Only when joy is found will the ultimate have been found. In this also Raja Rao and I are too much alike: it is joy that eludes us. We do not live in 'eternity's sunrise'. Ramu told me on my first visit to India that I was 'too sad'. Kishori, asked why she wanted to paint my portrait, spoke of my eyes that were 'compassionate and a little sad.' There is no wisdom in sorrow. I was at Chisholme to expound to the Sufi community there the story of Job, as Blake understood it and expressed it in his twenty-two engravings. Blake is not, like Jung, one of those who say—as Jung's friend Gershom Scholem said to me also—that 'God never *did* give an answer to Job.' The Jungians are very well satisfied with Jung's *Answer to Job*, which gives Job the last word and the moral victory. A brilliant, but not a wise book—psychology is not that ultimate. God is himself the answer—in God there is no longer either question or answer. What does Jung suppose God to be? How could such a Being answer Job's 'question' in terms of his own ignorance? An enlightenment transposes the questioner into another order of knowing altogether than that of question and answer. By his own confession Job did not know, had not seen, God: 'Oh that I knew where I might find him! That I might come even to his seat! I would order my cause before him, and fill my mouth with arguments. I would know the words which he would answer me!' Job was looking for an answer to questions of his human transient selfhood in its own terms. No Indian seeking God would 'fill his mouth with arguments', the knowledge of God is not of that kind at all: how could Jung have supposed such a thing? When God 'answered' Job what arguments could be put to epiphany? To Blake it was clear that God's self-revelation was the 'Divine Humanity' the God within, the universal Self.

❧

Last of all came my Prince of Rama's kingdom. He had been in Paris with his little community there, for the bi-centenary celebrations of the Revolution. (I see little to celebrate in that revolting slaughter or that the *sang impur* of victims of the guillotine *abreuve nos sillons*, or the enthronement of the Goddess Reason in Paris's Cathedral of Notre Dame; whose statues were also decapitated; the bonfires of harpsichords, the Napoleonic wars.)

As usual Kumar admonished me to write poems. I read him those I had written since last we met; he didn't think they were enough. But I read him also passages from this record, especially those relating to Tambi. These he enjoyed, but returned with ever more urgency to reminding me of my appointed (and neglected) task, the writing of poetry. That alone, a hundred years from now, he said, will remain. Yes, I tell him (and myself) soon now, very soon. The poems are there whenever there is a blank sheet of paper before me, and a time of quiet. But for how much longer? And will the civilized world last so long.

I told him of Raja Rao's visit; showed him the books of Sri

Krishna Menon, and spoke of Raja Rao's quest for the Ultimate. It is like those people so anxious to go into 'space', he said; as though we were not in 'space' already. We do not have to go there, we *are* there. So with the 'ultimate' we are already there, the quest for the 'ultimate', the 'absolute' is its own fallacy, like Job's 'search' for God who is ever-present. 'Oh! That I knew where I might find him!' But what a world of Blind Man's Buff we have been thrown into!

We spoke, of course, of India. I might, said Kumar, have found India many years ago, but instead made a lifelong detour working on Blake, and Yeats, and Thomas Taylor the Platonist and the rest. But could I really have reached 'the India of the Imagination' by a shorter way? And was not my task precisely to make that long detour in order to weave that slender bridge? Tambi's India was not what I was looking for, that dear Bohemian. Such knowledge as I gathered in my many studies is vanity of vanities only for those who have passed through it. Nor would I have wished to sit at the feet of some 'Babaji', true or false, in a state of enchantment. Illumination comes, if it comes at all, in its due season. No, all has had to be as it has been; I was not ready for India, nor perhaps was 'my' India ready for me. I have no regrets, no wish that I had 'reached' that far India sooner. There are no short cuts to our destined times and places. My task has been with Blake and Plotinus and Yeats, to uncover the lost traces of an excluded knowledge in our own inheritance, and only having done so am I free. If India—my small parcel of India, my dearly valued Indian friends, some of whom, like my friend Dr. Sethna, I have never even met, have received me with love, the journey had to be life-long. It was Kumar, not I, who used the word 'home'. Perhaps Tambi had seen, perhaps Kumar had seen, long before I had discovered it to be so for myself, that the India of the Imagination is that homecoming. Only, of course, in a manner of speaking, for 'home', by whatever

[289]

way we reach it, is everywhere and nowhere. As is the exile
of those for whom 'this is hell, nor am I out of it'.

POSTSCRIPT

'In Vishnu-land what avatar?'

And yet again there is more to tell as this record comes full
circle and I seem to discern in it a pattern in which my own
story is only one small strand. Long ago Mr Rasgotra had
spoken to me of meeting in one life those with whom we
had been associated before; as if he had divined in me
(being, as an Indian, more sensitive than I to such things)
such a one. A metaphor, perhaps, which we ourselves
realize? Who knows the One Mind that weaves the pattern?
After my return from the United States India remained with
me; I was invited to read at India House with the Bombay
poet Nissim Ezekiel, who had been one of Tambi's many
friends; and on another evening India House played host to
the launching of the long-deferred memorial volume for
Tambi himself. Presently there came from the High Commissioner the text of an address he was about to give at the
eighth Convocation of the Sathya Sai University at Prasanthi Nilayan, on the twenty-second of November, 1989.
This Institute of Higher Learning is almost exactly contemporary with *Temenos*, whose first issue appeared in February 1981. As I read that address my heart was warmed to
read that 'This Institute is well on the way to become the
model for tomorrow's Universities in India and elsewhere.'
It was as if a single mind—Raja Rao's 'eruption from the
cosmic ground'?— had been the agent of both, so similar
were our purposes, and this address, given by Sri Rasgotra

at Prasanthi Nilayan in Andra Pradesh spoke of a programme in all essentials identical with what we are hoping
to realize for a Temenos Academy of Integral Studies here in
London; a course for students in all the essential Humani-
ties, but grounded not in those current illusions that impri-
son the modern mind, cluttering the minds of the young
with theories, prejudices, and false or trivial facts, but in the
perennial wisdom. Just that 'learning of the Imagination'
our prospectus sets forth has already, it seems, become a
reality—a new pattern of education brought into being at
the behest of Bhagwan Sathya Sai Baba, whose ashram I had
not visited in 1982, on my first visit to India. The first
Vice-Chancellor, I now learned, had been Professor V. K.
Gokak, with whom I had corresponded and whom we had
published in *Temenos*. I had known him as the President of
the Indian literary Akademy, ignorant as I was of the existence of a University at Prasanthi Nilayam. This, evidently,
was a University of importance and by no means some
counter-culture experimental venture. Sathya Sai Baba
clearly could call upon India's best minds in many fields.

Presently the High Commissioner himself came to tea, to
tell Keith Critchlow and myself of this new University, and
to advise us. How many students are there? I asked; twenty
thousand at present, taking five-year courses. And how
many listened to your Convocation address? A hundred
thousand: a *lakh*! Mr Rasgotra was sure we would have no
difficulty in raising the two (or maybe three) million pounds
needed to realize our Academy; for the divine Will can
bring into being what is needful no less in London than in
Andra Pradesh. Such thoughts I believe were in all our minds
as Mr Rasgotra told us more of the Holy Man, whom
many regard as an avatar, at whose behest this University of
the future has arisen. Laurens van der Post, who has so
lovingly supported our project throughout, he too believes
that this reversal of the premises of a materialist civilization

[291]

is now inevitable and timely, and therefore a new education grounded not in an obsolete materialism no longer supported by the newest discoveries of science itself, must come about; an education grounded in a deeper and a truer understanding of the nature of Man. The seed is sown, he wrote to me; and if not we, then others will bring the new education into being. The germination of that seed will come about with the same certainty with which all seeds germinate in their due season. The one Spirit that over and over again has manifested itself in India's Holy Men—and in how many others throughout the world at all times—is everywhere and always at work. We are not separate, as we think, but, as Blake wrote long ago, only 'forms and organs' of the one Life.

And so for a moment it seemed that 'India Seen Afar' had allowed me to discern, even to touch, the miraculous centre of her mystery, taken me to her heart. In his address Sri Rasgotra had spoken warmly of us as fellow-travellers with that *lakh* of Indian scholars and devotees whom he then addressed. It seems that he had already spoken of us to Sai Baba himself. He quoted from a letter I had written him in 1984:

'It is with regret, with sorrow, that I see the worst Western culture has to offer being exported world-wide, and so willingly accepted even in India where traditional culture has survived in a purer form and to a greater degree than elsewhere. The time has come to challenge and to reject values that threaten East and West alike. We suggest that a centre should be established—and this surely must be in India—devoted to the study of the true alternatives to the cultural and spiritual malady of our time.'

Kathleen Raine's suggestion has merit and I thought I should put it forward for the consideration of our revered Chancellor. For if there is a place in this country which can project to the world the 'spiritual knowledge' of which Kathleen Raine speaks, that place is here. For this Institute of Higher Learning was created by Bhagwan Sathya Sai Baba precisely for this purpose so perceptively defined by Kathleen Raine.

A few weeks later arrived a copy of the monthly journal issued by the ashram (sent, as I think, by an English member of the Community) quoting extensively from Sri Rasgotra's address, and including a photograph, in brilliant Southern Indian technicolour, of the governing body of the University, in full academic dress, moving in dignified procession, under the ashoka trees and paper streamers, towards the auditorium. Heading the procession were Sri Rasgotra and the present Vice-Chancellor. But for the Indian sunlight, the ashoka trees and the streamers, the same procession might have been seen in the Cambridge Senate-House, or on any University 'campus' in the world; and for the presence, between the Guest of Honour and Vice-Chancellor Saraf, of an Indian Holy-Man in a red robe, smiling and blessing the spectators with upraised hand—a figure from another world—one might almost say from another dimension—than that of Academia.

Ice seemed to melt in my heart at this unlooked-for confirmation (as it seemed) that this world is not abandoned. Can there be a greater happiness than to be instrumental in some sacred purpose? Long ago I sought 'To know in order to serve', and if I have still one last small part to play in the service of sacred knowledge I am indeed happy. Even have I contributed a small drop to that great river of India?

'God or man, what's the difference?' my dear Kumar had said in princely nonchalance, of his ancestor King Rama; but he intended the words also on other levels, embracing vast sweeps of Vedantic doctrine of the Self, of

[293]

Sufi mysticism, and including the deepest mystery of all, before which all humankind must bow, *'et homo factus est.* And does not that love between devotee and *guru* that has repeatedly mystified me in my Indian friends, rest in the reality of divine Incarnation ever present? We in the West are habituated to thinking of Raja Rao's ultimate, the absolute, the unknowable, as the inhuman universe of 'nature' understood in terms of the 'laws' of the natural sciences; 'real' no doubt within their own terms. But the forever unknowable may turn towards us a face—one of the innumerable faces of the Divine Humanity; not a face of flesh and blood but seen 'not with but through the eye' by multitudes who know the difference between a cluster of sense organs and a face. India's immemorial wisdom which I have 'seen afar', what is it but love? 'Go with the flow': have I too been caught up into a miraculous order, that 'more than a quarter' of reality I seemed for a moment to discern operating not only in India but even in my own story?